PHOENIX CHILD

Book One of the
Children of Fire Series

Alica McKenna-Johnson

I dedicate this book to my mom Becky and my dad Bobby who always supported and encouraged me. I miss you both.

Acknowledgments

I had SO many people help support and encourage me while writing Phoenix Child. My husband Rod, my kids Logan and Tala, my sister Brandy and my step-mom Sue. Mary, Kim, Jill, who critiqued, monitored my pacing, held my hand, and copy edited for me. Kilian my main editor, friend, and cheerleader. Theresa, who never stopped bugging me to get it finished. Amber, who listened to me whine and complain while dragging my butt to the gym. To Saguaro Romance Writers for their encouragement and holding amazing programs so members can become the best writers possible. And thanks to Kristen and my WANA family for their support and hand holding when I felt like this would never happen.

Chapter One

"Change is the constant, the signal for rebirth, the egg of the
phoenix."
~Christina Baldwin

Alien abduction? Extreme makeover? Witch's spell?

Something had to explain the changes that happened to me
overnight. Even the doctor Melanie dragged me to offered no
explanation, but apparently, I'm in perfect health. I barely
managed to stop myself from demanding to see his medical
license. How can it be possible to wake up looking completely
different and still be in perfect health? I looked down at the
coppery tint that appeared this morning on my skin. Stupid
doctor.

Thick fog covered the brightly painted row houses, making
them look dull and plain. Only the Christmas lights came close
to cutting through the cold gray blanket. I leaned back into the
seat of my houseparent's Honda as I took in the familiar beauty
of the city.

"Sara, we'll figure this all out, don't worry," Melanie said as
she drove down one of San Francisco's seven hills. My stomach
did a little flip as we crested the top. One would think after
driving over these streets all of my life I would have become
numb to them, but they still made my stomach flutter.

"With all the tests the doctor ordered, he'd better figure
something out." The nurse had trouble finding a vein for the lab
draws, and a bruise had formed in the bend in my elbow.

Rubbing my temples, I pushed back the headache and tears. This morning had been hell.

My fingers twitched in shock as they touched the soft curls resting on my forehead. I tugged my bangs down and tried to hide my eyes, which had also changed. Instead of the dull gray-green I'd grown-up with, now they were a clear pale green with flecks of gold. My first day as a fifteen-year-old and already the drama level had reached insane.

I ran my hands over the bandana covering my hair. Until I knew what had happened to me, I wanted to keep the flame-red streaks that highlighted my midnight curls hidden. I didn't recognize myself, and didn't like being so out of control. If I couldn't control my hair color, I could at least control who saw it. Maybe it's childish, but hey, I'm only fifteen, no one expects me to make good choices yet.

Melanie flipped through her CDs, her eyes darting between bright jacket covers and the foggy road. I adore Melanie, she's a great houseparent, but every time I get into her car, it's a near-death experience. "I'm going to have to file an incident report with your caseworker. Between the fever last night and the changes this morning, he needs to know what's going on."

"I'm fine. The report will make Five worry." I crossed my arms and scattered a pile of half empty water bottles as I stretched out my legs.

"I know, but these are the rules," Melanie said, her voice soft and even. I called it her 'calm houseparent' voice. She uses it to try to keep us kids from losing our tempers. I hated having it used on me. "And your caseworker's name is David. It's rude to call him Five."

I rolled my eyes and chose not to say anything.

"Are you sure you want to go to camp? Maybe you should rest today," Melanie said.

"I'm sure. If I sit at home, I'll worry." I shifted so I could see the clock. Damn. "I'm going to be so late."

"It'll be fine. I bet they haven't started anything important yet. The first day always starts with introductions and rules anyway."

I sat back. There wasn't anything I could do about it now, and Melanie would get irritated if I kept complaining. She's in charge; it's best to keep her happy.

I could feel how close we were to the school before I could see it. The itching need to get in that building intensified. My fingers and toes twitched and every cell in my body vibrated with nervous excitement. I sat on the edge of my seat and stared out the windshield, my breath catching as the bright, multi-colored swirls on the outside of the converted warehouse came into view.

I'd first seen the San Francisco Center for the Circus Arts months ago when Melanie and I stopped at the cafe across the street. Instantly I wanted—no, needed—to go there. I felt like the building called me, invading my dreams and my thoughts. It took six months and a rather crafty plan, but I made it. I hoped whatever part of my brain latched onto this place would feel happy now that I was finally attending classes here.

"Here we are, come on," Melanie said, yanking me out of my obsessive thoughts.

Melanie has the best parking karma of anyone I know. She always finds a parking space in front of whatever building she's going to, and in San Francisco that is a miracle.

I ran my fingers over the school's huge front window, the need to go inside as physical as if a rope were around my waist pulling me. A flash of red caught my eye. In the window hung a red crystal bird with a long tail. It flashed again, like it was winking at me.

When we entered the building warm air surrounded us, carrying the smells of floor wax, sweat, and incense, and the happy sounds of Celtic music. The converted warehouse looked like a huge dance studio with its scuffed wooden floor and wall of mirrors. The ropes, trapezes, hoops, and fabrics secured to the two-story high ceiling, and other circus equipment around the room let me know I'd have a lot more fun than in some stuffy dance class.

I glared at Melanie as we walked to the tall front desk. Divided into groups, the other campers were already learning circus arts. She ignored me and looked over the fliers and brochures scattered over the counter.

"Why don't you put your stuff away?" Melanie pointed to the wall of brightly painted cubbies. Maybe my staring bothered her. I strengthened my glare before doing as she asked.

I tucked my stuff away, and checked out the class closest to me. Their feet were bare. I took off my shoes and socks. I made it inside the stupid building, so when would this itching need stop? My fingers twitched in sympathy; they didn't like this either.

"The teacher over there has hair like yours," Melanie said softly, when I came back.

Following her glance, I saw a teenage boy teaching one of the classes. My instincts screamed 'run' when I saw his tight black curls that looked to be studded with rubies. The draw to come here, could it be some implanted beacon from a government experiment our parents had been a part of? Or perhaps we were alien/human hybrids and the mother ship called out to us to take us home. Or were we mutants drawn to this school by a psychic call from a group of superheroes? Or maybe I should stop reading things recommended to me by geeky staff?

I tried not to stare at him; however, my eyes kept being drawn back to the tall ebony boy with hair so close to mine in color. Looking over the rest of the students I didn't see anyone else with hair like ours. There were several Mohawks, a few people with dreadlocks, a girl with orange spiky hair, and one boy with black- and blue-streaked bangs. Maybe this wasn't some great conspiracy. Maybe he'd dyed his hair that color and this was nothing more than a freaky coincidence.

"Sorry for the wait, I'm Philip. How can I help you?"

Philip looked young at first. He wore sweats, cut off at his knees, and a faded David Bowie concert tee shirt. His ears were decorated with silver hoops. Only his three-inch salt and pepper Mohawk that curved between the sides of his shaved head, caused me to wonder at his age.

"No worries, this is Sara Fokine, she's here for the winter camp," Melanie said.

"Great, I have a few things for you to sign." Philip walked behind the high counter and handed Melanie some papers and a pen. Melanie scooted down to find an empty spot on the cluttered counter and began to read the papers.

Ignoring the mess, Philip crossed his arms on the counter, his eyes sparkling. Why did he look so happy? Part of me wanted to smile back, another part wanted to know what he was up to.

"Are you having a good birthday, Sara?" he asked.

"How did you know it's my birthday?" The itching need faded as he spoke, and a sense of safety and calm moved through me. I didn't trust it, or him. Could he be the government agent or alien in disguise? I stepped away.

He tilted his head toward Melanie. "The paperwork."

"Of course. Um...it's been different. I went to the doctor." Why would I tell him this? I never gave away personal information. I narrowed my eyes, as if that would help me find out the truth.

"Well turning fifteen can be challenging. I'm sure your mom wanted to take care of you."

I didn't bother to correct Philip. I didn't correct people when they mistook Melanie for my mom, or (her preference) my older sister. Most people didn't know about houseparents, which meant I needed to explain that I belong to the state. That got looks of pity or suspicion. I found it easier to keep my mouth shut.

I needed to get the conversation off me. "Nice tattoo." I pointed to the faded picture of a mermaid sitting on an anchor.

I could barely see it through the coat of white hair covering his arm.

Philip shook his head, a sheepish smile on his face. "I can't believe you can see it. That's a mark from another life, one full of adventure, danger, stupidity, and a scary lack of both condoms and common sense."

I slapped my hand over my mouth, trying not to laugh out loud, my face heating up. I thought Philip was an interesting person, even if he wasn't an alien here to take me back to the home planet.

"Excuse me?" Melanie handed back the papers, her eyes narrowed to the 'mom' look.

"Sorry, I need to edit better." He looked over the papers. "She's all set."

"Thanks, I'll see you at four?" Melanie searched around the counter top.

I handed her the set of keys she searched for. "Yes."

"Cool, I'll see you later. Call me if you need anything," Melanie said as she walked away.

Melanie's leaving never bothered me before, but today I wanted to call her back, to ask to go with her, or to beg her to stay with me. My voice stuck in my throat as the door closed.

"Come on, the group I'm working with could use one more person. This morning I'm teaching juggling." Philip held out a cloth ball.

I turned away from the door and took the ball. It squished a little between my fingers, like it was filled with sand.

Philip explained the basics of juggling. His calm, steady voice made me feel like I could learn to juggle easily.

"So once you can toss one beanbag back and forth without moving your hands to catch it, try it with two." Philip easily tossed them between his hands.

It didn't look too hard. I ignored Philip as he watched me toss the beanbag from my right hand to my left hand and back to my right. I moved my right hand in order to catch the beanbag; I normally don't throw things with my left hand. It felt awkward but not impossible.

"Good job. Try and look up when you toss them, it will help later on when you have three or more in the air. If you need any help, call for me or Shin." Philip nodded towards a muscular, stocky boy with black hair cut short, except for his blue-streaked bangs, which fell to his chin.

It took all my concentration to keep two beanbags in the air. One by one, all of the worries and wondering were pushed away, and my mind focused on juggling. My body relaxed as the pressure faded away.

Light reflected in the mirror, blinding me.

"You need to remember..." Philip's voice faded, and I heard an unfamiliar woman speaking in his place.

"You'll remember..." Images flashed in my mind.

Holding my mom's hand, running down a street, seeing a red bird in the window winking at us.

Inside the torn-up building, wood and paint cans everywhere.

My mom on her hands and knees in the bathroom, reaching into the wall, hiding something.

The sun sets behind her, I can't see her face. Her lips touch my forehead as she whispers something. It sounds like a song. When she's done, fire dances in her eyes.

"You'll remember when it's time," my mom says. "It will get dark soon, and the bad men will come. You need to go into the police station across the street. Give the nice officer this letter, and they will take care of you for me."

"I'm scared. I want to stay with you." Hot tears fall down my cheek.

"I can't let the bad men get you. I can't. You're my Jewel. I must protect you." Arms wrap around me hugging me tight. I breathe in the soft scent of flowers.

"You'll come back for me, right, Mommy?"

"They're close, baby. I have to go. I need you to be brave, and remember I will love you forever."

"Sara. Sara, are you okay?" Philip shook my shoulder.

"Sorry...I...I need a drink of water." I wrapped my arms around myself trying to hide the trembling. What the hell just happened?

"Are you all right?" Philip frowned looking me over to make sure I'm okay.

"I'm a bit dizzy, maybe something left over from the fever last night?" That made sense; it had been a bad fever. Maybe the vision came from my dream last night. At least I hoped so, but my gut told me something important just happened.

"Okay, go get a drink. If you need anything, I'm here." Philip stepped back, his frown still there.

"Thanks, I'll be right back." I reached up to rub my forehead where I could still feel my mother's lips. The spot felt warm, not body heat warm, but sitting in the sun warm.

Sitting down on a bench against the window I took a long drink of water. I didn't need any more weirdness. Wasn't there a limit, like a law of physics or something that maxed out how much weird crap can happen to you in one day?

A spark made me turn. Above me the red crystal bird spun in the window. Gripping my bottle so tight my fingers ached, flashes from my dream or memory lay over the room. Was this the same building? Had I been here before with my mom? I never dreamed about my mom, not that clearly. The memory of what she looked like and the sound of her voice had faded long ago. For all I knew I made the whole thing up. Maybe it was some post-fever-induced daydream.

Putting my water away, I went back to class. Crazy, fever-induced visions were not going to have me searching the bathroom walls. I picked up the beanbags and began tossing them again, trying but failing to find that peace and focus from before.

Staying to the back of the class, I watched the next teacher, Kayin Mangwiro. His voice sounded warm and rich with an African accent. Kayin went over a bunch of information about jumping on a trampoline safely. Even though I learned about the trampoline, I learned nothing that would give me a clue as to why his hair was black and red like mine.

When my turn came, Kayin helped me up onto the springy surface of the trampoline. My stomach flipped, and I barely suppressed the urge to wave my arms around as I fell back down. Bending my knees I tried to keep my balance, but took off towards the side of the trampoline. This was much harder than it looked.

"Try to keep in the middle," Kayin said, making sure I didn't fall off.

"Okay." I felt I did pretty well for my first time on a trampoline. When Kayin bounced, he controlled his movements. I felt lucky I hadn't fallen on my face.

"Time to switch." Kayin held out a dark hand to help me down.

"Thanks," I said, my breath coming in gasps. He nodded and went to help the next kid up.

Kayin seemed nice and answered questions when asked, but he wasn't playful like Philip. I twisted the hem of my shirt trying to get up the courage to ask about his hair. My new hair color made me look like a child dressing up for Halloween. Kayin's made him look like an African prince. His proud posture, wide flat nose, and high cheekbones looked elegant with the small ruby curls scattered among the ebony black ones.

Waiting for my second turn, I held my breath as Kayin stood next to me. How could he stand so still and with such perfect posture? I shifted from one foot to another and tugged on the sleeve of my shirt, smoothing out the embroidered silver dragon.

"I like your hair," I said, my voice barely more than a whisper. Hoping he heard me and hadn't heard me at the same time. Hey, I'm a teenager; I'm allowed to feel conflicted.

"Thank you. I woke up like this on the morning of my fifteenth birthday. It's a shocking thing, to change so suddenly, isn't it?" Kayin's gaze held mine. After a moment I felt warmth fill me and I knew. Kayin was like me. Whatever was happening to me already happened to him.

"We're family now," he said.

"I don't ...I'm not sure..." Turning away, I tried to calm my thoughts so I could make a complete sentence.

"I know this is hard to understand. I'm here if you need to talk." Kayin touched my hand, and a spark of heat ignited beneath my skin.

I rubbed the back of my hand as Kayin left to help another kid onto the trampoline. While I felt happy to know I'm not alone in this, the heat thing was strange. Oh well, one more thing to add to the 'list of weirdness'. I moved on to the next class.

Hearing Taliesin Gadarn tell us about the walking globe, a large ball that we were going to walk on, I realized he would not be here for me if I needed to talk. He looked like snow and ice. His attitude, the way he moved, the color of his hair and skin chilled me. If it weren't for his blue eyes I would have thought he was an albino.

"Are there any questions?" Taliesin asked, looking over us one by one. I tried not to feel insignificant under his cool assessing gaze. Did his high school teach him how to act like a snob, or did it come naturally?

"Line up," Taliesin said, flipping his white braid over his shoulder.

When my turn came, Taliesin braced the knee-high walking globe against his shins and held out his hands to me. Taking his hands, I climbed onto the ball. It teetered, but I managed to stay on. Clenching my stomach, I tried to find my balance on the wobbling ball.

"I'm going to start walking," Taliesin said taking a small step back.

I gripped his hands, took a small step and then another. Standing straighter, I made my steps a little bit faster. Taliesin easily adjusted. When we got to the end of the track my cheeks hurt from smiling so big.

"Thank you, that was fun." I looked up, my smile fading at Taliesin's emotionless face.

"Birds like the air," he said as he walked back to the beginning.

What did that mean? Birds? Is this some new slang? Or something to do with the changes? And how would he know? He didn't feel like Kayin, and I didn't feel any warmth or attraction to him. At this point I needed to make another entry to my list if I hoped of keeping up with the craziness of today.

*   *   *

Stalling without being obvious is a gift. In a classroom, the teacher is your best ally. Ask questions or offer to help. Today, I helped move mats while the other kids got ready for lunch. I wanted to sit alone. Once everyone else started eating I would venture out and claim a nook to myself.

Not everyone had settled down for lunch once the mats were put away, so I went to the bathroom - another good stalling technique.

I took a breath and prepared for the inevitable stream of questions that would race through my mind when I spent any time looking in a mirror. Running my fingers under the black bandanna, I checked to make sure my hair stayed secure in the bun. It crunched from the mass of gel and hair spray I'd used.

Did my mom have almond-shaped eyes, too? Did my dimples come from my dad? Did I look like my parents, or like another family member? Who else in my family had a nose that turned up a bit at the end?

These questions were familiar. Having no memory or pictures of my parents, I'm a mystery to myself. I have no idea who I am or where I come from. I hope that someday I will either know who I am, or let it go and get on with my life.

Looking at my changed reflection, I found new questions filling my mind. Did I look more like my parents now, or less? Was I now proof of a mistake made in their youth? An ancient family secret revealed? Would they be proud of how I looked, or lock me in the basement so no one else could see me?

I glared at myself in the mirror. "Sara, get a grip, go out there, make a list of all the craziness, and eat lunch."

Looking around the bathroom, I felt both grateful and disappointed that I didn't get any flashes of memory. My hands itched to touch the walls, hoping to find where my mom hid the package almost ten years ago. I flung the bathroom door open, refusing to give in to hallucinations.

People-watching is a sport in San Francisco, so the other students sat near the huge front windows. Philip, Kayin and Taliesin were gathered in an office behind the desk, with the door open. Shin brushed his blue and black bangs away from his face as he ate with the students. He must have drawn the short straw.

Eavesdropping is wrong; sitting where you can hear people talking is an 'accident.' The key: don't sit so close they know you hear them. Looking busy helps. Luck was with me today; a stack of mats stood a few feet from the open office door. Sitting down, I leaned against the mats and took out my lunch.

"I don't know if she's the Jewel, but she's definitely a Child of Fire," Philip said.

What is a Child of Fire? I took a bite of my vegetable sandwich. Pickle juice dripped down my chin. I grabbed my napkin before it could drip onto my shirt. I didn't want to smell like dill pickles all day.

"How did classes go?" Philip asked.

"Fine," Taliesin said.

"I'm looking forward to Gavin and Anali being here. Teaching is new to me, and I'd rather help than be in charge," Kayin said.

I thought Kayin did a good job.

"Do you think you will be ready to teach a class in January?" Philip mumbled. I guess he was eating.

"Yes. Once I get used to teaching, I should be fine," Kayin said.

"You did well today," Taliesin said. Wow, he could be nice.

"Thank you," Kayin said.

I jumped when the phone rang; not good, way too obvious. I finished my sandwich, took out a notebook, and began listing all the weird things that happened so far. Philip's one-sided phone conversation wasn't that interesting anyway, something about hoping the storm cleared and that they would arrive here tomorrow, whoever "they" were.

I kept one ear on the conversation, in case something interesting came up, but focused on my list: high fever, my hair, skin, and eyes changed color, I saw a flashback/daydream/hallucination about my mom, Kayin said we were family, and I felt heat when we touched. I didn't know what any of it meant, or what would happen next. I had a feeling the weirdness wasn't over.

The list didn't help. I hated change, even change within my control. Closing my eyes, I leaned my head against the mats.

What should, I do? What could I do? I liked Melanie and trusted her, but nothing could be a secret between us. She needed to report everything out of the ordinary to my caseworker and the group home supervisor. The physical differences were bad enough. If I added these weird feelings and visions, I could wind up in the hospital for crazy people. That was not an option that appealed to me.

I guess I would have to wait and see what happened next. Maybe this was leftover brain bubbles from the fever. Just odd stuff leaking from my subconscious, and after a good night's sleep it would all go away. Yes, a good plan. I liked this plan, especially the all going away part.

An image flashed into my mind of an old leather-bound book, one I memorized and which brought me comfort and words of wisdom when I needed it. It was the only thing I had from my mom. On each page she wrote a quote, and then offered advice in small neat letters.

"Change is the constant, the signal for rebirth, the egg of the phoenix." -Christina Baldwin.

"Every life is full of changes and challenges. Some changes are small, while others will alter the rest of your life. Some changes you will have hoped and prayed for, while plenty of others will make you want to hide under your covers and stay in bed. Just know that your strength lies within you. No matter what, remember who you are. Change happens, finding out what new opportunities lie before you is a sign of the wise and brave."

"All right everyone, I'd like you all to finish up and meet in the middle of the room in ten minutes," Philip said.

I wasn't sure what was to come, what changes would be forced on me, or what opportunities would present themselves. What I did know was that I needed to be very careful.

Chapter Two

"Opportunity is missed by most people because it is dressed in overalls and looks like work." ~Thomas Edison

The bus ride home was uneventful by San Francisco standards. I shared the bus with a pack of punked-out teenagers, some people arguing about the best way to prevent the government from reading their minds, and two drag queens. One sported Dolly Parton curls and a pink feather boa, and the other wore short black hair and a gold, sequined gown. Looking down at my hands, I jumped, having forgotten for a moment about my new skin color. Maybe I should try and talk to Kayin about all the crazy happening to me?

Hopping off the bus I switched to the cable car, which would drop me off near home. I love riding the cable car. I always stand on the outside, even in bad weather. As we clanked and groaned over the hills, I looked down on my neighborhood.

I tried to focus on the beauty of the city, but I couldn't drag my thoughts away from the changes happening to me. I didn't have any answers, nothing new to add to my list of possibilities, so letting my thoughts run crazy wasn't going to help anything. If being rational was enough, I would be able to stop the swirling tornado of questions, what ifs, and wild theories tearing through my mind. Unfortunately it wasn't enough, and the whirlwind continued.

Getting off at my stop, I waved my thanks to the driver.

I tried to calm my thoughts, and pull my focus back to the here and now. I couldn't fix anything today, and I hoped to wake up in the morning and find this was all a dream.

Resting for a moment, I stared up at the cheery Victorian row house which had been my home for the past three years. Volunteers had come by recently and repainted Hope House. The white trim gleamed against the sunny yellow walls. Not only was Hope House the best group home I ever lived in, it also looked the prettiest.

Walking up the stairs I groaned. Who knew you could over-work your butt? For afternoon classes Shin taught acrobatics, Philip and Kayin taught clowning, and Taliesin taught poi, the fluffy, bright-colored balls on strings which we spun around in patterns, or at least we tried to. It had been fun, but now my body ached.

I skipped the steps that squeaked, to see if I could sneak into the house. On the second floor I stopped and listened as the kids in House One sang along to some Disney show. No sound came from House Two; the sibling set of five must have gone out on a visit. All clear, I continued my trek up the stairs.

When I reached my floor, I heard shouting coming from House Four. Teenage boys are loud, especially when playing video games.

Pressing my ear against House Three's door, I could hear voices and music; maybe today I could sneak in. I opened the door, making sure it didn't creak or open too wide, and peeked into the house. Melanie's back faced me as she played Go Fish with Caitlin, Rhonda and Myra. No one looked up from the table as I walked into the room.

"Hello Sara, how was your day?" Melanie asked, causing all of us to jump.

I glared at the back of her head. One of these days I was going to sneak up on her. Hey, everyone needs a goal.

"I finished my homework," Shante shouted as she barreled at me, hugging me tight. The preschool she goes to sends home coloring sheets. Shante liked having homework like the "big girls."

"Good job. How was your day?" I said, running my hand over Shante's dark brown pigtails.

"Great, Miss Kimberly said I sang the ABCs louder than anyone else!"

I believed her.

"Go fish!" Caitlin yelled, sticking her tongue out at Myra.

"Quiet down," Melanie said. "Now that Shante is finished, why don't you go watch TV?"

Shante didn't follow the rest of the girls. Her big brown eyes inspected me carefully. "You look different."

"Well, I am fifteen now." I hoped she'd buy that as an excuse.

"I have something for you, don't move." She ran down the hallway, and then came back waving a piece of paper. "Happy birthday!"

I took the handmade card she thrust at my face. "Thank you Shante. It's wonderful."

Shante poked her picture with a chubby finger. "It's a picture of all of us. There's you and me and the house you're going to buy for us, and there's my mommy."

An art therapist would have a field day with this drawing. Shante and I were bright smiling people with arms and legs standing in front of a hot pink house that apparently I would buy. Off to the side sat a shapeless blob of swirling gray, Shante's mom Sophia.

"I love it, I'm going to go and hang it on my wall right now." I hugged Shante tight.

Shante squeezed me, then ran off to the living room.

"Can you get ready to leave in fifteen minutes?" Melanie asked. "Rachel should be here by then, and we can go."

Deep sigh, my poor body. "Yes, let me shower and change."

I could hear the thumping bass of Crystal's music through our bedroom door. "Hello, Crystal. How was your day?"

"Awful, the camp sucked and the food was so horrible, I couldn't eat any of it." She twisted her honey blond hair around her finger. "I have split ends, I need a haircut, but not from the woman down the street, she sucks. My roots are showing, I need to get a box of dye, but the stupid people here don't trust me enough to dye my own hair!"

I winced at her voice and kept my head down hoping Crystal wouldn't notice my hair. It could happen. I'd had entire conversations with Crystal, and she'd never once looked up from the magazine she was reading.

Gathering up my clothes, I didn't notice Crystal had moved until she ripped the bandanna off my head. "You dyed your hair! Melanie, Sara dyed her hair!"

I went deaf for a moment, Crystal continued to scream, and the other girls all ran in, squealing at my black and red hair. Melanie came in, and everyone calmed down.

"Sara got straight A's on her report card, and she's never caused any problems or broken any rules," Melanie said, her voice firm. "So dying her hair was her reward, and a birthday present. I don't want to hear any more about it."

The younger girls shrugged and went back to the living room. Crystal complained and demanded to call her caseworker because this was "totally unfair."

I ran to the bathroom before anything else could happen. Hiding is underrated; it's my top problem-solving tool.

As quickly as I could I washed the gel out of my hair and got dressed. I wanted to put my hair into another bun and hide the strange new color, but Melanie wouldn't be okay with that, so instead I dried it as best as I could then wove it into a braid.

Tossing my clothes into my laundry basket, I waved good-bye to Crystal who now moaned to her caseworker about my going with Melanie. I left without saying anything.

I opened the door to Melanie's room and glared at the mess all over the floor. I cleaned her room last weekend. Oh, well, this meant she would pay me to clean it again.

"We have to go."

"Go out to the car, I need to find my stuff," she said stepping out of the bathroom.

"I have your bag, keys, and phone." As if I didn't know exactly what she needed.

"You're the best. All right, let's go."

Melanie dressed comfortably, but far dressier than most days. She was wearing makeup and had also pinned up her hair! This created a lovely cascade of rich brown curls down her back and accentuated the heart shape of her face.

Why was she so dressed up? "You look nice."

"Well, we are going out for your birthday. I'm surprised you didn't dress nicer."

"What?" I asked making my eyes wide with fake innocence as I looked down at my blue jeans, blue blouse, and gray sweater. "This is nice for me."

Melanie glared at me. I couldn't help but laugh. She huffed and walked off, but I knew she wasn't mad. I followed behind and as soon as I stepped towards the door a little body slammed into me.

"Do you have to go?" Shante pressed her face into my stomach. I always tucked Shante into bed and read her a story. I felt bad about leaving.

"Yes, Shante, but I'll see you in the morning, okay? Be good for Rachel while we're gone."

"Okay, night, Sara. I love you."

"I love you, too, Shante."

*   *   *

My fingers gripped the seat and my eyes were tightly shut. I wished it was foggy because Melanie drove more slowly in the fog. Right now, she texted as she drove. I hated driving with her. Hearing the clicking of CD cases, I snapped, "Can I help you? I'm not driving right now."

"Find the Rent soundtrack and put it in." Melanie glanced at the road before looking at her phone.

Hunting through the stack of CD's I found Rent and put it in the player. "Thank you for taking me out tonight."

Melanie smiled. "This is what you wanted for your birthday gift, a movie and dinner with me, which I totally understand, because I am awesome."

"And yet you left two new outfits on my bed this morning."

"You needed those for camp."

I rolled my eyes, I didn't need new clothes. "Thank you for them. I don't think I said thanks because of all the crazy this morning."

Melanie set her phone down and patted my leg. "You're welcome and with all you do for me, you deserve it. I wanted your birthday to be special."

I didn't help Melanie out in order to get stuff, but because my mom advised me in her journal never to waste an opportunity.

"Frequently people will open up opportunities to you because they need help, and by helping someone you never know what will come of it. It might be something simple like finding out about a great pizza place, because that's where they order lunch when you help them move. It could also lead to meeting new people, people who could become friends, or know of a job, or a place to live. You never know what you can gain by accepting requests for help. Opportunities are everywhere, so don't be afraid of a little hard work, you never know what it'll get you."

"I like helping you, and you pay me." I said feeling guilty. Melanie was generous and some of her friends took advantage of her. I didn't want to become one of those people.

Melanie laughed. "No worries Sara, I know that. I like hanging out with you, and anyway I've wanted to see this movie forever."

*   *   *

I slumped into the car, my stomach pooching out from the huge Mexican dinner we'd eaten.

"Thanks for helping me finish my Christmas shopping," I said.

Melanie started the car and turned on the heater.

"No problem, I had fun. The girls are going to love what you bought them."

"Thanks for dinner, it was so good." I rubbed my tummy.

Melanie shook her head. "I can't believe you ate that much. Do you have everything you need for Christmas now?"

I nodded. "I got Shante, Caitlin, Myra and Rhonda baby dolls, two CDs for Crystal, and a little something for you while you were looking at the DVDs."

Melanie pulled into the garage. "Okay, everyone should be asleep, so make sure to be quiet."

"Of course." I didn't want to deal with anyone anyway.

After washing my hair three times and failing to get any of the black or red out I went to bed. Maybe I'll be back to normal in the morning. Laying my head on my pillow, I closed my eyes. Images from this morning flashed in my mind: the old building, my mom hiding something in the bathroom wall. Then new ones began: a dragon, a unicorn, and a bird on fire. I tried to open my eyes, to collect my thoughts.

"No, my Jewel, you need to come to us," a man said, pulling me into sleep.

Chapter Three

"Life shrinks or expands in proportion to one's courage."
~Anais Nin

I was on fire! I beat at the flames with my hands. Taking in a deep breath so I could scream, instead I froze. The air didn't burn; it felt warm but not hot. Looking up, I saw a bird, flames coming from its feathers. What in the world was going on? And how do I get out of here?

The bird blinked his gold eyes, then began to sing. Its voice was a mix of bird song, human voices, and musical instruments, yet at the same time much simpler than that. My whole body relaxed as a sense of peace filled me. My sore aching muscles were soothed with each note. Flames continued to dance along my skin, but I no longer felt afraid.

"This must be a dream." I closed my eyes and relaxed. None of this was real.

Blinking, I tried to get my bearings. I was no longer on fire, which was great, but I knew that something had happened, something changed, and time passed. I did something or had been told something, and now it was lost to me.

"Remember us, I know it will be hard. Dreaming is a new skill. But try your hardest to remember us," a woman pleaded with me. Her long black curls flowed in the flower-scented breeze. She wore a toga of blue, purple and green. Her copper skin glowed darker than my own.

"You will be able to find what your mother left for you, as we have restored your memories," her husband said, as he slid an arm around her waist. His flame-red hair and pale skin made him look otherworldly. Behind them stood a herd of unicorns feasting on the unnaturally green grass. Above us a griffin and a dragon raced across the turquoise sky.

My eyes opened with a jolt.

I ran my hands over my face trying to rub away the images. Shakily, I got out of bed, surprised that I wasn't sore at all. Stretching my arms, I felt the ghost of the warmth and peace from the bird's fire. This was crazy! I grabbed my outfit for the day and went into the bathroom.

Catching my reflection in the mirror, I jumped. *How long would it take to get use to my new appearance?* Quickly, I twisted my hair into a tight bun. I made sure to separate my black bangs from the red, and covered my hair in a bandanna then put on a gray long-sleeved shirt, and plain black sweatpants.

I tried to forget my dream, tried to ignore the hum of magic on my skin. Every time I moved without pain, my suspicion grew that my dream healed me.

I do not believe in fairy tale creatures! Dreams are nothing more than my subconscious working on a problem!

Turning, I glared at myself in the mirror. This is not good, you're arguing with yourself about something you don't even believe in! Wait, did that even make sense? I'm going crazy! Okay, calm down. I gritted my teeth knowing if I actually talked out loud, Melanie would wake up and ask was going on. What would I say?

Okay, Sara, get a grip. Deep breath, take a deep cleansing breath. Now put your things away, get your yoga mat and figure this out.

Moving from one yoga pose to another, I thought over the problem and the mysterious dreams I'd been having. I knew I had experienced the same kind of dream that I'd had on my birthday, even though I couldn't remember the details. My brain kept going over how my body felt last night, dreaming of the faerie tale world, and how good I felt now. As I lay in corpse pose I came up with two options. First: I was wrong about how sore I felt last night; a perfectly reasonable option. Second: A magical being healed me while I slept.

As I put my things away I still felt confused about which reality to choose, the one where I didn't believe my own perceptions or the one where I believed in mythical creatures.

The others began to wake, and I turned my focus toward getting ready for the day.

"Melanie, I'm leaving," I said sticking my head into her room an hour later.

"Have a good day, I'll see you at four," Melanie called from the bathroom.

My eyes came to rest on her pink toolbox peeking out from under the bed. I dashed in and pulled out a screwdriver and stuffed it into my bag.

"The church group is coming tonight, right?" I asked.

"Yes, they're bringing dinner." Melanie mumbled as she brushed her teeth.

"Cool, see you then." Guilt gnawed at my stomach. I'd never taken anything from Melanie before. The image of my mom hiding something in the bathroom wall played clearly in my mind. I wasn't sure what to do about it, but I would need a tool to use if I decided to break through a wall at San Francisco Center for the Circus Arts.

Walking down the hill to the cable car, I felt the wind whip through my jacket and sweater. I kept my head down trying to keep the rain off my face. By the time I got to circus camp, I was glad for central heating. Heading to the cubbies, I peeled off my wet jacket. I wore enough layers that my shirt stayed dry; my pants, however, were not so lucky and completely soaked.

"Got caught in the rain?" An Indian woman asked, looking at the puddle around my feet.

"Yes, but they'll dry, I'm not worried." I sat down to take off my shoes and socks. I rubbed my blue toes trying to warm them up. My icy hands weren't much help. "I like the music today."

"Thanks, I got to the stereo before anyone else. I love Bollywood. I'm Anali, my husband and I are teachers here." A shoulder length black bob framed her sweet round face.

"Nice to meet you. I'm Sara."

"We're about the same size, if you would like to borrow a dry pair? If the floor gets wet, it could become dangerous." Anali gestured to my wet pants.

True, Anali was petite, only an inch or two taller than my five feet two and a half inches, and I suppose wet clothes could be a safety concern. I hoped they wouldn't be bright pink with turquoise embroidery like hers.

"Okay, thanks." I followed her up the narrow wooden staircase, hitching my backpack on my shoulder. A plain door opened into a living room. There were books everywhere. Books shoved tightly onto shelves, with more books stuffed on top of them, books stacked into corners, under tables, on top of tables, peeking out from couch cushions, and opened over the arms of the furniture.

"I'll come right back," Anali smiled.

I nodded and looked at the nearest bookshelf. My eyes widened; they were all about mythical creatures. Just a coincidence, look away, nothing to see here, citizen. Turning, I saw Kayin standing inside the kitchen looking puzzled, his dark skin glowing against the rich orange of his tee shirt.

Before I could explain why I was up there, a man with flame-red hair walked into the room, tugging on a gray tee shirt with Kermit the Frog on the front.

"Hurry up, the little monsters will get here soon!" He stopped short when he saw me, his mouth dropping open, eyes wide.

Well, this is uncomfortable.

"Not a good look on you, honey." Anali said as she walked past her husband, her head barely reaching his shoulder. "Here, Sara, these should fit you, they're a little short on me."

"Thank you." I took the soft cotton pants, grateful for the dark green color.

"This is my husband, Gavin. Gavin, this is Sara; she's a student here."

"Hello. You look a lot like my sister," Gavin said, as he continued to stare at me.

"Weird. Thank you for the pants, Anali. I'll go downstairs and change." I turned and ran back down the stairs.

I crashed into someone at the bottom of the stairs.

Taliesin frowned at me. "Oh, are all the little birds happy in their nest?"

"What exactly is wrong with you?" I asked looking him over as if I could see some kind of flaw. Unfortunately, I couldn't see any. He looked perfect in his slate blue sweats and white tee shirt, if you liked slender, muscular, GQ guys. "Is that some kind of new racist term?"

His sky-blue eyes narrowed. "Didn't your parents tell you about your heritage?"

"Taliesin, that's enough," Gavin said as he walked down the stairs, his voice firm.

Crap, more weirdness would happen today. Well, I didn't need a protector. "I don't have any parents. I haven't since I was five."

"What?" Gavin said behind me.

I turned. He gripped the banister, holding himself up, and looking horrified. What was his problem?

Taliesin's face went through a range of emotions, confusion, anger, and disbelief. He settled on pity. I pushed passed him, making sure my bag hit him in the chest and headed to the bathroom to change. If more strangeness was on its way, I wanted to be wearing dry pants.

I stepped into the empty bathroom and felt the memory of my mother wash over me. I went into the last stall, hung my bag on the hook, and changed into the borrowed pants. Had my mother really knelt here on the floor and hidden something in the wall? I locked the stall door and changed.

What was I going to do? Did I believe my mom hid something in the wall? What if someone found me lying on the floor? What if nothing was there? What if something was? What if I got caught? How would I explain prying open the wall?

I didn't want my life to change! Wrapping my arms around myself, I slid to the floor, my whole body shaking. I wanted things to go back to the way they were before! I wanted boring brown hair and ugly gray-green eyes.

I glared at the trashcan, which stood in front of the spot my mom had been in my vision. Okay, how about this, it could be like a coin toss, two choices. If there is nothing in the wall, I can say all the changes are due to hormones, the fever, becoming a teenager, and I can ignore all the weirdness.

I stopped shaking. Okay, good plan, but what if there is something in the wall? Well, I explained to myself (in my head: only crazy people talk to themselves out loud) well, then, whatever is in the wall will provide answers, and I'll figure out where to go from there.

Cool, two rational, logical plans. Now I just needed to cross the floor and look behind the trashcan. I sat frozen. I knew if I sat here long enough someone would come into the bathroom and my chance would be lost. Hey, I'm on a roll with the good plans this morning!

"Courage is a tricky thing; sometimes the right thing to do isn't always clear. Sometimes our choices are based on gut feelings, dreams, wisps of memory, or even an impression. It is these small guides that lead us to our true lives. Going down one street suddenly can change the course of your life. I met your father by following an odd feeling. I walked around the tables of the library. I felt so embarrassed when the other students stared at me. Then I finally found the right table, no one else sat there, only a messy pile of books. A few minutes later your dad sat down.

Don't be afraid of what others might think, my darling daughter. Follow your heart, trust your feelings, and live life fully."

I slid across the cold tile. Behind the trashcan, I ran my fingers over the tall baseboards separating the floor from the cheap wood paneling. Getting the screwdriver from my bag, I pulled the baseboard loose. The nails squealed in protest as they were pulled from the wall.

Thank goodness for poor construction. A two-inch gap came into view between the floor and the wall, plenty of space for my trembling fingers to reach into the gap. I reached in as far as I could, stretching my fingers hoping to find whatever my mom left. There was nothing.

Sitting back I stared at the wall. I could clearly see my mom reaching in and up into the wall. I grabbed the bottom of the wood paneling and tugged. The flimsy wood moved easily, and in a puff of dust, a wrinkled paper bag fell down. I pulled it to me.

I shoved the panel back into place, using the back of the screwdriver to force the nails back in. I finished putting the baseboard back as the bathroom door opened. Three Perky Girls giggled as they fixed their hair and talked about the cute boys in class. I grabbed the bag and moved further into the stall, almost falling onto the toilet. This is crazy! The dream, the memory, was real? Carefully, I opened the bag finding two bundles of cloth and an envelope.

"Hurry up, classes will start soon," one of the Perky Girls said to her friends.

Crap, should I read it now? Could I stand to wait until lunch? If I want to keep this a secret I needed to go back out there. I placed the bag in my backpack, making sure it was safe and wouldn't get squished. I washed up, plastered a bored teenage mask on, and went out to pretend my life hadn't changed again in ways I couldn't begin to imagine.

I sat away from everyone else and began stretching, grateful I wasn't as sore as most of the other kids seemed to feel this morning. Maybe the crazy dreams weren't so bad.

Philip and Gavin were at the desk searching for something. Gavin flung papers aside, while Philip tried to calm him down. Hoping I wasn't obvious, I continued to watch the two men while I warmed-up. Gavin froze, his confusion visible. Grabbing the phone he dialed, his eyes darting between the phone and a piece of paper. His mouth opened a bit, as if to say hello, but it must have been a message because Gavin closed his mouth and hung up the phone. Shaking his head he hid his face in his hands; whatever he'd heard upset him. Phillip placed an arm around him, comforting and supportive.

"Do you mind if I join you?" Kayin asked.

"Sure, no problem."

"You said your hair changed on your fifteenth birthday?" I asked once he'd sat down. If I couldn't read the letter, or spy on Gavin and Phillip, I was going to get answers from somewhere.

"Yes, it was quite shocking." Kayin reached out and grabbed his toes. "I went to bed with black hair and high fever and woke up with ruby red curls scattered around my head. It's part of our inheritance, they say it's a gift."

"There are more people like us?" My voice a whisper.

"Yes, not a lot, we're special, but there are others. Gavin, Anali, and Philip are all of the same line too," Kayin said.

"So we're all related?" Hello, weirdness level reaching critical mass.

Kayin shrugged. "A little bit. We are all descendants from a great king and queen who lived thousands of years ago in Babylon."

"This can't be real." I stared at the door, wondering if I could escape before any of them caught up to me.

"I didn't believe it at first either, then my gift came in and I couldn't deny it any more. I'm sorry this is happening to you. I know it's a shock. Some people actually grow up knowing the change is coming and it's celebrated."

"You didn't celebrate?" I didn't need to ask, his tone told me everything.

Kayin shook his head and looked away. "No, I did not."

"What kind of gift?" I asked keeping my voice soft enough that Kayin could pretend he hadn't heard me if he wanted. I hoped he would answer, I needed to know what else could happen.

"It's different for everyone. Some people can feel other people's emotions, or influence others with their voice, some can help heal, or manipulate fire." Kayin brought the soles of his feet together, let his legs fall open, and leaned forward to touch his head to the floor.

"Wow, first how you look changes then you can suddenly do freaky things." This was not good. I'm supposed to hide something like that, how?

Kayin's dry chuckle made me shiver. "It is rather scary. There are quite a few of us in town. Once your gift comes in, we will find someone to teach you how to use it."

Oh, yeah. I could just see Five letting me take classes from some stranger to control my sudden supernatural gift. "We'll see."

"Remember that I'm here, and I'm willing to help. I need to get ready, classes will start soon." Kayin stood up.

"Thank you."

"I know it's a lot, but it will be okay."

"It's not okay for you yet," I said without thinking.

Kayin turned away.

"I'm sorry."

"No you're right, it's not okay yet, but I'm hopeful," Kayin said, sounding more resigned than hopeful.

Feeling like a jerk, I watched him walk away. Just because I felt upset and confused didn't mean I had the right to hurt Kayin.

"Good morning everyone," Philip said. "Our two snow-bound teachers managed to get a flight from New York and are here now. This is Gavin and Anali."

"I hope you all remember your number from yesterday; we'll stay in those groups. Group one will go with Anali for tumbling, group two will come with me for poi spinning. I see those looks, and no, we won't use fire during camp." Several of the boys groaned. "Group three will go with Gavin, Shin, Kayin and Taliesin for stilts."

I couldn't remember what group I was in yesterday. Looking around, I found a girl with brown dreadlocks who'd been in my group yesterday and followed her.

"Good morning, I'm Gavin, and we'll be teaching stilting. The four of us will go around the room and help you put on the stilts. Please do not try to get up on your own."

I watched while Shin helped another girl put her stilts on, and followed what he did. I picked my feet up, it felt weird having two feet of wood tied to them.

"Good job, Sara," Shin said, testing the tightness of my knots.

"Thanks," I said, pleased I got it right, but then I felt a flash of jealously. Weird. Why would I feel jealous?

"Are you ready to try walking?" Shin turned his feet so they pointed out and were shoulder width apart.

"Sure," I said, although it came out more like a question. I wanted to try and walk on the stilts, but not excited about falling from that high up.

Shin smiled. "It'll be fine. That's why Gavin has all the assistants, so no one gets hurt. Now place the bottom of each stilt at the arch of my foot. Good, grab my hands and up you go."

I held my breath as Shin leaned back and I rose into the air. Once my stilts were straight, I stood up slowly. Gripping Shin's hands, I shifted from foot to foot as I tried to stand.

"Good, get your balance," Shin said stepping back a bit.

"Don't let go." I tightened my grip on his hands.

"Not until you're ready. Let's try and walk okay?" Shin raised his hand higher forcing me to stand straighter.

"Okay." I took a very small, very careful step.

Shin walked with me for a few minutes. Each step got easier, and I loosened my death grip on his hands.

"Kayin," Shin said. "Take Sara and I'll go get another one up."

"Sure." Kayin walked towards us. The boy he supported needed only one of his hands held for balance.

I wasn't sure about holding onto one hand. Shin's thin eyes crinkled in amusement. "Sara you'll do fine; you haven't slipped or lost your balance once."

I placed my hand in Kayin's dark one, feeling the warm spark just like last time. Kayin smiled at me. I relaxed a bit, maybe he'd forgiven me.

"Josh, why don't you try walking on your own, you seem to have the hang of it," Kayin said a few minutes later.

Josh nodded and let go of Kayin's hand. He walked next to us for a bit then rambled off on his own.

"I'm sorry about what I said."

Kayin squeezed my hand. "It's okay, Sara, don't worry about it. You're doing well. Do you want to try it on your own?"

"Will you stay next to me?" I asked.

"Yes, don't worry, I'm not going anywhere." Kayin's rich brown eyes held mine.

For a moment it seemed he was saying more, it made me feel safe and protected.

"Okay." I let go of his hand and took a step.

"Remember, your balance comes from your stomach an inch or two above your belly button."

After a few more careful steps I began taking more normal steps. I had a few tippy moments, then I walked without any trouble.

"I think you've got it. I'm going to help someone else," Kayin said.

"Sure, thanks." *I was stilting. I rock!*

"Class is about to end," Gavin said. "We will come around and help each of you down, then you can take off your stilts."

I made my way over the side of the room.

Gavin held up his hands. "Let me help you down."

When I touched him I got that same jolt of warmth I had when I touched Kayin. I looked up in surprise, meeting his pale green eyes in shock. Gavin smiled. Kayin said that Gavin was a descendant of the King and Queen like us, so I shouldn't be surprised to feel the same spark. Slowly, I lowered myself down using Gavin to keep my balance.

"If you have any questions or need anything, both Anali and I are here for you," Gavin said softly. I could hear a faint hint of a New York accent in his voice.

I nodded and began to undo my stilts. I didn't know what else to say. I mean how does one respond when a total stranger offers to help you as your world falls apart around you?

I sat alone at lunch again. Opening my backpack, I pulled out the thick envelope. I saw my name written across the front in neat, loopy letters. The paper crinkled as I opened the envelope and unfolded the pages. A strangely familiar scent of flowers came from the paper. Was that my mother's perfume?

My dearest daughter,

I would give anything to be with you right now. I tried everything I could think of to keep you with me, but in the end I wasn't able to. Know that I love you so very, very much. You are my Jewel, the most precious thing in the world to both your dad and me.

I hope you are reading this before your fifteenth birthday. Sometimes huge changes can happen almost overnight. Remember this letter, and know that everything will be all right.

You need to find your uncle, Gavin Marsh. He will help protect you and explain what is happening.

Love always and all ways,

Mom

P.S. On your fifteen birthday you'll be able to read the other letter. Try reading it out loud. It helps.

Wow, okay so this was some weird family thing, like Kayin explained. Nice to know he wasn't lying to me. Wait, Gavin Marsh? Turning, I peeked around the edge of the gym mats I sat behind. Gavin stood by the desk talking with Philip and Kayin, his hair the same shade of flame red as the curls in Kayin's hair.

Is he my uncle? I sat back staring at the letter in front of me, reading it over and over again. It couldn't be a coincidence, could it?

Okay, slow breaths, Sara, take slow breaths, you still need to read the other page. I switched the pages, and the images swam as my eyes filled with tears. My mom was crazy, these weren't words just a bunch of odd lines and shapes. She expected me to read this? Reading it out loud helps? What?

I felt so close to understanding what was happening. So hopeful that I would finally learn who I am and what's going on. The marks seemed to swirl as I stared at them, mocking me with hidden truths I couldn't decipher.

"I'm going to see if I can find her. I haven't seen her for a while." I heard Gavin say.

Quickly I put the letter away, pulled my curly bangs over my eyes, wiped away the tears, and picked up my salad, and took a big bite.

Gavin walked past the mats. "Oh, here you are, Sara. I was worried."

"Is it not okay to sit over here?" I made my voice sound timid. Most adults fall for the "innocent" voice.

"No, it's fine. I was doing a head count making sure we hadn't lost anyone, and I couldn't find you." Gavin sat down, a warm smile on his face.

My leg began to twitch. Crossing my legs, I tried to hide my nervousness.

"Why aren't you sitting with the others?" Gavin tilted his head to the side like a curious puppy.

"I don't get a lot of chances to be alone, so I take them when I can." It's my standard answer. Honestly, I think most people imagine that I live in a long hall filled with poor orphans like something out of Oliver Twist or Annie.

A wave of sadness swept over me. What was that? Looking up Gavin's eyes were filled with sadness. I could feel it coming from him.

Oh, this isn't good. Didn't Kayin say one of the gifts was feeling other people's emotions? My first conversation with the man who could be my uncle, and I have to deal with this too? Seriously, Universe, I can't take much more. I'm only fifteen. There's only so much I can deal with.

"It's nice to have time alone. I'll give you your space. I'm sure I'm supposed to help with something." Gavin's hand twitched as if he wanted to touch me.

"It's fine, thanks for checking on me." For some reason this made Gavin happy, if the bubbly warmth coming off of him was any indication.

"No problem. I know Kayin has been talking to you about things, but remember Anali and I are also here and willing to help," Gavin said, standing up.

"I'll remember," I said taking a bite of salad so I didn't have to say any more.

While playing red light/green light, I became dizzy from everyone's emotions. No wonder adults said teenagers were crazy. Emotions danced around me like light from a disco ball: joy, anger, lust, jealousy, embarrassment, and happiness.

"Stay out of my personal bubble!" one of the girls said to a boy who kept scooting closer to her.

A bubble, I wonder if I could make something like that work? Stepping to the back of the group I imagined a bubble surrounding me, blocking the emotions out. I imagined a bubble several time before I created it. The bubble seemed flimsy and it only toned down the emotions around me. Oh well, it's better than nothing. But maybe I'll get through the rest of camp.

I made it through juggling with Kayin and Philip, and learned to jump Double Dutch with Anali and Taliesin. In both classes I stayed far enough away from people to keep the impact of the other kids' emotions down.

I wasn't able to keep the same distance during clowning. Gavin watched me intently, his pale green eyes burning. His emotions went right through my pathetic attempts at shielding myself. Determination, confusion, protectiveness, and sadness flooded through me. They mixed in with all of the emotions from the students. I wasn't sure how I could get through class.

Stumbling with the intensity of emotion, I fell and sent three of us tumbling to the ground. I cried out as an elbow hit me in the nose. My eyes began to water, much to my embarrassment.

"Okay, let's get everyone up," Gavin said. The other two were lifted off of me. "Sara, are you okay? Let me see."

I looked up into Gavin's worried face, and slowly opened my hands. "Crap, you're bleeding. Come with me I'll get you cleaned up."

I let Gavin help me up and guide me over to the bathrooms. He opened a door, marked employees only, and pulled out a first aid kit.

"Here hold this on your nose." Gavin handed me a wad of gauze and an ice pack. "Are you okay?"

"Yes, it's sore, but I think the bleeding is slowing down."

"Good, I'll get some wet paper towels and get you cleaned up."

I opened my mouth to protest, I'm perfectly capable of taking care of myself, but he already grabbed a bunch of supplies.

"Here let me take that," Gavin reached out for the bloody gauze.

I pulled back and shook my head. "I'll throw it away." That's gross, he wasn't even wearing gloves.

"Sure." Gavin held out a small plastic bag. As I placed the bloody gauze in the bag I felt a quick wave of triumph hit me. "Here are the wet towels, and there's a mirror in the bathroom. I'll take care of this."

Weird, what was Gavin so happy about? Getting up, I tried to put it from my mind - there are times when trying to understand adults isn't worth the trouble. After cleaning up I re-joined the class.

*   *   *

Rain. I sighed as I gathered up all my things. Camp ended for the day, and it was time to go home. After changing back into my pants I looked for Anali.

"I'm going to have it tested." I heard Gavin say. It sounded like his voice came from upstairs. The door to the apartment stood open, so maybe Anali was up there too.

"That's fine, but please don't get too hopeful or do anything rash. It will take a week before we know anything for sure." Philip said.

"It could be her. If Gabriella died it would explain everything." Gavin's voice cracked.

I backed away, not wanting to intrude on a private moment.

"Do you need something?" Taliesin asked, with as much snootiness as possible.

"Anali," I said rolling my eyes at his attitude.

"Gavin, where's Anali?" Taliesin said loudly looking up at the apartment.

"In the shower. Why?" Gavin replied, coming down the stairs.

I held out the pants she'd let me borrow. "Will you give her these and thank her for me?"

"Of course. How are you getting home?" he asked, taking the pants.

"The bus."

"I'll drive you," Gavin said. His happiness bubbled around me.

"Thank you, but I'll be fine." I started walking to the door. I needed some space from all the crazy—at least the crazy that affected my life. Bus crazy is entertaining.

"It's pouring out there. Really, it's no trouble."

I saw Gavin's hopeful face, and Taliesin's curious one. I wasn't sure how to get out of this without being rude, and I wasn't at all excited about getting home in the rain. "I would have to have permission from my caseworker. I can't just go with people."

"Here." Gavin handed me his cell phone.

I dialed, not sure whether I wanted to face the rain or Gavin.

"Hello."

"Hey, Five, it's Sara. One of the teachers here has offered me a ride home. Is that okay?"

"That's nice of him," Five hummed. "He isn't a serial killer is he?"

"Hold on, Five. Gavin, are you a serial killer?" I looked at him with mock suspicion.

Gavin's green eyes widened for a moment, then a mischievous smiled brightened his face. "I have never killed a Frosted Flake in my entire life."

Five chuckled.

"What?"

"Frosted Flakes, cereal." Gavin grinned, rocking on his feet and obviously pleased with himself.

I rolled my eyes.

"As long as puns won't kill you it's fine," Five said. "Tell him thanks for me."

"Thanks, Five. Have a good day."

"You, too, Sara, take care."

I closed my eyes. Gavin radiated happy, it felt like soda bubbling against my skin.

"Ready?"

"Sure." I followed him out the back door. I saw a bright red, sporty-looking car and a white Prius parked in the alley. I expected him to head for the red car, but he led me to the Prius.

"Anali insisted we rent something practical." Gavin explained when he saw me looking at the cherry-red Mustang.

"You'll have to give me step-by-step directions. I haven't driven in San Francisco for seven years," Gavin said as we pulled out of the parking lot.

"No problem. Go right." I imagined my flimsy bubble getting stronger and thicker but I couldn't block Gavin's emotions.

"So while we're visiting,' where should we go? Things have changed in seven years. I know all the standard places, like Fisherman's Wharf and Chinatown, but what are your favorite places to go?"

"I don't get out much. Turn left at the light. This pizza place on the corner is one of my favorites," I offered. I didn't care for small talk, but tried being polite.

"What's your favorite kind?"

"The pesto."

Gavin beamed as if I'd given him some wonderful bit of information. "My sister Gabriella loved pesto. I'm a pineapple, onion, and green pepper fan myself."

I wasn't sure what to say to that so I stayed quiet. I suppose if I knew for certain we were related, it would be interesting information.

"What about places to visit? Is there something we shouldn't miss?"

"The Monterey Bay Aquarium, it's wonderful," I said, with a soft smile.

"Do you go often?"

"No, I've only been once. A charitable group donated a bunch of tickets, and we got to go." I could have sat watching the fish swim in the large tanks for days.

"That's nice of them," Gavin said. The happy, bubbly feeling faded as cool, smooth sadness took its place.

"We get donated stuff all the time." I didn't want him feeling sorry for me. "Last Saturday, one of the big law firms brought over a ton of Christmas gifts for all of us. I helped Melanie, my houseparent, go through all of it and pick out gifts for the other girls in my house."

"That must have been fun." Gavin still felt sad, but he tried to sound happy.

"I guess. Tonight another group is bringing fried chicken, stockings, and a Santa."

"You seem a bit old for Santa," Gavin said with a smile.

"I am, but there are a bunch of younger kids in the house. Turn right up there," I directed, pointing at the next street. "After this stop sign is a bright yellow house—that's mine."

He turned off the car, and unbuckled his seat belt.

"You don't have to come in," I said.

"A gentleman always walks a lady to her door."

"Thanks, you don't have to."

"I know, but I want to."

I walked through the little front garden and opened the door. "I'm on the third floor."

Gavin grinned. "I will be able to make it up the stairs."

I rolled my eyes and headed up.

"Melanie, I'm home," I called, opening my house's door.

"Thank you for the ride," I said to Gavin. I wondered how long he planned on staying.

Gavin peered into the house. His curiosity tugging at my skin. "No problem."

"Hey, sweetie. Thank you for bringing her home," Melanie said, all in one breath.

"No problem. I'm Gavin Marsh, one of the instructors at the circus camp." Gavin gave a bright smile and held out his hand.

"Melanie Klein, Sara's houseparent," she said shaking his hand.

"I wanted to make sure Sara got home safe. Is it okay if I bring her home again if the weather is bad?" Gavin asked.

"It's fine with me." Melanie turned to me.

"Sure, thanks Gavin," I answered automatically, my mind racing to make sense of everything. His last name was Marsh, he had to be my uncle. What do I do now?

"Great, see you tomorrow." Gavin waved.

"Bye." My stomach felt queasy, relief and sadness battled while I watched him leave.

Chapter Four

The ancient stones of Rome glowed in the magic light of dawn. Taking a deep breath, Cartazonon sat down in meditation and opened to the web of energy and power that connected all that he owned: businesses, homes, and those few people who were important enough to be his.

Church bells rang to mark the hour as a spark of power caught his attention. How interesting, he thought and followed the wake of energy. Something magical had just awakened, or had been born in San Francisco. The connection flickered. Cartazonon hoped something good was in San Francisco, he needed to recharge.

"Khan, I have your espresso and paper."

Sighing, he glared at Lee. His flat broken nose, pockmarked face, and straight black hair looked the same as when they had first met on the Mongolian plains. "You must stop calling me by that ridiculous title. It's Sir, or Mr. Cartazonon now."

His first and most trusted general shrugged his massive shoulders. "I hope eventually it will come back into fashion, everything else has."

Taking a sip of the bitter black coffee, he sighed. This is what made life worth living. "My poor General Lee, I fear the life of a modern warlord holds no interest for you."

"You have become a business man. I am more suited for riding horses, shooting a bow and arrow, and wielding a sabre."

Cartazonon wagged a finger at him. "Now, Lee, you know I like my people to be happy, so after you get me a list of those who owe me a favor in San Francisco, why don't you go hunting? I need to recharge, and you need to have some fun."

Lee looked out the window towards the sea. "Remember the huge mermaid colony here once?"

"Of course, you should take the yacht out. I swear after we did that stint as pirates, you miss the sea. Do we have any of those pixies left?"

"Yes. I'll bring you one with the reports."

"Perfect. Thanks."

Cartazonon took off his necklace—a simple crystal set in silver metal. It came from Akasha, a gift from the Phoenix King to his stupid family. *What a joke they were now,* he thought, *running around feeling proud that tiny little drops of his great power ran through their veins. They are so pathetic. The only reason to even keep an eye on them is because they have led me to some wonderfully strong magical creatures.*

He wrapped the necklace around his left hand and placed the crystal in his palm. When Lee came back he set the list on the desk and deposited a pixie on top of the crystal. Its dirty blond hair stuck up in messy clumps, and the leaves that made up its clothing crunched under Cartazonon's pale fingers. Lee waited and watched.

Taking a deep breath, Cartazonon pulled the magic and life from the pixie and directed it into the crystal. The pixie fought, and dug into his flesh with its tiny nails and teeth. A water glass cracked as it screamed, and the heat from its tiny tears warmed Cartazonon's cold skin. The pixie went limp, trembling as the very last bit of magic was pulled out from its body.

Cartazonon sipped his espresso and looked over the list of names. "I need to send a walk-in and see if any of the so called Children of Fire know anything about what created that delicious spark of power this morning." He pointed to a name on the list. "This one. They don't owe me a very big favor, so send a low level walk-in. It should only need to possess the human for a few hours. And I'm done with this. Feed it to the cats or something."

"Now Khan, you know pixies give the cats indigestion, but I think the hell hounds would like the treat."

"Of course, good thinking. The cat yowled all night last time."

Lee bowed low, the pixie hanging from his thick fingers. "I live to serve."

Cartazonon raised an eyebrow. "Send the walk-in and then go hunting. I always worry for my safety when you start cracking jokes."

Lee chuckled darkly. Cartazonon shivered, like he always did at that sound from Lee, and turned to the day's task of acquiring the largest Bollywood studio in Delhi.

Chapter Five

"I love you. Never doubt that, not for a second. No matter what you fear, or what you're told. I love you with everything I am." ~Mom

"I love you. Never doubt that, not for a second. No matter what you fear, or what you're told. I love you with everything I am." ~Mom

Leaning my head against the cold bus window, I tried to stay awake. Even the two women behind me fighting over whose turn it was to take out the trash couldn't keep me awake. Last night Shante threw a huge fit at bedtime because her mom wasn't able to take her for Christmas. I suspected that Sophia had dropped dirty. Shante cried and screamed as she vented her anger and pain. Her little heart couldn't hold that much rejection and betrayal. Chairs were knocked over, books hurled through the air, and anything else light enough for her four-year-old body to move became a victim of her rage.

Melanie took the kids into her room to keep them safe. I was foolish enough to try to help Shante calm down. I didn't duck fast enough and had a resulting black eye to show for it. I grabbed some ice on my way to Melanie's room. Shante didn't even notice she'd hurt me.

It took almost half an hour before Shante calmed down. She ended up in a ball on the floor crying. Melanie held her, soothing her sobs. It wasn't long before she fell asleep. My heart ached for Shante; she's so small and innocent, she doesn't deserve to feel unwanted and unloved. In a few years she'll be like me, unwilling or unable to form attachments and trust anyone. At least that's what a shrink wrote in my file, so it must be true.

After Shante fell asleep, Melanie calmed the other kids down and got them into bed while I cleaned up. It took forever. Afterwards, I couldn't sleep because Shante kept having bad dreams, and this morning I was dragging butt. Shaking my head to clear the memory, I pulled the cord to stop the bus.

The air around me hung thick with water that couldn't decide if it wanted to remain a cloud or fall as rain. I could barely see the cafe, but the aroma of coffee led the way. I rarely drink coffee, because I get hyper on caffeine, then crash. But today coffee was a necessity. As I neared the cafe door someone called my name. Turning, I saw a shape coming closer through the fog.

"Carlos, how are you?" I asked, as strong arms wrapped me in a hug. Carlos was a self-proclaimed flirt, sometimes charming, and frequently a total snot. He'd run away from Hope House three months ago.

"Hey, Sara. I'm okay," he said. His chapped lips stretched into a tired smile. His brown skin looked chalky and broken out and his normally rosy cheeks were sunken and dull, making his high cheekbones look painfully sharp.

Taking a deep breath, I tried to ignore the sadness and aching fatigue coming off of him. I hoped that feeling other people's emotions was a one-time thing, but no such luck. Arching my eyebrow, I looked into his brown eyes. We both knew he was lying to me.

"Okay. I'm not fine. My mom worked all night, and I had to stay out of the apartment. I love the freedom of being at home, but I miss regular meals and a warm bed every night."

Carlos lived at Hope House for three years, and they were about to sever his mom's rights when he freaked and ran. Apparently Carlos' mom was still hooking, and sending him out of the house at night. "Call your caseworker. One of the kids in your old house is leaving Friday; there'll be an empty bed."

"I don't know, maybe. What are you doing here?" Carlos looked around. Smooth change in the conversation, I let it go.

"I'm on my way to day camp at the circus school. I stopped to get a mocha." I pointed across the street to where I knew the Circus Center sat, invisible in the fog.

Carlos' eyes widened, and his face broke into a bright smile. "I've seen you on caffeine, why are you punishing them like that?"

I smacked him on the arm. "Shut up. I was up all night with Shante. Come on, I'll buy you breakfast."

Sighing in pleasure, I stepped into the warm café. We placed our order and waited under the 'pick-up here' sign, with a bunch of adults on their way to work.

"Are you going out with anyone?" Carols asked, his voice soft.

I looked at Carlos, I could feel his worry, but my shock at the question was the stronger emotion. "What?" Why would I want to date some boy?

"Your eye." He pointed to my black and purple eye.

"No need to worry. Shante threw a fit last night and I got hit with a book." I grabbed our order and found a free table, not giving Carlos a chance to leave. "Let's sit down. I have a while before camp begins."

"Cool. Tell me what's going on at Hope House."

I caught Carlos up on all the house gossip. Looking out the window I could see the faint shapes through the fog of parents dropping off kids at the circus school.

"I have to go," I said, cleaning up the table.

"I'll walk with you," Carlos offered, as he helped pick up the trash.

Crossing a foggy street is a leap of faith. The fog lifted some, but not enough to take away the danger. Carlos took my hand, we looked, listened, took a deep breath and ran across the street. Seconds after we reached the sidewalk a car drove past us.

I squeezed his hand before letting go. "Bye, Carlos. Please call and get somewhere safe. It's supposed to get even colder tonight."

"I'll be fine, but yeah, maybe I'll call. Take better care of yourself." Gently he rubbed his thumb across my black eye. "Hey, if I come back, maybe we could go out?"

I rolled my eyes. "I'd feel flattered, except you flirt with everyone."

Watching Carlos walk away in his dirty, oversized jeans, I wondered if I would ever see him again. I knew he wouldn't call, and even if he did, there's no way he'd come straight to Hope House. They'd send Carlos to a lock-down group home or juvy first.

Stepping inside the school, I took off several layers of clothes and was ready to go in a dry, all-black workout outfit. Finishing my mocha, I threw away the cup and began to bounce on the balls of my feet. I went over to the mat to warm up, hoping to channel some of my caffeine-induced energy.

"How are you this morning?" Gavin asked, his bare feet all I could see. They were very pale.

"Morning, Gavin. I'm great! How are you?" I asked looking up at my possible uncle. No. I felt too tired and too wired to deal with this today. Choosing to ignore any possible family connections, I went back to stretching.

Gavin's amusement faded and he dropped to his knees in front of me. "What happened? Did that boy do this to you? Do you need anything?"

"What are you talking about? And why do you care? And what boy?" Is it time for the crazy to start already today? "Nice tee shirt, I loved The Empire Strikes Back."

Gavin took a deep breath and closed his eyes. His mouth moved slightly, it looked like he was counting to ten. "Your black eye, the boy you walked up with, and you're my student. Of course, I care if you're hurt."

I lowered my head and stretched the back of my legs, my fingers tapping against my feet. "My eye is nothing. Carlos is a friend I ran into this morning."

"Do you need anything for it? Ice? Ibuprofen?" Gavin said.

"I'm fine, you should be much more worried that I drank an entire double mocha with extra chocolate and whipped cream." I pressed up into a backbend. "What are we doing today? When do we get started? Whose turn is it for music?"

Gavin chuckled. "I guess I should be worried. Warm-ups will start in five minutes, and we are doing large trampoline, trapeze and acrobatics this morning. Shin picked hip-hop and pop from around the world."

The beat of the music changed and someone started rapping in ... French, cool.

"Will we work on the high trap today?" I asked, lying down. Gavin's eyes crinkled as he smiled. "You have a scar," I blurted out, looking at a thin white line under the edge of his jaw.

"I got it when I was little and fell out of a tree, and, yes, we're going to have you in safety harnesses and up in the air."

"Sounds like a fun day. I wonder what I'll start with?"

My caffeine high didn't end until two-thirty, much to the amusement of the staff. Well, except for Taliesin, who seemed grumpy as usual. Closing my eyes, I leaned against the wall willing strength into my body. I was so tired I ached. I seriously overworked my muscles today. Thank goodness Melanie was picking me up today.

"Sara! I'm so sorry," Shante said, running through the door of the Circus Center.

I grunted when her little body hit mine. "Shush, it's okay. I'm fine."

"Your eye looks so bad. I didn't mean to." Large tears dripped down her face.

"Look at me, baby." I turned her face so I could look into her eyes. "I'm fine, really. My eye looks much worse than it feels."

She buried her head into my shirt, still crying. Rubbing her back, I looked around for Melanie.

"I figured you'd be crashed out by now," Melanie said walking over to us.

"Sara, you're hot," Shante whispered loudly into my ear.

It took a lot of energy to open my eyes. "I'm just tired."

"Melanie! Sara's hot!" The little brat ratted me out!

I groaned as an ice-cold hand touched my forehead. "Sara, another fever? This is not okay, something is seriously wrong!" Melanie said looking between me and the phone in her hand.

"I'm fine, I just need to sleep. I don't have a cut or cough, or anything else. I bet it's because I'm so tired." I did not want to go to the hospital. I hoped Melanie would be so busy she'd give in and let me sleep at home.

"I'm sure she'll feel fine in the morning," Gavin said, a strange tone in his voice, but I couldn't figure out what or why.

Melanie's phone rang. "Give me a second."

I closed my eyes again. I felt someone sit down next to me, but was too tired to look.

"For some of us it can take time for all the changes to come in. Remember that we are here for you. We can help you adjust to your new gifts," Gavin said.

I opened my eyes. What new weirdness was this? Gavin's green eyes were worried. He stared at my head. I fought the urge to make sure the bandanna covered all of the red in my hair. His gaze shifted and he tried to see my eyes through the curtain of curly bangs.

A beautiful woman walked in the door dressed in a pale blue suit. Her long, honey blond hair hung down her back, and her smile warmed up the room. "Taliesin, there are more bags in the car. Will you get them, please?"

"Sure, Mom."

"Cordelia," Philip said taking the plastic garment bags from her. "Thank you so much for getting the new costumes done."

"Thankfully, my assistants are good and were able to do the basic sewing for the wedding dresses so I could work on these."

Taliesin's mom, Cordelia, felt like the opposite of her son: warm, gentle, and soft. Their hair color matched their personalities.

Taliesin backed through the door, his arms full of garment bags, flashes of bright colors peeking through the layers of plastic.

"Thank you, dear. Put everything on the counter." Cordelia began to sort through the garment bags. "Anali and Gavin, you two need to try yours on in case I need to make any adjustments. I think you two are the only ones who couldn't do a fitting with me."

"They are so pretty," Shante said kneeing me in the gut as she got up.

"Thank you, sweetheart. Are you taking classes here?" Cordelia asked.

"Nope, but Sara is," she said pointing to me. I waved from my place on the floor.

"Come on, girls, let's go home," Melanie said before Shante could start asking even more questions.

I must have fallen asleep because suddenly we were at the house. "Sara, go to bed. I'll tell Penny to leave you alone, and I'll check in on you when I get home."

"Thanks, Melanie." I muttered and stumbled into my room. Kicking off my shoes, I burrowed under the covers.

A few hours later, Penny woke me to tell me that they were going to the dining hall for dinner. As soon as they left, I got into a hot shower. The pounding water felt wonderful as I washed the sickness off my skin. I would have stayed in the shower forever, but I began to feel dizzy.

I wasn't ready to go back to bed. Looking around, I realized I'd left my book out in the living room. I didn't want to get caught by Penny because she would fuss and coo at me. Sitting down, I began to organize my dresser. My first week of living in a group home, I saw staff going through a kid's things and throwing away what they decided was garbage. Ever since that moment I have always kept my things neat and tidy. I got rid of old papers, cards, toys, and clothes. Nothing of mine is ever going to be taken away without my permission.

All of my clothes were in good shape, neatly folded in the drawers. I didn't have a lot of stuff, but what I owned was precious to me. I kept it in an old pink backpack with faded yellow flowers. My mother packed this bag for me when she left me at the police station when I was five. The backpack held the journal she'd written for me and a scrapbook of photos.

I pulled out the package I'd found at the school. I'd been so busy I hadn't touched it since yesterday at lunch. I picked up the letter. After reading the first part again, I sat and stared at the second page. The shapes and lines shifted and swirled. I guess my fever must be worse than I thought. It's so weird. Nothing else pointed to my mom being crazy. And what did she mean I should try reading it out loud?

"Even if I wanted to read it, I wouldn't know where to start," I said, laying the page on the floor, then turned the page around several times. My finger settled on the top right corner. The words didn't turn into English, but somehow they were becoming clear. I ran my finger along the marks and began to read:

My darling daughter,

Happy fifteenth birthday! I hope you are safe and loved, and I hope the changes over your birthday haven't been too traumatic. You are very special: you are a descendant of an ancient king and queen.

This can't be real! How can I read this? My thoughts raced and I began to lose my focus, and the words faded. *Sara, calm down. Kayin said something about languages being a gift; maybe this is part of the gift. Just try not to freak out. Let it happen.* I took several deeps breaths before I felt calm enough to try again. Once again the odd patterns began to swirl and shift until I could understand the words my mother had written.

On our fifteenth birthdays the descendants of Shamash and Aya come into an inheritance. For some of us our appearance changes, and we get certain gifts.

In the white felt packages, I've wrapped up my jewelry. It will help you control your new powers and aid in your connection to Akasha.

I've done all I can to protect you, but I've failed. The Sons of Belial are after me. I don't have much time. Your real name is Sapphire Aya Rayner, my name is Gabriella Aya Rayner and your father was Keagan Michael Rayner. You need to find my brother, Gavin Colin Marsh. Contact the New York Center for Circus Arts; they will know how to get in touch with him.

I'm so sorry, my darling. I wish I could do more. I'd send you to Gavin directly but I fear someone has betrayed me. I have to hide you. It's the only way.

Remember I love you. Find Gavin. He will take care of you. Be strong and brave. I know you can do this.

Trust your instincts, baby; you know what is true and right.

I love you with all that I am,

Mom

I climbed into bed, tears running down my face, and clutched the letter to my chest. Slowly I succumbed to sleep, my fever so high that my breath felt hot against my lips.

Chapter Six

"Action is the antidote to despair." ~Joan Baez

"No!" I sat up in bed clutching my chest, rejection filling my body with bitterness. Closing my eyes, I shuddered and took several deep breaths. Images of the dream floated through my mind; copper and cream arms holding me, flames healing my body, and soft glowing gold fur—from a lion? I shoved the images and feelings down. And the words from my mother's letter, written in weird shapes, came rushing back.

How the hell did I go from having no family to an ancient, magical one? Clamping my hands over my mouth, I stifled the hysterical laughter and panicked sobs that bubbled inside of me. Looking over at the bunk beds, I made sure Shante and Crystal were still asleep.

This can't be true! How could it be true? What should I do? I moved, and one of the felt packages fell to the floor. Carefully, I picked it up. Was there jewelry in here? Jewelry an ancient king had given to his family?

With a shaky breath, I opened the smaller package. Inside I found a silver chain that looked solid, but flowed over my hand like water. A pendant a little larger than a quarter hung from the chain. The silver base was ornamented with gold designs along the edge. In the center of the pendant glowed a flame of green, blue, and purple. Red, orange and yellow flames surrounded it. I couldn't tell what the translucent colors were made of, they looked painted on, but felt like stone, as if someone melted down gemstones and painted with them. I'd never seen anything so beautiful.

As I held the pendant, it became warm. I felt a gentle, tingly energy flow into me. It reminded me of the dreams I'd been having. It felt odd to feel connected to that fairy tale world while still in this one. Closing my eyes, I let the feeling wash over me. With each breath I could feel Phoenix power flowing through me. It pulsed and sparked as it moved through my body. I placed the necklace back into the white felt, ignoring the cold loneliness that settled in my heart as the connection faded.

Opening the second package, I gasped as six bangles fell out. They rang softly as they hit each other. Pulling back the felt, I found a ring. It took my breath away: a silver band with a ribbon of deep blue running through the center. Within the blue ribbon were a hundred small stars, as if a piece of the evening sky was set in silver. I longed to try it on, to see how it would look on my hand, but if the ring also connected to Akasha, and my body filled with the warmth of home again, I wasn't sure I would be able to take the ring off. How could I possibly explain this jewelry to Melanie?

Turning my attention to the pile of bangle bracelets, I picked them up one at a time. Each bracelet was a different shade of silver or gold. They were about a quarter of an inch wide, with small perfectly carved silhouettes of magical creatures covering each one. There were at least a dozen creatures on each bracelet. A few I recognized, but most were unfamiliar to me.

I wrapped the jewelry up, and tucked it and the letter into my backpack. Now what? I asked myself as I set the bag on the floor. What I wanted to do was go back to bed and hide under my covers. Instead, I took a deep breath and placed my feet on the floor. My mom's advice whispered in my mind.

"There will be times in your life when it feels like nothing is in your control, and all you want to do is curl up in bed and hide. I understand. Everyone has times like this in their lives, but hiding doesn't help at all. Get up, put one foot in front of the other and do something: shower, walk, do the dishes, write, draw, or read. There must be something, even if it is

small, that you can do that will make things a little better. There are times when all we can control are our actions and how we respond to the chaos around us. Always find a positive action to take, and you'll feel better and a little more in control."

*   *   *

Today I planned ahead, so when I arrived at camp with soaking wet pants, I pulled an extra pair out of my backpack. Despite the rain, I managed to get to the Circus Center early enough that no one had come downstairs yet. After tucking my things into a cubby, I went into the bathroom to change.

I was about to leave the bathroom, happy to be warm and dry, when I heard voices outside the door.

"Tony called me this morning. He's the most experienced Dreamer in America, and he said that there was only one Child of Fire that came into power in the past six months in California. This means Sara has to be Sapphire!"

"Gavin, I hope Sara is Sapphire, I want you to find your niece. You know I do. However, we need to take it slow. We can't hurt this girl. You coming into her life is like a fairy tale, and if it's not true, it could hurt her beyond measure." Philip's voice sounded calm and firm.

"But the Dreamer said..."

"I know, but sometimes there are confusing signs in dreams. You sent off her blood to get tested right?"

What were they talking about? How did he get my blood?

"Yes, I sent it to Nathan," Gavin answered.

"He's your lawyer, right?"

"Yes, but he hasn't gotten back to me yet."

Something thudded against the bathroom door.

"You're going to give yourself a headache if you do that. And you know Nathan isn't going to call you until he knows exactly what is going on and what the next step is," Philip soothed.

"I just wish I knew for sure; we don't even know if she has had any other physical changes," Gavin cried out, his frustration clear.

Crap, now I felt bad. I looked in the mirror; my hair pulled back in a tight bun with all of the red carefully hidden under my bandanna.

The door thudded again.

"We don't even know for sure that your niece is the Jewel. I know Keagan dreamed about it, and your sister choose the name Sapphire because they felt she was going to be the Jewel, but dreams can be very hard to interrupt."

Thud.

"We do know she has the eye color of the first children, that alone shows how powerful and connected she is to Shamash and Aya. Most Children of Fire have no physical changes any more, and Anali said Sara feels empathic to her." I could almost see Philip counting off the different things on his fingers.

Thud.

"If only I saw her before her birthday, then I would know if her skin color changed. If she would let her hair down, we would know what color it is," Gavin said.

Thud.

"Gavin, if she isn't your niece, will Nathan still be willing to help one of us get her? We need to train her to use her powers, and I don't see how we can do that while she's still in the foster-care system."

"Yes, of course. But, Philip, she is the Jewel. I know in my heart Sara is Sapphire! Why did Gabriella hide her with Child Protective Services and change her name? Why not send her to me instead of to CPS? I have to tell her. I can't let her keep thinking she has no family."

"No! Gavin, no. You have to calm down and let your lawyer do his job. I agree it sounds like Sara is most likely Sapphire, but we will have to work within the system. Nathan will call you when he has the next step ready and in place. He knows you have no patience." Philip's voice filled with power. It felt strong and soothing, and my own anxiety receded against my will.

"Okay, I'll calm down, no need to go all Jedi Voice on me," Gavin said.

"Come on, let's go, classes will start soon," Philip said. Gavin's muttering got softer as they walked away.

I took a deep breath. Okay, this was intense. Gavin took my blood, I assume from when I had the bloody nose, and sent it to get tested. Who does stuff like that? Would Gavin be able to keep the secret a while longer? What would I say if he told me? I know he's my uncle, but I still hadn't figured out what to do about that. Now I didn't have a choice. When Gavin finds out for sure, he'll go to my caseworker. Once again, where I live and who I live with will be in chaos and beyond my control.

I held my head in my hands, breathing slowly, willing my body to stop shaking and forcing the tears away. Change doesn't have to be bad. And for most people being part of a family is a good thing, right? At least I wouldn't have to share a room with three other girls. Maybe I should go to him first? Or at least let my hair down. What was I going to do?

As soon as I opened the bathroom door, I ran into Anali. "Crap, oh crap, you scared me!"

"Sorry I didn't mean to scare you. Are you all right?" Anali reached out to steady me.

I plastered a quick smile on my face. "Of course I'm fine."

"Sara, I'm also a Child of Fire, and my gift is empathy. Your emotions are intense. Normally I don't invade people's privacy, but I could feel how upset you were from upstairs." Anali freed a lock of brown hair from her gold hoop earring.

"I'm not hurt; I'm not thinking of hurting myself or others; and I'm not running away," I rattled off the list of things that staff always needed to make sure weren't an issue.

Anali's brow wrinkled around her bindi. "Well, that is good to know, but that doesn't mean you're all right. It's okay if you don't want to talk. I'm here when you do want to talk. Did you overhear Gavin and Philip?"

I looked away, and my cheeks heated up. It always sucked getting caught eavesdropping, but how else was I supposed to find out what the adults were planning to do to my life?

"I don't sense surprise from you. Did you already know Gavin is your uncle?" Anali leaned towards me so she could whisper.

I breathed in her sweet jasmine perfume. I didn't know what to say. "Please."

"Hush, it's okay. I won't tell anyone." Anali rubbed her hands over my arms.

"Okay." I didn't believe her.

"Sara, know you can talk to me. I'll listen, without judging and without telling anyone else." Anali meant what she was saying, her honesty clear and light against my skin.

"Thank you, that's nice of you. I know Gavin's your husband . . ." I trailed off, unsure of what else to say.

"Yes, Gavin is my husband, which makes you my niece, too. I want you to feel safe with me. Now classes are about to begin. Are you okay to join everyone?" Anali's light brown eyes held concern even as her lips softened into a smile.

"Sure, of course," I said automatically. Would I ever feel okay again?

*   *   *

Kayin held my legs and I tightened my stomach, as Shin told us to do, and tried to hold the handstand while Kayin supported my legs.

"Your eye looks a lot better," Kayin said.

"I guess some good comes out of all these changes."

Kayin sighed. "Yes, but I'm not sure the trade is worth it."

I squeaked as my arms shook.

Kayin chuckled. "Let me help you down."

"Okay," I said and tried to keep from collapsing as he supported my legs down to the floor.

"You did well."

I glared at him from under my bangs.

Kayin smiled. "For your first handstand, you did well."

"I guess so. I'm sorry that you had a difficult time with the changes, too," I said, as cold sadness seeped from Kayin.

Kayin shrugged. "I grew up in small village in Zimbabwe. My mother was—is—very superstitious. I haven't seen or talked to my family since."

"That's awful. How long has it been?"

"Six months."

"But that means we're the same age. You seem so much older than me." I stood and looked up at Kayin.

"In my world, I'm an adult. I should be helping to support my family."

"Oh, this must be very odd for you."

Kayin nodded. "I feel like I'm in the middle of a story my grandmother use to tell us around the fire at night."

Yes, trapped in a fairy tale is exactly how I felt. "Do you sometimes wonder if you'll wake up?"

"I used to," Kayin smiled at me. "I don't anymore."

"How did you get from Africa to here in six months?"

"Good job, everyone," Philip called out. "Let's finish up, and we'll switch groups."

"On an airplane." Kayin winked then held out a hand and helped me up. "It's a long story. I'll tell you later."

"Time for poi," I said, watching as the others picked a set of fuzzy poi and giggled as they tried to pull the cords apart.

The phone rang, startling me. I shook my head. You need to focus and not stay lost in your thoughts, I scolded myself.

"I've got it," Gavin said leaning over the counter. "Good morning, San Francisco Center for the Circus Arts. How can I help you?"

I watched Gavin hum and nod to the person on the phone. Happiness began to swirl around him.

"Of course we can add her to our after-hours program."

"We don't have an after-hours program," Philip said walking over to Gavin. Gavin held up his hand, stopping Philip.

"Sure, I'll get her right now. Sara, phone." Gavin held up the receiver and wiggled it a bit.

I blushed as everyone stared at me.

"Gavin, what have you done?" Philip hissed.

I took the phone. "Hello."

"Hey Sara, it's Melanie. I have to take one of the kids from house one to the emergency room. I've signed you up for their after-hours program, but just for today, I swear."

Trapped here with my uncle and the other Children of Fire, with no buffer? No other people around to keep conversations short and not invasive? This isn't good. "What about the Shante and the others? I can take the bus home."

"Anyone who doesn't have a visit is being sent to another house. I couldn't find staff to work for me. I found a spot for everyone but you. I can't believe they can keep you until eight. I'm sorry. Maybe I can think of something else."

I sighed. "No, here is fine. I don't want you to have to spend extra money on me."

Melanie chuckled. "You're a good kid and don't worry about it. I owe you big time. I hope you can have fun. I'll make it up to you."

"Go save the day and no worries, Melanie. I'm sure it'll be great."

"Bye, Sara."

I handed Gavin the phone. His excitement exploded around him like Pop Rocks. "So, there's an after-hours program," I said.

Gavin grinned. "There is now."

Philip rubbed his hands over his face. "I hope you don't mind hanging out with us. I don't have anything planned."

"No, its fine. I should get back to poi."

"Yes, can't keep everyone waiting." Gavin walked to his group.

Philip patted my arm and walked away.

Worry squirmed in my belly as I joined my group. Nothing good could come from this, I just knew it.

*   *   *

My shoulders ached and I suspected they were bruised from my failed attempts at graceful somersaults. I helped fold up mats and put away equipment as the other kids got their stuff and left.

Gavin clapped his hands together. "How about we go upstairs and have a snack?"

"Are you coming, Taliesin?" Anali asked.

"Sure, I have an hour before my class starts," he said. Why would they included him? He's not a Child of Fire.

Kayin stood next to me, and together we walked up the stairs. The feeling of dread increased with each step.

Chapter Seven

"Nearly all men can stand adversity, but if you want to test a man's character, give him power." ~Abraham Lincoln

We gathered in Philip's apartment, trying to find a place to sit among all of the books. I sat on the floor next to the chair Kayin chose. The books on the coffee table were about myths, legends, and magical creatures.

Philip's living room felt warm and cozy, furnished with dark wood and deep forest green couches and chairs. It looked more like a fancy library than the home of a mohawked circus performer.

"Before I start, do any of you need anything for our Christmas Eve charity show? It's tomorrow, so speak now or forever hold your peace." Philip set down a tray of glasses, small plates, and a pitcher of lemonade.

"Friday is going to be exhausting." Taliesin poured a glass of lemonade. "I don't need anything."

"Camp ends at three and the show starts at five, so hopefully that's enough time to rest and get ready," Philip said.

I poured a glass of lemonade and passed it to Kayin before getting my own.

"Thanks," he said.

"Sure."

"I don't think we need anything." Anali walked in carrying a platter of sliced fruit.

Gavin followed with a plate of crackers and cheese. "We are good to go. So on with the story telling. The kids should know how all this Phoenix stuff started."

Philip rolled his eyes and waited until everyone filled their plates.

"Shamash flew over Earth checking on his people, making sure they were safe," Philip began, his Phoenix gift weaving power into his voice, drawing us into his story. "His feathers were yellow, orange, and red flames streaking across the sky. The people below stared at his beauty, some fell in worship, while others ran in fear.

"Shamash only laughed at the people's behavior. He didn't understand humans and their need for more. More power, more wealth, more land, more things, more, more, more!

"As the Phoenix King flew away from the city, he felt something that reminded him of Akasha. Searching the green land below him, Shamash's golden eyes spied a young woman sitting next to a sparkling river. Silently he landed, wanting to get a better look. Her thoughts were silent as she connected heart and soul to the world. She sat in meditation, completely open, and vulnerable. There was no fear, no worry coming from her, just a sense of peace and joy.

"Shamash sat quietly watching the strange woman. Her black hair curled around her copper shoulders and fluttered in the breeze. Her lips formed a soft smile as she emerged from her meditation. Shamash delighted in the pale green eyes which opened, looking at him in curiosity without fear or worship."

I floated on the sound of Philip's voice as the images he described filled my vision as clearly as a movie.

"'Hello, I am Aya,' the young woman said. The musical sound of her voice drew him closer, and Shamash decided to find out more about this young woman. He changed into the form of a man with flame-red hair, gold eyes, and pearl white skin.

"Aya blushed at his nakedness, but didn't look away. 'I'm Shamash,' he said. Walking closer to her, he held out his hand. Aya placed her small hand into his and let Shamash lead her away.

"Together they lived a wonderful life. They had six children, three boys and three girls. Each a blend of their parents; midnight black hair with ruby red streaks, peridot green eyes with gold flecks, and creamy copper skin."

I gasped momentarily breaking from the spell of Philip's voice. It sounded like he just described me.

"After a long life together, Shamash and Aya lay dying. Their children, grandchildren, and great-grandchildren surrounded them with love and prayers.

"'Aya, my love, my wife, you are my heart, and I do not wish to live without you. Come with me, rule by my side in Akasha,' Shamash, begged holding out his hand as he had all those years ago. As she did the very first time, Aya took his hand with an open heart. As the couple took their last breaths, their bodies dissolved into a pile of ashes.

"The family knew more was to come and waited, sometimes crying, sometimes laughing, but always loving each other and their parents. As the sun set, a soft trill sounded and a magnificent bird with flames for feathers burst from the ashes. Pearly tears dripped from his eyes onto the ashes, and moments later another bird rose. She was smaller, and her flame feathers were purple, blue, and green, showing that she was indeed the heart of the Phoenix King.

"A prophecy said that a child will be born looking like their first Jewels: onyx and ruby, peridot, gold, copper and pearl. And this Jewel, along with the Treasures, shall have the power to open a doorway back to Akasha to help their people left behind." Philip paused taking a sip of his drink. I felt his power leave. I blinked as my mind cleared and the images faded.

"Shamash and Aya's grandchildren and great-grandchildren look like the Treasures, like Kayin, with one or two traits of the Phoenix King and Queen." Philip explained.

I looked up at Kayin's soft ruby-studded curls. "Before, when Aya and Shamash were on Earth, was it easy to go between the...worlds?" I asked not sure if "worlds" was accurate, but I lacked a better word.

"Yes. Akasha is another world, another dimension if you like." I nodded. I have seen enough Star Trek and Dr. Who to understand other dimensions. "Well, there were doorways all over the world for magical creatures. However, as people became more fearful, greedy, and hungry for power, the doorways began to close. They couldn't stay open, something about inharmonious vibrations," Philip said with a wave of his hand.

"Where did the prophecy come from?" Kayin asked.

"Before the doors closed all the way, several scrolls appeared before Children of Fire whose hearts were still pure. Some were found in churches, temples, and monasteries while others appeared before individual people. I'm sure the original prophecy rhymed beautifully and embodied the wonderful mystical tone all prophecies should have. Unfortunately that has been lost in the multitude of translations."

"Why are there still magical creatures here?" I asked. "Shouldn't they all have gone home when the doors closed?"

"Well, no one's sure exactly what happened." Philip leaned forward as if sharing some secret. "We do know over time many of the portals closed, so at the end there were only a few left open. Some magical creatures lived on Earth for years and didn't know how weak the portals had become. And some beings wanted to stay, at least until the last minute. Shamash and Aya found everyone they could."

"Why would they want to stay?" Not that Earth wasn't nice, but Akasha seemed nicer in my dreams.

"Some were enjoying being gods. Some liked the food, and some had created homes and families here," Philip told us.

"When did the last portal close?" Taliesin asked.

"No one knows for sure, but the guess is around two thousand years ago," Philip said.

The images his story painted danced through my head. Did I believe that the story is real and that I'm a part of it? A fairy tale in which I am the magical princess whose people are waiting to be saved. Unfortunately, I stopped believing in fairy tales long ago.

"Never stop believing. The world is so much more than you could possibly imagine. Someday you will know all there is, and see amazing magical things, but until then believe. Believe in the possibility, believe in hope, believe in magic, love, laughter, and joy. I know it will be hard, and people and times will try to crush your beliefs, but hold onto them. I pray you will remember the wonderful things you have seen and felt while we were together. It is real, and it will always be real. Believe."

I never understood my mom's words until now. For the first time I couldn't accept her advice at face value, despite everything happening around me, or maybe because of it.

Who wants to be so very different from everyone else in world?

The conversation flowed around me, but I didn't hear any of it. My mind tumbled the new information around and around in my head. I rubbed my queasy stomach. Guh. I'd never thought so hard I'd made myself sick before.

"Are you all right?" Kayin asked, rubbing the back of my neck.

I relaxed. "Yeah. I must have eaten too much."

Suddenly, all the conversation stopped. "You didn't eat very much. Did you feel bad during camp?" Philip asked, leaning towards me a bit.

I scratched my arms. "No, maybe all the thinking I'm doing is making me ill."

Taliesin snorted. Rude.

"Sara, honey, do you have a rash?" Anali asked.

"No, I feel weird, like ants are crawling on me."

Philip stood up. "And your stomach feels queasy?"

"Yes." Damn it, new weird was coming.

"Does anyone else feel bad?" Gavin asked as he walked to the window and looked out.

Everyone said no. Of course, this is my own special weird. Well, good. I don't like to share anyway. I'll keep all the weird to myself.

Philip's blue eyes looked me over. "She must be sensitive."

"Or it's something totally normal." I offered, in a pathetically hopeful way.

"Maybe," Gavin as he closed the curtains. "But we'll go and check it out. How you feel right now is how Children of Fire feel when they are close to a walk-in or the Sons of Belial."

"Who?"

"The Sons of Belial are a group that hunts magical beings, then drains them of their energy, power, and life. They use the stolen energy to increase their own power and extend their lives." Philip explained as he put on his jacket.

Oh, good. The only thing this crazy party was missing, a good dose of evil, had arrived. I sighed and leaned my head against Kayin's leg.

"How far should we check?" Anali said.

Gavin stopped, his expression blank. "You're staying here."

"No, I am going to go and help check for a walk-in. So, Philip, how far away should we check?"

"Let's go about three blocks out."

"Anali," Gavin began. The look she gave him stopped him from saying any more.

"You three stay here. Taliesin, you have my number, right?" Philip asked, putting his phone in his pocket.

"Yes."

The adults left, leaving us 'kids' behind. If they hadn't been looking for some creepy thing out to kill us, I might have protested.

"I should have gone with them," Kayin said. "I am a good hunter."

"Have you dealt with a walk-in yet?" Taliesin asked.

Kayin sighed. "No, but I do have my contacts in to keep me safe."

"Are they stronger, or faster, or anything?" I asked. In movies and shows people possessed tended to gain super strength and the ability to projectile vomit. "And why do contacts help?"

71

Taliesin shook his head, his white braid falling over his shoulder. "No, they are bound by the person's body they possess. They can sense magic, but that's it. They even lose their psychic connection to their leader while possessing someone."

"How do you know that?" Kayin asked.

Taliesin shrugged. "It's in one of the books on magical creatures Philip has. I believe that information came from a Dreamer."

"Well, it's good to know. As long as we don't look them in the eyes we should stay safe," Kayin said. "The contacts hide the fire burning in our eyes. If they see that fire they can track us magically. Don't look at one until your contacts get here. I know Philip ordered some."

"Wait, you're not a Child of Fire." I remembered touching Taliesin's hands, I'd felt no spark of heat just coolness. "Why are you here?"

Taliesin glared at me, his ice blue eyes hard. My stomach lurched. Rude. It was just a question, he didn't have to answer if he didn't want to.

The door knob jiggled then a scraping sound. Someone was breaking in!

"What do we do?" I whispered.

"Out the back door," Kayin hissed leading us through a small kitchen and a door which lead onto a rickety, creaky fire escape.

"Are you kidding?" I asked.

Taliesin pushed my shoulder. "No, and hurry up."

I followed Kayin, shivering in the damp winter night. This was not good, not good at all.

When we reached the bottom, Kayin and I turned to Taliesin.

Taliesin pulled out his phone. "Let me text Philip."

The door slammed open and Kayin pulled me and Taliesin into the shadows. A woman stood at the top of the stairs scanning the parking lot.

"We need to run," I whispered.

"Where?" Taliesin snapped.

She began to walk down the stairs.

"Away from her would be a good start."

We turned and ran, Kayin in the lead.

I shouldn't have suggested running, I hadn't actually meant running, more like quick walking. My sides hurt. Panting, I did my best to keep up with the guys. Or more accurately, not slow them down too horribly much.

She came closer. My sick stomach and itching skin hadn't let up. Kayin turned down an alley. A dead end. This was turning into a bad horror movie. Turning back, we could see her outline against the darkness.

Above us the clouds parted and the moon illuminated her.

"Damn it, the moon is out," Taliesin muttered.

Slowly, I turned expecting to find Taliesin's perfect features morphing into some kind of hideous were-monster.

Taliesin was glowing. The moon's rays illuminated his skin and hair, creating a soothing silvery glow.

"Taliesin?" I asked.

He sighed. "I'm a unicorn, or part unicorn. My father is one, apparently."

"Master will be so pleased." She, or more accurately the walk-in inside her, hissed. "A unicorn, alive and well. There has been no other unicorn for so very, very long."

Taliesin stepped back as she came closer. "They can't know. The Sons of Belial can't know about me."

"Where are the adults?" I asked. "Maybe they can do something?"

Taliesin fumbled for his phone. "Does anyone know where we are?"

Kayin and I both shook our heads.

"Can Philip do the voice thing over the phone?" I asked putting myself between the walk-in and Taliesin. Kayin moved in front of me.

"I don't think so, he's not that powerful," Taliesin answered.

I took a deep breath. Okay, fairy tale world, let's see what you've got. Closing my eyes, I thought of how I felt in my dreams. How connected to Akasha I felt when I'd held the jewelry. A tiny spark of warmth flickered in my belly.

Legend says that the Jewel is powerful, and I'm the Jewel, so maybe, just maybe, I could do what Philip did. I focused on that little spark of warmth and moved it to my throat.

"Stop," I said forcing as much power as I could into my voice. "Stop moving."

She wavered, and her face hardened as she fought the command.

"Stop," I said forcing more power into my voice, it had to work.

Her body froze. I stepped out from behind Kayin and walked forward, careful to keep my eyes down.

"I want you to forget. Forget about us."

"Never," she hissed.

I tugged on the power, pulling more into me. My hands shook as heat flooded my body. My throat vibrated with power. I needed to talk to the thing inside of the woman. I closed my eyes and followed the sick feeling to a dark presence inside of her.

"You will forget," I insisted, wrapping my power-filled voice around the creature. "You will forget about all of us. You will have no memory of a unicorn, or anything magical here."

"Forget," it hissed.

I opened my eyes. The woman's mouth went slack, and her body swayed. Oh, God, had I done that? My eyes swam with tears. I blinked, trying to force them back. "Go back to the circus school. Look around as ordered. Tell your leader you found nothing."

"Go back," she said, lips barely moving, her voice a hissed whisper. She turned, her movements choppy as her body swayed.

Still energetically attached to her I frantically pulled at the connection, reeling back when it finally snapped. The walk-in shook her head and walked away, her movements normal.

"Thank you," Taliesin said.

My hands shook.

"Are you okay?" he moved closer.

I shook my head. My stomach clenched. I forced someone to do what I wanted. I ran to the nearest garbage can and threw up. Hands rubbed my back as I emptied my stomach. This is a gift? What if I hurt the woman? My stomach convulsed as I threw up again.

"It's over; it'll be all right," Taliesin said.

But it would never be all right, because part of me reveled in this new power. Never again. I would never use it again. The dark part of me grinned, as I dry heaved as there was nothing else in my stomach to throw up.

"I'm going to use your bandanna, okay?" Kayin asked.

I nodded and felt him remove it. He walked away and I heard water running. He came back and wiped my face with the icy wet cloth. I focused on the cold and did my best to shut my brain down.

"Little Sister, we have the same hair," Kayin said touching my bun which crunched under his finger. "What do you have in your hair?"

I giggled. I couldn't help it. He sounded so offended by my gelled hair.

Kayin raised an eye brow.

My giggle turned into laughter. I clutched Kayin to keep from falling.

"Is she all right?" Kayin asked.

I laughed so much I began to cry. Crying led to sobbing. Kayin's strong arms held me close. I buried my face into his warm chest, the tiny bit of my mind that was still rational was mortified. I never cried, especially not in front of others.

"Kayin, I'll call Philip and walk to the street, so he can find us."

"Okay, thank you. I've got her," he said, his deep voice low and serious. It rumbled through me and I relaxed.

"You sure you'll be okay?" Taliesin asked.

I felt Kayin nod, his chin bumping the top of my head. "We will, and if I need you, I'll yell."

Kayin's warm hand rubbed my back. Taliesin's footsteps echoed as he walked away.

I took a deep breath and pushed everything I could back down to deal with later. I trusted Kayin and felt safe with him, but I wasn't ready to have some big therapy soul-baring moment. "I am so sorry, Big Brother." His shirt had a big wet blob on it from where I sobbed like a baby. "Your poor shirt."

"Little Sister, you saved us. My shirt is nothing. Thank you."

I looked up. His eyes were soft, and I could feel his concern like a tiny little finger reaching out to see if I was all right.

"Wow, fire is dancing in your eyes."

Blushing, I looked down. Yay for being a freak.

"It's not a bad thing," he said.

"Sara! Kayin!"

"Over there, Gavin," Taliesin called out.

I wiped at my eyes and reached up to fix my bandanna, but my fingers found only hair. Oh, crap.

"What happened?" Philip asked.

"Sara, are you all right?" Gavin grasped my shoulders and turned me around to look me over.

I stepped back. "Yes, I'm fine."

"You've been crying. Your hair..." Gavin reached out, but I stepped back again bumping into Kayin, who steadied me.

"Sara saved us," Taliesin said, stepping over a pile of trash. Gross, I looked around the alley for the first time. Trash cans, dumpsters, puddles of what I hoped was water surrounded us. And the smell, my tummy lurched. Oh, I didn't like this smell. How had I not noticed it before?

"Is anyone hurt?" Gavin asked, his tone professional and cold.

I bit my lip and shook my head. I hadn't meant to hurt his feelings, but I hadn't expected him to reach out for me.

"Okay then let's get back to the school. Anali is already there," Gavin said.

"What? No." My chest tightened as I fought to take in enough air to speak. "No, the school isn't safe. I sent it, her, back there. You have to call Anali. I didn't know. Or I wouldn't have." My vision began to gray at the edges, and my hands shook.

Gavin held my face still and looked into my eyes. "Philip is calling Anali right now. I need you to breathe. You're having a panic attack. Listen to me and do your best to follow."

I gripped Gavin's wrists, hanging on as my sight dimmed. He took loud, slow, breaths. I could feel his exhalation on my face. My gasps changed to match his.

"Good," he said soft and slow. "Very good. Keep doing that."

"Anali is safe, she saw the walk-in go back into the school, so she left. I told her to meet us at the cafe down the street," Philip said.

I blinked. Gavin's peridot green eyes were the only thing I could see. My breath returned to normal, and the pressure on my chest left. Okay that sucked. Mental note to never have another panic attack ever again.

I dropped my hands from Gavin's wrists. "I'm sorry."

He smiled, but I could feel his worry and sadness. "You have nothing to be sorry for. Let's go to the cafe, and get you guys warmed up."

"I'll need to borrow a jacket," Taliesin said, stepping into the moonlight and glowing again. It was as if the moon loved him and wanted the world to see his beauty.

Gavin took off his coat. "Here, there's a hood too. I'd forgotten you're a unicorn."

"Thanks." Taliesin hid beneath the big coat.

"Come on." Philip wrinkled his nose. "This place stinks. Let's go get something hot to drink, and then you can tell us what happened."

I wanted to walk behind everyone, I needed a moment to myself. To regroup. To calm down enough to ensure I wouldn't throw up again. Gavin and Philip had different ideas. Philip led us, walking the tiniest bit in front, chatting like nothing was wrong, and Gavin walked behind, surrounding me with a sense of protection and security.

I liked being cared for, but it would be nice to only feel my own crazy emotions right now.

Chapter Eight

"How blunt are all the arrows of thy quiver in comparison with those of guilt." ~ Robert Blair

Anali waved to us as soon as we entered the cafe. My fingers and toes burned as they began to warm up. From now on I would carry a jacket with me from room to room. Anali hugged Gavin. "I'm so glad you're all okay."

"I was scared when I thought you were in the school with that thing," Gavin said burying his face in her dark brown hair.

I tugged on Kayin's sleeve. "I'm going to go to the bathroom, will you let them know?"

"Of course, do you want anything?"

"Something hot to drink, whatever you get."

Kayin's brown eyes were soft as they looked into mine. "We're safe now, try to relax, Little Sister."

I nodded, and tried to fake a smile before slipping between the packed tables. The bathroom was clean, small, and with room for only one person. I exhaled, letting my shoulders relax as I leaned against the sink. I needed to try and re-create my flimsy bubble. Right now I could feel everyone's emotions. And the energy I received from Akasha still sparked inside of me.

I rinsed out my mouth and splashed water on my face. Looking in the mirror, I groaned. My eyes were puffy, red, bloodshot, with small flames flickering in the iris, and pieces of my hair stuck up as it escaped the bun and gel. I couldn't put it back together so I reached up and began pulling the pins out of my hair. With numb fingers, I combed through the messy curls, trying in vain to make my hair look less like a Halloween costume for an '80s rocker.

"Just a second," I called out to whoever knocked on the door. I guess this was as good as it was going to get.

I walked back to the table and sat in the empty chair between Kayin and Gavin. A steaming cup of spiced apple cider waited for me. I took a sip and felt warmer instantly. Taliesin and Kayin were taking turns telling the others about our encounter. It was nice of them to make me sound heroic instead of like a scared child, pathetically trying to find something to save us.

"Wait," Philip said, holding up a calloused hand, "Sara, how did you know what to do?"

I shrugged. "I thought of how it felt when you told us the story and how the energy feels when I dream, and tried to connect to Akasha."

Philip sat forward, resting his arms on the table. "I felt you, I didn't realize it at the time, but I felt you tugging at me. You realize you're the Jewel right?"

"I thought we agreed not to bring that up?" Gavin said between clenched teeth.

"Gavin, it must be important, or he wouldn't have," Anali said her voice soothing.

"I, um, yes. Yes, I know," I said grasping the warm mug and drinking some more.

"Your gift is all about connection. You'll be able to do other stuff too, but you can open the doorway to Akasha because you can connect other Children of Fire, specifically Treasures, to Akasha and increase the energy. And it would seem you can use the gifts of other Children of Fire near you."

"I didn't mean to. I won't do it again."

"No, no, sweetie, it's fine." Philip smiled, the light behind him making his salt and pepper mohawk throw a weird sinister shadow over his face. "It didn't hurt."

"Do you have any gifts unique to you?" Gavin asked.

I shrugged, how exactly was I supposed to know that?

Anali sighed. "Gavin, really. Sara, are you willing to tell us if you've experienced any of the other gifts?"

"I suppose, but I don't know much about them. I mean, Kayin told me a little bit."

Gavin's face looked warm and open. "The strength and focus of the gift varies, but there are six basic types: telepathy, language, healing, fire, empathy, and dreams."

I must have looked as confused as I felt because Gavin immediately began explaining. "Each gift can be broken down into a few basic skills. Healing for instance, can be the ability to heal others, or regeneration also called, speed healing, which is my gift.

"People with the gift of language can easily learn other languages, have the ability to understand any spoken or written language." Gavin paused, waiting for a moment, and when I nodded that I understood, he continued. "The gift of dreams usually is one of two skills, either having prophetic dreams, which are dreams that come true, or the ability to dream and talk with those in Akasha and remembering the dream clearly the next day."

"Those who have the gift of fire can create fire, control fire, or are completely fireproof. Then there are those with the gift of empathy, being able to read other people's emotions or the ability to influence how other people feel. This is usually done through our voices. The whole Phoenix song thing," Gavin said waving his hand around. "And finally the Children of Fire with the gift of telepathy can communicate with animals. Some can hear what animals are thinking and some can project their thoughts to animals."

"Most Children of Fire have only a small portion of the gift," Philip explained. "Treasures, like Kayin, have the full range of their gift."

"And as the Jewel, what am I expected to do?" I asked before telling them anything.

"No one knows," Gavin said. "But it seems like as long as you are near someone with a gift you can tap into it."

I took a sip of the apple cider. "Well, I believe I am feeling other people's emotions, but I honestly haven't tried to do anything else."

"Why didn't you say something?" Gavin asked. "And why did you hide your hair?"

"I don't know you, any of you," I protested. "Do you have any idea how scared I am? I'm changing! My life is chaos, and the people in control of what happens to me, they wouldn't understand any of this. I need to have a better understanding of what is going on, to be more in control of myself before I figure out who to tell what."

Gavin leaned forward reaching out a calloused hand, excitement and hope flooded over me. "Sara, I'm ... ouch! You kicked me." He shot an accusing look at Anali, sipping her drink not meeting his eyes.

Philip smiled. "Sara, we are all here for you. And other than Kayin, I don't think any of us understand how scary these transformations can be when you didn't know they were going to happen."

Gavin ran his hands through his hair, making the damp red locks even wilder. Taking a deep breath, I felt him pull in and lock down his emotions. Anali patted his arm. "You're right" Gavin said."I'm sorry if I sounded like I was accusing you. I forget that this isn't always a welcome change."

Guilt feels like brain freeze, sharp and cold. I didn't want Gavin to feel like that. "It's all right."

"We all will help you, Little Sister," Kayin said.

"Thanks, Big Brother," I smiled faintly.

"So how long do we sit here?" Anali asked. "The cafe is open until midnight, but I'm not interested in being trapped here that long."

"What was a walk-in doing here anyway? I thought the Sons of Belial rarely go after Children of Fire," Taliesin asked.

"She was looking for something," I answered. "Searching. I could feel it."

"Are you sure she wasn't after us?" Kayin asked, his brow furrowed.

Gavin shook his head. "If a walk-in sees the fire in our eyes they'll track us, or if we get in the way of a magical creature, they'll fight us, but most of the time the Sons of Belial keep an eye on us."

"Most of us aren't powerful enough to bother with. They must have felt a power surge," Philip said.

Taliesin turned cold blue eyes to me. "So this is because of you."

"What?" Guilt swept through me.

"When a Child of Fire comes into their power they tend to have dreams of Akasha. They are brought there by Shamash so he can mask their power surges and help them learn to use their gifts. This can't be anything Sara has done." Gavin sighed and rubbed his eyes. "Most of us don't even remember the dreams unless dreaming is our gift."

I could remember bits and pieces of the dreams, but no point in sharing that bit of information, or the fact my mother left me a letter written in another language.

"This is no one's fault," Philip said his voice firm.

I opened my eyes staring firmly at the table, remembering when Shamash pulled me into the dream because I hadn't wanted to go to Akasha. This was my fault. If someone got hurt or worse, I'm the one to blame.

"Guilt is such a vicious debilitating emotion because we wield it on ourselves. We tear apart our own actions, thoughts, motives, and desires. Do not let guilt consume you, my darling daughter. If you have done something wrong, intentional or not, work towards a solution. Can you fix things, or will you need to do better next time? We all make mistakes, and we are all deserving of forgiveness. Please, my darling, allow forgiveness to always follow guilt. Wash the guilt away as you fix things and forgive yourself with as much love and compassion as you would forgive a friend."

Kayin's large dark hand covered mine. "Everything will be fine."

"I'm just saying we should figure out if Sara is attracting the Sons of Belial so we can deal with it in the future," Taliesin replied.

"And we will," Anali said. "But right now we need to figure out what we are going to do tonight."

"I have an idea, let me make a few calls." Philip got up and walked outside.

I watched him for a moment, his frown quickly turned to a smile. I guess his plan was coming together. I took another sip of my drink and stared at the table. Was this all my fault? Had that poor woman been possessed because of me? Did I put everyone in danger?

"Okay, I've got it all figured out," Philip said interrupting my wallow in self-pity. "My friend, Lucas, is going to have a couple of his faeries go over the school and lead the walk-in away. His husband, Zachary, is working tonight, so he'll pick her up for being intoxicated in public and take her to the hospital to get evaluated because she's talking about trying to capture faeries."

"Philip, you're a genius!" Anali said.

"Yes, well, I try and tone it down so as to not make people nervous around me. Anyway, Zachary will text me as soon as she's in custody," Philip replied.

"What time is it?" I asked.

Gavin looked at his watch. "Five-thirty. Why?"

"I want to make sure I won't be late for Melanie."

Philip's phone chirped. "Looks like the faeries are working, and they are headed south, which means we can head back once everyone is ready."

*   *   *

"Oh, good, you're back," Shin said as we walked through the door. "Philip, did you see Nat? She was acting weird."

"No, did she ask for me?" Philip took off his jacket.

Shin shrugged. "Not really, she muttered to herself about looking for something."

"I thought she looked familiar," Taliesin whispered. "She's new, in the advanced contortion class."

"I'll try and call her later," Philip said with a tight smile. "So what are you guys up to?"

"Well, we finished practicing for tomorrow night, and this fool bet everyone he could do more handstand push-ups than anyone else," Shin answered running his fingers through his blue and black bangs.

"It is the true test of awesomely superior strength," said a man with short blond hair. His brown eyes sparkled with mischief.

The heater clicked on. I looked up and, finding a vent, went to stand under it, sighing in pleasure as warm dry air flowed over me.

"Any of you want to join us?" Shin asked.

"Of course," Gavin said. "Come on, Kayin, you can help me represent the New York school."

Kayin walked over, swinging his arms. I assumed in order to warm them up.

"Okay, everyone line up. On the count of three, into handstands and begin." Philip raised his arms over his head.

I took slow breaths, and tried to focus on strengthening my feeble attempt at creating a bubble to keep out other people's emotions, while the six men and three women popped up into handstands then lowered their noses to the floor and pushed back up.

How in the world could they do that? I could barely do a regular push-up. Once they did five, people began to fall out. The first a man and woman I didn't know, then Kayin and Anali came down after their eighth. The blond guyand the other girl stopped at ten. Philip and Gavin grunted, shook, and cursed their way to fifteen before collapsing to the floor. After which Shin and Taliesin gracefully came down from their handstands. Both of them were sweaty but calm.

"So what did that prove?" I muttered under my breath.

Anali giggled. "That youth always wins."

"Come on, I'll order some pizza for dinner," Gavin said once he'd caught his breath.

Taliesin sighed. "I need to call my mom, she was expecting me home by now."

"I can give you a ride home if she wants," Gavin offered.

Taliesin rolled his eyes. "She's a bit over-protective sometimes, she'll probably come to get me."

I felt Taliesin's embarrassment and irritation at his mom, but I couldn't help feeling jealous. He didn't know how lucky he was.

* * *

I debated having a third slice of pesto pizza when Cordelia swept into the room. A measuring tape hung around her neck, flapping as she rushed over to Taliesin. Her worry and fear grated against me like sandpaper.

"Are you okay? Did they see you?" The glitter in her blue nail polish sparkled as her hands fluttered around her son, checking for injuries.

Taliesin's pale cheeks flushed pink. "Mom, I'm fine stop fussing."

"I'm not fussing, it's my job to make sure you're okay." She huffed and fidgeted with the measuring tape while staring at Taliesin.

A small wave of guilt swept over me as Taliesin pointed at me. "Mom, you remember Sara, right? Sara, this is my mom, Cordelia Gadarn. Sara saved me. She forced the walk-in to go away and forget all about us."

Cordelia rushed at me in a blur of blue clothing and honey blond hair. Wrapping her arms around me, she hugged me tight as she thanked me over and over again.

"I didn't do much, Ms. Gadarn," I said as she squeezed the breath out of me.

She pulled back, her blue gray eyes shining with tears. "You did so much more than you can possibly understand. Thank you."

Heat burned my cheeks. "You're welcome."

She grasped my hands. "I shall make you the most wonderful costumes. Gavin, you will bring her to me to get measured. You're so lovely, let me know what acts you'll perform in, and I'll start drawing right away."

I opened my mouth, but Taliesin's mom turned and began walking towards the door. "Come on, honey, let's go home. You can tell me all about your adventure on the way."

Taliesin rolled his eyes, grabbed another slice of the pineapple, onion, and bell pepper pizza and followed his mom out the door.

"How are you feeling?" Anali asked.

"Fine," I answered, leaving out the part where my skin felt gross as if ants had been crawling on me. Until I showered I felt sure the grossness wouldn't leave. And of course, if I let my thoughts wander I would see the woman's empty eyes as I forced her to do what I wanted, which made my stomach feel sick. But other than that, I was peachy keen.

"Do you want me to talk to your houseparent?" Gavin asked.

I frowned. "Talk to her about what?"

He waved a hand in the air. "About everything that is going on."

"No, are you crazy?" I screeched. "She has no idea about what is going on, and it needs to stay that way."

"Well," Philip began calmly a touch of power in his voice which simultaneously soothed and irritated me. "What does she think is happening?"

I leaned back in my chair. "I have no idea. The doctor said I'm fine, and Five, my caseworker, said that was good enough for him, so no issue."

"Maybe she thinks you dyed your hair," Anali said.

"She checked for that, hair dye leaves a distinctive smell."

"I don't like you going back there after such a traumatic experience and not have someone who can support you," Gavin said. "What if you have a nightmare?"

"Then I make something up. Look if you want me here tomorrow, you can't say anything to Melanie." I took another slice of pesto pizza and began to eat. The grown-ups all sighed and didn't argue with me. Kayin bumped his arm into mine. I smiled and bumped him back. Another crisis averted, hopefully the last one for the night.

Chapter Nine

"When you have eliminated all which is impossible, then
whatever remains, however improbable, must be the truth."
~said by Sherlock Holmes in 'The Adventure of the Blanched
Soldier' by Sir Arthur Conan Doyle

*Claws gripped my leg, their cold points drawing blood as my skin tore.
I screamed and fought to get away, my fingers digging into the ground.
Something howled. I fought harder. I broke free from the claws but my shoe
was ripped from my foot as the monster tried to hold onto me. I shifted,
ready to push up and run, when saliva dripped onto my back. Hot breath
ruffled my hair; the putrid smell of rotting meat made me gag.*

Screaming when claws and teeth pierced my flesh.

"No," I gasped, sitting up. My chest ached as I took in
heaving breaths. I wiped the sweat and tears from my eyes with
shaking hands. First I can't sleep, and then I have nightmares.
Great. I sat up in bed and looked around the room. Shadows
moved and changed in the dim light.

I looked at the floor. What if there is something under the
bed? I laughed, but it sounded dry and brittle. When was the
last time I worried about monsters under the bed? My small
room seemed extra tiny, and it had one exit. Sure there was the
fire escape, but how often did people in the movies get away
using the fire escape?

Shante muttered in her sleep.

I tried to relax, but the feeling of something coming after
me wouldn't go away. Risking the monster-under-the-bed, I put
on my slippers and crept down the hall to the living room.
Jumping at every creak the old house made, I turned on the

table lamp. The living room looked safe and inviting under the warm yellow light. However, it did make the hallway look like a dark pit of terror.

I couldn't turn the TV on, that would be rude, so I scanned the shelves for something to read. The books were a chaotic mix with no rhyme or reason that I could find. Maybe Melanie would pay me to organize them. I was tempted by a copy of Neil Gaiman's Coraline, but decided against scaring myself further. My finger bumped along the spines as I read the titles, trying to find the perfect book.

"Sara," said a sleep rough voice.

I jumped and turned with a yelp stuck in my throat. "You scared the crap out of me."

Melanie shrugged. "I walked normally and cleared my throat three times. I guess those books are really interesting."

"No," I sighed and rubbed at my eyes. "The words are blurring and I was trying to force myself to read them."

"Why don't you go back to bed?" she asked sitting on a chair.

I plopped down on the couch and curled my legs up underneath me. "Maybe I'll sleep out here."

"Why?"

"Because in the movies nothing ever gets you on the couch," I said, blushing as soon as the words left my mouth. Okay, I was seriously tired if I said that out loud.

Melanie snorted. "Bad dream?"

"Yes. I know it's silly but . . . " I shrugged.

Melanie laughed. "Just this once," she said as she left.

I guess I wasn't entertaining. I nestled my head down on the arm of the couch and stared at the gaping dark pit where the hall started. Anything could be waiting in the darkness. I curled up tighter. I was safe on the couch, right? I'd never seen any movies where the person was attacked on the couch, so I had to be safe.

Something creaked. Maybe I should go back to my room.

"Here," Melanie said, making me gasp. She spread a blanket over me.

"Thank you." I lifted my feet and tucked the blanket under them.

"I hope you have happy dreams. And remember I won't let anything bad happen to you." Melanie patted my head and shuffled back to her own room. I waited but didn't hear her door shut. I smiled as I snuggled into the couch, knowing Melanie watched after me.

Sighing, I looked around. I didn't want one of these dreams! They were confusing, and my life always changed once I woke up. I sat in a meadow with iridescent green grass and bright flowers that looked like they were made from spun glass. Above me a Pegasus flew. My skin tingled, as if electricity danced over me. I tried to fight the feeling of being home, of belonging, but each breath of sweet air connected me more deeply with this faerie land. Around me a large circle of mythical animals formed, many I didn't recognize. A seal slid out of the crystal blue water, squirmed, then its skin split and out stepped a naked woman. Blushing, I turned away. What in the world was she?

Two streaks of fire came straight at me. I backed up. I hadn't been hurt in these dreams yet, but I wasn't taking any chances. Landing easily, the red, orange and yellow Phoenix trilled. Instantly I felt calmer, but at the same time felt irritated that I couldn't help feeling calmer. Next to the flame-colored bird, landed a smaller Phoenix with feathers of purple, blue and green. With the ease and quickness of a breath, they both transformed. I recognized them from my other dreams.

"Hello, darling, you look so beautiful, so much like our first children, I can't get over it." Aya walked over to me. Her black curls flowed around her, moved by her magical force.

"Yes, she is very lovely." Right next to me stood Shamash. My eyes darted back and forth between them.

The highlights in my and Kayin's hair, along with Gavin's hair were the exact shade of fire red as Shamash's. The light, clear green of Aya's eye matched Gavin's and mine. I tried to see how else we looked like them. Eye shape, chins, noses.

"Slow down and breathe," Shamash said, his gold eyes held mine until I calmed.

His intense gaze felt like he looked at my soul. Guh, so cliché. Breaking away, I looked down and my knees trembled. Aya and Shamash were holding my hand. My new skin color a perfect blend of Shamash's pearl white and Aya's dark copper.

"We're family," I said. I knew this, but something felt different this time. I began to accept it and them. My heart fluttered. I have a family. I'm part of a real family.

"Yes, we are." Aya smiled at me with love. I had never seen anyone look at me like that before.

A warm hand cupped my check and wiped away a tear I hadn't even known I'd shed.

"It's okay, Sapphire. We're here for you, and now that your powers are growing, you'll be able to remember more of your dreams," Shamash said.

"We'll start teaching you how to control your powers. First, of course, we'll have to get your dreams strong enough to remember when you wake up. So, for today how about we have some fun?" Aya grinned at me.

"What are we going to do?" My voice trembled a bit.

Shamash's grin matched his wife's. "The faeries built this huge swing; all three of us can fit on it."

At the edge of the meadow, the swing hung from an oak tree three times the size of any other tree I had ever seen. A moss-covered wooden bench hung by braided vines covered with big white flowers.

Together we swung up into the turquoise sky. I sat between my many times great-grandparents, feeling safe, warm, loved, and like a regular child.

In the morning when I woke, I was still filled with happiness and at the same time my heart breaking at having to leave them. I wondered if this is how the other kids felt coming back from visits with their families. If so, no wonder they were in horrible moods and threw fits. This was the most confusing feeling ever.

Wait. I left my family. Really? I believe this? I am going to believe that my long-lost uncle has found me, and I have four-thousand-year-old grandparents I play with in my dreams, and that I am some kind of magical being?

True, I had the letter from my mom, part of which is written in some ancient language that I could read, and I could feel people's emotions and control them with my voice. All of which seemed like rather compelling evidence.

I needed to decide if this was all some weird Twilight Zone episode I'm dreaming while trapped in a coma kind of thing, or reality. Everything happened so fast, and so far I'd gone with the flow of things, but waking up missing my grandparents felt like a huge step towards the crazy.

Did I believe all this? That I found a long lost family? Did I remember some horrible accident that left me trapped in a coma?

Right now I needed advice, and the journal my mother left with me when I was five always helped me. I hoped it would help me now. Reaching under my bed I pulled out my old flowered backpack. Holding the journal, I stared at its worn cover. I knew I was going to a biased source for advice on this issue, but this what I had. Opening the journal at random I read the page.

"Sometimes life defies explanation. There are going to be events in your life that no logic or science will help you make sense of. You are going to have to trust your instincts and your heart as you look at all the possible options. When the mundane doesn't explain what is happening, then look to the magical and mystical which will guide you."

I shut the book with a soft snap and carefully put it away. Well, there you go. I'm a many times great-granddaughter of the Phoenix King and Queen, and my long-lost uncle has magically found me. Grabbing my clothes for the day, I tried to remember if I had been hit in the head anytime in the past week or so.

*   *   *

"Normally we would have one more lesson, but because it's Christmas Eve, I thought we would spend the last hour celebrating. So while you pick up from class, the other teachers and I will bring out the party," Philip said to loud cheering.

"Sara, will you help me with these mats?" Kayin asked.

"Sure." It was Christmas Eve. When did this happen?

We each grabbed an end and folded the large gym mats and dragged them to the side of the room.

"How are you doing today?" Kayin asked as we grabbed another mat.

"I'm okay, and you?"

Kayin shrugged. "I'm fine. My life isn't as exciting as yours is right now."

"Yes, it's thrilling," I said, rolling my eyes.

Kayin tugged on my shirtsleeve. "Come on, Little Sister, let's go get something to eat before it's all gone."

Looking over at the table surrounded by kids, I chose not to move. "Yeah, I'll wait until it clears up a bit."

"I'll brave the crowd and get you something to eat," Kayin said, taking my hand.

"My Big Brother, the brave hunter." I fluttered my eyelashes.

"Not quite the hunting I was brought up to do, but I should be able to handle it." He grinned and walked into the crowd.

Sliding up to the table, he quickly returned with two glasses.

"Do you like this?" Kayin handed me a glass of thick eggnog.

Taking the glass I smiled. "Yes, I love eggnog. I have to have it at Christmas."

"I'm going back in for food," Kayin said, puffing out his chest.

"I'll hold your cup, you might need both hands to survive." I laughed as Kayin stalked the crowed before sliding in.

I could feel Gavin coming closer. All day his crazy emotions shifted between excitement, sadness, joy, and confusion. It drove me nuts. In my next dream with Aya and Shamash, I'd ask for help blocking other people's emotions.

Taking a sip of eggnog, I was surprised at how familiar it tasted. It was different than any other eggnog I'd ever drunk, and yet I'd tasted it before. Taking another sip, I saw images flash through my mind. Me sitting on a man's lap, his gold eyes warm as he held a cup for me to drink from. A huge tree being decorated by a woman with creamy copper skin and long black curls, and a young man with flame red hair throwing tinsel at her.

"Sara, are you okay?" Gavin asked.

"Yes, thanks. I just, um, . . . it's really good eggnog," I managed to mumble, as Gavin stared at me with concern.

"Oh thank you, it's an old family tradition, there's a secret ingredient," Gavin whispered loudly.

"I guess I shouldn't ask for the recipe, then."

We both froze in painful, obvious silence. I needed to learn to keep my mouth shut! I now knew without a doubt that a single second could go on forever.

"It was hard, and I wasn't sure I would make it out alive, but I got you strawberries and cookies." Kayin handed me a plate filled with treats.

"Thank you," I said taking the plate and giving Kayin back his cup.

"Do you kids mind if we old, boring teachers join you?" Anali asked, slipping her arm around Gavin's waist.

"Hey, I'm not boring or old," Gavin said, trying to joke after the uncomfortable silence.

"Of course you can join us. We're going to sit over there by the window," Kayin said, tilting his chin to the corner on the other side of the room.

"We'll be just a minute." Anali tugged Gavin towards the table of goodies.

As Kayin and I settled ourselves in the corner I couldn't help but wonder how awkward this was going to be. Sighing, I leaned against the stack of mats and watched people walk past the window, holding bright umbrellas to keep them dry. Picking up a strawberry, I hummed along with Deck the Halls.

"What are you doing for Christmas?" Kayin asked, taking a bite from a Santa cookie.

"Tonight I'll make cookies with the little girls, and tomorrow I'm going with Melanie to her family's house," I said, hoping I didn't have pieces of strawberry between my teeth.

"Who's Melanie?" Anali sat down gracefully, not spilling her full plate or cup. Gavin was not so lucky, shockingly his packed plate only lost two cookies as he sat down.

"She's my houseparent." And now for the barrage of questions.

"What's a houseparent?" Kayin asked.

"I live in a group home, and Melanie is in charge of taking care of me." I didn't look up from my plate as I explained.

"Is she nice? I mean she seemed nice the other day when I dropped you off," Gavin asked his voice barely above a whisper.

I looked up, surprised by the question. This time Gavin was the one looking down.

"Melanie's great, she's the best person I've ever lived with."

"How many people have you lived with?" Anali asked.

"I've lived in five different placements, three group homes and two foster homes," I said, picking out a Mexican wedding cookie, and stuffing it in my mouth.

"Why so many?" Kayin's brow wrinkled into a frown.

"Oh, that's nothing. I have always been a good kid, no real behavior problems. There are kids that easily go through five placements within a year. Oh, these are good," I said, after biting into a cookie with pieces of candied ginger.

"I made those," Anali said with a pleased smile. Yes, topic change.

Kayin looked at his plate and pouted. "I don't have one."

Rolling my eyes, I held out the rest of my cookie. Kayin leaned over and took a bite. "Ouch, you bit my finger."

Kayin grinned. "That is a good cookie. I like the spiciness."

"You're such a brat. What are you doing for Christmas?" I asked, hoping to keep the attention off of me.

"Philip invited all of us to a big dinner he has with a bunch of friends every year. I'm not sure what else is going to happen, it's the first year I've celebrated Christmas in America," Kayin said.

"Don't worry I've only celebrated with Gavin since we got married three years ago. We'll stick together, and get through it," Anali said, patting Kayin's arm.

"We're going to have a great time. Merry Christmas," Philip said, passing out shirts.

Printed in fancy letter on one side of the soft white cotton tee shirt were the words, San Francisco Center of the Circus Arts. Next to that a man in green with what looked like thorns on his costume. He held a woman above his head; she wore a red frilly outfit curled up tightly. Together they looked like a rose.

"Thank you, it's beautiful. Is that Shin?" I asked, pointing to the man in green.

Philip beamed. "Yep, I think it turned out well."

"It's perfect." Anali smoothed her hand over the picture.

"I should get going," I said, looking up at the clock.

"I'll drive you home," Gavin said, jumping up so fast he almost fell over.

His sudden excitement hit me like a wave of prickling heat. "You don't have to."

"I know, but Melanie gave me permission, and I want to. You shouldn't have to walk home in the rain."

Blushing, I nodded. "Okay, let me get my stuff."

"I'll meet you at the back door." Gavin beamed and took off leaping up the stairs to the apartment.

Anali patted my shoulder, and followed her husband up the stairs. I hoped that meant she would talk to him.

"Ready, Sara," Gavin said, as he tucked a light blue fuzzy scarf into his brown leather bomber jacket.

I followed him out into the drizzling rain. The cold wind went right through my jacket. I was very grateful that I wouldn't have to take the bus home.

"I hope it's all right but I, um, we got you a little something." Gavin pulled an envelope out from inside his jacket, my name written across the front.

If my fingers trembled when I opened the envelope, it's because of the cold I lied to myself. Inside was a gift certificate for up to three classes a session for as long as I wanted to take classes at the San Francisco Center for Circus Arts, and passes for tonight's show. "Thanks, this is great."

"I know it's not much." Gavin's fingers gripped the steering wheel, the plastic creaking under the pressure. Prickly hot excitement quickly changed to something cold and bitter. I needed to get Gavin calmed down. His mood swings were making me queasy.

"No, really, it's great, it can be hard to get money for classes. I can use this, thank you," I said, hoping he would believe me. "And the show sounds like a lot of fun. We didn't have big plans anyway."

"You're welcome, I'm glad you like it. I know it's not much. I'm sure you have a Christmas list as long as your arm." Gavin gave me a shy grin.

I rolled my eyes. "I don't need anything. All I asked for was an mp3 player. I'll also get two outfits and a pair of pajamas."

"I thought teenagers loved to get lots of stuff?" Gavin sounded as if I told him gravity wasn't real.

"I guess I'm weird that way. Anyway I don't have room for a lot of stuff."

Gavin sighed as he pulled in front of my house.

Down another level in the awkward pit. "Sorry to be such a downer. I do like the gift certificate. I know as long as I keep my grades up, Melanie will let me take three classes a session. There wouldn't have been any other way for me to take classes, so I do appreciate it."

"You're very welcome. Come on, let's get you upstairs." Gavin tried to act cheerful, but failed.

"You don't have to, it's raining hard." I twisted the thread I picked loose from my sweater.

"A gentleman always walks a lady to the door." His voice firm as he opened the door and stepped out into the cold winter rain.

I reached for the door handle when Gavin opened it for me. His eyes crinkled with mischief as he bowed low and held out his hand to help me out of the car. I giggled, I couldn't help it.

"Thanks," I said, rushing towards the door.

"Be careful." Gavin followed close behind me, his arms out for balance as we ran over the slippery rock walkway.

I made it over the rocks, up the stairs, and through the door before slipping.

"Whoa." Gavin reached out, his strong hands grabbing my arms, steadying me as I got my feet back under me.

"Thanks, that was close!"

"Maybe we should walk slowly up the stairs." Gavin smiled, holding onto my arm until I steadied myself.

I looked up the polished wooden staircase then down at my dripping sneakers. Reaching down I pulled off my shoes and walked up the stairs in my dry socks.

"Good thinking. I like your socks."

"Thanks." I wiggled my toes, making the bright tree frogs on my socks move.

With each step the tensions rose between us. I wanted to run up the stairs to get away from the emotional chaos radiating from Gavin. I mean, I had enough crazy of my own right now without sharing his. Instead, I took slow steady breaths, and the scents of Christmas filled my nose.

"When are we going to pick mom up?" Rhonda asked as she came down the stairs.

"Tomorrow. She only gets a six-hour pass right now," said a woman, following behind her holding a small suitcase.

"What time tomorrow? Oh, hey, Sara, we'll see you Sunday," Myra said, hoping down the steps.

"Bye, have a good time," I said as we passed each other.

"Are you the only one staying behind?" Gavin asked, his voice barely above a whisper.

"No, Caitlin doesn't get picked up 'til tomorrow morning, and Shante is going to stay here for Christmas, too."

The front door flew open, Crystal's face morphing from a bright smile to a scowl in seconds. "Oh, it's just you."

Gavin looked shocked as Crystal stormed away.

"She's waiting for her grandmother to pick her up. And she hates me," I said with a smirk.

Gavin grinned. "You don't seem heartbroken over that fact."

"Not even close. Anyway, she's going to run away soon."

Gavin opened his mouth to answer, but Melanie interrupted him. "Sara, are you going to stand in the hallway all afternoon?"

"I just got here. Look what Gavin gave me for Christmas." I held out the gift certificate.

"This is a very nice gift. Thank you, Gavin," Melanie said after reading it.

"Isn't it great? I know I'll have to keep up my grades, and I can take the bus so it won't cause any schedule problems," I assured her. I could feel Gavin's happiness bubbling in the air.

"I'm sure you will. Do you know what you want to take?" Melanie asked.

"No, not yet, but the class schedule is in the envelope. When do I have to sign up by?" I turned to Gavin.

"At least a week before classes begin, but the earlier the better in case they fill up."

"Okay, I can do that."

Melanie snorted. "Please. You'll have it all sorted out by Monday morning. Sara is a very quick decision maker, she knows exactly what she wants."

Gavin smiled. "I'm sure she does. Monday is fine. Give Philip your list and he'll get you all signed up."

"And," I said dragging out the word and waving the passes in front of her. "We got tickets to their circus performance tonight. It starts at five."

Melanie snatched the tickets from me with a grin. "This is very generous. Thank you so much."

"I hope you can come. We weren't sure if you had plans," Gavin said.

Melanie shook her head. "Nope. The girls were going to make cookies, but we can make them later, and Crystal should get picked up soon, so we can go."

"We're going to the circus?" Shante asked.

"Yes," Melanie said.

"Caitlin, we're going to the circus," Shante screamed, running back into the house. "We should wear our best dresses."

Gavin chuckled. "I should go and get ready for tonight."

"Thank you. Have a Merry Christmas, Gavin."

"Merry Christmas, Sara," Gavin said, his shoulders hunched as he walked away.

"I'll see you tonight at the show right?" I said.

Gavin smiled. "Yep."

I watched him go, and for a second I wanted to tell him I knew who he was. Tell him I wanted to get to know him better. Instead, I turned and went inside.

Chapter Ten

"Discipline is the refining fire by which talent becomes ability."
~ Ron L. Smith

My eye twitched as Shante and Caitlin jumped out of their seats again to dance to the music filling the theater. Shante began to twirl so she could look at her skirt as it spun. I caught her before she fell onto the people in front of us. I was tempted to ask Melanie if it was five yet, but I'd already asked three times and I didn't want to press my luck.

"What's that? What's happening?" Caitlin asked, pointing out into the crowd. We were seated on the first tier in the middle of the auditorium with a perfect view of the clowns. The lights were still up, there wasn't a spot light, yet two clowns, the woman in a baggy purple tuxedo and the man in rainbow tights and short puffy skirt that looked like the sky, were playing with the audience. I was glad the clowns didn't have painted faces and orange wigs, those clowns freaked me out.

Shante laughed and sat down, her dress bunching up behind her in the seat. "They're clowns. Look, he sat in that man's lap."

Caitlin sat giggling as the female clown began going through the man's pockets and running off when she got his wallet.

I relaxed and watched the clowns, blushing as they embarrassed and teased people. "I'm glad we're not down there," I said as one woman's shoes were tried on by the male clown.

"I wish they would come up here," Shante said.

The music changed to a thumping drum as the lights dimmed. The clowns rushed to the stage trying to look busy, as if they'd been there the whole time. Philip came out, his salt and pepper mohawk gelled into a spiky arch over his head and dusted with glitter. His face was painted half black and half white like a Harlequin doll and his suit was a dark blue and silver patchwork of different types of fabric.

"Welcome everyone to the annual San Francisco Center for the Circus Arts Winter Performance." The audience clapped and cheered, and cameras and video recorders were held up ready to capture the show. "I must ask that no one take flash photography, some of the acts can be dangerous and all require focused concentration. Please, no flash."

Another clown ran up on the stage in a large tan trench coat 'flashing' the audience. When his coat opened light burst from it, blinding us for a moment.

"See," Philip said with a smirk. "No one likes to get flashed. Now on to the fun."

The music changed into something that seemed to flow and swirl. The lights dimmed, focusing on a tiny spot, a glimmer of silver and then a man walked towards us inside a large wheel.

Shante tugged on my sleeve. "What's that called?"

I opened the program. "German Wheel."

"Oh," she said.

The man spun inside the wheel around the stage, poised like Vitruvian Man, holding onto rungs placed between the two large wheels. He somehow tipped it over and moved the wheel like a dropped coin. Pulling himself and the wheel back up, he flipped in and out of spaces between the two circles while still rolling around the stage.

It was mesmerizing, even Shante and Caitlin were silent and still as he performed. I hadn't thought how difficult sitting in an enclosed space with so many people would be. Thankfully, they all seemed to feel the same thing as me, so the wonder and awe that swept over me matched my own. I breathed slowly and tried my best to strengthen my flimsy bubble.

"Can you do that?" Shante asked as we all clapped.

"No," I answered as a length of pale blue silk fluttered down from the ceiling.

"Shush," Shante hissed at me as she settled back into her seat.

I rolled my eyes and watched as a man walked out onto the stage. Each step fell slow and perfectly timed to the rhythm of the classical guitar music. I gasped as he came into the light. Taliesin stood on the stage wearing skin tight white pants and makeup which made him look like an ice prince.

He backed up to the edge of the stage, the pale blue fabric fluttering in front of him. Then running, he leapt into the air and soared around the stage supported only by his grip on the silks.

Landing, he climbed up the fabric hand over hand, stretching out one hand to his side and bringing it up to the silk pulled himself up, then the other hand would do the same slow movement. His body held hard as a board and his legs perfectly straight and not helping him as he climbed. I held my breath, my heart pounding. Shante grabbed my arm and held it tight.

I watched in awe as Taliesin wrapped himself in the silk in a complicated pattern, then dropped. The silk tightened before he hit the floor. I gasped and clapped with the rest of the audience as he unwound himself.

Taliesin continued to climb, twist, slide, and wrap himself with the silk, showing his strength and flexibility. I was amazed and envious, and if he wasn't such a jerk, I would ask him to teach me how to do silks. Oh, well, maybe Gavin or Anali could help me. When he finished and bowed low, the audience got to their feet clapping for him. Taliesin waved and walked off the stage as a group of clowns ran out to entertain us.

"Having fun, Little Sister?" Kayin asked slipping into the empty seat next to me.

"Yes, it's wonderful. I had no idea it would be this beautiful. Are you performing?"

"No, I'm not good enough yet. But if I practice enough I should be by this summer."

"Ssshhhhh," Shante said, glaring at us.

"Sorry," I said, holding in my laughter at her angry look.

Hula Hoopers, rope-jumpers, clowns, and a group of contortionists all kept our attention fully focused on the stage.

"Shin's group is next," Kayin whispered, careful not to anger Shante-the-Fierce again.

Eight people walked onto the stage. Their costumes looked like someone wrapped them in silver, white and light-blue ribbons. Four of them carried tall wooden poles which they secured into the floor, then climbed the poles. Their feet kicked out, one at a time making it look like they were dancing. Once they reached the top the second group climbed up the same way.

It took a moment to find Shin, as the performers never stopped moving. They went from climbing to using their legs and arms to hang from the poles in intricate poses, then sliding down the poles, sometimes head first.

A sharp cold wave of fear hit my shield, I'm guessing from the parents of performers. Their honest fear felt stronger than the pleasant anxiety most people experienced.

Two performers went to the poles and began to pull themselves up using only their arms, their bodies about a foot away from the pole. As they went up, they spun around the pole. Reaching the top, they paused for a moment, and I finally saw Shin. He smiled as they began to go down the pole in the same way.

To end the performance, they all got on the poles. As a group, they leapt from one pole to another in unison. One guy almost slipped, and I grabbed Kayin's hand at the same time Shante grabbed mine. I didn't breathe until they were all on the ground and safe.

The crowd erupted into applause and cheers. They bowed, removed the poles, and walked off stage.

A juggler came out, moving to the Latin music as he juggled five balls. For a while he did tricks in the air, then switched to juggling with the balls hitting the floor.

"He's reverse juggling," Kayin whispered. "I just started to learn how to do that."

He never stopped moving to the music even while he juggled eight balls.

We clapped for the juggler as deep notes from a cello pulsed through the hall. Gavin and Anali glided onto the stage. His leggings looked like someone painted fire on his legs. Anali's sleeveless leotard also looked like painted fire.

Gavin stood at the front of the stage and placed his hand palms up on top of his shoulders. Anali's dark hands slid into his and then he lifted her up over his head. Her silver eye shadow was so thick it glowed in the spotlight, making her look alien. Inch by inch, she moved into a hand stand. I couldn't breathe as bit by bit they moved so Anali's shoulders were balanced on Gavin's, then he began to turn in a circle, somehow Anali stayed statue still as they moved.

I grabbed Kayin's hand again as a wave of amazement and worry swept over me from the audience. He chuckled and gave it a squeeze.

They glided from one pose to another, finishing their routine with Gavin's feet on the ground. He leaned back and he balanced parallel to the floor, holding Anali's hand as she balanced on the one hand upside down.

I sucked in a deep breath and clapped as they bowed low. The music became light and playful as everyone came out on the stage bowing and waving to the audience.

"Thank you for coming," Philip said. "There are refreshments in the lobby and in a few minutes the performers will meet you out there to say hi."

"That was the bestest ever!" Shante said. "Melanie, can we meet them?"

"Maybe they'll sign our programs," Caitlin said, waving hers in the air and almost hitting Melanie in the eye.

"We can stay for a while, but if you want to have time to make cookies tonight, we'll have to go soon," Melanie said not glancing up from her phone.

Shante and Caitlin looked at each other and smiled. "We'll be super-fast."

Kayin smiled as Shante and Caitlin ended the two hours of silence by describing each and every thing we all just saw.

"Sorry, they're very excited," I said holding their hands so they wouldn't get lost.

Kayin chuckled, but I felt sadness flow from him. "It is fine, I have little sisters. I'm sure they would be acting like this."

"You must miss them."

"Yes, and my little brother. When I changed, my mom threw me out of the hut I was born in and held my siblings back as she made me leave the village. She has a very superstitious nature."

"Oh, Kayin, that is awful. I'm so sorry."

Kayin shrugged. "It might have been different if my dad had been there, but he was off leading a safari."

"Hurry," said Caitlin, pulling on my arm.

Shante joined her. "Yes, what if they run out of cookies? Come on."

"Don't worry, Gavin took care of refreshments, I don't think we will ever run out of cookies," Kayin said, smiling at the girls even though I could feel his sadness. I wish we could go somewhere quiet so we could talk, but for tonight the conversation was over.

Laughing children covered in cookie crumbs filled the lobby, running around and rushing to talk to the performers. The girls let go of my hands and grabbed my legs.

"They look kind of scary," Shante said.

"It's make-up," I said, putting my hands on their shoulders. "They're people in costumes."

The girls didn't move.

"How about some cookies first?" Kayin suggested.

"Cookies," they yelled and ran for the nearest table.

"Sara," said Melanie. "I'm going to sit on the couch by the front door. Watch the girls."

"Sure thing." I took Kayin's hand so I wouldn't lose him in the crowd, although he stood taller than most of the people here. If I was watching the two terrors, I wanted help.

They stood at the table, cheeks bulging with chocolate chip cookies, looking at the pitchers of juice trying to figure out how to get some.

"Let me help," I said pouring them each a bit of apple juice into a cup. "Would you like to meet some of the performers? Kayin and I know a few of them, we can introduce you to."

"Yes, please," Shante said.

Victory. I guided them away from the sugar. Scanning the crowd, I spotted Gavin's red hair. We made our way through hyper children and tired but indulgent adults to where Gavin and Anali stood.

"Sara, did you enjoy the show?" Anali asked.

"It was amazing. It's hard to believe that what I'm learning now could someday become something so beautiful."

Anali smiled. "Thank you. And who do you have here?"

"This is Shante and Caitlin. They live with me at the group home. Guys, this is Anali. She's one of the teachers at the circus camp I've been going to." And my aunt, I added in my head.

"It's a pleasure to meet you," Anali said.

Caitlin's face scrunched up for a moment before she blurted out, "Will you sign my program?"

"I would be happy to, but I don't have a pen. Do you have one?"

Caitlin shook her head her blond hair flying around her.

"I have one." I held out the pen I'd gotten from Melanie.

Anali took the pen, flipped through the glossy program until she found her picture and signed a little message and her name.

"Me too, me too," Shante squealed, holding out her program.

"Of course," Anali said.

"What's going on over here? Sounds like too much fun to me," Gavin teased.

Caitlin held out her program, her lips pressed together in determination to get his signature, but fearful of the tall man with red paint on his cheeks, lips, and around his eyes.

"Gavin, these are my house mates, Caitlin and Shante. Guys, this is Gavin. He's another teacher at my camp. The girls are hoping to get everyone to sign their program," I said.

Gavin smiled, but it looked a little creepy with the make-up. "Of course, do you have a pen?"

"I'm just about done with it," Anali said finishing Shante's program.

Gavin took the pen and knelt down on one knee. "You're Caitlin right?" He asked as he looked for his picture.

"Yes," she said. "You're so strong."

Gavin laughed. "I have the easy job, Anali's the one who's super strong."

"He lies," Anali said running her fingers through Gavin's hair. "He is very strong."

Shante arched a tiny eyebrow as she handed over her program to get signed. "Like a super hero?"

"No, I'm not that strong," Gavin said as he signed her program.

"That's what a super hero would say," Caitlin whispered loudly to Shante. "They have to keep up their secret identities."

Gavin shook his head. "Are you having fun?"

"Yes," they both said.

"When we go home, we get to make cookies," Shante said.

"Sara said she'd help us 'cause were making them from scratch," Caitlin said. "Melanie can only make cookies from the tubes."

Anali frowned. "Tubes?"

"Pre-made dough, they come in tubes," I explained. "Shall we go and see the others? I'm sure there are other kids who want a turn."

"Bye, and Merry Christmas," the girls said before running off.

"Merry Christmas," Gavin said.

"Merry Christmas," I said quickly, following the girls so I didn't have to feel Gavin's swirling emotions.

After asking several performers for their autographs, the girls lost their shyness and began running around the theater scaring people as they jumped up waving their programs and demanded signatures.

"Calm down," Shin said with a chuckle. "Do these belong to you?"

"Yes," I said as I caught up.

"Will you sign, my program?" Shante asked.

"Me too?" Caitlin added waving hers as high as she could.

"Sure," Shin took their programs. "I've never had anyone want my signature before."

"You were awesome," Caitlin squealed.

"Like a lemur," Shante said with a nod.

Shin's mouth twitched. I also tried to hide my laughter knowing Shante would pout for a very long time if we laughed at her.

"I agree," said Kayin. "They were very good."

"Thank you," Shin said passing the programs back to the girls who slid over to the Chinese pole artist. "Did you two enjoy the show?"

"Very much," I answered. "The amount of discipline needed to become so good seems overwhelming."

Shin shrugged. "It takes a lot of work to get from beginner to performer, but you can do it if you feel passionate about your art. It doesn't feel like discipline when you are doing what you love."

I smiled, that sounded like something from my mom's journal.

"Discipline is a great strength to cultivate in yourself. Have the discipline to eat healthy, get enough sleep, get your homework done on time, or whatever it is you want or need to have in your life. However, don't

overdo the discipline. When you love something, when it brings you joy, the act of discipline should support you and your passions, not force you to live in a way that is stifling. Self-discipline should help you reach your goals and commitments, not force you to live in a way others think is important or good."

Kayin tugged on my sleeve. "The girls are gone."

"Crap. Bye, Shin. See you Monday."

"Merry Christmas," he said.

"Merry Christmas." I headed for the refreshment table and found Shante and Catlin with red and green frosting covering their chins as they ate cupcakes.

"Did you get everyone's signature?" I asked.

The girls flipped through their programs. "Everyone but him."

Taliesin stared up from the page looking like a winter prince. "Okay, I'll see if I can find him while you finish your cupcake."

I looked around but wasn't tall enough to look over the crowd. "Kayin, do you see Taliesin?"

Kayin pointed to the other side of the room. "He's over there, by the staircase."

I wiped as much of the frosting off the girls as I could and then followed them through the crowd. Being smaller, and oblivious to proper social behavior, the girls wove in-between people and quickly got ahead of us. By the time I caught up, they were being cooed over by Taliesin's mom while he signed their programs, his cheeks pink.

"Did you two lovely girls like the show?" Cordelia asked.

"Oh, yes, very much," said Shante.

"Do you know him?" Caitlin asked pointing to Taliesin. "He was good."

She smiled. "Yes, he's my son. Are you here with your moms?"

"Melanie and Sara brought us." Shante looked behind her.

"You two are supposed to stay with me," I said. "Hi, Ms. Gadarn. How are you?"

"Hello Sara," she said hugging me. "I'm well, did you enjoy the show?"

"It was awesome, these two stayed quiet for the entire time." I pointed at the girls who were currently talking at Taliesin.

Her face lit up as she looked at her son. My heart clenched, as it always did, when seeing a parent's love for their child. "I'm going to miss him so much when he travels with the circus. I guess I'll have to get a hobby."

Somehow I doubted Ms. Gadarn lacked in things to keep her busy.

"We're done," said Caitlin.

"Can we go make cookies now?" asked Shante.

"Yes, we can go. You were great Taliesin, I've never seen silks before."

Taliesin tipped his head forward, his white braid sliding over his shoulder a smile curving his normally frowning mouth. "Thank you."

"Have a lovely holiday, girls," Ms. Gadarn said.

"Thank you, happy holidays," we said and headed to where Melanie waited for us.

Her thumbs flew as she typed on her phone. Without looking up she asked, "Are you ready?"

"Yes," Caitlin and Shante said, telling Melanie all about their adventure.

"Good night, Big Brother, have a great holiday," I said turning to Kayin.

"You too, Little Sister."

I walked out of the theater with my group home family, leaving my real, but still secret, family behind.

The wind whipped around me. My nose and ears were cold before we'd even walked to the end of the block. Thankfully, the car wasn't far.

"Who's that?" Shante said holding my hand tighter.

"I don't know, a homeless person." I glanced at the poor man curled up in the doorway of a shop. "Wait, Carlos?"

Dull brown eyes looked up at me. A livid bruise marked his check and his dry ashy skin was dotted with blemishes. "Hey, Sara."

"What the hell?" I snapped.

"Sara!" Melanie said looking up from her phone. "Carlos? What are you doing here? You look like crap."

Carlos stood up and moved away from us. "Hey, Melanie. I'm fine. My mom's working and needed the apartment empty for a while."

Melanie's eyes narrowed. "It's Christmas Eve, you shouldn't be out on the street. How did you get that bruise?"

Carlos' face went blank. "I tripped and fell."

"Well, that's original. You should come back with us. We'll call and get you somewhere safe and warm."

Carlos shook his head.

"Please," I said he turned and looked at me. "Please, Carlos, this isn't right. Let us help you."

"Yes, come home with us," said Shante.

Caitlin stepped forward. "Please, Carlos, we're going to make cookies. You can help."

Carlos' smiled, the sadness in it made my heart ache. "Sorry, I have plans for tomorrow. See you around."

Turning, he ran down the street.

"Police please," said Melanie into her phone as she walked to the car. "Yes, I've seen a runaway child."

Carlos disappeared around the corner. I doubted they would find him, but Melanie needed to try. "Merry Christmas, take care of yourself Carlos," I whispered.

*　　　*　　　*

There was far too much sarcasm for this to be a tooth-achingly sweet Hallmark Christmas, but it was a happy Christmas. Melanie and her family teased each other as they opened their gifts, while the younger kids danced around showing off their newest treasures.

I tucked myself into a chair off in the corner. Piled around me were far more gifts than I expected. Looking over the tags, I smiled. All of Melanie's family gave me something. It was obvious where Melanie's generosity came from.

"Hiding back here in your chair, I see." Melanie's mom smiled at me, letting me know she didn't mind my sitting off to the side, and handed me a glass of eggnog.

"Thanks," I said, taking a sip of the festive drink; Gavin's tasted better. I sat back into the squishy beige-on-beige striped chair. "I didn't realize I had my own chair."

"Sara you have sat in this chair every holiday for the past three years. You should open some of your gifts. I know for a fact there are several books to hide behind." She patted my head and went to sit next to Melanie's father.

"Cookies," Shante cheered as she danced around with the large platter of cookies, a smear of red frosting across her soft brown cheek. "We made them last night. It was so much fun!"

"Melanie made cookies?" her sister asked, hand frozen in mid-air.

"Are they safe to eat?" Their brother sniffed his cookie.

"You two are the worst siblings ever," Melanie said.

Shante, being five, answered honestly. "Of course Melanie didn't cook. Sara helped us. Caitlin and I made such a big mess it took Sara forever to wash the dough out of our hair."

Caitlin's straight blond hair had been easy to clean, but Shante's thick curls, a mix of her mom's Mexican heritage and her dad's African, took forever to get clean.

*   *   *

I reclaimed my chair after stuffing myself with dinner. I was about to hunt through my pile of gifts to find my new books when Shante came up to me.

"Will you read to me?" Shante held out a stack of picture books.

"Of course," I said, sitting back so Shante could climb onto my lap.

"Will you play your music box first?" She asked, pointing down at the pretty gold and lacquer box with a Phoenix blazed across its top that Five had given to me for Christmas, an odd coincidence.

"Sure," I said and opened the box. The tune inside sounded fast and vibrant, and I could imagine the Phoenix streaking through the air to the music. There wasn't any note or sticker on the box giving what the name of the piece. Maybe I would ask Five the next time I saw him.

Once the song ended I smoothed down Shante's green velvet skirt and began to read.

It wasn't long before Shante fell asleep. I pushed her pigtail out of my face and relaxed. I wish I'd thought to grab one of my books, now I would have to sit here until Shante woke up.

"Do you want me to take her?" Melanie asked, as she walked by.

"No, thanks. Would you get me one of my new books?"

"Sure, Sara." Melanie hunted through my pile of gifts. "Where are you going to put all this stuff?"

"I'm not sure. I'll have to get rid of some of my clothes to make room for all the new ones."

"I'll help you, we can get you some bins for the closet or something," Melanie said handing me a book. "Here you go, give me a shout if you need anything else."

I smiled as Melanie plopped on the couch with her family. I knew I could join them, but it didn't feel right. Melanie was kind enough to share her holiday with us, but it wasn't right to sit in the middle of her family.

I couldn't help but wonder what next year's Christmas would bring. Would I be with Gavin and Anali? Would we celebrate in his home in New York or in some strange country? Would I be Sara or Sapphire?

I forced the questions down. I was supposed to celebrate today's Christmas not wallow in angst.

Chapter Eleven

"Call it a clan, call it a network, call it a tribe, call it a family. Whatever you call it, whoever you are, you need one." ~Jane Howard

Everyone bounced around Monday morning, showing off their new clothes, telling their friends about their favorites gifts, and still high from Christmas candy. Philip planned well for hyper students and we were busy all morning: stilt walking, globe, and acrobatics.

As usual I held back, waiting until the crowd cleared before trying to get to my lunch.

"Sara," a male voice called out.

"Five, what are you doing here?" My caseworker looked a bit nervous but determined. Nothing good was about to happen.

"I need you to get your things and come with me." He spoke with as much authority as his baby face and sweater vest would allow.

Not good, David didn't even correct me when I called him Five. "Why? What's going on?"

"Please, Sara. I promise to explain, but right now I need you to get your things."

"Fine." I went to get my stuff, glaring at Five as frequently as possible.

"Who are you? Where are you going with Sara?" Gavin demanded.

Five held the front door open for me. "I'm Sara's caseworker, David Holden. I've signed her out."

"Gavin, stay inside," said a tall, thin man, sliding between Five and me, his navy blue suit very out of place in the circus school.

"Nathan, what is going on?" Nathan? Is this Gavin's lawyer?

"Gavin, we'll talk inside," Nathan said taking Gavin's arm and tugging him towards the office.

"When will I be coming back?" I kicked empty fast food wrappers out of the way as I sat in Five's battered hatchback.

David closed his eyes and took a deep breath. "You won't."

"What? Why? I haven't done anything wrong." This sucked!

"Sara, this isn't your fault. Your teacher, Gavin, he says he's your uncle. Until I know more you can't be around him." Five brushed a hand over his messy brown hair.

I put my feet on his dashboard. "This isn't fair."

"I know. We'll try and get this all sorted out as soon as possible." I could feel how bad Five felt; maybe I could ease up a bit.

"Why does Gavin think I'm his niece?"

"Has he said anything to you?" Five asked. I hate it when adults answer a question with a question.

"The first day I met Gavin he said I looked like his sister." My finger twisted the hem of my sweater.

"You must look a lot like her for him to go through all this trouble. Gavin ran a DNA test on your blood. It came back positive; he's your family," Five said.

"I did get a bloody nose last week," I tugged my bangs down over my eyes.

"Well, that explains the DNA test. How do you feel about Gavin being your uncle?"

"I don't know. I never thought I'd have to deal with family." Seeing Hope House, I breathed a sigh of relief.

"I understand. I didn't know you had any family out there, either. We have an emergency Child Family Team meeting set up for Friday. So think about what you want. Bring a list of any questions you have. And please, Sara, feel free to call me if you need anything. I know this has got to be shocking for you." Five pulled in front of my building.

"Thanks. I'll see you," I said getting out of the car. Then I remembered the Christmas gift. "Hey, thanks for the music box; it's pretty, so is the song."

Five smiled. "I'm glad you like it. My mom forced me to go antique shopping with her. I found it tucked into a corner. Stravinsky's Firebird is one of my favorite ballets, and I wanted to share it with you."

"I like it; thanks for thinking of me." I relaxed; the music box was just an odd coincidence. "See you Friday."

"Bye, Sara," he said then drove off.

I shut the door to my house. "Melanie, are you here?"

"I'm in my room."

I walked over and kicked aside some clothes to make a clear spot on the floor.

"Did Five call you?" I asked as I sat on her bedroom floor and unpacked my lunch.

"Yes. How do you feel?" Melanie shut her laptop and gave me her full attention.

"I don't know. I don't know Gavin or his wife Anali. They're both nice enough at camp. Am I going to have to go and live with them?"

"No, you're old enough to say where you want to live. We'll see what plan they present on Friday."

"Will you be at the CFT?" I asked before stuffing a cracker and cheese in my mouth. A Child Family Team meeting is boring! I try to avoid them.

"Sure." Melanie popped open her laptop and tossed her dark brown curls over her shoulder. "What do you want to do now?"

I stared at her computer. Normally I wasn't allowed anywhere near the Internet, as all contact must be supervised. "Do you think we could Google Gavin? I don't know anything about him."

Melanie patted her bed, and I stretched out next to her. "Spying— good plan."

We found several articles that mentioned Gavin Marsh, including his parents' obituaries. I didn't expect to feel so disappointed that I would never get to meet my grandparents. Until I saw their obituary I hadn't even thought about them.

"It looks like your uncle is quite wealthy," Melanie said pointing to an article on the Forbes website. "It says here his great-great-great grandfather, Clements Marsh, started an import-export business that is still running. The Marsh family also owns galleries, antique stores, and auction houses all over the country."

"Is there other family?" I asked as I read over her shoulder.

"The article is about five years old. At that time his parents, Miriam and Jonathan, were still alive. It says they only had two children. I don't see any mention of other family, but you never know. I guess you'll have to ask Gavin." Melanie lay back on the bed, letting me read the rest of the article.

"Wow, he's about perfect on paper. I bet I'm the only group home kid who is secretly a long-lost princess," I said with a chuckle, trying to make light of the situation. Most people would jump for joy knowing the family they were going to was rich. Right now it felt like one more hurdle. Would I have to learn fancy, snooty manners? Go to a boarding school? Did rich people talk and act in a different way like on TV?

"I know this is a lot to take in, Sara; you know that I'm here and willing to help in any way I can." Melanie pulled out a notebook and a pen. "Let's make a list; you like lists."

True, I do like lists. They help keep things organized. I looked around her room, which completely lacked in organization.

Melanie held the pen over the page and waited for me. "David said there would be a CFT this Friday. What questions do you have? What do you want to know? What are your concerns?"

"Where will we live? Will I have to change schools? Will they change my last name?" There were other questions, magical Phoenix-based questions, but I would leave those for another time.

"Just remember, you do have some say in what happens. You might need to compromise, but Gavin is a stranger to you, and David won't force you to live with a stranger." Melanie looked up from the page, her brown eyes warm and comforting. "What do you think about changing schools or having to move?"

"When they were introduced at camp, they said they lived in New York. I don't know about moving that far away and changing schools. It's a lot, but it seems mean and unfair to ask them to give up their lives. However I also promised Shante I wouldn't leave her, and moving across town would be bad enough, but going all the way to New York?"

"Sara, I know you and Shante are close, and I'm glad she has you. But you can't live your life to make other people happy."

"I know," I whispered, guilt eating at me. Shante wouldn't understand.

Melanie sighed. "I wish I could make this easier for you. It's a huge amount of change for you. Try and be selfish for once. Take care of yourself. Shante will be okay."

"I'll try," This was going to suck, big time.

*   *   *

Gavin and Anali were already in the conference room when Five led Melanie and me into the room for the CFT.

"Sara," Gavin said, jumping up. He wore khaki slacks and a white button-down shirt. His earrings were gone. "Your hair is down. It looks great."

Blushing, I tucked my hair behind my ear and breathed through the intensity of Gavin's emotions.

"Thank you."

"Hello, Sara," Anali smiled at me, at ease in her long, flowing tunic and pants. Pale blue beads decorated the hems. Her bindi looked freshly painted on, and a small silver stud pieced her nose. I guess both of them were trying to look respectable. Obviously, they had never seen CPS workers before.

"Did the doctor ever get back to you with the results of her blood work?" Five asked Melanie, as he set down several thick folders on the cheap conference table. Five looked very young today. His round face, big blue eyes, and wild brown curls made him look even younger with the faded blue jeans and Captain America shirt he wore.

"He said Sara was healthy. All of the tests came back within normal range," Melanie said.

"It's so weird how much you have changed," Five said, looking me over. "And you feel okay?"

I nodded trying to avoid Gavin's inspection. I stared at the ugly blue and gray office carpet. "Yeah, I feel fine, and I've stopped jumping every time I look into a mirror."

"I'm glad you're all right," Five said. Then he turned to Gavin and Anali. "I'm David Holden, Sara's caseworker." They all shook hands and introduced themselves.

I moved to sit at the end of the table so I wouldn't get stuck in between any adults. Melanie sat next to me. It wasn't long before the facilitator and Gavin's lawyer joined us, and the meeting began.

"Good afternoon, everyone. I think we have all introduced ourselves, but just in case, I'm Patricia Pinter, and I'll facilitate the meeting today. Please sign in on this pad I'm passing around, with your name and phone number so we can all contact each other later if needed. Now first, David, do you have the results from the tests?" Patricia sounded professional, but looked like she belonged at circus camp. The edges of tribal tattoos peeked above the collar of her fifties style white and yellow flowered dress. Silver gauges expanded her earlobes, and a silver tongue ring glittered in her mouth as she spoke.

Five opened a thick orange file. "Yes, the DNA test shows Mr. Marsh is Sara's uncle. The handwriting on the letters Mr.

Thompson gave us matches the handwriting on the letter left with Sara when she walked into the police station."

"Sara, how do you feel about all this?" Patricia asked. "This is a lot of change."

All the adults turned towards me, the intensity of their eyes making me uncomfortable. I could feel curiosity from Patricia and Nathan, Gavin's hope, Anali's worry, Melanie's support and sadness, and Five felt completely blank. Why didn't I feel anything from him? I looked at him and he winked at me. Weird.

Thank goodness Aya and Shamash were teaching me how to block people's emotions. It was difficult, and I wasn't that good at it yet, but I could now tell what someone felt without their emotions invading me. Some of the time, anyway, if I focused hard.

"I'm not sure," I answered honestly. "I never thought I'd leave the system until I was out of independent living."

"That's what we talked about last time, right?" Patricia asked going over her notes. "You said you wanted to stay at Hope House until you were old enough to go into independent living, finish high school, and then go to college."

"What are you hoping for, Gavin?" Patricia asked, refocusing the conversation.

"I have a large house in New York. Anali and I can take Sara home with us as soon as she's packed." Wow, he didn't have high expectations did he?

"Mr. Marsh . . . " Five began.

"Please call me Gavin."

Five nodded, "Okay, Gavin. Sara doesn't know you. We don't know you. Even though you are family, we can't release her into your custody. There are steps we need to go through to make sure placing Sara with you is in everyone's best interest."

"I'm her uncle!" Gavin started to stand up until Nathan placed a large hand on Gavin's shoulder and restrained him.

"Let's calm down," Patricia said firmly. "Anali is your wife, correct?"

"Yes," Gavin answered, trying to rein in his emotions.

"Sara, do you know Anali?" Patricia asked me.

"Yes, she teaches at the Circus school. She's nice." I sent Anali a small smile across the table. She smiled back and linked her hand with Gavin's, calming him down.

Patricia turned to the white board, marker poised to write. "David, what steps need to be taken?"

"Well, we need to know Gavin and Anali's physical and mental health. We need to establish a relationship between Gavin, Anali, and Sara. We need to know what kind of life Gavin and Anali will provide, that Sara will be safe and taken care of, and Sara has to agree to go with them." David said, looking over his list.

"I have copies of Gavin and Anali's last physical exams, which were six months ago, a financial statement, copies of their drivers' licenses, and their fingerprint ID cards." Nathan handed over a folder. "Sara's birth certificate is also in there."

"This birth certificate is for Sapphire Aya Rayner," Five said, as he read it over. "Born to Gabriella Aya Marsh Rayner and Keagan Michael Rayner. We'll have to run a search on them both and any possible family."

Nathan pulled out another folder. "These are the death certificates for both parents, and, both sets of grandparents. Gavin is Sara's only living relative."

Five looked through the new folder, nodding to himself and making notes. "How did you get all of these?"

"I started searching for Gabriella and Keagan as soon as I realized they were missing," Gavin said. "I knew Keagan's family and attended both his parents' funerals. He didn't have any siblings or close family, so Keagan inherited his parents' estate. I was the executor of Keagan and Gabriella's estate."

Gavin ran a hand through his hair. "Gabriella sent me a letter about six months after they went missing, saying that 'they' killed Keagan and were now after her. Every few months I would get a letter from another place. They were always cryptic.

"Two years after they disappeared, Gabriella began making references to keeping her Jewel safe. A year later she ended her letter with, 'don't worry, the baby and I are fine. I think we lost them.'" Gavin rubbed his eyes. "That was the last letter I got."

That's what happened? It sounds like my mom was crazy or running from a drug dealer or something. I kept my eyes down and my face blank. What Gavin said didn't feel right, and it didn't match my mom's letter.

"Due to the letters, private investigators' reports, and lack of contact, Gabriella and Keagan were declared dead." Nathan explained. "Once Gavin saw Sara and found out her birth date, he asked me to check through the letters Gabriella sent. There was one post marked the day after Sara was born. It didn't take long for a private investigator to find her birth certificate."

"Let's take a moment here," Patricia said. I could feel her looking at me. The next thing out of her mouth would be some caring phrase from her training. "Sara, this is a lot of information, and whatever you're feeling is fine. This is a safe place."

Guh, how predictable. Unfortunately it wasn't over.

"Sara, how do you feel about all of this?" All the adults went silent. Oh yeah, this sure felt like a "safe place."

I kept my eyes down and my voice soft. With adults, timid always works better than angry. "I'm not sure. I'm sorry all these people have died, but I didn't know them."

Patricia and Five both hummed and nodded in understanding.

"I'm not sure what to think about my mom running from people. And my name—, I'm used to Sara. I don't know that I want to be called Sapphire." Sapphire's the Jewel, Gavin's niece, the girl with a powerful destiny. Sara's a group-home kid trying to make a future for herself. I didn't feel like Sapphire, I don't even know who she is. But Sara felt like an illusion my mom created to keep me safe. Sara faded with each new change and truth I discovered, with Sapphire waiting under the illusion.

"Thank you for sharing, Sara," Patricia said when she realized I wasn't going to say anything else.

I zoned out as the adults began to go over everything. Questions were asked and answered. Papers switched hands and information exchanged. Patricia would recap the meeting at the end and say what was going to happen next. I wouldn't miss anything important. Two weeks ago the swirling chaos of my thoughts would have upset me, now it felt normal.

Patricia, Five, and Nathan stayed professional and focused, determined to get what they each needed and wanted. As Gavin became more and more excited, Anali tried to soothe him, while grinning excitedly herself. Only Melanie and I sat back calmly. Melanie was there for me and in case anyone asked questions about my home life.

"Okay, we're close to the end. Let's recap what needs to get done," Patricia said. See, I knew it. I sat up and focused on the meeting.

"I will need Gavin and Anali to have a psychological evaluation with one of our psychologists," Five said, looking over his notes. "Due to Gavin's being family, and all of the information he has already provided us, and as long as Sara is comfortable, I'll ask my supervisor to approve unrestricted phone access and one six hour visit on the weekends to start with. Do you want Saturdays or Sundays?"

"Saturdays," Gavin said.

"Saturdays are fine," I said with a shrug. It wasn't like I had a busy social life.

"Great, let me go and run this by my supervisor, I'll be back in a minute."

"Wait, can she take classes at the Circus Center again?" Anali asked. Oh, good point. The winter/spring session started Monday, and I had the gift certificate Gavin gave me.

Five smiled. "Yes, that's fine."

When I got into the car with Melanie I was exhausted. All the emotions and changes had overwhelmed me.

"Gavin and Anali seem very nice, and it's obvious how much they want you in their lives."

"I know, but it's so different from what I planned." I sighed and leaned back. "I finally thought I would have a little control over my life, and now this. I can't even imagine what living with them will look like."

Melanie patted my leg as she made a sharp left turn. "Don't even try, just be open to them. Find out what they're like, and how they live, without throwing in a bunch of what ifs and worries."

"Thanks," I whispered, trying to believe her. I knew this was what my mom wanted for me, yet I wasn't convinced that I wanted it.

"Someday you will find a family, it may be one of your own creation, and I dearly hope it includes those I have loved and cherished. I don't know how long it will take, or what will happen before you have a family again, but know this is what I want for you. To have people you can turn to, to love, to take care of you. Families can drive you mad, and make you want to run away, but they will always be there for you, and they will accept you no matter what. Please, my dearest, make a family for yourself, fill it with people who love you, care for you, treat you well, and support you."

Chapter Twelve

Cartazonon snarled as the ass-kissing businessmen left his conference room. Standing, he pushed on the wood-paneled wall. A hidden door opened directly to his office so he wouldn't have to deal with any of those idiots loitering in the hallway. If only Lee would let him bring one of his daggers to these meetings, life would be so much better.

Sitting in his chair, he propped his feet up on his antique rosewood desk and pressed the button for his assistant. "Please bring me a coffee," he said in slightly old-fashioned Italian.

"Si, signor," said his secretary.

He flipped through a few pages of paperwork and set it down with disgust, tired of the same old thing. Day after day of papers, meetings, and business people trying to get whatever they could from him. He missed the good old days when you ran a man through with your sword, took his women, enslaved his children, and owned all that had been his.

Running a hand through his shoulder-length black hair, Cartazonon remembered the little walk-in he'd sent off to San Francisco. Closing his eyes he found the walk-in. The shadow spirit showed him what it saw. He watched the memory several times. Something seemed off.

A faerie being born could have caused the energy spike but it was unlikely. And what about the missing time? Had the woman the shadow spirit taken over fought back for a while? Or did something else happen? Maybe he should go to San Francisco himself and check things out.

"Your coffee sir," his assistant said as she set the hot drink down.

Cartazonon thanked her and watched her walk out of the office. She was one of the best secretaries he'd ever hired, didn't ask questions, typed fast, understood all this strange new computer nonsense, and the little bit of siren's blood in her would make a lovely snack, one day.

Chapter Thirteen

"When people talk, listen completely. Most people never listen."
~ Ernest Hemingway

Staring out the window Saturday morning, I watched the rain while waiting for Gavin and Anali to pick me up from Hope House. It had been a very odd week. People who normally ignored me at school suddenly came up to me exclaiming over my hair. Telling me how great I look. I kept my hair done up in a tight braid, but my school didn't allow us to wear bandannas so I couldn't cover it completely. Gavin called every evening. I hadn't gotten a phone call from someone since my mentor left for a job in another state two years ago. Gavin sounded so chipper over the phone, asking me about my day, school, friends and stuff like that. I tried my best, but small talk over the phone is not my thing.

Thankfully it was easy to get him to talk. Asking Gavin "How was your day?" could lead to a twenty minute play-by-play of what he'd done. I didn't mind listening to him talk. Gavin was as animated over the phone as in person. Most people like to talk about themselves. A few well-placed questions, and I change from socially challenged to their favorite person to talk to.

"Listening is a great skill. A good listener is the best of friends, the most trusted, and said to be a great conversationalist. Asking questions and then listening to the person's answer will tell you a lot about them. Don't think of your own story to share, or what you need to do later, just listen. Your father was a very private person, frequently forced to socialize at large

parties. He hated it; however, everyone loved to stop and chat with him because he would calmly ask questions and then listen. Everyone was so busy talking about themselves they never realized he'd never said anything about himself."

Planning our first visit took all week. Gavin started Tuesday, ending the phone call by asking me what I wanted to do Saturday. I had no idea what I wanted to do. I didn't plan outings, I went along with them. I tried to find out what he would like to do, if he was willing to spend money, or if the outing needed to be free. I even casually suggested a few things. Unfortunately, Gavin could tell. By Friday night he seemed rather tense.

Anali saved the day. She suggested that we would all take turns planning a Saturday and she got to go first. Gavin sputtered at her smug proclamation, and I breathed a sigh of relief. I bet Anali would play peacemaker between us for a long time.

*   *   *

Gavin's white Prius pulled up in front of the house. He jumped out of the car. I grabbed my coat, hat and gloves, and picked up my backpack as he knocked on the door. I waited for Melanie to open it. That's the rule.

"Hey, Sara, ready to go?" His smile was bright, but it didn't completely reach his eyes.

"Yes. I don't need anything special do I?"

"Naw, Anali's cooking us lunch, and then we're going to a museum." Gavin wrinkled his nose.

"Where are you going?" Shante demanded, her brown eyes looking at me suspiciously.

"I'm going with my Uncle Gavin." I said, pointing to him as he filled out a visitation form.

"Will you be back?" Shante's asked in a small voice.

"Yes, I will, about six tonight, okay?" Shante hugged me and nodded into my stomach, then darted off.

"Go, have a good time," Melanie said.

I waved bye and followed Gavin out to the car. He fairly bounced with excitement. "What has you so happy?" I asked, unable to keep the smile from my face; his emotions were overwhelming.

"We have a surprise for you," Gavin answered, his grin so wide it must have hurt his face.

"Where are we going?" I asked as we turned right, the opposite direction from the school.

"That's part of the surprise."

I shook my head at Gavin's excitement and watched as the neighborhood changed. The houses became bigger and more expensive with gold leaf decorating the scroll work. Gavin pulled into a driveway in front of a dark blue house with lavender and cream trim and brilliant gold accent on the scroll work. I looked up at the huge building. It looked at least twice the size of Hope House.

"I own this house," Gavin explained excitedly as we drove down a narrow drive to the back of the house. "The bottom floor is an antique shop, the second floor is where the manager of the shop lives, and the top floor is where my family used to stay when in town."

"Oh, cool. Why were you staying at the circus school before?" The driveway stretched much longer than I expected. This was a big house.

Gavin blushed getting out of the car, then headed for a narrow wooden staircase. "I'm not a morning person, and it was easier to be right there. Come on, Anali's expecting us."

"Is Kayin here, too?"

"No, he's staying with Phillip until we get custody of you." Gavin explained. "I didn't want anything to mess up your coming to live with us."

It was my turn to blush. His commitment to my living with him flustered me. It wasn't like I didn't want to live with him, but I wasn't sure that I did want to live with him, either. If Gavin and Anali wanted me, I would worry that once they got to know me they'd change their minds. However, they needed me; the Children of Fire needed me, and I knew they wouldn't back out. I had a destiny to fulfill. I did wonder if Gavin and Anali would regret having to take me in, and if they would say goodbye as soon as all the magical creatures were back home.

"Perfect timing," Anali said as we stepped into the apartment. She laid white cloth placemats on the glass table. Her yellow sari flowed around her reminding me of Aya, their skin almost the same shade of copper-brown. "I'm about finished cooking."

"I'll help put things on the table," Gavin said as he tossed his coat up on the coat tree. "Make yourself at home, Sara."

I nodded at his retreating back and looked around as I hung up my coat, scarf, and hat. The room was open and airy, and the hardwood floor shone from being recently polished. Large windows let in the sun, and the many houseplants soaked it up. In front of me stood a glass dining room table with four white upholstered chairs around it, and to the left was the swinging door Gavin went through to the kitchen. On the right was the living room, which had a large fireplace in one corner, and a couch, love seat and chair, all with polished wooden legs and white upholstery. In the middle of the room sat a coffee table with the same scroll work as the couches, and a large, dark red oriental rug.

This wasn't a home for children. I was terrified to even walk on the floor, let alone sit down at the table. Everything looked so clean and delicate. Gavin burst through the door carrying a pitcher of lemonade, three plates with three glasses balanced on top of them. I bit my lip to keep myself from telling him to be careful. Anali came next holding two steaming bowls that smelled so good that for a second I didn't care about getting the glass table dirty.

"Come and sit," Gavin said as he laid out plates and glasses. As I got closer he smiled and pointed to the seat in the middle. I carefully sat down and stared at the thin plates; they were white with a delicate gold circle half an inch from the edge.

Anali smiled as she set down rolls and condiments for the sandwiches. "I know they look fancy, but this is the 'everyday' china." I smiled as she rolled her eyes and made air quotes. "It took me a while to get used to it."

"Most places I've lived have thick plastic plates that you can't break," I confessed, touching the finely cut water glass.

Anali leaned closer. "In my village in India we used wooden plates, and our glasses were metal or cleaned-out coconut shells. I was so scared I would break one of Gavin's dishes that when he wasn't home, I'd eat out of pots or put food on a napkin."

I giggled as she blushed. Leaning closer to me she whispered a secret into my ear. "One day I couldn't take it anymore, and I flung one of the plates to the floor. It shattered into a million pieces."

"What happened?" I whispered holding my breath. Gavin must have been so mad.

Anali's face softened as love and tenderness washed over her. "Gavin rushed into the kitchen demanding to know if I was all right. When I apologized for breaking the plate he looked at me as if I was crazy and said..."

"I don't care about some stupid plate; I care about you. Then I cleaned up the mess." Gavin laughed as we both blushed. "Sara, I don't know how you grew up; heck, I don't even know your favorite color. This is how I grew up, and how your mom grew up. They are nice things, but they are only things. So don't worry about the dishes. Just enjoy the meal. Do we need anything else? I'm ready to eat."

"No, dear, we have everything. Go ahead and sit down." Anali smiled at him, and I could tell how much she loved him. Gavin's pale green eyes became lost for a moment in her warm brown ones, showing he loved her, too.

Gavin helped me put together my first vegetarian cheese steak. He slathered a soft roll with mayonnaise and mustard, then added several slices of provolone cheese, grilled onions, bell peppers, mushrooms, tempeh, spinach, and topped it off with pickled sweet peppers. It was huge and dripping with juice and melting cheese. I looked at it suspiciously. Watching Gavin take a bite of his sandwich I couldn't help but smile at the moan of happiness as he chewed, oil dripping down his chin.

I carefully picked up the drippy sandwich and opened my mouth wide in order to take a bite. Yum! The gooey cheese melted around the grilled vegetables, and the sweet pepper cut a bit of the richness. Gavin looked at me expectantly, and I smiled around my mouthful. He puffed up proudly, and went back to his own lunch.

Melanie was always easygoing about my being a vegetarian. She even bought me veggie burgers and cans of beans to add to the food cooked at the house. Even then, I didn't have access to a lot of different foods. I looked forward to eating more meals with Gavin and Anali.

We ate quietly for a while, and Gavin began making a second sandwich.

"Where are we going today?" I asked.

"The de Young Fine Arts Museum. There is a traveling exhibit there for ancient pottery and jewelry from the Middle East. It leaves next week, and I want to see it," Anali said.

Gavin pouted, but I could tell it was only to tease Anali. I could feel his playfulness—it tickled.

"That sounds like fun. Maybe I can tie something we see there into my report for history." An easy way to get a good grade on a paper is to do something different from everyone else. I mean, how boring can it be to read thirty papers on ancient Egypt?

"What's your report on?" Gavin asked.

"I'm thinking of doing it on ancient Babylon." It seemed like a good idea to learn how Shamash and Aya lived.

"Do you like school?" Anali asked.

"I guess. I get good grades, mostly so I can get scholarships to college and get rewards at the group home." I answered before taking another bite.

"What about friends?" Gavin asked.

"I don't have any." It wasn't that big a deal. Most of the kids in my school are into drama so they weren't fun to hang out with. "I have some people I hang out with at lunch but no one I'm close to. It's not like I can go and hang out with anyone after school or on the weekends."

"Why not?" Gavin tilted his head to the side in confusion.

"Hope House is a 24/7 group home. I can't go hang out whenever I want to." Gavin looked upset, and I wasn't sure why. "It's fine. Melanie takes us out a lot, and I don't have a lot in common with the kids at school."

"Gavin, why don't you show Sara around the apartment while I clean up from lunch." Anali suggested carefully changing the topic.

"Okay, thanks." Gavin kissed her cheek. "Come on, Sara, I'll give you the grand tour."

We started in the clean white kitchen, which looked big enough for several people to help cook a meal. Pale blue forget-me-nots were painted on random tiles along the walls and counters. Down the hallway the family room held a large TV, stereo and comfortable cream couches, another oriental rug protected the hard wood floor, this one with a dark blue background.

"The living room is for entertaining in a formal setting. This is where we hang out and relax." I wasn't sure I could relax in such a fancy room. "I got a new gaming system, I wasn't sure if you like to play, but if you want to, we can."

"I haven't played in years. My second foster placement owned one. I don't remember what kind. It was fun," I offered.

Gavin's smile wavered a bit, but came back full force the next moment. "Here, I'll show you your room."

I have a room?

Down the hallway were four doors; the one on the left opened to a bathroom, white and sea green. The first door on the right had been Gavin's room as a child. "Our parents let us decorate them," he explained, blushing a little. The room was black– the walls, sheets, and the furniture all painted black. The only breaks in the blackness were the books on the shelves, and posters of heavy metal bands on the walls.

I raised an eyebrow at him in question.

"I was fourteen," Gavin mumbled. "And Metallica still rocks."

I smirked and followed him to the next door. I should have realized what the next room had been, maybe then it wouldn't have been such a shock. Unfortunately, it didn't occur to me.

"This was your mother's room," Gavin said softly, opening the door. "It's your room now."

I couldn't breathe. I didn't blink. The walls were painted warm lavender and the blanket on the four-poster bed was made of white lace. The shelves matched the white pine bed frame and held books, delicate figurines, and a few swimming trophies. Behind the white lace curtains, crystals hung in the window, catching the sunlight and turning it into rainbows which danced on the walls. There was a white pine vanity with a large mirror. On the top sat a silver brush set, a jewelry box, and a half empty bottle of perfume.

My hands shook as I picked up the bottle and sniffed a light floral scent, nothing I would ever wear. Tears ran down my face as I looked around the very feminine room. There were several books of sheet music on one shelf, below that a row of books, most of which looked like romance novels.

I never cared about being labeled a tomboy until I stepped into my mom's room. Angrily, I wiped at my face. I couldn't help but think my mom would have been so disappointed in me. I straightened my plain black shirt.

"We can redecorate it if you like," Gavin offered softly.

"I don't...I'm not sure..." I stopped trying to talk. I couldn't. This wasn't my room.

"It's okay." Gavin placed a hand on my shoulder. "You don't have to decide now. Once Gabriella and I went to college, we stopped coming here on family vacations."

I nodded silently, afraid to talk. I could tell Gavin wanted to offer a hug, but held back. Part of me wanted to bury my face in his shoulder. I pushed that part down. I didn't know how long he would stick around. It would be better if I dealt with this alone.

"Let me show you the rest, then we can go."

"Sure." I shut the door behind me.

"Anali decorated it." Gavin shrugged and opened the door at the end of the hall.

I blinked. Wow, this room was bright. The walls were sky blue; yellow translucent cotton draped over the four-poster bed; the sheets and pillows were bright pinks and oranges. The room felt vibrant and happy. I guessed the two other doors lead to a closet and bathroom.

"You have a lovely home," I said, remembering my manners. My first foster mom was big into manners.

"It's yours, too," Gavin insisted. "I know nothing is official, but when they let you move in with me you'll live here, too."

"What about New York?"

Gavin smiled. "We'll get there eventually. I run the business, but I don't enjoy it. They can send me important papers to sign, and I'll delegate the hands-on work to those who like it. I plan on doing that once when we begin traveling with the circus, now it will happen a bit earlier. Anyway, Anali and I thought it would be good to stay here until after the end of the school year. We want to make things go as easily as possible for you."

"Thanks, it's much easier to stay in the same school." I hated changing schools.

"Anali keeps reminding me that while I'm very excited, that this whole thing could be scary for you. If you need or want anything, let me know. I'll do my best," Gavin said.

"Thank you," I said. "I can't think of anything I need right now."

"Well if that changes, please tell me or Anali."

"It's time to go," Anali called out to us, again saving me from an awkward conversation.

We piled into the car. Gavin's spicy scent blended perfectly with Anali's light jasmine perfume. We sat in uncomfortable silence for several minutes. Anali once again came to the rescue. "Have you decided what classes to take at the Circus Center?"

"I'm thinking about taking beginning acrobatics and aerial arts, because they are required for other classes I want to take later, and I'd like to take juggling."

"Good choice, especially if you want to do any of the cool classes," Anali replied.

"Then you can take mine, I'm teaching Chinese pole and trampoline," Gavin exclaimed. "Hey, if the classes you're taking end around the time mine end, I'd be happy to drive you home."

"Okay, thanks." I didn't mind taking the bus or walking, but sometimes at night it did get a bit creepy. "You'll have to get permission from Five, um, David."

"Why do you call your caseworker Five?" Anali asked.

I shrugged, "He's my fifth caseworker."

"It sounds like you're talking about, Dr. Who. I love that show. Nine is my favorite. Okay here's the museum," Gavin announced and started looking for a place to park.

Thirty minutes later we walked into the museum. People were milling about quietly, some looking bored, some enthralled, and some trying to feel inspired. Despite Gavin's seeming reluctance to go to the museum, he made a great tour guide. He knew all about the pieces displayed, where they were from, what they were used for and how they were made.

We walked past a couple arguing and I was grateful my empathy seemed to be turned down. I couldn't remember when I last dreamt of Akasha, but I appeared to have better control.

"How do you know all this?" I asked, after Gavin explained yet another display of artifacts from Assyria.

"Oh, well, I have a master's degree in art history, with a minor in archeology. It helps with appraising pieces for auctions and finding authentic pieces to help the Children of Fire," Gavin explained with a shrug.

Wait, this didn't make sense. "Why didn't you want to come here, then?"

"I did; I just like being a pain." Gavin moved on to the next display case.

I rolled my eyes and Anali giggled next to me.

The amount of talent ancient people possessed amazed me. What they could create from stone, wood, and pottery made some of our current creations look pathetic. They didn't have the tools we have today, and yet the intricacy and detail they created with their hands and a few simple tools was awe inspiring.

We came to a case filled with artifacts from Phoenicia. In the center of the case stood a glass vase, some of the first glass ever made, more than five thousand years old. The pieces were dark blue glass with ribbons of yellow and green glass. I couldn't take my eyes off the delicate vase. How did they discover sand could be melted into glass? Who thought of adding different ingredients to get colors? I leaned forward almost touching the case, as if by getting a little closer the answers would suddenly be revealed to me.

The soft noise of the museum faded away.

A young woman sat by a fountain in her father's house. Nervously she trailed her fingers along the bright mosaic tiles. Tomorrow she would get married, and today she would meet her husband for the first time. Her father was a kind man who loved her very much. She knew he would pick a good man for her, but she couldn't help being nervous.

She stood as a throat cleared, and a tall figure walked towards her. The sun shone behind him and she couldn't see his face. Servants set out a tray of mint tea and dates, then stood back to wait in the shadows, silently chaperoning the visit.

"Good afternoon, would you join me?" she said, offering her future husband a seat.

"Yes, thank you, Tanith." His voice sounded warm and confident.

Tanith smiled at him. "My father said your name is Sikarbaal."

"Yes, sorry, I should have introduced myself."

As he stepped closer and sat down, Tanith's smile widened. Sikarbaal's eyes had soft lines around them from smiling; he was a handsome man. Tanith poured the tea and handed him a cup.

He took a sip of the fragrant mint tea then set down the red and white painted cup. "I have a gift for you, a wedding present."

"That is very kind of you." Tanith held out her hands to accept the cloth-covered package. Carefully she opened it. "It's beautiful, thank you very much."

"It has perfume in it, I hope you find the scent pleasing."

Tanith pulled the blue glass stopper and took a sniff. "Roses. Oh, Sikarbaal, it's lovely."

I saw flashes of their lives, happiness, sorrow, births, deaths, and through it all, a lovely dark blue glass vase with ribbons of green and yellow filled with rose perfume sat next to their bed.

My eyes flew open as I came back to the present. Gavin held me in his arms walking quickly to the doors.

"Let's get her outside," Anali said. "Maybe if we get her away from everyone, she'll be able to calm down."

I tried to tell them I was okay but my voice didn't work. I could hear Anali assuring someone that I was fine and needed some air. Gavin didn't say anything. He moved quickly to the doors, and we both gasped as we hit the cold, wet air. Sitting down, Gavin held me close, as if shielding me from anything bad with his arms.

"I'm okay," I managed to whisper.

"What happened?" Anali asked as she placed a hand on my forehead checking my temperature.

"I wanted to know more about the glass vase and suddenly I was in Phoenicia watching this girl being given that vase by her fiancé. She'd met him that day." I shook my head as if to clear it and leaned closer into Gavin.

"You have come into a lot of power." Gavin explained. "It will take a while to learn to control it, and while you're getting used to it, gifts will flare up."

"So I could be sitting in school and suddenly what? Talk in another language? Burst into flames? Know what everyone around me is thinking?"

"Unfortunately, yes, but we are here to help you. You can call either Anali or me whenever you need us. We will teach you how to use and control your gifts."

"I thought Shamash and Aya would teach me how to use my gifts."

"They do," Aya said. "But dreams happen mostly in your subconscious. Information they give you helps, but you need to practice here so you can consciously control your power."

I took a few deep breaths and began to sit up, pulling away from Gavin. "Shouldn't we be doing that instead of going to a museum?"

"No," Anali said. "We don't know each other, and without some basis of trust and understanding, it would be too hard."

"And," Gavin interrupted. "I want to get to know you. I want us to be a family."

I didn't know what to say.

"Do you know how to block out other people's feelings?" Anali asked.

"A little bit. I can imagine a bubble around me, and that blocks people's emotions from overwhelming me. But I still know what they're feeling, and if their emotions are strong or directed right at me, the bubble doesn't help at all."

"I'm happy to help you with this," Anali offered. "I'm empathetic, not as powerful as you, but I can show you techniques that will help."

"That's great, thank you," I said, my shoulders relaxing a bit. It helped knowing I wasn't in this alone.

Gavin looked at his watch. "We still have time, how about we head downtown, do some window shopping or actually shopping if something catches our eye, then have dinner?"

"Sounds good to me," Anali said. "I still haven't gotten to explore San Francisco yet."

"Sure," I stood and straightened my jacket. "I'm always up for wandering around."

* * *

Over a dinner of Vietnamese noodle soup, Anali and Gavin taught me some new meditation techniques to help block out other people's emotions. The new techniques built upon deep breathing, which I learned in yoga, and felt vaguely familiar. Maybe I dreamed about it.

My bubble felt much stronger. I knew what people were feeling like I knew the color of their shirt. It was something there, but not invasive.

After a rowdy game of Rock-Paper-Scissors-Lizard-Spock, Gavin won and would pick next weekend's destination. I was surprised by how much I looked forward to next week's adventure.

Chapter Fourteen

"The greatest gift you can give another is the purity of your attention."
~Richard Moss

"So, how was the visit?" Melanie asked as I cleaned up her room.

I hadn't said much after getting home last night; I needed time to figure everything out. I still didn't have any idea what I wanted, what I thought of everything, or what name I wanted to use.

"It was fun. Anali cooked lunch, then we went to the museum to see an exhibit of ancient jewelry and stuff." Sitting on the floor, I began to sort through her clothes.

"Gavin seems nice." Melanie typed a comment to one of her friends on Facebook.

"He is." I sprayed stain-remover on her pink blouse and tossed it with the other light-colored clothes. "He's very excited."

"About finding you?"

"Yeah. The house they live in was owned by his parents. My mom's room is still there, just how she left it when she was a teenager." I put the clothes, now sorted by color, back in the basket and shoved them by the door, ready to wash.

"What was that like?" Melanie kept her voice gentle, inviting me to talk, but not demanding it.

"Let me get the wash started," I said, postponing my answer for a minute. What had it been like to see my dead mother's childhood bedroom? Odd, uncomfortable, special, overwhelming, sad, all of these things mashed together into a giant emotional mess.

"It looked all girly," I answered when I came back into Melanie's room. My face flushed hot with embarrassment. I grabbed some hangers and began to hang up the clean clothes I found on the floor. Who would take care of Melanie if I left?

"Girly?"

"White and lavender with lace, there were even a few outfits still hanging up in the closet——-all dresses." My explanation sounded lame.

Melanie stopped typing, her brown eyes now focused on me. "That must have felt uncomfortable."

"It was just so . . . not me," I whispered, my chest tightening.

"Most of us aren't much like our parents. I mean, can you see me spending my day baking like my mom does?" Melanie said with a soft smile.

I shook out a skirt before hanging it up. "How do you know exactly what I need to hear?"

"It's a gift; I'm awesome like that." Melanie pulled her laptop closer. "Don't forget to clean my bathroom."

"I never do." Melanie understood when to talk and, more importantly, when to stop.

*   *   *

My eyebrows rose in surprise when I saw Five waiting for me when I got out of school Tuesday afternoon. He leaned against his beat-up hatchback, sunglasses on, brown hair blowing in the wind, faded blue jeans slightly baggy, but nice. His ultra-cool look finished off with a brown sweater vest over a blue shirt and brown loafers. I shook my head at Five, I couldn't decide if he didn't know or didn't care. He was nice looking, for an adult, but dressed nerdy.

"Hey, Five, what's up?" I asked.

"Sara," he said, stressing my name. He couldn't pull off a stern look with his baby face. "I thought I would drive you to class so we could chat for a bit."

"Okay, well thanks, it will make things easier." I got into his tiny hatchback.

"What time does your class start?" he asked as he pulled away from my school.

"Four." I gave Anali the class registration form on Saturday. When Gavin called on Sunday, he told me I got all of the classes I wanted.

"Great. Let's get something to drink at the café across the street and talk before your class starts. Which one is it today?"

"Today is beginning acrobatics; it's a requirement for a lot of the other classes." I bet Five was waiting for the "right time" to ask lots of irritating questions I didn't have the answers to yet.

"That sounds like fun. What other classes are you taking?"

"Well, Wednesdays I'm taking juggling, and on Fridays beginning aerial arts, another required class."

"They all sound like a lot of fun. Here we are," Five carefully navigated the small parking lot and managed to find a parking spot.

Sitting down on the cool metal chair, I sipped my chai latte, enjoying the hot drink and the cool breeze off the bay. The sun was warm on my skin, and the birds chirped as they flitted about.

"I thought the hot chocolate was your favorite here."

He actually remembered that? "It is, but it's too rich for me to drink right before working out."

Five nodded his head and took a sip of his cappuccino. "I wanted to find out how your visit went."

"It was good. We had fun. Gavin and Anali are nice."

"I'm sure they are. Gavin is very excited about finding you. He's ready for you to move in. Today." Five smiled at me. "Everything has checked out. What we are waiting for is for you to feel comfortable being with Gavin and Anali."

"Oh." I took a sip of my drink so I wouldn't have to answer right away. That's quite a bit of pressure on me.

"I haven't told Gavin that," Five reassured me. "You need time to get used to the idea of having a family. He's been hunting for his sister's child for years. For him this is a dream come true. I suspect you gave up the dream of being rescued a long time ago. This must be a lot for you to take in. So I wanted you to know that I'll give you as long as I can. I want this to be your decision." Five sat back in his chair sipping his drink.

"Thank you." Five's a good guy. I'm grateful he's my caseworker. Four would have packed and moved me already.

*   *   *

"Welcome to beginning acrobatics," Shin greeted us. His long blue-streaked bangs were tucked behind his ear. "The focus of this class is to build strength, increase flexibility, and make sure your foundational skills are strong. I know this class is a requirement for many of our other classes, and it is important that when you pass this class you have acquired a set level of skills and ability. You may not pass this class the first time through." Shin paused for a moment. We all waited patiently; no one seemed bothered by this.

"In fact, three of you I remember from last session." Shin smiled. Two girls and a boy smiled back. There were seven of us in today's class. They all looked older than me by at least two years, but that's fine. I was here to learn, not to make friends. "For our first class we will go over warm-ups and exercises. Then we'll do some basic tumbling."

Shin was as patient as I remembered from camp. Carefully, he went through each exercise, pointing out the exercise's importance and how it would prevent injury and build core strength. One by one Shin went by each of us, adjusting our position, so we were doing the exercises properly. I could do them all, but just barely.

I blushed through the partnered stretches, as Shin used me to demonstrate to the class how to do each one. I didn't know my legs could stretch that far back!

"Okay everyone, go get some water," Shin said, as he offered me a hand and helped me up from the floor.

"How's class going?" Gavin asked. He'd been watching since he got here ten minutes ago.

"Good. Shin's a great teacher. It's a lot harder than I thought it would be. Class is much more intense than camp. We haven't even started tumbling yet."

"Have you ever taken gymnastics before?"

I shook my head as I drank some water.

"Well, the point of taking classes is to learn, right?" Gavin said, with a smile.

"True. What are you up to today?" I asked, putting my water bottle away.

"I'm teaching a trampoline class in a bit. Looks like you'd better get back to it," he said, pointing to my class.

"Thanks, see you later," I said, walking back to the mats.

"Let's start with somersaults. I'll show you a few then I want each of you to do three going down the mat and three coming back." Shin, of course, did a perfect somersault, tight and controlled. Picking up a clipboard and pen, he took notes as he watched us.

I did my best, but there was a big difference between my tumbling and those of the three kids who were back for a second time. I tried not to feel embarrassed.

"Everyone did really well. Next class I want you to come in and start with the stretches we did today. That way we'll have more time to work on acrobatics. The doors open at three-thirty, so get here as early as you can to warm up." Shin flipped through the papers on his clipboard. "To help you succeed in this class, I have a list of some of the core exercises we did today, plus exercises for each of you that I think will help you personally. You don't have to do them, but you will improve much faster if you do them at home. Does anyone have to go right away? I need a few minutes to go over the paper with each of you."

"My mom is here, and we need to pick up my sister from piano," said one of the boys from class.

"All right, we'll start with you. Anyone else?"

I raised my hand. "I have to catch the bus home, but I have about fifteen minutes."

"You'll go next. If the five of you could pick your order based on who needs to leave while I talk with these two, that would be helpful,"

I heard Gavin's voice from the other side of the refurbished warehouse. "Everyone take a quick water break, and then we'll work on turns."

I walked over to say goodbye to Gavin, knowing he would feel hurt if I left. "Hey, my class is over, so I'm going to leave soon."

"Oh," Gavin replied. "David hasn't called me back yet. I'll call him again tomorrow, but if you want to wait until I'm done, I don't mind driving you home."

I didn't tell Gavin that Five probably waited until he spoke to me before agreeing to put us together more. "Thanks, but I think you would have to work out something with Five and Melanie for me to be able to do that."

"I'll talk to them," Gavin smiled. "You certainly are a well-behaved kid."

I shrugged. "I get a lot of privileges because they trust me to follow all the rules. It's worth it."

Before Gavin could answer, Shin called me over. I waved to Anali, who walked in. You couldn't miss her, she wore a lime-green outfit. "Hello."

"Hey, Sara, how was class?"

"Good. Are you teaching?"

"Yep, I'm doing kid's beginning acrobatics with Shin, then this evening adult beginning acrobatics."

"Trying to get all of us newbies out of the way," I teased.

"Of course," Anali smirked, "that way the rest of the week is easy."

"Shin is waiting; maybe I'll see you tomorrow?"

"I'll be here." Anali went to greet Gavin.

"Sara," Shin began, turning his clipboard so I could see the paper. "You are quite flexible and have good strength. You practice yoga right?"

"Yes."

"Do you take classes?" Shin asked his brow furrowed.

"I take yoga at school for my P.E. credit, and sometimes I do it at home."

"Okay, that makes sense. You need to work on your core strength. I've added a few yoga poses that I would like you to work on holding. Once you can easily hold them for sixty seconds, let me know and we'll see what you need then."

"Okay," I nodded reading over the poses; I was familiar with some of them. "I thought yoga built core strength."

"It does, but most classes for kids simply don't push you as hard as an adult class can. The classes I take do lots of challenging inverted poses, like headstand, and the class lasts for an hour and a half," Shin explained.

"I know of few of these like, up and down dog, plank, and push-up," I said pointing to his list. I felt a little sad that my yoga practice wasn't as good as I thought.

"Okay, great. Can I see them? These other poses build on those and I want to make sure you don't need any help with them."

Nodding, I went through the poses that I knew. I hoped people thought my face turned red from being upside-down and not from the embarrassment I felt at sticking my butt up into the air.

"You have a very strong practice," Shin complimented. "That's wonderful; it will make these a lot easier. Add these poses to your routine after you have warmed up your body. We'll start with dolphin."

*   *   *

I arrived at the Circus Center Wednesday afternoon, grateful to be somewhere I could burn off my anger. I tossed my backpack into a cubby with more force than necessary. It bounced out and landed on the floor. I picked it up and shoved it into place. Taking off my shoes, I shoved them into the cubby, then remembered I needed to change, so I yanked my backpack out, which knocked my shoes onto the floor. I tore open my bag and began to dig for my workout clothes. Once I found them, I shoved my bag back into the cubby and stomped off to the bathroom to change.

"Having a bad day?" Gavin asked. I could hear the smile in his voice as I shoved my bag, now full of school clothes, back into the cubby.

"Oh no, everything is peachy keen." I grabbed my shoes, dropped one, cursed, then shoved them next to my backpack.

"What happened?"

My eyes narrowed, I could tell Gavin was trying not to laugh. I was afraid if I turned and saw him I'd want to smack the smile off his face. It had been a craptastical day.

I moved to the floor and began to warm up, not looking at Gavin. "In history, Bruce Danbury decided to act like the moron we all know he is, and he got half the class riled up. Mr. Kaplan was so pissed he gave the whole class lunch detention! I didn't even do anything. I tried to talk to him, but he yelled at me."

I could feel my face heating up and my hands clenched into fists as my anger flared. "Then during lunch detention, some stupid seventh grader decided to start throwing food. I hid under the table, and the vice principal spent the next thirty minutes trying to figure out what happened, and refused to give anyone passes to class, so I now have a tardy and got a lecture in front of the whole class by Miss Patton."

I switched to stretching my arms and wrists since I had juggling class today. "And then stupid, slimy Kevin Brock slaps me on the ass and asks me if I want to go out on Friday! I mean really! First of all, when have I ever even looked at the jerk, and second, what girl would ever say yes to that! I never got noticed before my hair changed!"

"Wow," Gavin said barely toning down the mirth he felt. "That is a lot to happen in one day. I completely agree with you about the boy, maybe I should talk to him?"

I glared at Gavin through my bangs and started doing wrist circles.

"Okay, okay, maybe not. But Sara, I can't believe that the teachers punished you for no reason."

My stomach got tight and hot with anger.

"I mean are you sure you didn't do anything?"

"Excuse me?" I hissed glaring, at him. How dare he! Was I sure I didn't lie, and I didn't cause trouble! I don't even hang out with those stupid kids!

"Sara, calm down." Gavin sat down on the floor next to me. "Sara, your hands are on fire. You need to calm down. I'm sorry I didn't believe you."

Looking down, I wiggled my fingers, small orange flames surrounding them. I couldn't even be angry today, and I had every right to be angry! Hot tears ran down my face, which pissed me off even more. I wanted to scream and cry and apparently burn something, or someone, maybe Kevin Brock.

"Sara, I can't touch you when you're on fire. I can't help, and class starts in fifteen minutes. A lot of people will arrive soon. Please, honey, try to calm down." Gavin pleaded, his hands twitching in front of him. I could tell he wanted to soothe me, but his gift wasn't fire. Taking a deep breath, he held his hands over mine to hide the fire as best as he could without touching me.

I wanted to stay angry, but I needed to suck it up unless I wanted someone to call the fire department because I was on fire. With one last glare at Gavin, as he was the only one nearby, I closed my eyes and began to breathe. Breathe in to the count of five, hold to the count of five, exhale to the count of five, hold to the count of five. After three sets I could feel my body temperature cooling. A few more sets, and I unclenched my fire free hands.

"Good, Sara. I can tell you've been practicing the breathing. I'm glad that it's helping." Gavin fidgeted next to me.

I kept breathing to a count of five and slowly, I opened my eyes. I found that I kept calmer longer if I ended my breathing with my eyes open. I had no idea why; it just worked.

On the other end of the school I saw Anali. "Is Anali teaching yoga?"

"Um, yeah."

"I didn't know she taught yoga." I let go of my breath, allowing it to return to normal and turned to Gavin. I felt a little bad; he looked very worried.

"We both do." Gavin tilted his head to the side in confusion. "Are you okay?"

"Yeah, I'll be all right. It was a really sucky day."

"I'm sorry if I made it worse." He looked down at his hands and flinched. The skin on his palms bright red and blistered.

"Gavin," I reached out but didn't touch him. Why had he held his hands so close to mine?

"It's fine, my gift is regeneration remember?" Closing his eyes, Gavin's breath deepened and I could feel the hum of Akashic magic. The skin on his hands darkened and then crumpled leaving a fine ashy powder. Gavin shook his hands and the skin under the ash looked healthy and fine.

"Does it hurt?" I asked looking at the newly healed skin.

"The healing hurts a bit, and it can get hot if I have to heal something big, but it feels better quickly enough."

"My class is starting, will you be all right?"

Gavin smiled. "I'm fine. The new skin needs some lotion, and I need to eat a little something. Go to class."

I bit my lip and walked over to Kayin, looking back at my uncle several times. I needed to be more careful.

I did much better in the first juggling class than I did in my first acrobatics class. It was fun and relaxed. Kayin did go through a few stretches for arms and wrists before beginning the juggling. I hadn't juggled at all since the camp, but what I learned came back to me quickly once I held the bean bags in my hands.

Kayin was warm and encouraging as he spent time with each of us, helping and guiding how we were throwing the bean bags.

"You're doing well," Kayin said as he came up to me. "Remember to throw to your hand, and not move to catch the ball, that will keep your movements smoother."

"Okay, thanks." I felt better listening to Kayin's rich voice.

Kayin smiled. His teeth flashed bright against his dark skin. "You're welcome. How have you been? I haven't seen you in weeks."

"Good. The adjustments have been hard. My powers are still out of control, but I'm working on it," I said while trying to continue throwing and catching. Unfortunately, I wasn't successful and the bean bags fell to the floor with a soft thud.

Kayin patted my shoulder. "Keep trying, you'll get the hang of it."

I finally managed to keep three balls in the air for several minutes when Kayin ended the class. "All right, everyone, put the juggling balls away, and we'll do some cool-down exercises before you go."

Turning, I looked at the clock, five already, the hour had gone by so quickly. I tossed the round, sand-filled balls into the basket. I needed to get a set of my own so I could practice at home.

"Kayin," I called once the rest of the students left.

"Yes, Sara?"

"I was hoping to buy some juggling balls, do you have any?"

"I think Philip has several kinds in the office. Did you want rubber ones or the bean-bag style like we use in class?" Kayin asked holding up one of his own. It was a round, sand-filled ball like the ones I used in class, but this one made from fabric with a bright geometric pattern.

"That is lovely. Are there more like the kind you have?" The ones used in class were red, blue or yellow.

Kayin smiled and tilted his head down a bit as if embarrassed. "No, I made these."

"Did you? Can I see them?" I asked excitedly.

Wordlessly, he handed me the three bean bags. They were perfect. All the same size and such great colors. Bright bold patterns of animal prints, geometric African prints, and pieces that looked as if the fabric had been painted with watercolors were patched together to make a lovely wild pattern.

"These are beautiful," I said giving them back.

"I'd be happy to make some for you," Kayin offered.

"Are you sure? I don't want to be a bother."

"Yes, I'm sure. I enjoy making things. I do not like to be idle; I'm not used to it."

"I would love some. I brought money; let me get it," I said moving toward my bag.

Kayin touched my arm. "No, Little Sister, these will be a gift." His deep brown eyes let me know he wouldn't be swayed.

"Thank you." Impulsively, I reached up and gave Kayin a hug.

"You are very welcome," he replied as he wrapped his arms around me.

"There is no greater gift than something made by hand. It doesn't matter if it's cookies, a poem, a painting made by a small child, or a knitted scarf, they are all precious. The care, thought, and time, which goes into something made by hand, can't be duplicated with money. I know it can be frightening to give a handmade gift, not knowing if the receiver will appreciate how much has gone into the gift. How much of yourself you are giving can make you feel vulnerable, but be brave, my darling, be strong and open. Once you find someone you care about, give something made of your time, your skill, and yourself."

Chapter Fifteen

"Being deeply loved by someone gives you strength.
Loving someone deeply gives you courage." ~Lao Tzu

When I got to the Circus Center Friday afternoon, I saw several classes in progress: Philip teaching clowning, Shin taking a Chinese pole class, judging by the tricks he was doing it was an advanced class, and Gavin teaching a conditioning class, where they focused on strength and flexibility for specific skills, such as pole, acrobatics, and trapeze. I didn't see Anali anywhere.

"Beginning aerial arts for teens, come over here," Taliesin called, his hand high in the air so everyone could see him. As if anyone could miss his snow-white hair.

Taliesin began his class much like Shin, going over rules then into stretches and core strengthening exercises. Taliesin stressed the importance of doing these before class, and doing the exercises daily for faster improvement, just like Shin.

"Now we are going to move on to the class warm-ups," Taliesin said. "You will use the trapeze bars to warm-up. There are three bars, so pair up and share. I'll show each exercise and then come around making sure you are doing them properly."

Four giggling girls paired off instantly; they seemed to know each other. Smiling, I approached the remaining girl. She was not in the best shape; the warm-up left her panting and sweaty. She was plump, with a sweet face and short spiky orange hair.

"I guess it'll be the two of us," I said. "I'm Sara."

"Cool, I'm Jane."

"Come on, it looks like Taliesin is ready to start." Taliesin crossed his arms, drawing his blue tee shirt tight over his back, and he tapped his foot.

The other girls glared at us then turned back to watch Taliesin hang from the trapeze bar, as he went through the different exercises.

"Shockingly enough, I think my hands are going to wear out before my arms do," Jane moaned as she rubbed her sore hands.

"Let me see," demanded Taliesin. Where did he come from? Wasn't he helping the Perky Girls?

Jane held out her hands. Taliesin looked them over carefully running his thumb over the red skin. "I don't see or feel any blisters," he said.

"There are two things you can do to strengthen the skin on your hands." Taliesin raised his voice so all six of us could easily hear him. "Do the dishes, with hot soapy water and no gloves, this helps a lot. You can also hold damp tea bags in your hands, the tannin in the tea will toughen up the skin."

"How long do you need to hold the teabags for them to work?" Jane asked, her voice softer and more breathy than I heard it all afternoon. Oh no, she wasn't crushing on Taliesin, was she? I mean sure Taliesin looked all GQ and perfect with his tight, blue tee shirt, gray track pants, and his hair in a long white braid down his back, but he's such a snot.

"Sit with them while you're doing homework or watching TV," Taliesin said with a shrug.

"Taliesin, are my hands okay?" One of the Perky Girls asked, holding out her hands for inspection.

Taliesin looked at me, his pale blue eyes pleading. I quirked an eyebrow, silently asking, 'What?' Taliesin glared and walked over to her, keeping his touch much lighter and quicker than with Jane. One by one, each of the Perky Girls held up their hands for him to check. They all blushed and batted their eyelashes at Taliesin. One of them even leaned forward showing how low her top could go.

"Okay, everyone has done well. We have about thirty minutes left in class and I want to spend the last ten minutes cooling down. So before then let's try a simple hip hang. You need to find your point of balance, and let your body hang, trust that the bar will hold you." Taliesin placed his hands on the trapeze and pushed himself up and over the bar. His torso and legs hung on each side of the bar; he let his arms go and hung, his body perfectly balanced on the wooden bar.

Jane looked at me, her brown eyes wide. "Oh, please, you go right on ahead."

Chuckling, I shook my head and pushed myself up. The first time I lay on the bar, I positioned myself too high up and squished my stomach, forcing my breath out of me. I quickly jumped down.

"Ouch," Jane said. "Try again."

"Sure." My second try I settled too low on the bar and when I let go of my hand I began to tip forward. I may have squealed before grabbing onto the bar and flipping forward landing with a less than graceful thump.

Jane cupped her hand over her mouth trying not to laugh.

"Your turn," I said with a halfhearted glare.

"Okay, wait a second everyone." Taliesin paused until all of us were looking at him. "Now the perfect spot to balance is a little different for everyone, but it's usually about three inches below your navel. Place your hand, thumb side up, below your bellybutton. The bottom of your hand will lay lie close to where your center of balance is."

Jane looked down at her hand against her lower belly. She quirked an eyebrow at me then moved to the trapeze. Taking a deep breath she bent her legs and hopped onto the bar. She squeaked as she fought to keep her balance. Then she leaned forward. Slowly, she removed her hands and hung on the bar.

I couldn't help myself, I clapped for her. "Good job, Jane."

"Thanks." She landed with a thud. "It's not very comfortable, but I think I could get used to it."

"You'll work up to it," Taliesin said, startling us both.

"Crap, you scared me!" I said.

"Sorry," Taliesin said. He didn't sound sorry. "Your turn, Sara."

Rolling my eyes, I placed my hand on my stomach, making sure I knew where I needed to aim for and hopped up on the bar. My arms protested. I would only be able to do that one more time tonight. Carefully, I adjusted and leaned over. It took a bit of shifting but I finally found my balancing point. Removing my hands, I hung on the slowly turning trapeze. Within a minute the bar became uncomfortable and I jumped down.

"Go, Sara!" Jane grinned.

"I think the other girls are waiting for you to help them," I told Taliesin. The Perky Girls were currently glaring at us.

Taliesin closed his eyes and then looked up at the clock. "Okay everyone to the mat, time to cool down before class ends."

"Chicken," I whispered as Taliesin walked over to the mat. I could tell he'd heard me because he squared his shoulders and lifted his chin.

After leading us through the cool down, Taliesin passed out a paper, which listed the exercises he wanted us to do outside of class. Only two were different from those Shin wanted us to do.

"Next week, we will learn more hangs on the trapeze, so remember to come a bit early and warm-up before class, and I'll see everyone next Friday." Taliesin took a few steps away from the group. "Sara, can I speak with you for a moment please?"

"Sure." I turned to Jane. "I'll see you next week."

"Yep, I'll be here; we can partner again," Jane answered with a bright smile.

"Cool." I followed Taliesin all the while feeling the burning glares of the Perky Girls.

"What's up?" I asked once we were in the office.

"How did you like the class?" he asked as he placed papers into a file.

"It was fun, and styled a lot like Shin's beginning acrobat class I took on Tuesday."

"Yes, Philip has a system he likes to follow, it's designed to reduce injuries, and people who do the exercises at home find they improve faster which makes it more fun."

"So, what did you want to talk to me about? Melanie should get here soon to pick me up, and I want to change first."

"I wanted to check in, we haven't seen each other in a while," Taliesin answered, looking anywhere but at me.

I folded my arms. That was utter crap, what did he want? I stared at him, waiting until I figured it out or Taliesin gave in and told me.

Taliesin kept looking out the open door. I followed his gaze to the Perky Girls. Seriously? "Are you hiding from them?" I couldn't keep the shock out of my voice.

"Maybe," he said evasively.

"Why?" I didn't like the Perky Girls, but they were pretty enough, I guess.

Taliesin fiddled with his clothes, smoothing imaginary wrinkles. "Class is for learning. I don't want to encourage them. I'm hoping by ignoring the flirting, they'll stop."

"Good luck with that," I snorted. "Look, I need to go change, will you be okay without me here to protect you?"

Taliesin rolled his eyes. "Yes, I'll be fine."

"Is everything okay?" Gavin asked as he walked in.

"Taliesin is using me to hide from the pretty girls in his class," I teased. I may have found a new hobby.

Taliesin blushed. Oh, yes, this could be a lot of fun.

Gavin placed his hand over his heart. "I understand it is a burden to be so good looking, but I have learned to live with it, and someday you will too."

Rolling my eyes, I headed for the door. "I'm sure you have lots of good advice to offer, so I'll leave. I need to get ready."

"Hey, my class is done, do you want a ride home? David said it was fine."

"No thanks, Gavin. Melanie is picking me up; we have dine-out tonight."

"What's dine-out?" Taliesin asked.

"Once every other month we get to go out to eat," I explained.

"Oh. Where are you going?" Gavin wore that sad, lost look on his face he got it whenever I talked about the group home.

"I don't know. Usually we go to a buffet. I need to go; Melanie will expect me to be ready when they show up. I'll see you in the morning, right?" I asked Gavin.

"Yes, I'll pick you up at eight. We're going to have a lot of fun. David said we could have a twelve-hour visit."

"Cool, I'll see you then."

*   *   *

Putting the tray down, I placed Shante's plate in front of her as she settled herself into her booster seat.

"Thanks for helping me, Sara."

"You're welcome, Shante." She picked a bunch of different foods, and her plate was packed. I wasn't sure she could eat that much.

"When I'm done, I can get dessert right?" Shante asked as she took a big bite of macaroni and cheese.

I set the tray down and sat next to Shante. "Yes, I'll take you to get dessert," I promised.

"Cool. Tomorrow Melanie said she's going to take us roller-skating. I've never been roller skating before. Will you help me?" Shante looked at me, her big brown eyes begging me to say yes.

"I'm sorry, sweetie, but I won't be here tomorrow. I'm going with my uncle."

"How come she gets to go with someone she doesn't even know, and I can't even call my mom?" Crystal demanded, setting down her plate overflowing with fried shrimp and fish.

"Everyone is different; we can't compare cases. You know this," Melanie said as she set her and Caitlin's plates on the table. Rhonda and Myra followed behind her. Myra's plate was covered in greasy pizza. "Where's your fruit or vegetable?"

"There's pineapple on the pizza. See, Melanie," Myra said holding up her plate for inspection.

Melanie pursed her lips. "Well, I suppose since it's dine-out, I can let that be enough."

Myra beamed and dug into her food.

"Are you going to live with your uncle?" Caitlin asked.

"I guess so, eventually." I wasn't sure how to answer.

"You're so lucky," Rhonda said. Her mom was doing better, but she needed to get and keep an apartment and job to prove she could provide for Rhonda and Myra before they could move back with her.

"You don't want to leave do you, Sara?" Shante asked.

"Of course she does," snorted Crystal. "Who in their right mind would want to stay here?"

Leaning down, I bumped Shante's forehead with my own. "I don't want to leave you, Caitlin, or Melanie, but I'm thinking of ditching Crystal right now. What do you think, should we make a run for it?"

Shante giggled, nodding her head, her mouth too full of food to answer.

"Okay, calm down or you'll choke on your fried chicken." Shante grinned at me, the gaps in her teeth showing half chewed chicken. Gross.

I would miss this once I left, as odd as that sounds. I always knew that life in a group home was temporary and that people would come and go, but I planned on being the one to stay. A few months ago I sat in a meeting and told all of the people involved in my case, yet again, that yes, I did want to stay at Hope House and no, I didn't want to go to foster care or get adopted.

Now I didn't know what would happen, or what was coming next. I used to have a plan, but now everything has changed. All the adults were happy and seemed to think this was a good thing, but I wasn't sure.

*   *   *

"Nope, I'm done. I'm not doing anymore!" I sat down in the vibrant green grass and curled myself into a ball, my forehead pressed against my knees. All week I fought to control the so-called 'gifts' from my Phoenix ancestry. I knew I'd been having dreams, but so far couldn't remember much about them. Some mornings I woke tired, my brain aching as if I'd taken a hard test in school, yet I couldn't remember anything that happened.

Delicate copper-brown toes entered my vision. I felt the warmth from Aya as she knelt next to me in the grass. Slender fingers ran through my hair soothing me.

"I'm sorry you're having such a hard time," she said, her voice infused with the magical song that Phoenixes are known for. "It is a great burden, these gifts, when one doesn't have proper understanding or support on how to use them."

I nodded, not lifting my head.

"My poor Sapphire. I wish you could remember our teachings. Both Shamash and I have been trying to help you in your dreams. Unfortunately your dream powers haven't come in fully yet, and you can't remember everything the way you'll be able to do one day." Aya continued to soothe me.

They always called me Sapphire. I was slowly getting used to it.

"You have your mother's jewelry, don't you?" Shamash asked, his voice deep, with a musical lilt.

"Yes, I have the fire pendant, the night sky ring, and the bracelets with the magical animals on it. I hid them to keep them safe," I answered, still not lifting my head.

"Where you live, it isn't safe?" Shamash asked.

"No, at least not for something as special and important as your jewelry." My hands moved as I talked. I still kept my face pressed into my knees.

"If it isn't safe for jewelry, how can it be safe for you?" Shamash demanded. "You are a far greater treasure then some trinkets."

I'm more important than four-thousand-year-old magical jewelry? I don't think so.

"Aren't you living with Gavin now?" Aya asked.

With a deep, self-pitying sigh I looked up. "I'm safe enough, but it's too easy for other kids to steal things and hide them. Gavin is trying to make it so I can live with him. It takes a while. The people who have been taking care of me want to make sure that my moving in with him will be a good thing and that I'll be safe."

"He's family!" Shamash exclaimed as if that was the ultimate answer.

"Not all family is nice or safe. They are being careful. Everything will be fine, don't worry," I said, trying to explain without making things worse.

"Sapphire," Shamash said with concern. "You need help and support. Our descendants with only part of a gift find this time challenging. As my Jewel you have all this uncontrolled power running through you. You need help, let us help you." Gold eyes pleaded with me. Pearl-white hands grasped mine. Their warmth and strength offered protection and love.

I knew I couldn't say no, not only did I need help, but I could also feel how sad they both were. "How?"

"Wear the jewelry," Shamash said firmly.

"I can't; it's too much." I began to panic. The jewelry is so special and important and connected generations of my family together. The thought of losing even one piece made my heart ache.

"One piece," Aya said quietly. Shamash and I visibly relaxed at the song she wove into her voice.

"I suppose, I could keep one piece safe." I wasn't sure how I could explain it to Melanie.

"Wear the pendant, you never have to take it off. Water doesn't bother it and the chain adjusts. It won't even be a problem during the circus classes." I could see Gavin in Shamash at that moment, his exuberance at finding an answer and his desire to help.

"We'll talk with Gavin and Anali so they can help you remember that you need our pendant," Aya said.

"You'll remember, won't you?" Shamash leaned forward and kissed my forehead. "You'll remember this for your old grandpa, won't you?"

I couldn't help but grin. In front of me sat a beautiful man. He looked no more than twenty, and he could easily be a model in any magazine.

"I'll remember Adadda." The Babylonian name flowed into my mind.

Suddenly I was swept up in his strong arms. "It has been forever since I was called grandfather in the language of my first children."

"Amagal," I said softly, holding out a hand. My grandmother came to us wrapping her arms around us both.

I wanted to stay there forever, surrounded by their loving, protective arms, but the intensity was too much. After a few minutes, I began to squirm.

"Come on, let's go have some fun." Shamash helped both of us off the grass.

I woke up laughing. I felt light, free, and happier then I could ever remember. Humming to myself as I got ready for the day. I packed my bag and for some reason added the felt-wrapped jewelry my mom hid in the wall of the Circus Center.

"Sara, Gavin is here for you," Melanie called out.

"Coming," I hollered grabbing my coat, scarf and hat. "Bye, Shante, bye, Caitlin, have fun roller skating. I'll see you tonight."

Shante followed me to the door. She stood there glaring at Gavin, looking as fierce as a newborn kitten.

"Hello," Gavin said cheerfully as he handed back the visitation form to Melanie.

Shante looked at Gavin again. "I don't want you to take Sara away."

Gavin looked stricken for a moment and didn't know what to say. "I'm sorry," he stuttered. "I don't want to take her from you either, but I want her to come and live with me." He paused for a moment. "Maybe you could come and visit us?"

"Really?" Shante's eyes glowed with hope.

"You know I will always want to hang out with you." I bent down to give her a hug. "I have to go now. You be good, all right?"

"Okay, Sara, bye."

"Bye, Shante," Gavin waved cheerfully as we left.

"You shouldn't have said that," I said, as we walked down the stairs.

"What?" Gavin asked totally confused.

"That she could come and visit."

"Why not?" Gavin opened the car door for me. I waited until he sat to continue the conversation.

"Because she will remember you said it, and when it doesn't happen she'll be hurt and confused."

"Why wouldn't it happen?" Gavin cocked his head to the side for a second. Then straightened up as he was driving.

A thousand reasons raced through my head, because we'd get busy, CPS wouldn't let us, Gavin didn't mean it. Instead I asked. "Why would it?"

"Because Shante is important to you, so I'll make it happen," Gavin said. To him it was so simple. If I wanted it, he would make sure I got it. Gavin lived in a very different world from mine.

I wasn't sure what to say, so I didn't say anything. I sat there and let Gavin flip radio stations at every commercial.

"I wanted to go out to breakfast," Gavin said breaking the silence as we pulled into the driveway. "But Anali felt it's important for us to show you how we live so you knew what you were in for, and adjustments could be made before you came."

"Well, that sounds kind of ominous."

Gavin ran a hand through his hair nervously. "I guess so. I didn't mean it that way. Anali's made breakfast, so nothing to worry about there at least. She doesn't want me spoiling you, and thinking that is how we live day-to-day life."

"I understand."

Gavin opened the door and I was instantly hungry. Breakfast smelled wonderful, sweet and spicy.

"Come on in, breakfast is ready," Anali called. "We have fruit salad and hot rice cereal."

"It looks fantastic," Gavin said, kissing Anali on the cheek.

"Thank you, sweetie." Anali began dishing up bowls of hot rice cereal. "My mom use to make this for breakfast when I was growing up. We weren't sure if you would like it, due to the different spices," Anali explained, handing me a bowl.

"This is delicious." The cereal was so creamy and the spices reminded me of pumpkin pie. "Thank you for making breakfast."

"You're welcome," Anali replied.

"So we're going to the arcade today!" Gavin said excitedly between bites. "I found one that has laser tag, mini golf and a ton of games. We can eat cheap greasy arcade food for lunch."

How could he get excited about nasty cheap food while eating the breakfast Anali made for us?

"It sounds like fun," Anali said very unconvincingly.

I tuned out their playful bickering. My hand began to twitch and the thoughts which bounced around in the back of my head got louder and louder. I tried to find something to ground me, and then my mom's words came to me, helping me once again make a decision.

"Sometimes when we truly love someone we find ourselves capable of amazing things. Great feats of strength, courage, understanding, and forgiveness. The most powerful thing we can do is to be more vulnerable. I know being vulnerable sounds like a weakness, but in fact it's a great strength. Opening yourself up doesn't put you at risk of being attacked; instead, it shows how strong you are, and how much you care for the other person, and more importantly, yourself. When you hide your true self and true feelings, curling around them like an armadillo, you become small and defenseless. You can't see or meet what is coming at you. When you unfold and show who you are and what matters to you, you become big, and you shine, and the light you cast can scare away fear and worry. Be courageous in love, be vulnerable, be strong, and you will be powerful."

"Shante's mom lived in my first group home," I blurted out suddenly, startling both Anali and Gavin. "Sophia took care of me, and now I take care of Shante."

"Is she the little girl who came with Melanie to pick you up during winter camp, and came to the show?" Anali asked softly.

"Yes," I said swirling my spoon in my bowl.

"She isn't happy about Sara coming to live with us. I said she could come and visit," Gavin said softly. They both seemed wary of scaring me. As this was the first time I volunteered personal information, it was a fair concern.

I snorted. "Everyone says that. I'll write, you can visit, I'll call, it's always a lie, and I try very hard to not lie to Shante."

"What was Sophia like?" Anali asked.

"Hard and jaded, but sweet to me, I was so scared at first, and Sophia showed me the ropes. She taught me the rules and how following the rules meant the staff would trust you more and the more privileges you would get." I smiled. I knew it looked bitter and sad. "Sophia and I shared a room and she would hold me after I had a nightmare. I don't know what I would have done without her those first six months."

Gavin cleared his throat, and even then his voice rough with emotion. "What happened to her?"

"A boy. She was fourteen when she began dating this boy from school. He was older than she was, and she started sneaking out. She'd come home with bruises, and then she came home pregnant. She went to a lock-down home for pregnant teens. Now Sophia is using drugs and stripping for money, so Shante is in the system." My eyes stayed firmly on my breakfast.

"I'm sorry." Gavin's large hand covered mine. "I'm sorry people didn't stay in touch with you, and left you alone." He paused for a moment, maybe waiting for some reaction from me. I kept my face blank, done being vulnerable this morning. "I meant what I said. I'll do everything I can to make sure Shante can come and visit, especially now that I know how important she is to you."

"Thank you," I whispered, my eyes still not leaving the table. I took a deep breath and began eating again. Anali and Gavin got the hint and went back to their breakfast.

We were about to leave when Anali suddenly stopped. "Sara, do you have your mom's jewelry?"

"I do." I grabbed my backpack and pulled out the two white felt packages, as images from the dream flitted through my mind.

"I dreamt last night that you needed to wear the fire pendant," Anali said.

I held out the necklace. The pendant spun and caught the light. The purple, blue and green flames looked like they were dancing inside the red, orange, and yellow flames.

Putting it on, I felt the warm, gentle buzz of the Akasha magic beginning to flow into me. At first it felt like coming home, then I was overwhelmed with power. I could feel the energy of my different gifts shifting and spiking inside of me.

Reaching behind me, I tried to find something to hold onto as images from dreams filled my mind. A warm hand grabbed mine and helped me to the floor. I began to panic. I didn't want more power. I already had too much! I could barely keep myself together, and now more power was pouring into me. Why did Shamash and Aya do this to me? I trusted them. They said wearing the necklace would make things better.

"Breathe, Sara, remember to breathe," Anali said.

I took in a deep breath. I could smell Anali's jasmine perfume and Gavin's spicy cologne. I did my best to stay present, while memories of lessons taught by Shamash, my Adadda, and Aya, my Amagal, filled my mind. My head ached with sudden knowledge. It was like a Vulcan mind-meld gone wrong. I almost laughed at the geekiness of my inner thoughts. I must have made some kind of sound because Gavin wrapped his arms around me.

"It's okay, they won't hurt you. Let it happen," he whispered, his deep voice soothing.

I did my best to let go, but I couldn't. I knew, I mean deeply within myself knew, that if I could relax, this would all be easier. Yet, I couldn't. Apparently relaxing is a skill I have yet to learn.

I don't know how long it went on, but slowly it all began to sink in. The intensity faded like someone turning the volume down on a radio one notch at a time.

Blinking, I looked around, and my vision cleared. I found Anali's warm brown eyes and held them.

"Are you okay?"

I wasn't sure I could speak, so I nodded.

"Did the necklace connect you to Akasha?" Gavin asked.

I nodded again.

He breathed a sigh of relief. It ruffled my hair.

"That was some power surge," Gavin joked.

"I don't know how I'm going to control all of this. I had enough trouble before." I ran my hand over my face trying to rub away the tingling.

"It might help," Anali said hopefully.

I raised an eyebrow. I wasn't buying it.

"Did you know," she began. "That you're more likely to get cut with a dull knife then a sharp one? A dull knife you have to fight with more, use more force to get it to cut properly. A sharp knife is easier to cut with, so you have more control and can cut slower and more carefully. Maybe this increase in power will make things, easier and not harder."

I kept my eyebrow raised. I still wasn't buying it.

Gavin laughed. "I guess you will have to wait and see for yourself."

Chapter Sixteen

"It is exercise alone that supports the spirits, and keeps the mind in vigor."
~Marcus Tullius Cicero

We sat on the floor in silence for several minutes. My body twitched as my new power pulsed through me. My tennis shoes squeaked against the wood floor when my legs jerked.

"Do you need anything?" Anali asked softly.

"I...I'm not sure." My body felt strange and uncomfortable, I wasn't sure how to read it any more.

"Well," Gavin began thoughtfully. "You've been through a big change, so I'm not surprised you're confused. Can you tell if you need to sit still, or sleep, or move around?"

"We could rent movies and stay in today," Anali suggested.

My feet twitched as a wave of energy went through them. I couldn't imagine sitting still all day, and I was too wired to sleep. "I think I need to move, but I'm not sure I want to be around a lot of people."

"The energy from Akasha is very connected to nature, maybe we could go for a walk or something," Anali offered.

"Hey, Golden Gate Park is a few blocks away. We can tour the gardens, or feed the ducks, or walk around," Gavin suggested. Getting up, he looked out the window. "It's cold, but not horrible outside. I bet if we bundle up we'll be fine, and I doubt very many other people are out and about."

Cool green leaves and fresh air—that might help. "That sounds good." I stood up, happy to find the dizziness passed.

"Give us a minute," Gavin said, grabbing a brown leather messenger bag by the door. "I'll get water and some bread."

"I'll get our warm coats and scarves," Anali offered, and then she turned to me. "Do you need anything?"

"I don't think so. I have a coat, scarf, and hat," I said sorting through my pile of stuff on the floor.

"I'll pack an extra sweater for you in case it gets cold," Anali said grabbing a large yellow bag. "I have some gloves you can use."

"Thanks, do you need any help?" I asked. My hands were shaking, I wasn't sure how much of a help I could be, but I felt I needed to offer.

"No thanks, we'll just be a minute," Anali said as she walked away.

I stood by the door keeping my breath slow and steady, hoping it would help. For a moment I felt calm and still, then the energy spiked and my arm twitched. If Melanie saw this, I would be in the emergency room. I needed to find a way to get my body back under control.

"Okay let's go," Gavin said with a grin. He wore a fuzzy blue-and-green hat, which made his red hair even brighter. When he turned, I saw that the top of the hat came to a point and hung down to his shoulders. He looked like a mutant elf.

The air felt cool and damp as the winter sun slowly burned off the fog. Taking a deep breath, I felt the energy inside me settle a bit. Maybe going for a walk would be a good thing. We strolled past old Victorian row houses, all brightly painted, lined up like ladies at a ball waiting to be asked to dance.

Stepping onto the path lined with weeping willows and solid pine trees, I felt the power in me thrum happily. This had been a good idea. We walked along, Gavin and Anali holding hands and enjoying the cold winter day.

Each step seemed to settle the energy in me, like shaking out a bed sheet to get rid of the wrinkles. I could still feel the connection to Akasha through the necklace, now a soft gentle flow instead of a hot surge of power. The spikes of energy slowed down and so did the random twitching. My hands still shook, but I knew it would be okay as long as we kept walking.

We stopped at a pond to feed the fat ducks and geese. "How are you feeling?" Gavin asked as he handed me a slice of stale bread.

"Much better. I'm a bit nervous that the shaking will start again now that we have stopped walking," I said, tossing a chunk of bread onto the gray water.

"If it does, let us know, and we'll start moving again," Anali said. She dug into Gavin's messenger bag. "Here, the purple water bottle can be yours."

Taking the bottle, I drank. "Thanks, I hadn't realized I was so thirsty."

"You have a lot going on," Anali said, with a motherly smile.

"That's the last of the bread." Gavin tossed the last few crumbs into the water. "Do you want to keep walking?"

"I don't know, I'm not shaking anymore, but the energy still feels unsettled."

"That's fine," Gavin said. "It's pleasant out, for winter, and I enjoy walking." Gavin smiled, he looked lost in a memory. "Your mom always made me walk places. I wanted to take the bus, or a taxi. Gabriella would grab my arm and say some quote from some Roman philosopher about exercise being good for the soul."

"'It is exercise alone that supports the spirits, and keeps the mind in vigor.' Marcus Tullius Cicero," I recited without thinking.

Gavin turned, his green eyes blazing. "What? Where did you hear that?"

I cleared my throat. "Mom left me a journal. She filled it with quotes and lessons she wanted me to learn."

Gavin turned away from me, trying to hide his tears.

"Did she explain the quotes?" Anali asked, allowing Gavin to turn from us as he wiped away his tears.

"Yes, each page has a quote and then mom wrote the lesson she wanted me to learn from it," I answered, not looking up.

Taking a deep breath I decided to share the most precious thing I owned with them. Closing my eyes, I focused on that page in the journal and began to recite it. "I don't know how I would cope with the stress of life without exercise. This morning we practiced yoga. You slid under me so we could do down dog pose. I could see us together in the mirror, my triangle above yours, protecting and supporting you.

"Your life will be filled with stress and difficult choices. I encourage you to find a type of exercise that you enjoy and which helps you cope with life. It won't help if you hate every minute of it. There will be something you love to do: dancing, running, swinging, swimming, walking, sports, climbing, or yoga. Find something, take care of yourself, and you will be able to handle everything life throws at you."

"Your mother loved quotes," Gavin said, his deep voice rough. "She also swam. Gabriella was on swim team through high school. She wasn't a strong enough swimmer to make her college team, but she never stopped swimming." Gavin paused for a moment his eyes darting from side to side as if searching for something deep in his brain. "I think her high school swim coach suggested she do yoga."

"I didn't know she was a swimmer. I, um...I guess I could bring her journal, if you want to read it."

"I would love to read it. She started it while pregnant. Gabriella was afraid that she would be a bad mother and forget to teach you all sorts of important things, so she started the quote journal," Gavin said with a sad smile. "Maybe I'll finally learn some of the things she was trying to teach me."

Anali laughed. "I'm not that lucky."

"Hey!" Gavin protested. The tension faded, although I could still feel Gavin's sadness.

Taking his arm, Anali tugged softly. "Let's keep walking. It's too chilly to stand in one place for long."

Gavin placed his gloved hand over hers. "Of course, love. Sara, are you done with the water? If so I'll put it back into my bag."

I took another drink, then handed the purple bottle to him. "Thanks."

"No problem." Gavin paused for a moment. "I know it's hard for me to talk about your parents, but I do want to tell you about them."

"I like hearing about them," I answered, then hesitated. "I'm not sure what to feel."

Anali once again smoothed everything over. "Both of you will be fine. Gavin is mourning the loss of his family; Sara, you're learning you have one. There is no right or wrong to feelings; stop worrying so much."

Gavin kissed her cheek. "You're right of course, my dear. I don't know why I didn't think to ask for your help sooner."

Anali blushed, her large almond eyes softening with love. "I'm always here for you."

"Then I am the luckiest man on earth."

Oh gross! They're getting all mushy. Turning away in case they started kissing, I began walking, kicking the dry leaves on the ground. Behind me Gavin and Anali chuckled.

"Oh, look, what's that?" Anali asked about twenty minutes later.

I followed where she pointed through the trees, shifting to see through the dense leaves. There, shining in the filtered light, stood a white building. Even through the cloudy sky the sun reflected off the bright white walls.

Gavin shrugged. "Let's go find out."

As we walked the trees thinned out, and we finally saw the whole building. It looked old-fashioned with a large dome in the center and a smaller dome on each end. The spires and arches made it look like a building from an old romantic movie.

"It's a greenhouse," Anali said, standing on tiptoe.

"It must be the Conservatory of Flowers," Gavin answered. "I think I went here as a kid. Do you want to go?"

"I would love to," exclaimed Anali.

"Sara, will you be okay? It doesn't look very crowded, but there are people," Gavin said, pointing to the front.

There were a few people in the front walking up the stairs, admiring the winter flowers, and checking the time on the large garden clock. The shaking had stopped. I could feel the increased energy, but it now felt smooth. It seemed to flow gently through me. "I'm willing to try it. I like flowers."

"Okay, but if you need to leave at any time, just let us know," Gavin said, reaching out to touch my shoulder.

"Okay."

Judging by the spring in Anali's step, she really liked flowers. As we passed people I could feel them, but just an awareness of them and not an assault of emotion.

I took off my coat and hat as soon as we entered the warm, humid greenhouse. The white wooden frame was soft against the clear glass windows.

"They have one of the largest collections of orchids in America," Anali read from the brochure provided.

Gavin and I followed along as Anali pointed out everything of interest. I had never seen such fascinating plants and flowers in my life. The orchids took my breath away.

I looked through the dense foliage trying to find any hidden flowers. Most of the orchids were easy to find. Their bright colors and wild, alien-looking blossoms caught my eye. Anali decided to find as many orchids as possible. Since the Conservatory grew hundreds, a hunt began. Any time Gavin or I found some small hidden blossom she hadn't seen yet, Anali would give a soft cry of delight.

Peering past leaves as big as my head, I saw a young couple sitting on a bench. The man reached into his pocket and went to the ground on one knee. The woman's eyes filled with tears, and her hands shook as he proposed to her. I was hit with a wave of emotions: love, excitement, and nervousness all jumbled together. Without a thought, my power flared, and the foreign emotions were blocked. I could tell what the couple felt, but it no longer bothered me.

"Are you okay?" Anali asked.

"I think so. I'm not sure what happened." Well, I knew what happened but not how I protected myself.

"It feels like you put up a shield to block people's emotions."

"How could I have done that, and how could you know?" I asked turning to Anali.

"My gift is empathy, remember?" Anali explained. "At first it was hard for me, also. I could feel everything. Then I began dreaming, and Dadi, my grandmother, gave me a necklace. I began to remember my dreams, and I learned to control my gift." Anali reached into her shirt and pulled out a necklace like mine, a golden circle with a bright flame. "Give it time, Sara, you'll be able to remember the lessons Aya and Shamash have taught you. Until then things like this might suddenly happen when you need extra help."

I nodded. This was better than feeling every single emotion around me, but I wasn't excited about being able to do new things without knowing what I was doing. "Okay. Did you find any new orchids?"

Anali patted my arm, a soft smile on her face. "There is a small pale green one under that plant over there. Have you seen one like that?"

"No, not yet," I said, grateful Anali let the subject drop.

It was almost two o'clock before our hunger won out over our desire to find all the orchids.

"Sara," Gavin said once we were away from the crowd around the conservatory, "have you thought about your name?"

Crap, I hadn't thought about that at all. "A little bit. Aya and Shamash call me Sapphire." Sapphire and Sara were two different people, and I wasn't sure who I was or who I wanted to be.

Gavin ran a hand through his hair. "Sure, you're used to being called Sara."

I twisted the hem of my sleeve around my fingers. "But you've been looking for Sapphire."

"I have. I held you on the day you were born, celebrated birthdays and holidays with you, and knew you as Sapphire." Gavin looked at me and waited.

First my mom's journal, and now giving in on my name? What is it about Gavin that makes me want to make him happy? "I don't think I want to change my name, but if you would like to call me Sapphire, that would be okay."

I squeaked as Gavin swept me up into a hug. "Thank you. It means so much to me."

My stomach growled.

"We better get some food into you." Gavin beamed and moved ahead. "Come on, Anali. Come on, Sapphire. There's a great diner between here and home."

Anali touched my arm. "You have given him a great gift today, thank you."

My checks heated up as I blushed. "It's not that big a deal."

"It is. Gavin is very connected to Sapphire. It's Sapphire who is his niece, not Sara. I know you still feel like Sara, not Sapphire."

Note to self: don't bother lying or trying to hide around Anali.

I began walking towards Gavin. "I need to start accepting who I am."

"You can take all the time you need. We will support you no matter what." Anali wrapped her scarf tighter around her neck as the breeze picked up.

"Come on, I'm getting cold." Gavin's hair whipped around him in the wind.

Gavin read the list of twenty different types of pie they served while we waited for our lunch and ate homemade bread with butter. I don't think I'd ever eaten homemade bread before. New favorite food.

"Sapphire," Gavin's face lit up when he said my name. "Do you think it would be okay if the other Children of Fire call you by your real name? It's just that it might get confusing if everyone is calling you by different names."

"Gavin," Anali said, her tone calm but letting him know she wasn't pleased.

I hoped they weren't going to fight. Even the nicest-acting people could get mean and nasty when angry, and I wasn't ready to find out if either of them had a split personality. I did feel pressured into being called Sapphire, but it made Gavin so happy.

"Here you go." The waitress set down large bowls of steaming soup.

What did I think about everyone at the Circus Center calling me Sapphire? I took a bite of the rich soup enjoying how it warmed me up. It was just a name, it wasn't that big a deal, right?

I didn't remember Gavin from before. I wasn't excited about living with him or being the Jewel, but I could give him this. I still didn't know why I care about how Gavin felt. Maybe it was a side effect of the empathy. Of course I would still be Sara at home and at school, so it wouldn't be all that bad.

"It's fine with me if the others call me Sapphire."

Gavin beamed. I focused on my meal.

*   *   *

"How was your visit on Saturday?" Five asked when he called Monday afternoon.

"Good," I answered while I worked on my algebra homework.

"What did you do?"

I told him about my visit. Reaching up I touched the necklace. I felt cool and calm since after the first day I'd put it on. I had an awareness of my connection to Akasha, but wasn't bombarded with energy anymore.

"It sounds like a fun day." Five hesitated. "How do you feel about staying with them for the whole weekend?"

I set down my pencil. I didn't have anything against spending the weekend with Gavin and Anali; however, I wasn't hoping I could spend the weekend with them. I knew that things needed to move forward.; Five had his pointy-haired masters to report to, and no matter what I felt about the situation, it would end with my living with Gavin and Anali. "I guess that would be okay."

"Great. I'll call Gavin and let him know. I'm sure he'll be very excited," Five said. "Gavin also asked if he could drive you home from classes, maybe even have dinner after?"

"That's fine with me. I can do homework while I wait for his class to end," I said.

"Sara, if it becomes too much, let me know," Five said, concern in his voice.

I smiled, grateful Five was on my side. "I know, but the sooner I get used to them the better, right?"

"Gavin called you Sapphire several times," Five told me.

"Yeah, Gavin asked if he could, and I said yes."

"Remember I'm here to help. I don't want you to feel pressured," Five insisted. "Now let me talk to Melanie."

"Sure," I passed the phone off and went back to my homework trying to ignore the queasy feeling in my stomach.

*   *   *

The moment I stepped into the circus school Tuesday afternoon, Gavin bounded over to me. "Five called and said I could bring you home after classes, and we could have dinner together, and I have to have you home by seven-thirty, and you get to spend the whole weekend with us!" Gavin's face shone with joy.

Cold guilt crept through me. I wasn't nearly as excited about this. My whole routine was about to change. I would spend even less time at home. Less time with Melanie and Shante. But wasn't that the point, to make Gavin and Anali my home? I was out of my depth. I didn't know what to feel, what to hope for. Part of me felt excited at the idea of having a family and being special. Another part wished I could go back to being just some group home kid.

"We'll have to stop by my house after class on Friday night to pick up a bag for the weekend," I said trying to sound enthusiastic.

"I don't teach in the early afternoon; I could pick it up and then get you from school." Gavin's cheeks must hurt from smiling.

"Cool, that will work." And be easier on Shante if she didn't see me leaving for the weekend. "What are we doing tonight?"

"My class ends at six-thirty and Anali's ends at six so we thought we could grab something to eat between here and the group home," Gavin answered. "Tomorrow night we're done at the same time you are, so we can go home and eat dinner, and on Friday Anali doesn't have any classes and I end at six, so we we'll eat at home again."

"Sounds good. I should probably get ready for class."

"I came early so we could talk. I'll go entertain myself with something," Gavin said with an embarrassed grin.

"Do you want to warm up with me?" I offered.

"That would be great. I'll go change."

Gavin chatted happily while we warmed up, telling me what he and Anali had done since Saturday night. I made the socially appropriate sounds in the right places and even asked a few questions. I deserved a gold star.

"Beginning acrobatics," Shin called once he was ready to begin class.

"I'll see you after class," I told Gavin with a wave and walked over to Shin.

"Good afternoon, class," Shin greeted us. His hands were clasped behind his back, and he looked rather imposing. "I'm glad all of you arrived early and went right to work, I can already tell which of you have been doing the daily exercises I suggested." Shin walked over to me, tucking his blue streaked bangs behind his ear. "Everyone pair up for partnered stretches."

I let myself get lost in the class and managed to quiet my mind while focusing on the exercises. I wish it lasted longer.

"You did well this afternoon," Shin said after class.

"Thanks, it's a fun class. I'm learning a lot." Yeah, like I suck at cartwheels! "Is there a place I can sit and do some homework while I wait for Gavin?"

"Sure, I'm going into the office to eat dinner before my next class, you can sit with me," Shin offered.

"Cool, thanks. I'll go change and I'll meet you there."

Closing the office door behind me I sat down and began to pull out my books.

"What are you working on?" Shin asked as he started the microwave.

"Geography and science, today. What are you eating?" I asked, as the room filled with tangy and spicy smells.

Shin pointed to a small container on the desk. "Kimchi, and I'm heating up pork stew with rice."

"It smells great."

Shin bowed his head towards me. "Thank you. I will pass on your compliment to my mother. My classes are far enough apart that I can actually eat a good meal before nine in the evening."

"Are you in school?" I knew Shin was older than me, but that was all I knew about him.

"Yes, I'm a senior in high school. I only have to take four classes this semester, so I've got my homework done already."

"That has to be nice," I sighed, opening my science book. Shin ate quietly while I worked on memorizing the first twenty elements on the periodic table.

"Crap!" I snarled glaring at my geography book.

Shin jumped. "What's wrong?"

"Everyone seems to think all kids have easy access to a computer, and I have to look up and plan a trip to an Asian country," I explained. "I hoped to get this done tonight, now I'll have to spend lunch tomorrow in the library and hope to get a few minutes on one of the computers."

"I can tell you about South Korea," Shin offered, setting down his chopsticks. "My grandparents live there, and I've spent several summers there."

"That would help a lot." I grabbed my purple gel pen ready to take notes.

Shin told me about the best places to go, museums, temples, fortresses, and shopping. He told me the proper greetings and described Korean pottery in detail. "My grandfather is a master potter. He lets me make small things for fun, but I have cousins that are apprenticed to him. It's very demanding."

"It sounds amazing. Okay one last question. 'Foods: what should you try and what should you be careful of?' " I read from the book.

"Well, a lot of Korean food is spicy, so be careful with condiments and what you order," Shin said, thinking the question over. "Almost every meal will be served with kimchi; that's spicy fermented cabbage. There is a large variety of foods to choose from: noodles, rice, seafood, chicken, vegetarian dishes," Shin said with a shrug. "Oh, one thing to look out for is dog meat. Not an American-friendly dish."

"I've never tried Korean food; I'll have to try it. I like spicy food, but not eye-watering, mouth-on-fire spicy."

Shin stared at me for a moment, his black eyes looking for something. Using a different pair of chopsticks he picked up some kimchi and held it out over the desk. "Here, you can try some my mom made. The recipe has been passed down for generations."

I stood up a bit in order to reach the food being offered. It tasted cool, crisp, and tart with a warm spiciness. "That's good," I would need to find a way of getting more of his mom's kimchi.

Shin smiled brightly, "Would you like some stew?"

"No, thank you I don't eat meat."

Gavin knocked, then opened the door. "Oh, there you are, Sapphire. Are you ready for dinner?"

"Yes!" I gathered up my things. "Thanks for all your help, Shin, and please tell your mother that her kimchi is delicious."

"Is that what I smell? No wonder you're ready to go to dinner." Gavin walked over to Shin and stared at the kimchi.

Shin rolled his eyes, but was clearly pleased as he wordlessly offered him a piece.

"It's as good as the potluck party. If I weren't married, I'd try to steal your mom for myself. I'll be right back, Sapphire. I need to grab my stuff." Gavin whirled out the door.

"Gavin told us about your name change," Shin said, watching my reaction carefully. "So you want to be called Sapphire now?"

"Yeah, it's a bit weird, but I'll get us to it." I shrugged and put on my jacket. "Bye, Shin I'll see you later, and thanks again for your help."

"Goodbye, Sapphire."

Chapter Seventeen

Cartazonon woke, his chest pounding. He felt another power surge. Breathing deeply, he tried to pull some of the power into himself, but it had only been a dream. There was nothing in the air. Closing his eyes, he tried to remember the dream he'd been having but the images faded, and the people so blurry that he couldn't even tell their gender. However the skyline was unmistakable; something powerful lived in San Francisco.

Getting out of bed he cursed, almost tripping over the dead body of a young boy. The boy foolishly bragged about his gift of dreaming of the future in front of Cartazonon's assistant. She told him right away, not knowing it would lead to the boy's death. His assistant simply thought he was eccentric and interested in the occult.

Dead brown eyes stared up at him. Long ago he would have eaten the boys' eyes to try and gain his powers of sight. Thank goodness he didn't have to do that anymore. Picking up his phone Cartazonon texted his assistant. *Get me on a plane to San Francisco as soon as possible.*

Setting his phone down, he grabbed the boy's arms and dragged him to the edge of the carpet. Flipping the carpet over revealed a trapped door. The hinges squeaked as he opened it. The barking started instantly. Cartazonon smiled and pushed the boy down the chute. "Yes, don't worry. I have a treat for you."

Happy yips greeted the dull thump as the boy hit the floor of the Hell Hound's cage.

With a yawn Cartazonon went back to sleep. He could usually get three to four nights of helpful dreams after feeding on the power of a **Dreamer,** and he wasn't about to waste a moment of it.

Chapter Eighteen

"Certainly, travel is more than the seeing of sights; it is a change
that goes on, deep and permanent, in the ideas of living."
~Miriam Beard

"That's a cool bag," Gavin commented after juggling class
on Wednesday.

"Thanks. Kayin made me a set of juggling balls and this bag
to keep them in." I held up the black-and-tan, geometrically
patterned bag for him to see.

"May we see them?" Anali asked as we got into the car. They
had finished early today, so we were headed to their house for
dinner. Yesterday Gavin surprised me by choosing the pizza
place I pointed out the first night he drove me home. He'd even
ordered a pesto pizza, my favorite. I couldn't believe he'd
remembered and felt bad that I knew next to nothing about
what he liked.

"Sure." I pulled out the three sand-filled balls, each one
made with a different pattern. One made from animal prints,
another geometric patterns of black, brown, and white, and the
last ball covered in fabrics with prints of colored flowers and
plants.

"Should I be worried?" Gavin asked with an arched
eyebrow.

"What do you mean?"

"Well, yesterday Shin was feeding you and now Kayin is
giving you gifts," Gavin teased.

"Okay. First of all, Kayin calls me Little Sister and Shin is three years older than I am," I explained. "Second, I don't date."

"Why not?" Anali asked, adding at Gavin's growl, "Not that I'm complaining."

"I don't see the point. Nothing good comes from dating, and after listening to staff complain all these years about how bad teen-aged boys' hygiene is, why would I want to get close to them? Or teen-aged girls for that matter?" I muttered with a shudder. I cannot tell you how many times I've heard staff reminding teenagers that they need to shower, with soap, every day.

"Someday you'll meet someone you think is worth the risk," Anali replied sweetly.

I raised an eyebrow, I didn't think so.

"Hey, leave her alone," Gavin insisted. "Boys are gross and you should stay away from all of them. I'm behind that one hundred percent."

Anali laughed.

*   *   *

I sighed at the first bite of creamy potato leek soup, and felt the warmth take the chill from my body. Anali is the best cook. "Gavin, how are we going to travel around the world? And what exactly am I expected to do?" I asked.

I had thought about it for a while, and I couldn't make sense of how it all fit together.

"We will travel with the Cirque du Magique Fue. Michael, who runs the New York Center for Circus Arts, is starting a touring company. It's an easy way to hide and to get in and out of countries." Gavin dipped a piece of crusty bread into his soup. "You, as the Jewel, and the other Treasures will perform a ritual to open a portal to Akasha, and the magical creatures nearby will go through it, returning home."

That was it? What kind of help is that? What kind of ritual? I watched Gavin for a minute; he focused on eating, his eyes firmly staying down. I turned to Anali. Her brown eyes were warm, but she didn't offer any other information. Okay, going in blind, that's always fun.

"Will we fly everywhere?"

Gavin wiped his mouth with a white cloth napkin before answering. "Not most places. We will buy an RV and drive. That way it'll be easier to stop when we need to."

"You know Kayin and Taliesin. You'll meet Miu and Sasha once school ends. They will be traveling with the three of us," Anali told me. "We have been looking at RVs. Some of them are huge. We plan on sleeping in hotels or camping, but we could sleep in the RV if we have to."

"I don't have a passport." As if that fact was the most important thing right now.

Gavin made a sound, somewhere between a growl and a sigh. "We can't get you one until you're legally part of our family. Don't worry, we'll get everything taken care of in time. We won't leave until after you've finished the school year anyway."

I nodded my understanding, my mouth full of food.

"We planned on signing you up for the online school Kayin uses," Anali said. "I have a folder with information and classes offered for you to look at. If you don't like it let me know and we can try and find something else."

"I was wondering what I would do for school."

Anali smiled. "Do you have any other questions?"

"Where are we going first?"

"We're not exactly sure," Gavin answered. "It depends on when we get full custody of you."

"How long do you think it will take to save all the magical creatures?" I asked.

"It could take years," Gavin said. "There are magical creatures scattered all over the world. We might have to tour the world several times in order to save them all."

"Oh." How would I ever save so many creatures? What would my life be like once I fulfilled my destiny? How would I find them all? What if I left one behind? What if I failed?

Anali placed her warm hand on top of mine. "Don't worry. We'll take it one day at a time. There are a lot of people helping us, and most of the places where these beings live have a Child of Fire watching over them. We are all in this together."

"Does anyone know how I'm supposed to open the way into Akasha?"

Gavin ran a hand through his hair. "Not exactly. We know we need seven Children of Fire to open the portal. We have you, Kayin, Miu, and Sasha. We need to find three other Treasures to complete the ritual. Any Child of Fire can help, but the portal will be stronger if we can find Treasures. They have strong physical traits, like you and Kayin and full access to one type of gift."

"Shamash and Aya know what you need to do. I'm sure they will teach you," Anali reassured me.

"It's a lot to take in." I felt overwhelmed. "What about the Sons of Belial? Won't they be out there too?"

Gavin's jaw clenched. "They will, and we'll have to be careful to not draw attention to ourselves. But we will take precautions. Staying with the circus should help us hide."

"Okay." I went back to eating. I could do that. I don't even like attention.

"Try to look on the bright side," Anali said, sitting back in her chair. "You are going to travel all over the world, getting to see things most people never get a chance to, and having grand adventures. Also we have chocolate cake for dessert."

"Someday you will travel the world, you will meet interesting people, see the most beautiful things created by people and nature, and most of all you will learn more about yourself. Each new place you see, each ancient monument you touch, and each person you meet will change you. You'll grow as a person, expanding your mind and your heart. Even though change can be hard, embrace the journey."

Laughing, I shook my head. Anali reminded me of my mom in that moment. "True, those are all wonderful things, especially the cake."

*　　　*　　　*

Looking at the clock, I fought to keep myself from drumming my fingers against the desk. I ignored the droning lecture of my science teacher as I wondered what we would do over the weekend. Gavin said he wanted it to be a surprise and wouldn't tell me what he had planned. I was pretty sure I'd enjoy it, but I'm still against surprises as a general rule.

When the bell rang, I grabbed my backpack and headed for the main entrance. Gavin waved when he saw me. I hopped into the car.

"We have about an hour before class, do you want to get something to eat?" Gavin asked as he pulled into the street.

"Sure, something light."

"There's a smoothie place not far from the Circus Center will that work?" Gavin suggested.

"Yes, thanks."

We listened to the radio. Gavin hated commercials and changed the station when one came on. It made for an interesting blend of music during the drive.

"Sapphire, do you ever wear your hair down?" Gavin asked out of the blue. I was slowly getting used to his random questions.

Self-consciously I ran my hand across my tight French braid. "Not really. Sometimes, if I'm going somewhere special."

"Why?" Gavin asked

"It gets in the way, and attracts a lot of attention. I thought I was supposed to try to keep a low profile." I pulled my braid to the front. "See? Most of the red is hidden when I wear it this way."

"Sapphire, this is San Francisco, having some red streaks in your hair isn't going to attract attention."

"Oh." He had a point, but the kids at school seemed to notice me more now. No one else gave me a second glance. "I guess you have a point."

"We can get it cut if it's too long."

"Thanks, but I actually like it long. I prefer it to not get in the way. Most days having it in a braid or pony tail is easier."

Gavin's smiled sadly. "Your mom always kept her hair long."

"Oh." I never knew what to say when Gavin connected me with my mom. I felt like I was letting him down by not being more like her.

Gavin found a parking space and we went into the small store. I ordered a small mango smoothie, and Gavin chose a large banana berry blast with protein powder, anti-oxidants, and a shot of B vitamins.

"Your contacts came in today," Gavin said, in between big loud sips.

"What contacts?"

"The ones that will block people from seeing the fire in your eyes. I thought I mentioned them."

A vague memory of something like that floated around in my head. "Oh, yeah. I haven't had anyone say anything to me about seeing fire in my eyes."

"That's because you never look anyone in the eyes."

I gave him a quick glare through my bangs. "So do the contacts change the color of my eyes?"

"No, they have protection woven into them."

Okay, this sounded familiar but I couldn't remember what Kayin had told me. "What?"

Gavin rubbed his forehead, and brushed a lock of hair behind his ear. "It's hard to explain. It could be called a spell or a ritual. They set the contacts on a crystal table, surrounded by pieces of jewelry from Akasha, like the jewelry your mom left you." I nodded in understanding, and Gavin continued. "Then someone with the gift of dreaming, telepathy or empathy, but it could be any Child of Fire I'm told, asks Shamash and Aya to protect us. I guess they are specific, and keep what they want focused firmly in their mind, and the energy, gift, blessings, whatever, is transferred from the jewelry into the contacts."

Yep, more weirdness. "Does it only work with contacts?"

"No, they have asked for protection for lots of different things. Plus they ask for healing, strength, and blessings— general good stuff for the group. They have strict rules about not using the jewelry for selfish or harmful purposes."

Interesting. "Okay, should I put them in now?" I asked.

Gavin relaxed. "No, we'll wait until we get to the school. Are you ready to go?"

"Sure." I picked up my smoothie and headed for the door.

As soon as I walked into the Circus Center, Jane called to me.

"Hey, how was your week?" I asked.

Jane rolled her eyes and began stretching. "School sucked, every class had a test in it, and the drama level was out of sight. Lots of fights and yelling in the hallways. How are you?"

I shrugged. "Fine, busier than normal, but I survived. Did you do the exercises?"

Jane nodded, her orange spiked hair so stiff it didn't move. "Yes, every day, and I did dishes and used tea bags on my hands. My mom was super happy about me doing the dishes." Jane flexed a plump arm. "Look I think I can see a bit of muscle."

I couldn't help but admire Jane's determination. "I guess we'll see if a week is enough to make a difference."

"Okay, everyone who has done ten minutes of warm-up can start on the trapeze," Taliesin announced.

"He looks good today," Jane whispered to me as we headed to the trapeze.

I agreed; he wore a gray tee shirt and matching sweat pants. His white hair flowed softly around his face and over his shoulders. "He always looks like that."

"Yes, and he's yummy."

I laughed. "He's all yours."

"I don't think so," sneered one of the Perky Girls. "If he belongs to anyone, it's one of us. Why would he want either of you, anyway?"

All four of them looked us over with obvious distaste.

Normally I would walk away, but I could feel Jane's shame and desire to hide, and that pissed me off. "Well, I'm sure if Taliesin is into cheap and easy, he'll hand you his phone number any second." I pointedly looked at all of their exposed cleavage.

Jane choked on her laughter and tugged on my arm trying to pull me to the trapeze.

"If you've got it, flaunt it, right girls?" Perky number two cheered. The others agreed with her.

"Flaunting and advertising a fifty percent off sale are two different things," I retaliated. "Seriously, look at Taliesin. Everything he wears is designer brand, clean, and perfect. Why would he ever go for common, used goods?"

"Ladies," Taliesin said his voice cold. "Is there a reason no one is following my instructions?"

I could sense how uncomfortable Taliesin felt; he'd heard every word. I was glad I wasn't getting the full intensity of emotion from everyone.

"No," I answered before anyone else could. "We were discussing how refined your tastes are."

"Somehow I don't see how that will help you in this class. Get to work." Taliesin held out his hand and ushered us to the far trapeze. "Jane, I overheard you saying how much work you put into the exercises this week, I'd like to see if it has helped." Taliesin held out his hand and ushered us to the far trapeze.

"That was so awesome!" Jane whispered.

I could feel the angry glares in my back, and smirked. "Thank you, I'm rather happy right now."

"The bar, ladies," Taliesin said, re-directing us. He's such a spoilsport!

Jane went first. I could sense someone looking for me. Scanning the room, I found Gavin's eyes. He cocked his head to the side. I grinned a bright, unrepentant, evil grin. Gavin's laughter filled the converted warehouse.

At the end of class my hands ached, my muscles trembled, and I was happy. Jane and I chatted quietly while we stretched to cool down.

"Good job today," Taliesin said. "Jane, I think you improved the most this week. I hope you'll continue doing the daily exercises."

Jane blushed and nodded, looking away quickly.

"Next week, we'll work with silks, so make sure you have long pants and long sleeves to wear so you don't get fabric burns. Have a good week, and remember tea bags and washing dishes without gloves will help your sore hands."

The Perky Girls all jumped up, asking Taliesin questions. Jane shook her head, and we went to get our stuff.

Something was wrong, though I wasn't sure what. Looking around the room, I didn't see anything wrong. I went back to packing my stuff, but I felt uneasy.

"Hey, I'll see you next week. I need to go and wait for the bus," Jane said, bumping shoulders to get my attention.

"Sure, I'll see you next Friday."

Jane's brown eyes sparkled with happiness. "You were awesome. I'll be re-telling this afternoon for days!"

I was pretty awesome. "No big. They're insecure brats."

"You're still my hero," she cooed at me, fluttering her eyes.

"Go away," I laughed.

Once Jane left the building, the feeling of wrongness changed into something colder and focused. I looked around. The Perky Girls were leaving. They couldn't be the source, could they? I walked across the room toward the door.

"Sapphire?" Taliesin asked as I rushed by him.

"Not now," I said, not slowing down.

Bursting out of the door, I found Jane surrounded by the girls.

"Are we clear, Fatty? Stay away from Taliesin."

"Leave her alone!" I shouted moving closer.

"Oh, isn't this sweet, you're going to protect your girlfriend," sneered one of them.

Please, as if I'm stupid enough to be offended by being called gay. "Listen, losers, get away from Jane and go away."

"Or what?"

"Or I'll ban you from my school," Philip walked towards us, the school door banging shut behind him. "I won't have bullying here. This is a safe place, one where everyone can come to learn. Hatred makes a person ugly. You girls might want to think about that. Jane, Sapphire, inside now."

I grabbed Jane's hand and pulled her inside.

"Are you two okay?" Philip asked. His salt-and-pepper hair wasn't up in a Mohawk today but hung down to one side and over half his face as he looked down at us.

"Yes," Jane whispered.

"Yeah, thanks, I wasn't looking forward to beating the crap out of them." I held Jane's hand, not willing to let her go. She shook, and her eyes shone with unshed tears.

Philip chuckled. "I like your confidence. I have a book for you; I'll be right back." Philip walked up the stairs to his apartment.

Jane looked out the window. "There goes my bus."

"How are you going to get home now?"

"Sapphire, is everything okay?" Gavin asked.

"Aren't you teaching?" How big a scene did I cause?

"I finished. Do you need a ride home?" Gavin turned to Jane.

"Oh, no, I can wait for the next bus," Jane said shaking her head.

"Don't be silly, we're happy to help. Right, Gavin?" I asked my eyes pleading.

Gavin's face softened. "Of course. Should you call your mom or dad first to ask permission?"

"No, Mom's at work so she can't answer right now anyway," Jane said. Her eyes darted around the room. "Are you sure it's okay?"

"Of course. Let me grab my stuff, and we'll go," Gavin said, smiling.

Philip came back down the stairs. "Sorry it took so long. It was hiding."

The book had a worn dark blue cover with gold letters for the title: Common Mythical Creatures from Around the World. "Thanks, I haven't even thought about researching yet."

"Is that for school?" Jane asked looking over my shoulder.

"Yes, for an English project. Thanks Philip, I'll be careful with it."

Philip waved a hand. "It's for you."

"Thank you," I answered holding the book closer.

"You're welcome."

"Are you girls ready to go?" Gavin asked.

"Yes, we're coming. Bye, Philip, and thanks again."

I sat in the back of the car with Jane. Gavin called Anali to let her know we were going to get home a bit late.

"Your name is Sapphire? I thought it was Sara?" Jane asked.

"Yeah. Gavin is my uncle, he found me. My mom named me Sapphire, but no one knew that." I rolled my eyes. "I can't even begin to explain the crazy."

"Start at the beginning," Jane said and leaned against the gray seat while I told a short, non-magical version of what happened to me.

Jane looked at me in shock. "Are you kidding, that's like a fairy tale or something." Jane directed us to her house, getting more nervous the closer we got. I was confused, until we began driving into a poorer neighborhood.

"It's the apartment building up on the right," Jane said, clutching her bag.

"Okay." Gavin pulled next to the curb. "If it's okay with your mom, I'm happy to give you a ride home on Fridays after class."

Jane blushed. "I'll ask, and thank you for the ride."

"No problem," Gavin answered with a smile.

"Bye, Jane."

"Bye, Sapphire, I'll see you next week."

Gavin walked her to the front door of her building and came back. "Next time I'll walk her to her door. She seemed nervous like she didn't want me to go inside."

"She's embarrassed."

"About what?"

I rolled my eyes. Gavin was so clueless. "This is a very poor neighborhood, rent controlled, full of drug dealers and prostitutes."

"How do you know that?!" Gavin demanded.

"Shante lived in this building."

"Oh," Gavin said. "So how about telling me what all the fuss was about."

I could feel the evil grin creep over my face as I told him what happened.

Chapter Nineteen

"Life isn't fair. It's just fairer than death, that's all." ~William Goldman

Twisting my fingers together, I hummed in the appropriate places as Gavin talked about his class. I focused on my breath, keeping it slow and steady, trying to keep as calm as possible. I didn't think I would feel this nervous about a sleepover.

I jumped out of the car when we pulled into the driveway, grabbing my backpack. Gavin smiled. I could feel his happiness. I guess he mistook my nervousness for excitement. That would work.

Following Gavin up the stairs and through the front door, my mouth start to water. Anali had cooked dinner, and the rich aroma of Indian food filled the air.

"Anali, you didn't have to do all of this," I said, as my stomach rumbled in delight at all of the food laid out on the table. Anali asked me what I wanted for dinner, and I asked for a curry, a simple curry, but Anali cooked a feast! She made naan, samosas, lentil dal, two different curries, a pitcher of mango lassi, and fragrant rice.

Anali smiled and patted my shoulder. "I don't make a meal like this very often, and I enjoy cooking. It's a fun way to keep my connection to my family back in India. Anyway I don't teach on Fridays, so I had plenty of time."

"It looks wonderful, is there anything I can help with?" Gavin asked as he hung up his coat.

"No, thank you. It's all done. Go wash up, and we can eat." Anali kissed Gavin and headed back into the kitchen.

Gavin handed me the duffel bag he'd picked up from Hope House. "Why don't you put your stuff in your room; you can unpack later."

"Okay." I grabbed the bag and walked down the hallway to my mom's room. Gavin offered to make the room mine; pack things up, redecorate, and buy new sheets—anything I wanted, but I said no. I didn't see this as my room, or my house, at least not yet. I wasn't ready to make this place mine; it was too soon. I set my stuff down and went into the bathroom to wash my hands for dinner.

The soft, clean smell of ginger scented the bathroom. I couldn't believe it. I had told Anali about this bath stuff and how much I liked them. Melanie's sister had given me a set for Christmas and I had pouted about almost being out, but I never expected Anali to actually buy bath things for me. I looked around the cheery white and pale green tiled room finding several bars of soaps in different scents, new bottles of the ginger shampoo, conditioner, and body wash.

Maybe, just maybe, they really do care about me and want me here? Maybe having me live with them is more than needing the Jewel of the Phoenix King and Queen? Washing my hands, I allowed my thoughts to roam for a moment, about what it might be like to live with Gavin and Anali.

I continued daydreaming as I went to the table for dinner.

"Anali, this is even better than your mom's," Gavin moaned as he took another bite of the warm garlic naan.

"Thank you, sweetheart." Anali smiled softly.

"You've been to India?" I asked between bites of the delicious spicy curry. "Is that how you met?"

"Well," began Gavin, with a mischievous grin letting me know I was in for a story. "I was looking for antiques and art throughout India. I don't always go on buying trips, but something about this one called to me."

Anali looked at her husband with fond exasperation as the drama began to unfold.

"I heard of Anali's village from a friend of mine who deals in art. I planned to go at the end of my trip after checking the better-known markets." Gavin described his trip through India with wild hand gestures and outrageous theatrics all while he continued to eat. Somehow he never spilled anything nor talked with food in his mouth.

"The moment I set foot in Anali's village I knew my destiny was about to be revealed to me. Then I saw her, the most beautiful woman in the world. My heart pounded in my chest as I walked toward her."

Anali rolled her eyes.

"When our eyes met, magic, an instant connection so intense I rushed towards her. I barely caught her in time as she fainted from the power of our meeting. I knew she was the love of my life and I fought for her hand." Gavin finished with dramatic flair, kissing Anali's hand and looking deeply into her brown eyes.

Anali laughed. "I remember it a little bit differently."

"I know dear," Gavin replied, a little sadly patting her hand. "The power of our meeting was too much for you to handle."

"In fact," Anali continued, "I remember taking care of you for a week when you first came to my village. You had a fever and vomited for days."

Gavin sniffed indignantly. "I'm sure Sapphire won't believe such silly lies, and can easily tell the truth from fantasy."

"I also remember you begging my father on your knees for permission to marry me. The fear that you would stay in our village and harass him forever finally changed his mind."

"Your family loves me," Gavin gasped, hand pressed against his chest in pretend shock. He tried to keep a straight face, but his lips twitched as his smile tried to break free. I grinned into my mango lassi as they teased each other.

Cleaning up after dinner turned into a happy TV family moment. I did my best to accept it and not analyze it.

"What time do you need to wake up in the morning? I'm hoping to leave about nine," Anali asked.

"I want to do yoga in the morning, so seven," I said.

Gavin groaned. Anali playfully smacked him on the arm. "Sapphire, I want to help you with your gifts this weekend. I know a specific type of yoga that uses deep breathing along with the poses. I'd be happy to teach it to you." Her wide almond shaped eyes were soft and hopeful.

Yoga has been a refuge for me—something that I do alone. It helps me to center myself each day. Something I shared with my mom, according to her journal. I didn't want to share that time with someone else, but I did need help controlling my powers.

"Okay. How long will we need? Should I get up earlier?"

Anali tapped a frosty pink fingernail against her lips. "If you wake up at seven, when will you be ready to practice?"

"Within fifteen minutes, as long as there is a warm-up."

"Let's see, for the first time we'll practice for thirty minutes, so that will leave you almost an hour to get ready for your day. Is that enough?" Anali asked.

"More than enough." What did she think I need to do? I didn't wear make-up or do anything special with my hair.

Anali looked thoughtful. "How long do you normally practice yoga in the mornings?"

I shrugged. "About an hour."

"Maybe we'll play it by ear and see how you're feeling. The style of yoga my village practices is called Garuda yoga. It's designed to help descendants from the Phoenix King and Queen learn to use their gifts. It focuses on the breath and prana, or energy, during each pose."

"Are the poses very challenging?"

"Not any more than any other type of yoga. However, the goal of Garuda yoga is to get the energy of your gift flowing through your body. This way you can easily access your gifts, and they won't slip out of your control when they're not wanted. The intensity of the energy can feel overwhelming," Anali explained.

"If you're not used to the energy, it can feel like your nerves are overloaded. I decided I could easily do it, and after an hour-long session, I wound up shaking with hypersensitive nerves for three days. After that I took it slow," Gavin said with a soft grin.

"I pay attention to my breath while doing yoga, but I've never done yoga that focuses on breath," I said. Honestly, I'm not even sure what she means by yoga that focuses on the breath.

"We'll start with thirty minutes, then; I want you to enjoy it." Anali smiled encouragingly at me. "Come on, let's watch a movie."

"I get to pick," said Gavin, as he darted from the room. Soon I got sucked into an action-packed movie full of explosions and car crashes. Next time I would try to beat Gavin, so I could pick the movie.

"Do you want to watch another one?" Gavin asked, as the credits rolled across the huge flat screen TV.

"No, thanks. I need to get to bed if I want to get up on time." It was already after nine and I typically wasn't allowed to stay up this late.

"Well, good night then. I'll be ready by seven fifteen," Anali said, settling back onto the couch next to Gavin.

"Good night," Gavin said. "I hope you sleep well."

"Good night," I replied with a soft wave.

I got ready for bed, enjoying the peace and quiet. No one banged on my door, threw clothes around the room, or asked me for anything. I kept my eyes down as I settled into bed, not wanting to see the ghosts of my mother's childhood around the room. I pushed on the pillow a bit. I was used to having a new bed, and I didn't mind so much, but I wish I had brought my own pillow. I hadn't, because Gavin insisted on being able to provide me with everything I would need. The worst part about being in a new house and a new bed was the new pillow. Each one felt different, smelled different, and the fabric that covered them was different. I hated adjusting to a new pillow, and wasn't expecting to sleep well tonight at all.

Giving in, I laid down. My mom's pillow was so soft I sank into it. The cotton pillowcase felt smooth against my check and smelled faintly of the perfume on her dresser. Taking a deep breath I relaxed, and my empathy flared. I could feel her happiness. My mom had been happy, so very happy, the last time she'd slept in this bed. She felt safe and loved. The faint shadow of my mother's last night here crept over me covering me like a blanket as I slipped into sleep.

*   *   *

The next morning I met Anali in the living room at seven fifteen. She pushed the furniture out of the way, laid out yoga mats, and set down a wooden statue of a man with a beak-like nose and large wings extending skyward from his back. She lit a stick of incense, and smoke curled from the red tip.

Anali pulled back her shoulder-length dark brown hair with a headband, then started us with a breathing exercise. Once our breath synced, Anali moved us into simple poses. "Keep your breath slow and even, let your feet evenly take your weight, shoulder blades moving down your back and reach your fingertips away from each other."

I made the small adjustments to the pose, while keeping focus on my breath.

"Keeping your eyes open, focus on the center of your body and find the fire there. It may be a ball of fire, or a little flame, or several spots of fire. Don't worry about what it looks like, feel it."

It took a while for me to find what Anali wanted. A fire inside me, really? Was this supposed to be literal or did I need to imagine it? Each time I questioned what I should do, I lost my concentration. I took a deep breath and sank my thoughts into my belly, what I thought of as my core, and felt several warm spots, like small embers scattered about.

"I think I have it," I whispered.

"Perfect, try and keep your focus there while we move into another pose," Anali said, her voice soft, as if being loud would put the fires out.

I lost focus a few times but soon could move from one pose to another, while still keeping attention on the small fires. I wanted to close my eyes, knowing it would make focusing internally easier, but I kept them open as Anali asked.

"Sapphire, I want you to pull the fires together. Let them become one strong, clear flame," Anali instructed, as we stood with our palms together in mountain pose. "Once you have that let me know."

This was much easier. After a few poses, I could focus on the flame and how my body moved. The fire burned warm within my belly. It looked like my necklace, with an outer flame of vibrant red, orange, and yellows. The heart of the flame burned blue, green, indigo and violet. It filled me with a sense of safety and power. The necklace vibrated against my skin and warmed.

We held downward-facing dog, while she gave new instructions. "We're going to change our breathing for this last series of poses. We will use the five-count breath I taught you before, but add the fire element to it. When you inhale and count to five, I want you to expand the fire along your spine. Make it stay along your spine. Don't let the fire drift. Then hold the breath for a count of five. Exhale for a count of five. Pull all the fire back into your belly, and hold for another count of five before inhaling again. Count every time."

"Okay." Um, what?

"I'll keep the poses simple and moving slowly from one to the other. We'll hold each one for a few minutes so you will have time to focus on your breath and adjust your position."

I nodded, already counting and focusing on the movement of the fire up my spine. It felt hot, not uncomfortable, but hotter than when contained in my belly. I wasn't able to get the fire very high on the first try. In fact my second, third, and forth times didn't go much better. Keeping my eyes open, I held proud warrior, my legs apart and arms stretched away from each other. I began to count while pulling the Phoenix fire up my spine. With each number it rose, and when the fire reached my neck, the pendant vibrated. This time I managed to get the Phoenix fire to the top of my head and held it for a count of five. Then as I counted, I slowly pulled the fire back down to my belly. As the fire slid down my spine, little flames and sparks in my body joined the larger flame. With each breathing set I did, I felt more in control of my powers.

As we lay flat on the floor in relaxation pose, I pulled the fire into my belly. My breathing returned to normal. My body tingled with power. Around my neck, the pendent hummed with a life of its own, the connection to Akasha ready to open at any moment. Even as I felt protected by the connection to Akasha, a part of me hoped the necklace would grow cold again; I didn't like having this much power.

"You did very well, Sapphire," Anali said. "I recommend you do the breathing to the count of five and focusing your power up and down your spine each day. The more you practice, the quicker you'll be able to control your gifts."

I did feel more in control of my power, and that was the ultimate goal, even if the power made me uncomfortable.

"Let's get some juice, then we can get ready for the day." Anali sat up and began to roll up her mat.

I turned to ask her something and gasped. I could clearly see fire dancing in her brown eyes. She smiled in understanding. "Go look in the mirror. You'll need to wear your contacts today."

Racing to the bathroom mirror I looked and almost fainted at what I saw. Within my eyes, a flame moved, swaying as if dancing with the wind. I touched the mirror, unable to believe what I saw, but nothing changed. I had just got used to my eyes being a different color, and now this! I remembered seeing the flame weeks ago, a small flicker that vanished within seconds. This I couldn't hide on my own.

I opened the box of contacts and carefully put them in. My eyes watered a bit, then I felt nothing. Looking back into the mirror all I could see were my eyes, clear peridot green with gold flecks. Eyes that marked me as one of Shamash and Aya's children, as much as the fire hidden inside them.

Not yet ready to deal with anyone, I decided to get dressed for the day. I liked the idea of being able to take a shower after doing yoga. I couldn't shower in the mornings at the group home, there were too many of us who needed to get ready. Out of everything Gavin and Anali were offering me, privacy was the one thing I craved the most. It could become addictive.

Once I dressed, I went into the kitchen where Anali sat reading. I poured myself a glass of orange juice and sat down looking firmly at the table.

"There's nothing to be embarrassed about," Anali said softly. "You are allowed to take time to yourself. A lot is changing, and it is understandable that you will want and need time alone."

Feeling my cheeks heat up I took a sip of the cool orange juice. "Thank you."

"How are you feeling? Do you have any questions?"

I couldn't help but smile at the genuine concern in Anali's voice. "I feel good, maybe a little more sensitive." Anali nodded letting me know this was normal. "The necklace helps connect me to Akasha, whenever I want?"

"Yes." Anali reached up and touched the necklace she wore. "When we focus and activate our gifts, the jewelry responds and connects us to our beginnings—to Akasha and the Phoenix king and queen."

"Can it make the gifts stronger?"

"Yes, much stronger. Be careful about opening up the connection, especially if you're angry. You could pull huge amounts of energy into yourself and possibly get hurt."

I reached up to unclasp the pendant. Hello, shouldn't this have been mentioned earlier? "Is it safe? Should I give the necklace to you?"

"No, it's part of your legacy. The connection to Akasha will help protect you and help keep your powers in control. You need to know that it is possible for you to pull in enough energy to overload your nervous system, just be careful." Anali pulled my hands down, gripping them tightly in her own. "I can't imagine how insane this all must seem to you. I've grown up knowing these things. When I turned fifteen and could suddenly feel what others were feeling, I felt overwhelmed, scared, and sometimes angry that I wouldn't be like everyone else."

Looking away I clutched her hands tightly. I didn't want to let her go, but I couldn't face the honesty in her eyes. Accepting who I am and sharing that with others is two different things.

"It's okay, take your time, and honor how you feel. The sooner you can find peace with what your life is and who you are, the sooner you can feel happy and in control." Anali chuckled darkly. "Well, as in control as any of us ever are in life."

"*Life isn't fair, not to anybody. No one has real control over what happens to them, you can only control your actions and reactions. Right now I am full of self-righteous anger at how unfair life is. I want to cry, scream, throw things, and crawl into bed and hide. And I might do some of those. But that's not all I'll do. I will also enjoy your smile, and make breakfast, and watch the sunset, and run a little further, and hide a bit longer. While I can't control the actions of others I can control my own, and I choose to live every day I have left, and embrace who I am. I hope when life is unfair and overwhelming, you, too, will embrace who you are and live. After you've had a good pout.*"

Chapter Twenty

Cartazonon stepped out of his jet and smiled. He'd always loved the fog; it was so easy to hide in. His sleek black 1969 Mustang waited for him. Even after all these years, horses were his favorite. Sliding onto the black leather seat, he started the engine and let her warm up while he cast out his energy and found a small pocket of Akashic energy.

Cartazonon wasn't sure if he felt the source of the power spike he'd noticed before Christmas, but what he felt was the only thing within fifty miles that seemed big enough to be worth his time. As he drove towards the energy, his phone rang.

"Yes."

"I was successful, Khan," Lee said.

"Excellent, I'm in San Francisco right now," said Cartazonon.

"We'll arrive soon. Your newest assistant is very efficient."

He laughed. "I agree. I haven't thought of bringing anyone over in two hundred years, but she might be a keeper."

Lee sighed, and Cartazonon couldn't help but grin. Lee was the first general Cartazonon ever made his, and Lee got moody every time he'd brought another into their fold. Like a child disliking the newborn baby in the family. Of course he'd never tell Lee that. The last time they'd fought, Lee almost cut Cartazonon's arm off.

"I'm glad you found something. If I don't replenish soon, the protections might start to falter. The last time that happened several valuable plans were stolen and someone tried to embezzle money. Whatever happened to him?"

"I believe the Gorgons played with him for a few months before getting bored, and then the troll made a stew," Lee explained.

"Oh, good. I'm glad he didn't go to waste. I have to focus now; I'll talk to you later."

"Of course, Khan. I'll get the mermaid ready as soon as we get to the office."

Cartazonon turned off the phone and split his attention between the insane San Francisco traffic and the call of power.

Chapter Twenty-One

"There are times when fear is good. It must keep its watchful place at the heart's controls." ~Aeschylus

Gavin stepped into the kitchen, his hair still dripping from his shower. "Anali, will you please call Kayin and let him know we'll be about thirty minutes late. Sapphire, you're all packed for Monterey, right?"

I smiled at Gavin, pushing aside this creepy, worried, nervous feeling which seemed to grow worse with every passing minute. He told me over breakfast where we were going, yet again showing me that he listened and cared about what I wanted. Gavin planned to take us to the Monterey Bay Aquarium. "Yes, I'm all packed. I didn't realize Kayin was going with us."

"Phillip wanted some time to himself, and we haven't seen Kayin in a while. Is that okay?" Gavin asked.

"Yes, of course. I like Kayin."

"Kayin says, 'Of course Gavin is running late.' He was prepared and is in the middle of a movie," Anali said, snapping her phone shut.

"Hey, I'm not always late! Anyway I wanted to make you two breakfast."

"It was good," I said. Gavin cooked us cheese and tomato omelets with toast and fresh orange juice.

"Thank you, Sapphire," Gavin said, delighted at the compliment. "See I had to make breakfast for my niece. It was important."

"Yes, honey, and if you got up earlier, we wouldn't be rushing right now." Anali smiled and shooed him out of the room with her hands.

Gavin laughed. "All right I'm going! It shouldn't take me long to get everything together."

Squirming, I tried to get comfortable as I rubbed my hands over my arms hoping to get rid of the creepy feeling. Maybe it was from the energy increase during yoga? I'd ask Anali once we got in the car. I didn't want to slow Gavin down.

I sat on the very edge of the white couch, afraid to get it dirty, staring out the window watching cars go by. My stomach began to feel queasy, and my legs twitched with the desire to run. The itching sensation tormented my skin and I scratched trying to get rid of it.

"Sapphire!" Anali grabbed my hands. "What have you done?"

I looked down at my arms and slid to the floor. Long scratches covered my skin, several were bleeding. "I don't know. I just wanted to get rid of this slimy itching feeling. It's creepy and unnatural and my legs keep twitching. I want to run. Everything in me is screaming to get away to run because something is coming. I feel sick." I wanted to stop the tears from falling, but I couldn't. I felt out of control and fought to not push Anali away and run as fast as I could.

"Sapphire, is it getting worse?" Gavin asked his voice tight.

"Yes, can't you feel it? It's this sticky, slick, evil thing coming closer and closer. It's searching for us, for anything like us."

"Gavin, you don't think..." Anali's eyes grew wide.

"Fear is a warning, not a feeling. Fear is there to guide you, to help you know which path to choose. If you meet someone and your skin itches and you know something isn't right, then leave. Don't worry about being polite or kind, trust yourself and go. You might feel fear in your tummy, a weird flutter or queasy feeling; this is another warning that something is wrong. You may have to run, or hide, or fight, but always trust what you are feeling, my darling. Fear used as a warning will protect you."

"We have to run," I said, my mom's words echoing in my head. "It's a walk-in isn't it? Why didn't I recognize it sooner?"

"We don't have time. Sapphire, listen, we don't have time." Gavin gave my shoulders a little shake. "You're feeling the Sons of Belial, not just a single walk-in. I've never felt anything this strong. If there are a bunch of walk-ins out there we will not be able to get away. We have to become very, very small."

Anali rubbed my cheek to get my attention. "I know this is confusing, but you can do this. During yoga we worked on expanding your energy, now we need you to make it as small as possible." I nodded to Anali. I can do that. I can hide. I can be small.

"There is an artifact downstairs that gives off the same kind of energy we do. If we can make ourselves small enough, whoever it is will get it and leave." Gavin arranged himself crossed legged on the floor. "All right, close your eyes and pull your energy, light, power, gifts in. Make them go into a small little ball at the bottom of your stomach. Bundle them up so no light escapes."

I can do this. Closing my eyes, I began to pull in my energy. It didn't want to come in after all the work I had done to help it flow properly. I tried not to panic, but the slick itchy feeling became so strong that the air was thick with it. I whimpered.

"It's okay," Anali's voice took on a calm soothing tone. "Find the fire within you. The one you made at the base of your spine."

I listened to Anali's sweet voice and tried to block everything else out. "Okay."

"Perfect. Now you need to make the fire smaller. Find one small piece of wood and pull all the flames into it. The wood can get hot, let it turn into a dark red ember, but pull all the flame into it."

"Okay," I said. Turning my focus inward, I pulled each ribbon of fire into a small piece of wood, something that would fit into the palm of my hand. The wood began to glow and my body shook as I forced all of the fire down. "I have it," I whispered.

"Good job," I could hear the relief in Anali's voice. "Now, bury it under the ashes. This will keep it warm for later when it is safe to let the fire burn again."

As I began to bury the ember, I realized I couldn't feel whatever it was as strongly, and the necklace became cold against my skin. I buried everything, all connection, all power. Wait, wouldn't I need my empathy to stay safe? Isn't that what warned me of the dark presence? I didn't have time to figure it out. Quickly, I piled up more ash and packed it tightly around the rest of the ember.

"Now what?" I asked, gasping.

"We wait," Gavin growled.

My skin became clammy, and the air sticky with the evil presence. It felt like only one person to me. I wondered if this was how a rabbit felt, curled into the farthest corner of its den, hoping the fox wouldn't smell it and try to dig it out.

I jumped, squealing as Gavin took my hand. Instinctively, I reached for Anali's, and together we sat, hoping evil would pass us by.

It felt like forever, but finally the massive weight of the evil presence lifted.

"Whatever it was has left," Anali said.

I collapsed to the floor as soon as the weight lifted. I could feel hands checking my temperature and heard kind words. Gavin and Anali flew through the house grabbing what we needed.

I lay against the cool wood floor not sure what was going on. My body shook with the effort of containing my Phoenix gifts. My heart ached for whatever went against its own nature to become something so wrong that it was now an abomination.

Gavin kissed my forehead and scooped me up into his arms, carrying me down the stairs and into the car.

"Mr. Lindsey, the store manager, said a man bought the artifact in the back of the shop. He'll have the security camera footage set aside for us when we get back," Anali said opening the car door.

"Thank goodness. Will he warn everyone to expect walk-ins?" Gavin asked, as he set me in the car and pulled a blanket around me. As soon as the seat belt clicked into place I stopped fighting and fell asleep.

My eyes fluttered a bit when the car stopped and Kayin got in.

"What happened?" he asked.

I sighed at the sound of his voice. The car jostled a bit as he shut the trunk and climbed in. Kayin scooted close, and I shifted to lay my head on his shoulder.

"Are you okay, Little Sister?" I nodded and took in a deep breath. Kayin smelled of cinnamon and cedar; it was a warm, happy scent.

Gavin and Anali discussing what happened, but I didn't listen. Sleep pulled me down again. I fell into a nightmare.

The city glowed beneath him. Pressing his hands against the cold glass he looked down over the skyscrapers, buildings, houses, and cars. Closing his eyes he could feel everyone who belonged to him. He reigned over thousands of employees all over the world, but there were a few who belonged to him— some who stayed with him for centuries. Memories of looking down at other kingdoms overlapped the bright city lights: a Victorian manor on top of a hill, a castle made of stone, a Japanese pagoda, huts made of mud with thatched roofs.

He ruled over them all, surrounded them with armies, and increased the food, power, and money of his people. Even now he was seen as a ruthless businessman, a modern warlord, and his people prospered. He took care of all of them. He demanded perfection, the absolute best, no matter what your position. In return he offered a good salary, health plans, retirement packages, and job security. In the past he offered livestock, land, and women.

Turning away from the window, he reached up and touched the clouded crystal point at his neck; once part of a necklace Shamash gave to a beloved grandchild. The connection he created with his people and property wavered slightly. Smiling he moved the bookcase and walked through the hidden door into an altar room. In the center sat an oval table with symbols and pathways carved into its black marble top. His finger traced over the ancient Sumerian spell carved into it. A spider web of silver began at the center of the table and curved out to a bowl, composed of gems and metal from Akasha, which sat at one end. He placed his necklace in the bowl, and nodded to Lee, his first general, the one he stole from Genghis Khan.

"I captured a mermaid, Khan," Lee said, his upper arm bigger than her delicate waist. Her blue- green hair trailed on the ground. Lee placed her in the center of the table. Together they secured the straps which would hold her down. Her lavender eyes begged for her life, mercy, help, even a kind word.

"It will all be over soon. I'll work as quickly as I can. Your life and magic are very precious to me. Thank you for your gift." He smoothed a long pale finger over her cheek.

The time for magical creatures had come to an end. Like all life on earth they were tools, resources to be used for the greater good, protection for his people. The mermaid struggled against the restraints. It didn't matter, nothing could change what was about to happen.

He used to drink the blood of magical beings to gain power, but he could extract only a fraction of the magic they contained. Then he found a manuscript which led to the building of this table and ritual. It took him almost a century to buy, steal, and find enough artifacts from Akasha to make the table. Placing his hands on the bowl, he let his energy slide through the metal, down the pathways and pool under the mermaid. She screamed, agony clear in her voice. Chanting, he demanded that her life force, her energy, her powers come into the bowl. Bit by bit, he pulled it out of her. She screamed and fought, but she did not distract him.

When he extracted everything, he pulled his energy back in. Lee began undoing the straps and would take the lifeless body away. His large dark hands made quick work of the thick leather. He took what he needed, but others in the group could use what was left of her. Lee knew what to do with the body; something was always hungry.

His necklace glowed with her power. A silvery blue-green light, like moonlight on the Caribbean Sea, glowed from within the clear quartz. He took the necklace out of the bowl and put it on. He was filled with stolen power, energy, and life. Closing his eyes he reached out to his people, sending *power into them. Once again he felt connected to all that belong to him. His empire and people were protected.*

"Do you need anything else, Khan?" Lee asked, shifting the body in his huge arms.

Cartazonon froze for a moment. "Something, or someone is here." He turned, and his black eyes stared right at me.

I sat up screaming. Kayin knelt behind me rubbing my back. Gavin knelt in front of me his face filled with worry. "I'm going to be sick."

Kayin pushed me out of the car while Gavin scooted to the side and pulled my hair out of the way. Thankfully, it didn't last long. I hate throwing up. As I sat back, Anali swooped in with a damp cloth and wiped my face and mouth. The sweet jasmine scent of her perfume filled my nose and took away the smell of vomit.

"Are you okay?" Gavin asked. I shook my head. I was definitely not okay. I wiped at my face, angry that I was crying again. I had never cried this much in my entire life, not even when my mother left me.

Gavin scooped me up and held me as I sobbed. I cried because of the dream, of what I was expected to do, and of all the changes in my life. I hated this. I didn't want to be the Jewel and go against this monster to save magical creatures. I didn't want to cry every other day. I didn't want any of these powers or gifts or whatever they were called. I wanted everything to go away!

Once my sobs gave way to snuffles and hiccups, Gavin sat back a bit. Anali handed me a bottle of water. "Here, honey, can you sip this for me, please?"

My hand shook as I took the bottle. The water felt wonderful against my sore throat, and I needed to stop myself from guzzling it down. Absently, I heard cars driving nearby. Gavin must have pulled off the freeway.

"Can you tell us what your dream was about?" Gavin asked softly.

"The leader of the Sons of Belial pulled the life out of a mermaid into a crystal. He needed to replenish his strength so he could protect his empire. He killed her." My voice shook, but I managed to not cry.

"We knew he was doing something like that, but weren't sure exactly what it was. Can you remember exactly what he did?"

I shook my head. I didn't want to remember. I could still feel his eyes as he looked at me. "No, I'm sorry. It's already fading."

Gavin pulled me closer. "There is nothing to be sorry for, dreams fade quickly. Do you remember anything else?"

"I don't remember his name, but he seemed familiar to me somehow." I shook my head. "I can't remember any more. I can't even see his face."

"Don't worry about it," Gavin said patting my shoulder. "Do you think you can ride in the car a bit longer? We're just outside of Monterey."

"Sure, I can do that." I tried to give an encouraging smile. Judging by Gavin's expression I failed.

Climbing back into the car I was happy to see Kayin. "Come here, Little Sister."

I snapped my seatbelt on and snuggled under his arm. Kayin leaned down and rubbed his face on the top of my head, his wide flat nose tickled softly. "Are you all right?"

"I think so."

"Anali said we would order room service for lunch, and this afternoon we'll go to the aquarium, if you feel well enough."

"That sounds good. Have you been to an aquarium before?"

"No, I've been to a few zoos, and those had fish in them, but nothing this big. I'm looking forward to it. I grew up in grasslands; I find the ocean fascinating."

"It's one of my favorite places. I'm surprised Gavin remembered that I mentioned it," I confessed softly.

Kayin chuckled. "Little Sister, you underestimate his love for you."

Blushing I settled in, hoping my queasy stomach would make it to the hotel. As soon as possible I needed to take a shower. I could still feel his evil on my skin.

*   *   *

Drying my hair, I walked into the living room of the hotel suite. The room looked like something from a movie. Every window looked out over the ocean.

"Lunch is here," Gavin said. "Are you feeling better?"

"Much." The shower washed away the last memory of the dream.

"I wasn't sure what you wanted, so I got you tomato soup and grilled cheese. My mom always made it for Gabriella and me whenever we had a bad day. I thought maybe...," Gavin trailed off with a shrug.

"Thank you, it's perfect. Some comfort foods never change. I think every place I've ever lived in gives us tomato soup and grilled cheese when we needed to feel better." Sitting down I took off the lid and inhaled deeply. "Wow this smells wonderful."

"I've never eaten it before," Kayin said, removing his own lid.

"What did your mom make when you didn't feel good?" I took a bite of the creamy soup and it soothed my stomach. This was the only magic I needed.

"I didn't grow up with food that was easy to get. My mom made what was in season, and what the hunters caught," Kayin answered. "She would always try to have groundnuts for groundnut stew. It's my favorite."

"Groundnuts are peanuts," Anali explained uncovering her salad.

"Is it sweet?" Peanut stew, I'd never heard of that before.

Kayin shook his head. "No, it's spicy."

"Have you tasted Thai peanut sauce?" Gavin asked, twirling his fork in his pasta primavera.

"Oh yes, once. I liked it," I replied and then bit into the grilled cheese. Oh, my. It tasted so good. The crispy sourdough bread crunched around the gooey melted cheese. I dipped it into the tomato soup, which hadn't come from a can, and was full of fresh tomatoes and flecks of fresh herbs. This was the fanciest grilled cheese sandwich and tomato soup I'd ever had.

"I can make it for you, if you'd like," Kayin offered.

"That would be wonderful, Big Brother. I love trying new foods. I feel like I always eat the same ten things, over and over."

"Has it been difficult being a vegetarian while living in group homes?" Anali asked.

"No, most of the time I eat side dishes. A few people tried to push the meat thing, but it doesn't appeal to me."

"A lot of Children of Fire don't care for meat," Gavin said around a noodle.

"Why?"

"Phoenixes don't eat meat." Gavin shrugged. "Some believe that those who don't enjoy eating meat are more powerful or more connected to Shamash and Aya, but there's never been any proof of that."

So some of my behaviors are because I'm part Phoenix? "Philip gave me a book about magical creatures. I haven't read it yet. I didn't think it would tell me about me."

"Common Mythical Creatures from Around the World, I have one of those," Kayin said. "It's full of the most common magical creatures: faeries, gnomes, pixies, fire salamanders, nymphs and a bunch of others. I don't remember Phoenixes, though."

"Phillip has written other books. I think Royal Magical Creatures has a chapter on Phoenixes." Gavin looked to Anali for confirmation.

"Yes, there is a lot of very specific information on Phoenixes in that one."

"I didn't know he wrote the book; he didn't say anything." Now I felt bad for not having read it right away.

"Philip is a great researcher. We'll keep in contact with him as we travel," Gavin said. "He's written a bunch of books."

"Cool." I went back to my lunch. I would start reading the book he gave me when I got home.

*   *   *

Kayin ran down the sidewalk pulling me along, urging me to go faster. He was so cute; I'd never seen him this excited before.

"Gavin and Anali are way behind us, Big Brother, and they're the ones who are paying for us to get in. Maybe we should slow down?" I laughed as I tried to keep up without breaking into a run.

"I bet the entrance has something interesting to look at," Kayin insisted and tugged on my hand.

The outside of the aquarium didn't look very exciting, but I knew what waited inside, and I watched Kayin's face as we walked through the door.

His round eyes were huge as he took in the bits he could see from the ticket counter. "Look," he whispered, as if the huge model of a humpback whale hanging from the ceiling would vanish if it knew we were watching it. "Sapphire, it's beautiful."

"Wait, it gets even more amazing," I said, squeezing his hand. Kayin's joy and excitement bubbled through me, and soon both of us were bouncing on the balls of our feet waiting for Gavin and Anali to show up.

"All right, you two, where should we go first?" Gavin asked and handed us a map.

"There's too much to see," Kayin sighed, after looking the map over.

"I'm sure we'll get to see everything," I said.

"Maybe we should start here and see everything on the bottom floor, then move onto the top floor," Anali suggested.

"Okay, let's go," Kayin said as he tugged me to the first big observation window.

Kayin reached out to touch a round window and startled when his fingers didn't find anything. Leaning forward he stretched his arm into the recessed window, until he found the glass of the half sphere. "Oh," he gasped as he looked up into the water.

Kayin was mesmerized by a sunfish, when a shark suddenly swam over him. No matter how he tells the story, Kayin squealed a very unmanly squeal as he fell out of the window trying to get away from the shark.

"That was so amazing," he breathed, as we laughed. "Come on, Sapphire, you can protect me from the sharks."

"Sure, but don't you think the glass will do that?" I asked, lying back into the window with him.

"Have you ever seen anything as beautiful as this?" he asked ignoring my question.

Looking up into the water, I watched as huge ocean fish swam around us, their scales glittering as they moved through the water with enviable grace. "You're right, this is the most beautiful thing I've ever seen."

The smile Kayin gave me came in a close second.

As we walked through the aquarium, I felt something new. Carefully, I filtered the other people's emotions as Shamash and Aya taught me. It took a bit longer as my empathy wasn't picking up much beyond Kayin's joy anyway.

Standing in front of the seahorse display I felt it again--a soft hum of thought and emotion, a simple contented awareness. All I knew was that the hum wasn't human. Following Kayin, I tried to figure out what I felt.

"Look up," Gavin said. "They're stunning."

Silver sardines swam above us in a circle. Then I noticed happiness, like a little giggle, and three of the sardines suddenly changed direction. The rest of the fish exploded, frantic to swim the new way.

"Those little troublemakers," Gavin laughed. "Did you see those three mess up how the rest were swimming?"

I gripped Kayin's hand a bit tighter. Did I feel the fish? I didn't know I could feel animal emotions, too. They felt different, less complicated, and maybe shared?

"I changed my mind. This is the most beautiful thing I've ever seen," Kayin said, as we stopped in front of a new window.

The reverence in Kayin's voice brought me out of my thoughts. In front of me were dozens of jellyfish. Their translucent bodies pulsed as they moved through the water. The hum of contentment felt stronger here, but even more simple than the sardines.

It was odd sensing a creature without a brain. They didn't feel or think anything. They simply were in the moment, and that was all. Walking through the aquarium, I found most of the creatures felt that way, totally in the moment without thought, and most without emotions, just a sense of being.

I smiled at a particularly agitated octopus. Its fight-or-flight instincts were in high gear as a young child tapped on the glass of its home.

Placing my hand on the glass I attempted to send out a feeling of safety. My gift warmed and slowly moved from my lower belly to my hand. Confused as to why it moved so sluggishly, I waited as calmly as possible. I didn't want to send the poor creature fearful emotions.

Once the octopus calmed down, I stepped back onto someone's foot! "Oh, I'm so sorry."

"It's okay. They are very fascinating creatures, aren't they?" an old man said, his face alight with amusement.

"Yes, very." Quickly, I found Anali, Gavin and Kayin. So far no one had managed to sneak up on me since I changed, I could always feel everyone. As we walked up the stairs, I tried to discover why my powers were so weak.

"Let's see what's outside." Anali moved toward the door.

"Sure." Gavin held open the door for us. The first tank we saw slowly drained of water. Small creatures clung to the rocks, and seaweeds drooped as the water vanished. We heard a dull rushing sound, then a wave crashed into the tank. Jumping back I bumped into Gavin, and he laughed.

Kayin and Anali were both fascinated with the wave and began to read the information plaques about tidal pools. I sat down on a bench, using the moment to focus inward. Quickly, I checked the two main points of power. My necklace lay against my throat, cool and still——-the connection to Akasha gone! Checking deep in my belly I looked for the fire Anali helped me create. What I found instead was an ash-gray rock.

I was still all closed up from this morning! I remembered making my powers as small as possible so we couldn't be seen, and I guess I never released them. Mentally, I poked at the rock, it steamed a bit like a fissure in a volcano. My empathy began leaking out. Good, I wanted to feel the Sons of Belial if they came around again.

Well, now what? I didn't want to open up my powers here. What if I couldn't control them right away? What if people noticed? What if one of the Sons of Belial felt me? No, I couldn't let them go right now. I wasn't in any pain, so why not leave them alone? The Phoenix powers could stay hidden for a while.

"Sapphire, are you okay?" Gavin asked.

"I'm great." Smiling, I stood up. "Where to next?"

"The otters." Gavin pointed the way and I followed, happy that for today no weird out-of-this-world stuff had happened.

Chapter Twenty-Two

"Meditation brings wisdom; lack of meditation leaves ignorance.
Know well what leads you forward and what holds you back,
and choose the path that leads to wisdom." ~Buddha

I woke with the sun falling across my face. Looking around the room, I tried to remember where I was. My chest tightened and my stomach got queasy until I remembered I'd slept in the hotel suite Gavin and Anali rented for us in Monterey. I wonder how I'd gotten into bed. I remember putting on pajamas and then going to the living room to watch a movie, something with a car chase in it, I think.

I grabbed my stuff and went into the bathroom. First thing I ran saline solution into my eyes to soften the dried-out contacts so I could remove them. I will never fall asleep with my contacts in again, I vowed to my reflection in the mirror.

That's when I noticed I was shut down even more than yesterday. I felt no power humming under my skin, saw no flames in my eyes. I knew other people were in the hotel with me, but I couldn't feel any of them. For a moment I mourned the loss of the Phoenix gifts, but then I smiled. I felt normal. Only my own repressed emotions tugged at my heart. I didn't feel drawn to anyone. I didn't feel overwhelmed. I felt like me again, in a way I hadn't since my birthday.

I guess I did a good job of stuffing my power down. Reaching deep inside, I felt it, the warm spark of my inheritance and destiny. I thought about uncovering the ember and allowing the power to flow through me again, but I didn't want this power. I didn't want to catch fire, or feel other people's emotions, or experience the history of ancient vases. I knew Gavin wanted me as his niece, and I was pretty sure he would keep me even if the powers went away. I could always get them back later, right?

My stomach muscles clenched as I shoved the fire deeper down, ignoring its subtle call to me. Today, I would be me again. I put on my blue jeans and dark blue tee shirt with a silver orchid on the front, a gift from Gavin; he'd bought it for me at the conservatory.

"How are you feeling?" Kayin asked, as I stepped out of the bedroom.

"Good, and you?"

"Good, can I use your bathroom? Gavin's in the other one."

"Sure, I'm done."

"I'll be out in a minute. Gavin and Anali are already up." He shut the bathroom door.

With a smile I went out into the living room.

"Good morning," Anali said cheerfully.

"Good morning. You look nice," I said.

"Thank you," she replied, running her hand over the lavender silk blouse. "I had a pitcher of orange juice sent up if you want some. As soon as Gavin is out of the shower, we'll go and get breakfast."

"Thanks." After getting a tall glass of juice, I walked over to the big glass windows. The sun sparkled off the ocean and otters swam around the patches of floating kelp. "Kayin's up, he got into the shower before I left."

"Oh, Kayin's very quick, he'll be done long before Gavin's ready," Anali replied with a soft smile.

"Morning," Kayin greeted us, as he walked into the room. His skin glowed ebony against the white cotton sweater he wore. "I assume we're waiting on Gavin?"

"Yes, I'll go hurry him along," Anali offered.

"Let me put on my shoes, and we'll take off," Gavin said several minutes later. Sitting down he pulled on dark blue Converse high-tops.

"Cool shoes."

"Yeah," Gavin said, his face about to burst with his smile. "We can get you some if you want."

I thought for a moment watching him lace them up. "Okay."

"Great. We'll get them as soon as possible."

This was the first time I agreed to anything Gavin offered to buy me. I felt embarrassed by his excitement. "I don't need them."

Gavin snorted. "Not everything is about need. Now let's get breakfast—I'm starving!"

After breakfast we walked down to the beach. Yanking our shoes off, Kayin and I quickly rolled up the legs of our pants. We were eager to get into the water despite the cool winter temperatures.

"Before you two run off I would like Sapphire to practice creating fire. It's important that you learn to control tapping into other people's gifts. There is no one else out here this morning and being near water, we'll all be safe," Gavin said, as he set down a pile of driftwood. "Sit here, and if anyone sees you, they'll think you're making a fire."

Kayin walked over to Gavin, but I wasn't sure I wanted to do this. I didn't want to get caught by the Sons of Belial, or be on fire.

Dragging my feet in the sand, I walked over then plopped down next to Kayin.

"We'll give you two some privacy. Neither of us can help with this," Anali said, grabbing Gavin's arm and dragging him down the beach. Gavin looked like he wanted to stay, but he let Anali drag him away.

"How about this—I'll go through what I focus on to pull up fire slowly step by step, and we'll see if it works for you," Kayin offered.

"Okay," I agreed.

"First close your eyes and take a few deep breaths." Kayin's accented voice was deep and warm.

"Now feel the energy, the power of the Phoenix gifts flowing through you," Kayin guided. I continued to breathe, but I felt nothing.

"Now hold up a hand and imagine small flames dancing on the tips of your fingers." Okay, I could imagine that, I thought, while holding up my left hand.

"I want you to push your gift out onto the tips of your fingers, making the flames real." Well, this wasn't something I could fake. Reaching out I couldn't feel Kayin's power at all, so I turned my focus down into my belly. I found the hard sphere of ash. Only warm tendrils of smoke came through. Quickly, I grabbed one and pushed it through my body and out the tips of my fingers. Slowly I opened my eyes, grateful when I saw tiny dancing flames.

"I did it!"

Kayin opened his eyes and leaned forward to get a good look at the tiny flames. "Yes, you did. Now, pull out more power and make them bigger."

Was he kidding? Make them bigger; the bad guys could feel us then. I didn't say anything, and instead pretended to try.

"I can't," I said after a few minutes. I felt bad about lying to Kayin, but I needed to keep us all safe.

"Don't worry about it. You'll get the hang of it. We'll try another way," Kayin assured me.

With a sigh I settled in to try again.

Thirty minutes later nothing changed, all I created was a small pale flame. I knew I was letting Kayin down, but I couldn't let any more energy go. I even tried once, really tried, to let go and pull up more energy, but nothing more came to me.

Kayin's brow wrinkled in confusion. He'd been very patient, but I could tell he felt frustrated. "I don't understand."

"What's wrong?" Gavin asked, startling us both.

"Sapphire is having trouble creating a strong flame," Kayin said.

Gavin cocked his head to the side, his pale green eyes wide with concern. "Sapphire, what's wrong? Maybe we need to take you to a healer?"

"I'm fine." Standing up I brushed the sand off my butt.

"No, you're not fine, you should be having trouble with too much power not a lack of power," Gavin insisted. "We need to figure out what is going on."

"Look, yesterday I felt the most evil thing ever, and in order to protect myself and you, I had to shut down and hide all my power. Now you want me to open back up, to be sensed by the evil lurking out there waiting to steal our energy and our life? I don't think so!" I stormed off down the beach before anyone could respond.

I wiped at the tears running down my face. I hated how much I cried lately, it was another change beyond my control. Finding a group of rocks, I climbed up and stared out into the blue-gray sea.

A few minutes later, the others joined me and we spent an hour searching through tidal pools, poking small sea creatures and pointedly not talking about my outburst.

When we were headed home, Gavin cleared his throat. "I need to talk to the both of you before we get back to San Francisco. I called Philip, and he said after yesterday morning, there were a few walk-ins felt around town, but nothing since then. We think it will be safe, but if you feel the slick, creepy feeling get somewhere safe, and remember to wear your contacts at all times."

"What exactly are walk-ins? I know we dealt with one before, but you never told us what they are." I couldn't avoid them if I didn't know what they were.

"Walk-ins are spirits loyal to the Sons of Belial. They 'walk-in' or possess people to do whatever task they've been sent to do," Anali answered.

"Can they enter anyone?" Kayin asked, reaching over and clasping my hand.

Gavin ran a hand through his hair, making it even messier than the wind off the ocean. "No, they can only enter people who owe the Sons of Belial and their leader a favor."

"Do a lot of people owe him favors?"

"Well," Anali answered slowly, "we don't know. Most of them are basically good people who fell on hard times and someone helped them out. The person gets what they need and only has to promise the Sons of Belial a favor at some point. Then when there is a need, a walk-in takes the person over for a while."

"What if we're seen?" I asked. Kayin squeezed my hand. He seemed as nervous as I was about this threat.

"As long as you have your contacts in walk-ins can't use their magic to track you. They can sense you if they get close enough and will come after you, but once you get away, they can't find you again easily. Walk-ins don't like the sunlight, it's harder for them to keep control of the person in the light, so if it's daytime, get outside. They have to see the fire within your eyes to use their powers to hunt you down." Anali tried to make her voice comforting while making sure we understood the seriousness of the situation.

The memory of my mother's scared face as she said good-bye to me flashed in my mind. "Like they hunted my mother and father?"

Gavin's eyes met mine in the rear view mirror. "Yes, like they hunted your mother and father."

*   *   *

I stumbled, scraping my knees as I fell to the frozen ground. Fat tears dripped down my face and part of me wanted to lie down and give up. A fierce howl echoed through the forest, and I forced myself up on shaking legs. I was too young to try and find food on my own, let alone during winter. The injustice of it ate at my heart.

The sky was washed with color when I finally found some food, a bush with a few dried and frozen berries on it, and dried grasses hidden underneath. It wouldn't taste very good, but I grabbed the precious food and began to chew. Others tried to approach as they, too, were near starving. My mother would have welcomed them; I kicked rocks making them go away.

Suddenly I was running through the city holding my mother's hand. My body itched with the nearness of walk-ins. We ran as fast as we could. I fell, and my mom stopped, kneeling down to help me up. Hands descended on us grabbing, tearing us apart. I screamed and cried for her, but themonsters only laughed. Their huge shadowy bodies carried us effortlessly to their master.

Black hair framed a pale face, black eyes glowed softly in the dungeon. My mom kept fighting but was strapped to a table. The man pulled the energy out of her, filling his bowl, until her life and power threatened to run over the sides. I screamed and fought trying to get to my mom as she gasped for breath.

He stared at me. "I'll find you." His handsome face twisted into a predatory grin.

Gasping, I sat up looking around my bedroom until I realized I was safe in Hope House. I forced myself to calm down, and noticed I was alone in the room. I got up and opened the door. Someone had trashed the living room and the couch was torn into pieces. Books were thrown everywhere. Melanie, Myra, Rhonda, and Caitlin all lay in a pile, their bodies limp and unmoving. I looked for her, but I could not see Shante.

"I told you I would find you." He grinned, baring his bright, sharp, white teeth.

Lee stood behind him. His round face was pockmarked, and his flat nose was crooked from being broken. Shante hung limply from Lee's hand around her neck. He flung her down, and then he stood in front of me.

"You will come with us now," he said, as Lee grabbed my neck.

My eyes flew open as I gasped for breath, my hand clawing at my neck. I was drenched in sweat and shaking. I rubbed my hands over my face, trying to calm down. Thankfully, I hadn't screamed out loud, so no one woke up.

For the past three nights I'd been having nightmares. I was twitchy during the day, and worried the Sons of Belial would find me while at school, or at Hope House. I didn't want anyone else getting hurt because of me.

The only way to keep everyone safe was to move in with Gavin and Anali. At least they knew the risk, and they knew what to look out for. Turning to the clock I groaned, five-thirty in the morning. There was no way I could go back to sleep now.

I got up and begun my routine early. I lay on my yoga mat warming up, and for a moment, I thought about doing the breathing and energy exercises Anali taught me. I dismissed the idea. I was still enjoying feeling like myself, and being free of the so-called gifts. Anyway, having my Phoenix powers flowing normally would only make me easier to track. I couldn't risk jeopardizing Shante and the others.

By the time I finished with yoga, I knew what I needed to do. I would call Five and tell him I was ready to move in with Gavin and Anali. The only thing holding us back in the transition process was my reluctance. If I said I was ready, then they would speed things along, and everyone at Hope House would be safe. I wasn't ready to move in with Gavin and Anali; I would have liked to have had more time. Right now we were still doing fun things. I didn't have any idea what they expected from me or what the rules of the house were. I guess I would have to figure them out as I went along.

After I got ready for school and finished with my chores, I called Five. I was surprised when he answered, as it was only a little after eight in the morning.

"Hi it's Sapph...um Sara." Using two different names was becoming annoying.

"Hey, is everything okay?"

My fingers twisted the phone cord. I had to do this. I needed to keep everyone safe. "Yeah, I'm fine. I want to go and live with my Uncle Gavin."

"Are you sure?" Five asked. "You don't know them very well yet. You can have some more time."

"Yes, I'm sure. They're nice, and I like having my own room." Which was the truth.

"Okay. I'll talk to my supervisor and get things rolling," Five spoke slowly as if he wasn't sure he should go along with what I wanted.

"Do you know how long it will take?"

"Well, everything has come back fine. We are very happy with Gavin having custody of you. Now that you want to live with him, I'd bet two days. So on Friday when he picks you up for the weekend you can stay. Will that work?" I could hear Five flipping through papers.

I closed my eyes, trying to hold back the tears. "Friday will be great, thanks."

"I'll call you later and let you know, okay?"

"Sure, Five, thanks." I needed to do this It was the best thing for everyone.

Hanging up the phone, I sighed. It was done. I would move to a new home on Friday, with a new life, and new rules. The plans I made were beyond my reach now. I had no idea what I could hope for in my new world. What future would I have?

"You're leaving me?"

Oh, god, no. "Shante," I whispered, my heart clenching as she stared at me. Her brown eyes were full of hurt.

"You promised you would always be here. That you would never leave me." Her hands made little fists.

"I'm sorry you found out this way. I told you my uncle was trying to get custody of me. You knew I was going to leave eventually," I tried to explain.

"But you called, you chose! You don't want to be here anymore! I hate you!" Shante ran off to her room, slamming the door.

"What's going on?" Melanie looked around the room confused, her hair mussed.

"Shante overheard me asking Five if I could go ahead and move in with Gavin and Anali." I pressed a hand against my stomach hoping I wouldn't throw up.

"Oh dear." Melanie gave me a quick hug. "I'll talk to her, you need to head to school. You have to take care of yourself, Sara, never feel bad about that."

I nodded and left for school. The problem was I wasn't doing this for me, I was doing it for them, and they would never know.

I managed to stay focused during school despite the constant guilt and nervousness bubbling away in my stomach. I usually found the bus ride relaxing, but today I couldn't relax, and it had nothing to do with the homeless man and his alligator puppet arguing politics in the seat behind me. Well, maybe a little.

Getting off the bus, I smiled fondly at the sight of the café I stopped in all those months ago. I had plenty of time before class, so I decided to stop in and get a chai latte, no major caffeine for me.

Sipping on the spicy hot drink, I almost ran into someone as I walked out the glass door. One would think that being able to see through the door would help prevent such a thing.

"Sorry."

"No problem, Sara baby, you can run into me any time."

"Carlos!" I couldn't help myself. I threw my arm around him and gave him a hug. "How are you? What are you doing?"

He grinned, but it looked dimmer than the last time I saw him. Carlos' brownish-red skin was dirty, pale, and tight across his cheekbones, his brown eyes dull and sad. "I'm hanging in there. Hey, can I bum a cup of coffee off of you?"

"Of course." I went back into the café and bought him a coffee and two sandwiches.

"You still going to that school?"

"Yes, but I have a few minutes before class. Do you want to sit with me for a bit?"

"Sure, baby. I'll make sure no one bothers you." I grinned at Carlos' flirting. It was good to see him again.

"Are you still living with your mom?"

"Yeah. I thought about calling my caseworker, but I worry about what will become of my mom if I do."

"I know, but Carlos, you look horrible. You need some food, a shower, clean clothes..."

"Don't overdo the flattery," Carlos grumbled good-naturedly. "But what about family?"

I looked at Carlos, was he serious? "Carlos, your basic needs aren't being met. What could being in a family possibly give you that it's worth giving that up? I understand the freedom is appealing, but seriously this can't be worth it."

"What about love, affection, knowing you belong?" Carlos rolled his coffee cup between his hands.

"Are those more important than food, shelter, and being safe? And didn't you get that at Hope House? Maybe not from family, but from me and the staff?" I asked. "Look at you, Carlos. Is this how a mother expresses her love? What about your other family, why aren't they helping you if family is so important?"

Carlos looked like I slapped him in the face.

"I'm sorry. I shouldn't have said those things to you." I looked away and took a sip of my chai.

"They're true, though, aren't they?" Carlos asked, without needing or wanting an answer. He ran his fingers through his dirty black hair. "I bet you have wanted to say that to me many times. Why now? What's going on?"

I thought about blowing Carlos off or lying, but as I had been brutally honest about his situation, it seemed only fair to be as honest about mine. "I have an uncle, he found me over Christmas, and it looks like I'll move in with him this weekend."

"Wow, that's big."

"Yeah. I know I'll be taken care of, food, bed, clothes all that stuff. And he and his wife are nice, but I don't know what to do about the family thing. Gavin, my uncle, feels a connection to me that I don't feel or understand. I feel like it's a foster placement, like they are strangers. I don't know what to do."

Carlos squeezed my hand. "We lived together for two years, I saw some of us become special to you, and others you never bothered with at all. You created your own family in a way." Carlos lifted up the bag of food. "I mean, look—you take care of me, and encourage me to make the right choices. You want me to be safe and happy. That is what family members do for each other right?"

"Yeah I guess so," I mumbled. "But they're adults."

Carlos nodded. "True, it might take longer, and you'll have to let them take care of you too, but eventually I'm sure you'll figure out how to be a family."

I wasn't convinced, but I felt better. "Thanks. Is there any way I could get you to call your caseworker?"

Carlos gave me a sad smile. "Yeah, all right. I'm tired of sleeping on the street when mom works. And it would be nice to have regular meals again."

"Come on, I'm sure they'll let me borrow the phone." I pulled on Carlos' arm so he'd follow me to the Circus Center.

Thirty minutes later a caseworker drove up and took Carlos away. I gave Carlos Gavin's cell phone number along with Melanie's cell phone and email addresses so he could get ahold of me, even if it was unlikely I'd hear from him again. The caseworker said she would take him to the hospital first before placing him, so I didn't even know where he was going. I rubbed my eyes forcing back tears. Carlos would be okay and that's more important than me seeing him again.

"Are you okay?" Taliesin asked.

"Oh yeah, I'm fine." I tried going for sarcastic but I sounded tired and hollow.

"Are you sure? You look like crap." Oh, that's nice.

"I haven't been sleeping well," I said.

Taliesin straightened his sleeves. "Sorry, anything I can do?"

I stopped for a moment and looked into Taliesin's ice blue eyes. He seemed sincere. "No, I don't think so, but thanks anyway."

Taliesin carelessly shrugged a shoulder. "No problem. Have fun in class."

I watched him walk over to Gavin and whisper furiously. Gavin began frantically gesturing and running his hands through his hair. Taliesin's posture showed calm with a touch of defensiveness. Whatever Taliesin was telling him, Gavin didn't like it at all. I wasn't sure what he was upset about, but I bet I would hear all about it at dinner.

Going through the standard warm-up and stretches helped my mind begin to calm down, and I was able to fully focus on juggling.

"Meditation can take many forms. For some it is sitting quietly and allowing their mind to become blank and open. For others meditation happens with painting, knitting, cooking, or physical exercise. I know several parents who make time to meditate while cleaning. The point is not to focus deeply on a problem or issue, but to allow your worrying and 'what ifs' to shut down and leave so things can be clearer. You do not gain from meditation, but instead lose what is holding you back from following your heart."

I always found it easier to clear my mind through physical activity and today was no exception. I could feel my fear and worry leave as I tossed the juggling balls Kayin made me from one hand to another. As my focus narrowed to keeping the balls in the air, I could hear my heart and knew leaving Hope House was the right choice.

"You're doing well today," Kayin said. He'd been oddly distant today.

"Thanks. How are you doing?" I asked, amazed that I didn't lose my focus.

"I'm good. Maybe we can talk after class?"

That didn't sound good. "Sure. I have to wait a bit before Gavin and Anali are ready to go anyway."

Kayin smiled and tugged gently on my braid before checking on another student.

*   *   *

"I'm sorry about the beach," Kayin said as soon as class ended.

What was he talking about? "What about it, you didn't do anything wrong."

"I wasn't sure if you were upset that I told Gavin about your powers." Kayin shrugged, worry etched into his dark face.

Smiling, I scooted closer and bumped his arm until he moved it around my shoulder. "I'm not used to having privacy. I'm not upset and honestly I didn't expect anything different to happen."

Kayin held me close. "I was worried Little Sister, I don't like the idea of you being upset with me."

I wrapped my arms around Kayin's waist and relaxed, feeling safe for the first time in days. "Don't worry, Big Brother, you're stuck with me now."

Kayin held me tightly. "I'm very glad. I need to go warm-up for my class now, will you be all right?"

"I'm fine. I'm going to do homework while I wait."

I managed to get my homework done and all my stuff packed up before Gavin and Anali were ready to go. So I watched while they got their things together. Gavin tried to gather his stuff with one hand, and use his phone with the other. He always checked his messages right after class ended. I knew the minute Gavin got the message from Five. He froze, his whole body went rigid, even his eyes stopped moving. Then he began to smile. I'd never seen a smile start slowly and grow before, but there it was growing so big and bright Gavin's cheeks must ache. Turning, Gavin found Anali, laughing as he picked her up and swung her around.

When Gavin set her down, Anali's smile shone as bright as his. They both looked lighter, like a great worry or stress was suddenly gone.

Gavin looked around the school, his red hair whipping around his face. Once he saw me, he bounded over, and before I knew it I was scooped up into a crushing hug.

"You're coming home this Friday! David called and everything is all set, and this Friday you're coming home!"

Gavin set me down. I could see tears gathering in his peridot green eyes. Guilt began to sweep through me, chilling me to the bone. This meant so much to Gavin, being able to bring me home. I wish I felt as excited.

Quickly, I plastered a smile on my face letting Gavin's overflowing happiness fuel it.

"Come on, let's go to dinner and celebrate," he said.

I laughed softly. We planned on going to dinner anyway. "I'm ready."

Gavin danced all the way to the car. I felt a little nervous about him driving while so excited, but it wound up being fine.

Over a meal of tempura vegetables and yakisoba noodles, Gavin began making plans for Friday. It didn't seem to me that we needed big plans. All I needed to know was what time to have everything packed.

"Should we rent a moving truck?" Gavin asked.

"No, all I have are my clothes, and a box of stuff under my bed," I answered, picturing all of my things in my mind. "Oh, and some summer clothes in storage."

Gavin cocked his head to the side. "That's all? You've been gone nine years."

"There isn't a lot of space in group homes. We only keep what we need," I said.

"Well, we'll have to change that. Once you're unpacked we'll see what you need and go shopping."

Anali patted her husband on the arm. "Gavin, dear, we will be traveling with the circus soon, and we won't have a lot of space to store things."

"Well I suppose that is true," Gavin admitted, after pouting for a moment. "Okay we'll figure out what you need while we travel. But I will get you a few small things just for fun."

Gavin's happiness felt warm and soft against my skin, and in complete contrast to the cold sick guilt I felt. I wish I was happy about moving in with them. I wish I felt something other than fear about what was to come. I did my best to nod, hum, and smile in the right places as Gavin chatted away, changing topics quickly in his excitement.

Anali gave me worried looks and patted my hand. I knew I couldn't fool her, but I did hope she would respect my privacy, what little of it I possessed, and not ask why I felt so unhappy.

* * *

"Did David call you?" Gavin asked Melanie. He'd walked me to the door, as usual.

Melanie smiled, a sweet, indulgent smile. "Yes, he did. I know Sara has class Friday night, so tomorrow we'll have a little going away party for her. She doesn't have much to pack. We should be able to get everything done by Friday morning."

"I have a box in storage," I said.

"We can get it tomorrow," Melanie said.

"Great." Gavin clapped his hands together in excitement. "I don't work Friday afternoons until four. Would it be all right if I stopped by about two on Friday to collect her things?"

"That will work out fine. I'll have the paperwork ready for when you get here," Melanie said.

I could tell Melanie was happy for me, yet sad I was leaving. I felt the same way. Maybe we could watch a movie together Thursday night, one last time.

* * *

Friday night I stood in my mom's old room unpacking my few belongings. It didn't take long. After unpacking my box from storage, the shelves and closet weren't even half full.

I didn't pack up any of my mom's things; there weren't many. A few clothes hung in the closet, and a handful of books were on the shelves. It was obvious that while my mom liked staying here and loved her room, it wasn't her permanent home.

My collection of jeans and dark tee shirts looked odd hanging in my mom's lavender closet. I thought about taking Gavin up on his offer to paint the room, but it still didn't feel right.

I could hear Gavin and Anali in the kitchen. The steady hum of their voices sounded warm and comforting. I knew I should go out and sit with them, but instead I took the scrapbook Melanie gave me down and sat on the bed.

Melanie filled it with pictures from birthday parties, trips, Christmases, and other events. I didn't realize there were so many pictures of me. In the back people wrote me little notes wishing me well, or drew pictures. Shante took a whole page to draw the two of us holding hands. She wrote "best fiends foever" beneath the drawing. I smiled at her mistakes. I'm sure Melanie tried to help her, but Shante was stubborn. I was very glad she forgave me before I left.

"Sapphire, dinner," Anali called. Putting the scrapbook back into my old backpack, I forced a smile and went out to have dinner with my new family.

Chapter Twenty-Three

"Love is the flower you've got to let grow." ~ John Lennon

Crossing my arms, I glared at the salesman. Gavin ate it up, hanging on every word and being sold on the most expensive toys the salesman could come up with. Personally, I questioned whether they were the best.

Thirty minutes ago Gavin brought me into this electronics store, because I "needed" a laptop, and a smart phone. The man helping us took one look at Gavin and smiled. When Gavin said he wanted only the best and items that could work all over the world, the man practically drooled.

"Gavin is going to take you shopping today," Anali warned me after we practiced yoga that morning. "I'm leaving for Harbin Hot Springs in an hour. I'm going to a yoga retreat this weekend. Gavin had planned to take you shopping anyway, but now that you're living here, he's going to go crazy."

"But I don't need anything."

"I know you don't see it that way, but remember that Gavin grew up never wanting for anything. He feels guilty that he wasn't here for you for the past nine years. He wants to make it up to you. He wants to make sure you have everything you could ever want, or need." I started to protest, but Anali held up her hand, her brown eyes begging me to understand. "Please, Sapphire, let your uncle do this for you. Yes, we will be traveling soon, and we won't have room for tons of stuff, but let Gavin buy things for you now, let him spoil you. Gavin is a very loving man, and he expresses that love in many different ways. One of those ways is by taking care of the people he loves."

"Love isn't something you win, it's something you must grow and nurture every day. Love can grow and become strong enough to handle anything life throws at you, or it can wither and die due to neglect. Some gestures will be grand: huge life-changing moments. Most are going to be small simple things: remembering to say thank you, kisses goodnight, making a favorite meal, or a single flower picked on the way home. This is true for all kinds of love. Remember, my darling, to nurture the love you have in your life. Never take love for granted."

"Okay, I'll go shopping with him, and let him buy things for me. But I won't let him go crazy!" My stomach fluttered with excitement and nervousness.

Anali hugged me. I froze for a moment at the joyful spontaneous act, then softened and hugged her back. "Thank you, Sapphire, it will mean so much to him. Don't forget he wants to get you things you truly want. Speak up if you have an opinion."

I stood in the store, watching Gavin and the smarmy salesman go over the merits of the top three most expensive computers. Knowing nothing about pixels, megabytes, and hard drives, I was bored out of my mind. Turning, I randomly began looking through the DVDs.

"Sapphire, I think this is the one," Gavin said, his face lit up with happiness, as the salesman held up a laptop.

"Shiny," I said trying to soak up a little of Gavin's enthusiasm.

"What color do you want?" Gavin asked pointing to the screen of the laptop.

Walking closer, I could see there were pictures of six laptops all the same except for the color. I wanted the silver until I saw a dark black-purple. "That one, please."

"Oh, a very nice choice," The man cooed. Yuck!

"What color do you think Kayin would like?"

"Oh, you're getting two?" The man trembled in excitement. Yuck again!

"The lime-green one," Bright colors looked wonderful against his dark skin, and Kayin always wore bright colors.

"Okay," Gavin said. "Now we need cameras and cell phones."

"No, problem, in fact we have several of each that are proprietary to these machines, and come in the same colors." The man ushered us to where the cameras and phones were on display. "You must be very excited to get all these cutting-edge items."

I wanted to glare at the salesman, but remembering Anali's and my mom's words, I held it in. "My uncle is very generous; I don't know that I need all of this."

"It's not always about need," Gavin chanted. I had a feeling I'd hear that a lot today.

"You'll also want covers for everything, to protect them from being scratched and broken."

Taking a breath I took a chance, my stomach fluttering nervously. "Gavin, could we go to Japan Town to get mine?"

"Sure," Gavin beamed. "Maybe I should let Kayin pick out his own covers too? I'll ask him on Monday when I see him."

"Okay. Well, let's go ring everything up, and I'll activate the cell phones," the salesman said, his plastic smile never fading.

This time I hunted through the music selection while Gavin filled out paperwork and paid.

"Why don't you pick out some CDs?" Gavin suggested while waiting for what's-his-name to set up the phones.

"No, thanks, with all the traveling we're going to do I don't need to have the extra stuff."

"You can always buy music and movies on iTunes," the salesman suggested. "That way you can download directly onto her computer and iPhone without the clutter. We sell gift cards for it." He added pointing to the rack next to the register.

Gavin grinned at me and plucked two cards from the rack. I wasn't sure that I needed a hundred dollars' worth of music, but kept my mouth shut. I couldn't imagine being able to spend money as freely as Gavin did. Even Melanie, who loves to shop, was careful not to go overboard, and stayed within her budget.

"Let's go," Gavin called, holding out a bag to me. "We'll go to Japan Town first, then have lunch and see what else we need."

"It sounds like fun," I answered honestly. I loved anime and the cute gothic Japanese clothes and accessories.

*   *   *

"What?" I asked, turning so I could glare at Gavin as he drove. He'd been like this all through lunch. I tried to ignore it, but I couldn't take any more. His amusement bubbled against my skin while his curiosity poked at my brain.

"Hello Kitty?" he chuckled, crooking an eyebrow.

"And what exactly is wrong with Hello Kitty?" I mean, it's not as if I choose the bright pink Hello Kitty accessories. I got Badtz-Maru, a seriously fierce penguin.

"Nothing, I just wasn't expecting it. The tee shirt with sword wielding geisha yes, but Hello Kitty is so cute."

I rolled my eyes, Gavin didn't understand.

"I'm glad you had fun. I could tell the computer store wasn't your thing," Gavin said, turning into a parking garage.

I frowned. I didn't want Gavin to think I wasn't grateful. Uncomfortable, yes, but I still felt grateful for everything. "I like what you bought for me; thank you for everything."

Gavin smiled softly. "You've already thanked me. Don't worry, Sapphire, I'm glad you had fun and actually chose some things."

Blushing, I thought of the large bags in the trunk filled with clothes. I had bought a few pairs of jeans, some socks, and a bunch of tops—all with Japanese patterns and prints on them. I could have easily bought more, but I couldn't bring myself to ask Gavin to spend that much money on me.

"Where are we going now?" I asked, following Gavin out of the parking garage.

"To another store," Gavin said as we stepped out into Fashion Square. I wrinkled my nose. This was definitely not my part of town.

"More clothes? Gavin, I have like ten outfits now, that's more than enough," I said as he dragged me into a fancy department store.

"Sapphire, first of all, ten casual outfits isn't close to enough and second, we need some nice clothes, plus at least one fancy outfit in case we go to a party or something," Gavin explained as he took the elevator to the second floor, where teen clothes were sold.

I glared at his back. I didn't feel comfortable in here. Everyone dressed like they stepped out of a fashion magazine, and the amount of jewelry being flashed around was crazy.

"My clothes are fine," I pouted.

As soon as we stepped off the escalator a saleswoman pounced. What was it about Gavin that made these people know they could reel him in?

"Good afternoon, how can I help you?" she asked, her voice like syrup.

"My niece needs new clothes. I want her to have several casual outfits, shoes, at least one dress, and any underthings she might need, and Converse. We still haven't gotten those for you."

I hadn't seen Gavin like this. At the other store he acted calm and relaxed with the salesman, but here he was demanding, not rude but all "you-will-serve-me."

The saleswoman didn't seem to mind at all. "Of course, sir, right this way. We have some very cute skirts that are all the rage this season."

Skirts! Oh, I didn't wear skirts! Slowing down, I let them get ahead of me. Where were the jeans? Walking over to the racks, I began looking through them, hoping if I found a few pairs and some shirts I could save myself from having to wear skirts.

Flipping through the jeans, I grabbed a pair that looked nice, velvety black denim with purple flowers embroidered on the leg. Turing over the tag, I gasped. Were they kidding? There had to be sale rack around here somewhere. Looking around, I kept an eye out for Gavin. I didn't know where the saleslady dragged him.

I headed to the back of the store, still looking for the sales rack.

"Sapphire!" Gavin called. Oops, he sounded upset.

"I'm right here," I said cheerfully, hoping it would help.

His bright red hair filled my vision as he held me tight. "I couldn't find you; don't you ever walk off from me again."

"Okay." What was I, a little kid?

"I mean it." Gavin pulled back. His normally warm eyes were hard like green glass, and his hands tightened painfully on my shoulders. "I need to know where you are. Anything could happen to you. I can't believe I lost you again so easily."

Not good. Adults never touched me when they were angry; well-trained staff knew better. "I'm sorry, I'll stay with you," I whispered.

Closing his eyes, Gavin reined in his feelings. "Let's finish shopping. Did you find anything you liked?"

Showing him the black jeans, I wondered what punishment I would get once we got home.

*   *   *

"Do you need any help putting this away?" Gavin said as he dumped a load of bags on my bed.

"No, thank you," I said, shaking my head.

"Okay, I'll go check messages and make a snack. Then maybe we can watch a movie?"

"Sure that sounds good," I said.

Gavin frowned.

I acted very agreeable since he'd gotten mad at me. Standard technique to defuse angry adults: be extra good and agreeable until punishment is decided. It tends to lessen the consequences.

Scowling, I looked at the bed covered in bags. I had no idea where I was going to put everything. Oh, well, one thing at a time. I picked up the garment bag and hung it in the back of the closet, hoping I would never have to wear the fancy black dress inside. It was simple, no frills or flowers on it, but still a dress. One by one, I emptied the bags and sorted all the clothes into piles to be washed. New clothes were itchy, smelled weird, and other people touched them. Shoes went into the closet - I now owned two pairs of Converse, one classic black and a pair with green and purple checks, both high tops, of course. Gavin insisted on dressier shoes, and while I unpacked the black Mary Jane flats, the high heels that went with the dress were shoved into the back of the closet still in the box.

"Sapphire, I need to go downstairs for a minute. Mr. Lindsey has a package for me."

"Okay." Once I sorted all the clothes, I unpacked the computer and phone and plugged them in to charge.

It didn't take long to finish plugging everything in and throw away all the trash. I put my clothes in the washer off the kitchen when Gavin came back into the apartment holding a large box.

"All done?" he asked with a groan as he slipped through the doorway.

"Yes, everything is unpacked, charging, trash thrown away, and I'm going to start my laundry now," I answered.

"Wow, you're good." Gavin kicked the door shut. "When you're done, will you come into the TV room I have something I want to show you."

"Sure, no problem. Oh, did you ever see the video from when that nasty man came?" I forgot all about him going into the antique shop until right now.

"Yes, but unfortunately we didn't get a good look at his face, and even Mr. Lindsey can't remember what he looked like," Gavin explained as he went down the hall.

"Weird, I'll be there in a minute." Gavin didn't seem mad. Maybe I wasn't in trouble.

On the coffee table lay four large photo albums, a plate of peanut butter and jelly sandwiches, and two glasses of milk.

"I asked my house manager back in New York to pack up and send me several family photo albums. I realized that you hadn't gotten to see any pictures of your mom yet," Gavin said, running his hand through his hair nervously.

My hands shook. "Thank you. I hadn't thought about it, but it would be nice to know what my parents looked like," I said, sitting down near him. No one ever hands over a photo album. They always show it to you, which means sitting close so you can both see it.

"These are my parents, your grandparents," Gavin began, opening the first album. It looked like a fairy-tale wedding. My grandmother wore a long white gown with flowers and lace, and my grandfather stood proudly next to her in a tuxedo.

"They were lovely," I whispered.

"They were. I lost them a few years after your mom disappeared. They died in a plane crash. They loved you so much."

Page by page I got to see the life I should have lived. I got to see my mom and Gavin as children, opening Christmas gifts, acting in school plays, and going on family vacations.

"When your mom was five, she decided to join the swim team and said she wanted to play the violin. She did both all through school and still swam and played the last time I saw her." Gavin smiled fondly at a picture of a little girl holding up a third place ribbon, her straight brown hair cut into a neat bob.

"I, on the other hand, took different classes all the time. When I was in college a friend talked me into taking a stilt-walking class, and I fell in love with the circus."

School photos followed the others. Both Gavin and my mom had gone to a private school, at least that's what I guessed based on the navy blue blazers they wore in every school photo.

"I was twelve in this photo and your mom fifteen. We were on vacation in Greece. You look a lot like her."

Gently, I reached out and ran my finger over the picture. Both of them were smiling brightly, their arms wrapped around each other, in front of a clear blue ocean and ancient white pillars. My mom's hair was black then, and Gavin's hair brown.

"Our family has bad luck with pictures," I said pointing to a picture of white Greek columns with two white people-shaped blobs in the corner. A bunch of photos contained over-exposed people in them.

"Well, that is one of the protections the jewelry offers us," Gavin explained. "The Akashic energy makes magical beings that want to hurt us forget who we are and messes with cameras."

"Unless they see the fire in your eyes." I shivered thinking of the walk-ins.

"Yes, true." Gavin paused. "If you want to have your picture taken you need to take all of your jewelry off. Sometimes people would forget or don't realize that there is a photo being taken."

I touch the cool pendant laying at the base of my throat. Would it protect me right now while my power lay cold and hidden in my belly? I shoved the thoughts down and turned my focus back to the photo album.

Before my eyes, they grew up, going from awkward teens to beautiful young adults. Their hair, skin, and eyes changed as mine had.

"This was taken right before your mom went off to college," Gavin said. They looked perfect, wearing expensive tasteful clothing, and smiling as if nothing bad ever touched them. Would my life have been like that? Would I have younger siblings? Would we have taken pictures together?

I wanted to cry for what I lost. "It's a wonderful picture."

"There's more," Gavin said, his voice raspy.

Opening up the last album I saw my grandparents, Gavin, and my mom sitting around a Christmas tree, and joining them sat a young man with blond hair, golden eyes and pearl white skin. He leaned close to my mom, his hand clasping one of hers.

"Oh, my god," I choked out. So far I held in the tears that threatened at the very first picture, but seeing my dad with my mom was too much. A dizzy rush of déjà vu brought flashes of memories. Licking an ice cream cone with my dad. Playing with the big zipper of Grandfather's sweater. Baking cookies with Mom and Grandma. I knew these people. I had memories, happy memories, of my family.

"The moment Keagan walked in the door, I knew they would be together forever. They loved each other so much." Gavin wrapped an arm around my shoulders. At first I sat stiffly, then gave in and leaned against my uncle while tears fell down my checks.

They held a fancy engagement party; my mom wore an ice blue evening gown and my dad a soft gray suit. Next, their wedding photos. They looked a lot like my grandparents' pictures, a fairy-tale wedding with a huge cake, lacy white dress, and so much happiness. Everyone in that room looked so happy for them.

"These are your paternal grandparents," Gavin said pointing to a lovely couple with snow-white hair. "They were older when they had Keagan, and passed away a year after you were born." They had kind smiles and I wondered what kind of grandparents they would have been. They looked like movie grandparents, all soft and cuddly. The kind of grandparents who would read you stories, bake cookies, and teach you how to fish.

After a few more pages came a photo of my mom in bed looking tired but happy, and holding a newborn baby. My father sat behind her with tears in his eyes. My hand shook as I reached out to touch the picture. I turned into Gavin's shoulder and cried.

"I miss them," Gavin said, as he held me. "They were my best friends. They loved you so much. I wish you could remember them."

I nodded. "I'm starting to remember them. Thank you."

Gavin gave me a framed portrait of me with my parents. I placed it next to my bed that night where I could see it. My head ached from crying so much. Sticking out from under the bed was a bit of the backpack my mom left with me. The scrapbook from Melanie, the jewelry from Akasha, and my mom's journal were safely tucked inside.

I sat on the floor with a thump. I hadn't shared the journal with Gavin. I said I would, but I couldn't part with it, but now, after seeing the photo albums I needed to.

Reaching into the flowered bag, I pulled out the most important thing I owned and cradled the worn journal to my chest. I walked back into the family room where Gavin sat staring at the TV without seeing it.

"Gavin, I wanted to show you..." I held out the journal.

He turned off the TV, then took it from me and opened the cover.

"She started this when she became pregnant with you. She panicked one day, afraid she would be a horrible mom and forget to teach you all sorts of important things," Gavin whispered as he read the first page. "Thank you. I wasn't sure if you would ever feel comfortable sharing it with me."

"I didn't mean to keep it from you, it's just I've never shared it with anyone before," I said, twisting the hem of my pajama sleeve.

"Do you want to sit with me while I read it? Then I can give it right back."

I wanted to say yes, but I didn't like being that weak. "No, that's okay, I trust you."

"I will take very good care of it," Gavin said. "If you change your mind I'll be right here."

"Thanks, goodnight."

"Goodnight, sweetheart."

I finally drifted off to sleep when my door creaked open. Gavin placed my mom's journal on the nightstand next to her photo. Reaching down, he tugged the covers up over my shoulder. "I wish I could promise you nothing but happiness. I know the next few years will be hard, but I promise, Sapphire, I will be there right next to you every step of the way."

Chapter Twenty-Four

Cartazonon's skin buzzed with power. He loved the way he felt after a good feed. In the past he would have celebrated with such enthusiasm old Bacchus himself would get jealous. But now, in this modern era where information traveled the world in a single breath, he couldn't be seen for another week.

Stolen energy glowed about him, this time blue-green wisps swirled in his own murky gray energy. His black eyes danced with light, and around him power sparked like static electricity.

Closing his eyes, Cartazonon followed the energy as it spread out like a spiders' web connecting all of his properties and people. He noticed a few places where the energy wasn't flowing well, and one place where the energy was being consumed at a very fast rate.

Mentally he followed the trail and found one of the dark ones awake in the catacombs. Hunger gnawed its belly, and its teeth lengthened as it smelled the humans walking around above.

"Hush," Cartazonon hissed, lulling the creature back to sleep. His hands shook as the beast fought him. Sweat beaded on his forehead and ran down his cheek. The beast roared, and Cartazonon drew on his power forcing it to bend to his will. "You will go back to sleep. It isn't time for you to wake yet." The creature's growl turned into a snore as his yellow eyes closed.

Cartazonon wiped his face with a silk handkerchief. Sometimes he wondered if keeping these dark beasts was worth the energy it took to control them.

Groaning, he fell into a chair and allowed the soft leather to cradle his body. San Francisco popped back in his mind. He would have stayed and investigated, but meetings ruled his life and businessmen investing millions of dollars in a project wanted to talk to the man in charge.

Grabbing a piece of paper, he wrote a letter to Yilmaz. He wasn't far from San Francisco. Cursing he sucked on his finger, damn paper cut! He would find a way to drag his pasha into the modern world. There had to be something the old Turk wanted more than he hated technology. Some of his generals adapted to changes better than others. Yilmaz, while faithful and good at his job, needed to be dragged into each new century.

Chapter Twenty-Five

"If you have made mistakes, even serious ones, there is always another chance for you. What we call failure is not the falling down but the staying down."
~Mary Pickford

"Why do you keep looking over at the door?" Jane asked.

"Sorry," I said, going back to the warm-up stretches. "Shin left to try out for the circus that we're going to travel with this summer. He's supposed to get back today, and I'm hoping he'll stop by and let us know how it went."

"I hope he gets picked. Shin's the hot Asian guy with the blue streaks in his bangs, right?" Jane asked wagging her eyebrows, her right eyebrow looked like it was lifting weights with its barbell piercing.

"Shin is Korean, and he's cool."

Jane hummed through her smirk.

I rolled my eyes. "First of all, I don't date. And second, he's like three or four years older than me. Anyway, having another friend traveling with us would be nice."

Jane stretched over her legs. Her hair was gelled into short spikes, and I could see spots on her scalp where she dyed her skin pink along with her hair. "How are things going in fairy-tale land?" she asked.

Over the past month I told Jane a lot about Gavin, Anali, and growing up in group homes. I'd left out the Phoenix and magic bits. I hadn't planned on telling Jane much about my life, but with my sudden name change, Jane was curious and a surprisingly good listener. "Okay, I guess. I still don't know if there are any house rules. I keep my stuff tidy, clean up after myself, and go to bed about the same time every night. So far, no complaints from the adults yet."

"Not all houses have rules. I say do what works for you and see what happens." Jane moved into a one legged stretch, groaning as the muscles slowly relaxed.

Jane's mom worked two jobs, and her dad had been gone for years. She took care of the apartment and helped out by cooking and cleaning. Jane liked being independent and doing what she wanted.

"I guess. I don't like not knowing what to expect. Everything has been so mellow and free at Gavin's house. I don't know how to act. Seriously I think if I stayed up all night watching horror movies and skipped school the next day to sleep, no one would care."

Jane laughed. "Most kids would love that."

I shrugged and moved into a wide leg stretch. How could I explain that I didn't like not knowing the rules or consequences? That sleeping in a room alone scared me? And that, while I loved having a bathroom all to myself, I still rushed through my shower as if there were kids were waiting for me?

I suppose someday I'll adjust to life at Gavin's house. I bet it will happen right before we leave to travel the world in an RV.

Jane poked my foot with her big toe. The lime green polish on it made my eyes hurt. "Don't worry so much. This is a big change, give it time."

"You have no idea," I muttered. Looking for a way to change the topic, something shiny caught my eye. "Is that a new necklace? Maybe a Valentine's Day gift?"

Jane's blush clashed with her newly pink hair. "I think I told you about Jason?" I nodded yes. "Well, on Valentine's Day he brought me a rose, a card, and this necklace."

"It's very nice." The heart pendent was lacquered black with a pink rhinestone skull in the center. A perfect gift for Jane.

Jane smiled as she stretched her arms. "Thank you. He's very sweet, and he's in a band."

I wanted to go to Jane's school and make sure this Jason person was good enough for her.

"Okay, everyone, gather for class," Taliesin called out.

The Perky Girls reached Taliesin first, forming a half circle around him and blocking Jane and me from getting close. We rolled our eyes. They acted far more passive aggressive since Philip talked to them. They glared, interrupted, and stood as close to Taliesin as they could. Taliesin kept taking small steps away from them and, his jaw tightened every time they interrupted him.

"Today, as you can see, we have a trapeze, ring, and silk hanging up. Divide into pairs and practice the basics I've already taught you. I'll watch everyone to give advice and help," Taliesin explained. "We'll do about twenty minutes at each station and then switch."

Jane and I were put on the silk first. We chatted about school, and her new boy while going through the warm-ups. Then we climbed the silk. Jane went first since she lost at Rock-Paper-Scissors-Lizard-Spock.

"You're doing great," I cheered as Jane pulled herself up the fabric hanging from the ceiling.

When she climbed half way up, she stopped and secured her feet and arms into a resting position. I watched as she looked up the silk to the ceiling trying to decide if she should push herself further. I was about to say something when Taliesin spoke.

"Jane, don't push yourself too hard. You have gone much further today than you have before. I can tell you're doing the exercises at home." Every once in a while Taliesin would say something nice. It made me wonder if he had multiple personalities.

Jane nodded and slid down the silk.

"Very good. If you overdo it, getting down will be less controlled and could be dangerous," Taliesin said. "All right, up you go, Sapphire."

256

It took a couple tries to get my feet secure, but once in place, I pulled myself up the silk. I took my time, and used my legs and arms, as Taliesin taught us. I startled a bit when my fingers touched a hard knot. I made it to the top! Looking out over the school, I saw Gavin waving to me. I waved back delighted and scared to have made it to the top. The floor seemed far away.

"Rest for a minute before coming down," Taliesin said.

I locked my arm around the silk and checked my feet and hung there for a bit, before I slowly lowered myself back down.

My feet barely touched the ground when Jane squealed and hugged me. "That was so great!"

"Thanks, you did great too, you went so much further up today!" Oh, yeah, we rock.

"Please, we could do that on the first day!" Perky Girl number four said, the others agreeing with her instantly.

"So what improvements have you made?" Philip asked, appearing out of nowhere. "Can you go up more than once? Can you go up without using your legs? Taliesin, show them what they should work towards."

Taliesin sighed, but went to the silk and began to climb. He flew up the fabric using only his arms. Then came back down again with complete control. Holy crap, he's strong.

"Jane and Sapphire, you both have improved a lot. You should be very proud," Philip said, before going back to his office. Philip also rocks. And what is that I hear? It's the blissful sound of Perky Girls shamed into silence.

"All right, back to work everyone, we're not done yet," Taliesin said, shooing everyone back to their place.

Jane posed in hip-hang while I kept track of the time. We decided to help push each other into holding the poses thirty seconds longer each time. Suddenly, strong dark arms surrounded me and spun me around.

"I did it! I got accepted, and I'll be touring this summer!"

"Shin, that's wonderful," I turned in his arms so I could hug him. He laughed as he spun around again, his blue and black bangs tickling my neck. "What are you going to be doing?" I asked

Shin's black eyes shone with happiness. "Chinese pole."

"That is great, we'll get to hang out," I said, stepping back.

"That's right, Gavin and Anali are touring with the circus, too. So cool." Shin squeezed me again and lifted me off the ground. While I wasn't thrilled with being picked up, it did do wonders for my ego.

"Shin, could you please stop distracting my student?" Taliesin interrupted, his voice sounding colder than normal. What was wrong with him?

"Sure, sorry. I'll see you Tuesday." Shin blushed and went to share the good news with the others.

"Taliesin didn't seem happy about Shin holding you," Jane suggested, once Taliesin walked away.

I turned and saw Taliesin glaring at Shin's back. "Which of us do you think he's jealous of?"

Jane smacked my arm. "Oh, you're so bad!"

"Switch to the last station," Taliesin snapped.

I quirked an eyebrow at him, Taliesin turned and went over to the Perky Girls. Wow, he was pissed.

*   *   *

"Anali, this has gone on for too long. We need to do something!"

I hung up my towel and went into my bedroom as quietly as possible. What in the world were they talking about? Combing out my hair I sat on the bed and listened. It's not eavesdropping if people talk loudly enough for you to hear them.

"Gavin, I'm as concerned as you are, but please try to understand how many changes she's been through. Sapphire suddenly has all these powers, finds out there are evil beings after her, she's expected to save magical creatures she's grown up believing aren't real, her name has changed, and now she's living with an uncle she never even knew existed," Anali said.

"Living with me is not a bad thing!" Gavin yelled. Oh, crap, this isn't good. I thought about closing my door to give them some privacy, but I wanted to know what they were arguing about.

"Of course not, but, honey, it is a big change. She needs time," Anali said.

"It has been weeks, and Taliesin says he still doesn't feel any Phoenix power from her. We need to get her help." I didn't know Taliesin could do that. Is that why he would stand so close to me during class?

"What kind of help? We can't take her away right now, we have to stay here." Anali started to sound frustrated.

"I don't know, but maybe we should talk to her about it?"

"Gavin, she barely knows us. Let her have her space. I'm sure she knows things aren't quite right. When she's ready, she'll come and talk to us about it."

"I'm her uncle, she should feel safe with me."

"You being her uncle doesn't magically fix everything!" Uh-oh, now Anali was mad. Thank goodness my empathy had died down to almost nothing.

Their bedroom door slammed shut and while I could hear their voices I could no longer tell what they were saying. I sat in the bay window and pressed my head against the cool glass. I had never heard them fight before and now they were fighting over me. My stomach felt sick with guilt.

After a while their bedroom door opened and Gavin's heavy footsteps echoed through the house. The silence that followed the shutting of the front door settled over the house and suffocated the normal happy emotions. I saw Gavin walking down the street, his hunched form lit up by the street lamps.

"He'll be fine," Anali said, from my doorway. "He goes for walks when he gets upset. It gives him time to think and figure out what to do."

I nodded, my eyes glued to the street.

"Sapphire, Gavin will come back." Anali placed her hand on my shoulder. "Do you want to talk about it?"

"No," I said, but vowed to do better to get past my fears so Gavin wouldn't be mad and they wouldn't argue over me. I didn't want them to regret taking me in.

*   *   *

I walked carefully through the dark damp cave. In the distance I could see a faint light, I headed towards it, hopeful I would find the exit. Instead, I found Akasha. Light filled the cave as I got closer the bright turquoise sky. Once I could see where I was going I walked faster. I almost got to the opening when I slammed into a glass wall.

"No," I gasped, running my hands over the glass, desperate to find an opening. I couldn't find anything. The glass went from one side to another. In the distance I could see Shamash and Aya in the rich green meadow. Next to them sat Kayin, Taliesin, Gavin and Anali, they were laughing and having fun.

Banging on the glass I yelled for them, I didn't want to be all alone in this creepy dark cave. "I'm over here, help! I can't reach you!"

No one heard me. No one moved, or came to my rescue.

"Help!" I screamed, banging on the glass wall, my hands aching.

"Sapphire, Sapphire, wake up."

Jerking awake, I scooted away from the hand shaking my shoulder.

"It's okay, you're okay," Gavin said.

"I'm sorry. I..." My mind raced. I couldn't think straight. I knew it had been a dream, but I still felt scared.

Gavin sat on the edge of the bed. He wore a tee shirt and soft pajama bottoms. I hadn't heard him come home. "What happened?"

"I couldn't reach you. All of you were far away, and there was this wall of glass, and I couldn't reach you," I said, twisting the sheet around my fingers.

"Here, have some water," Anali said.

Taking a drink I began to settle a little bit, my mind and heart both calming down.

"Why couldn't you get to us?" Gavin asked. I could hear the worry in his voice.

Blushing, I looked down at the blanket. "It doesn't matter; it was a stupid dream."

"If you want to talk about it, you can," Anali said.

"I know, but now that I'm awake it seems silly."

"If you're sure," Gavin replied. He didn't sound convinced.

"I'm sure, thank you, and I'm sorry I woke you." I set my glass down and scooted under the covers.

Gavin reached out and smoothed down my hair. "We are both here for you, if you need anything."

"I know." It was nice to hear even if I didn't know what to do with them being "here for me."

*   *   *

It had been two weeks since the first nightmare. They continued, sometimes with walls of glass or fire, which burned me. Sometimes Gavin and Anali would drive away before I could get close to them. All I knew is that I was being left behind, and none of them noticed I wasn't there.

It's my fault. If I couldn't access my gifts, I couldn't be with them. Even though I was terrified, I tried to get my powers back. I practiced Garuda yoga with Anali every day and I focused into pulling my gifts out of the hard ball of ash I created weeks ago. I could feel my gifts, the heat from the fire making the rock hard sphere glow and steam, but nothing came out.

Every day I practiced, making fire, trying to read people's emotions, even the breathing meditation, and nothing worked.

*   *   *

"Hurry up!" Gavin called out. "I have a surprise for you."

"I'm ready," I answered, walking towards the door. It was a beautiful day, and Gavin insisted we go on a picnic. "Can I carry anything?"

"Thank you, sweetie. Will you take this, please?" Anali held out a large cloth bag with blue and white flowers all over it.

"Sure, anything else?"

"Nope, it's all packed," Gavin said, shooing us out the door.

"Spring is here," Gavin sighed, letting the sun warm his face. "It's perfect, the first weekend of March and bam, spring."

Anali smiled warmly. "It's a very nice day, dear. I'm glad the Universe is working with you today."

"As it should," Gavin said, puffing out his chest and strutting to the car. I now understood why some kids got embarrassed by their parents.

We drove to the west end of Golden Gate Park near the windmill. The tulips were blooming in a breathtaking array of colors. I lay the blanket out for the picnic when I heard someone squeal my name. Turning, I saw Shante running up the path, her black curls bouncing around her face.

"Shante," I whispered, my eyes filling with tears. Kneeling down I caught her in a hug.

"I missed you," she said, holding onto me tightly.

"I missed you too, Shante. How did you get here?" I asked.

"My mentor brought me." Shante pointed behind her. Taliesin's mom followed. Cordelia looked elegant in a light blue dress, her golden blond hair flowing around her shoulders. "She made me this dress too, isn't it pretty?"

"It's very pretty and such a lovely pink."

"I like pink, it's my favorite color," Shante said, twirling for me so I could get the full effect of the dress which shimmered in the sunlight.

"Hello, Sapphire, how are you today?" I felt scruffy as I stood next to her. It's easy to see where Taliesin's GQ perfection came from. Thankfully, Ms. Gadarn was much warmer than her son.

"Hello Ms. Gadarn, I'm well and you?" See watching British comedies does pay off. I learned some manners from them.

"I'm quite well, thank you. Please call me Cordelia, we're all friends. Shante and I made cookies to share with everyone." She held up a Tupperware container filled with cookies.

"Oh, what kind?" Gavin asked.

"Chocolate chip!" Shante shouted. "Sara, will you take me to look at the pretty flowers?"

"Sure, if it's okay with Mrs. Ga—... um, Cordelia."

"Is it okay, Cordelia?" Shante asked, her brown eyes wide and begging.

"It's fine with me. Go have fun."

Shante gave Taliesin's mom a quick hug, then grabbed my hand and dragged me to the flowers. For a while I listened to Shante ramble. She caught me up on all the gossip. It had been several weeks since we talked, and a lot had happened, according to Shante. Jessica, who went home with her parents six months ago, came back. This time we didn't have enough room for her siblings, so they were split up. Caitlin was spending a lot of time with her aunt, and Rhonda and Myra were going home with their mom tomorrow.

"Wow, things are busy," I said, once Shante took a breath. "When did Cordelia show up?" I felt bad I hadn't gotten to talk to Shante in so long. I'd called a few times but Shante hadn't been home.

"I don't know, a few weeks ago. She has a son. She left him a few cookies," Shante said, giggling. "Anyway, Cordelia said her son was getting older and going to be traveling soon, and she always wanted a smart pretty girl to hang out with, and she picked me!" Shante threw her hands into the air and twirled in joy.

Gavin arranged this, it was the only option. Gavin somehow arranged for Shante to be taken care of. "Of course, she picked you."

"She's very nice and very pretty." Shante stopped for a moment to sniff a bright pink tulip with a ruffled edge. "It smells sweet. Cordelia said she would take me to a class if I want. It can be anything, dance, or gymnastics, or music. Anything I want."

"That sounds like fun, want do you want to learn?" I'd never seen Shante this happy before.

"I want to be a ballerina like Angelina Ballerina." Shante twirled and danced all the way back to the picnic. I smiled as she danced away. Angelina Ballerina, Shante's favorite book for me to read at bedtime.

"Did you see any pretty flowers?" Cordelia asked when we got back.

While Shante went into great detail about every flower, I walked over to Gavin. I wasn't sure what to do or say and stood there uncomfortably.

"Are you all right?" Gavin asked his brow furrowed.

Stepping forward I hugged my uncle. "Thank you."

Gavin's arms folded around me gently. "You're welcome. I knew you were upset about leaving Shante. I couldn't fix that, but I could try to make it easier. At least now you know Cordelia will be with Shante, watching out for her."

"Thank you," I said again into his chest. His spicy cologne filled my nose and I knew it would mean safety to me from now on. I also knew that Gavin would listen to me and help with my problems.

"Everyone makes mistakes, some are small little things, and some are huge and rather scary. The key is knowing when you have made a mistake and working to fix it. Forgetting to pick up milk at the store is an easy mistake to fix. However, there will be times when a mistake is big, and you will need help. Never be afraid to ask for help from those who care about you. A true friend and loving family might be disappointed, but they will always help you as best they can. Even if help is holding your hand as you slowly work your way through the mistake and get back to where you want to be."

"I can't access my powers. I tucked them away so tight when that evil man came that I can't get to them anymore. At first I felt happy to feel normal, but I've been trying and I can't," I confessed, in a single breath.

Gavin's arms tightened around me and he began to stroke my hair. "Don't worry we'll get it all sorted out. Thank you for telling me."

That's it? No lecture, or interrogation, or consequences? Maybe I should ask for help more often.

"Can we eat now?" Shante said.

"Of course," Anali said, petting my hair as she walked past us.

Stepping back, I pulled a lock of hair forward, focusing on the ruby red streak instead of looking up at anyone.

"I promise that we'll figure this out. I will help make it better," Gavin insisted.

Looking up I smiled. "I believe you."

"Sara, come and eat!" Shante demanded.

"We better go, your princess awaits," Gavin said.

For the first time since I woke up on my birthday I felt like everything might turn out all right.

*   *   *

"We're going camping!" Gavin announced when he got home Monday evening.

Anali and I looked at each other than at him, waiting for more information.

"What are you making?" Gavin asked, coming further into the kitchen.

"Sapphire is helping me make vegetable soup with dumplings," Anali answered going back to chopping.

"Oh, that sounds good." Gavin lifted the lid on the pot. "It smells good too."

"Camping?" I asked. Like in heated cabins or in tents?

"Ah, yes. I talked to Philip, and he talked to some people he knows, and we think we have a way to help you. There is a group called the Guardians. They travel around the U.S.

checking in on magical creatures. Philip thinks they might know how to help us."

"Who are they? I've never heard of them," Anali asked.

"Well, they're Children of Fire, and they come from different Native American tribes. Philip says they are very powerful. They mix their Phoenix gifts with traditional spiritual practices from their own tribes. Philip went to a powwow the Guardians held and every Child of Fire began to glow with power." Gavin explained as he snatched pieces of carrot from my cutting board.

"When do we go?" I asked. I wasn't sure how I felt about meeting the Guardians or camping, but I was willing to try.

"Next week over spring break. Kayin and Taliesin are going to come with us."

Slowly, I took a deep breath and let it out. "Okay."

Chapter Twenty-Six

"Appearances are not held to be a clue to the truth. But we seem to have no other."
~Ivy Compton-Burnett

Sitting in a camp chair, I hid behind my journal. Anali bought it for me in order to help me figure out how I felt, hoping that would help release my gifts. I wrote diligently, doing everything and anything to try and open up the rock-hard ball I'd locked my powers in. Unfortunately, I had been unsuccessful, and here I sat deep in Yosemite National Park where we would camp for the next week. I wasn't looking forward to being trapped here. We were camping in tents, with no running water, and what they called a toilet was just a cold plastic seat over big stinky hole in the ground. I can't believe people actually do this for fun!

Kayin and Gavin were thrilled. Gavin was excited to try out all of the camping equipment he'd bought. Taliesin, Kayin and I had sat squished together in back seat of the Suburban Gavin rented to carry all of the camping gear.

Kayin, on the other hand, was happy to get out of the city. He loved the quiet, and currently sat with Storm and Elijah cleaning fish. Storm, named after a Steven Seagal movie character, was one of the three apprentices who trained with the Guardians. He wore his black hair short and the silky locks shone with a red tint in the sunlight. He had brown eyes, full lips and a pointy little nose. Storm felt mischievous and alight with joy.

Elijah emanated calm and quiet; his gray-green eyes seemed to see everything. His face looked like someone chiseled it from stone, with sharp cheekbones, a hawk-like nose, and a square jaw. Elijah hadn't said much since we arrived. I couldn't decide if he was quiet, just shy around new people, or didn't want us here.

"These fish are very nice," Kayin said, gutting a shiny silver fish about as long as his forearm. Gross.

"Mary has a gift. She always catches the best fish. Mine are the scrawny ones." Paul laughed. Mary's apple cheeks turned pink as she shook her head at her husband's words, her braids sliding over her back as she moved.

"Thank goodness I inherited my mom's ability to fish," Elijah teased, his voice deep and soft.

Paul reached out and tugged on a long lock of his son's hair. Elijah looked so much like his father, the only difference was Paul's long hair curled where Elijah's hair was straight and so black it shone blue in the sun.

I turned back to my journal before anyone caught me staring. Blah blah blah...I don't want to be here...blah blah...I can't feel my powers...blah blah blah, more deep emotional soul searching. It would be worth the pain of getting my powers back to no longer have to do this stupid journal. Maybe I could use it as a scrapbook? I could write about the creatures we find and add pictures?

"Fudge," Rebecca said. Looking down I saw a bunch of seed beads scattered over the ground.

I jumped to help her pick them up. Rebecca was about my age with a sweet round face, copper skin, and wore her long dark brown hair in a tight braid hanging down her back to her waist.

"Thank you," she said. Her voice sounded soft, but not weak.

"No problem. I've been watching you work on the bracelet you're making. It's beautiful. I can't imagine having that much patience."

"Thanks, it's not as hard as it looks At least it isn't that hard anymore," Rebecca answered with a soft smile. "It's also very meditative."

"I can see how that would work. I use exercise to meditate." I told her as I hunted the ground for the small glass beads. The bright colors were easy to find, unfortunately the browns, grays and blacks were probably lost forever.

"You're very quiet, is everything all right?" Rebecca asked.

That's an odd question. We'd only been here a few hours, so how could she know if I was being quiet or if this was how I normally am? "So are you."

"Well, yes, but most white people aren't as quiet as we are. Anyway our grandparents teach us that words have power and should be used with care."

What kind of power? Did she mean like how Philip can influence people when he speaks because of his Phoenix gift?

"Rebecca, Sapphire, can you two help with dinner?" Carol asked.

"Yes, Grandmother." Rebecca put all of her things away.

"Coming," I said, setting my journal on my chair.

"We are going to have tacos tonight for dinner," Carol explained as she set out bowls and ingredients. "We need to make fry bread, beans, fried fish, steak, and rice."

"We brought enough fresh vegetables to make a nice salad," Anali said.

"It sounds great. So how can we help?" I can cook simple things on a stove, but over a campfire, no way.

"Well, there are thirteen of us so we'll need a lot of fry bread." Carol gave us each a large bowl, and walked us through the process step by step. Watching Rebecca, I knew the step-by-step instructions were for me.

Soon I kneaded a bowl full of silky smooth dough under my hands, which I worked until Grandmother Carol was happy with it. Looking around, I saw everyone was busy doing some chore - the boys were cleaning fish, Gavin was re-packing the Suburban with the food we wouldn't use tonight. We were busy making bread, and the two other Guardians, Grandfather Bob and Grandfather George, were carving pieces of wood.

I watched them out of the corner of my eye. Each stroke of the knife looked effortless and without thought, but I doubted that was true. Both men were dressed in beat-up cowboy boots, old blue jeans and western-cut shirts. Bob's short salt and pepper hair stuck out from under a worn cowboy hat. George's hair hung down his back in a thick braid. Most of George's hair was gray, but there were also white streaks tinted with a faded red, letting me know at one time his black hair had been highlighted by ruby red streaks like my own.

I could feel they were all Children of Fire. Philip and Gavin told me they were powerful spiritual people, but they didn't look like it. Blushing with embarrassment, I thought of what I expected to find. I imagined the Guardians as beautiful glowing people wearing beaded buckskin and feathers in their hair. Instead, they were people with tummies, worn clothes, and chores to do. I found it all a little unsettling.

"Not what you expected, dear?" Grandmother Carol asked with a fond smile. Her wrinkled face lit up making her reddish copper skin shine.

"I'm sorry," I muttered looking down at my dough.

"It's quite all right. People frequently have a vision in their head about what we do and who we are," she said, her voice calm and clear. "I'm sure you will also find people shocked at how you dress and act when they know they will be meeting the Jewel. And you will disappoint some of them at first.

"Try and keep an open mind, my darling. I know it will be hard, but the clothes do not make the man, they only make a mask. The woman in the faded ugly pink flowered dress could be a leading physicist, and the man in the three-piece suit might not be able to read. You never know who someone is on the inside until you spend time talking with them and learn what occupies their thoughts and fills their heart."

"Oh, I'm not disappointed, not at all. You have all been so kind. It's just..." I fumbled for the right words. "I have no idea what to expect. When we got here I did have an image in my head, and now it's gone and I'm not sure what's going to happen or what to do."

"Well, first everyone is going to tear their dough into twenty even pieces and roll them into balls," Carol said, and then winked at me. "I believe the plan is for you to be. Be in nature, surrounded by its strength and beauty, around magical creatures, and around other Children of Fire without other things and people intruding. We will also drum, rattle, and sing around the fire tonight. For the next few days that will be all, we'll watch how you respond and then make plans from there. We are hoping you naturally release your powers in this setting, but if not we have some other tricks up our sleeves."

"Don't give away the surprise!" Grandfather George teased, kissing his wife on the cheek. "Are you making fish tacos?" His brown eyes lit up in delight as his leathery brown hand pointed to the balls of white dough.

"Yes, we'll have several filling options to choose from, and Anali is going to make a salad," Grandmother Carol said, her tone changing when she said 'salad' letting her husband know he would be eating some.

Grandfather George merely smiled. "Of course, dear, whatever you wish."

Grandmother Carol's grunt, and Grandfather George's twinkling eyes made me suspiciously suspect that the salad issue wasn't finished.

Dinner was delicious, and Grandfather George did eat some salad. Fry bread is now one of my new favorite foods, and Grandmother Carol promised to write down the recipe for me.

"Why don't you kids go for a walk down to the lake?" Gavin suggested, in an obvious attempt to get rid of us. "There is still plenty of light, and my three haven't been down there yet."

We "kids" rolled our eyes and headed to the lake after clearing away our dishes. I felt lucky I could even move after dinner, I had eaten so much.

"That was subtle," Taliesin sneered.

"I guess they want to talk privately," Elijah said with a shrug.

"Damn!" Storm shook his iPod. "It's dead and I can't charge it again until we're driving."

Rebecca rolled her eyes. "It's not that big a deal."

Storm pouted.

"We have a solar panel charger. I don't know if it works since we haven't used it yet, but I know where it is," I said.

"That would be great, thanks." Storm smiled. "I love music."

Rebecca snorted. "You love tuning everyone out,"

"Well, as soon as you guys are interesting, I'll bother to listen." Storm shoved her playfully, then danced away so she couldn't hit him.

"Oh," I gasped. Stepping through the trees we saw the lake, the surface a perfect mirror for the sky, which was on fire with the setting sun.

Kayin grasped my hand. "It's gorgeous. I don't think I will ever get over the beauty of water."

"You grew up in Africa?" Elijah asked, tucking his long hair over his shoulders.

"Yes, in Zimbabwe, on an animal preserve."

"Will you tell us about it?" Rebecca asked.

Kayin smiled and began to tell us about his childhood in the African savannah, while we skipped rocks into the lake. The sunset colors rippled on its surface.

As our laughter died down from Kayin's story about his pet goat getting loose in the village, I heard an odd barking, clicking sound. Looking around I couldn't see anything in the dim light. A breeze slid through my clothes making me shiver. I was no longer happy about being out here in the woods. I tried to look calm, but, hello, I'm a city girl in the cold, dark woods!

"It's squirrels," Elijah said.

"What?"

"The high-pitched barking, it's squirrels chattering at each other," he explained with a smile.

"Oh, cool. I've never heard them do that before. We have squirrels in the city, but I don't think I've ever heard them at all," I said wrapping my arms around myself trying to stay warm. Now that the sun fell below the horizon it became cold.

An owl hooted in the distance. The call sounded as eerie as the horror movies made it out to be.

"Brother owl says it's time to go back," Rebecca said, standing up and brushing off her jeans.

"We still have to pack up all the food into bear boxes and make sure the trash is thrown into the bear bins," Storm said with a sigh.

Elijah hummed in agreement as he stood up.

"Gavin was going to leave it in the back of the truck," I said.

Storm laughed. "Not a good idea. A hungry bear can break a car window."

"They are awake and very hungry right now," Elijah added. "In fact, you all want to make sure you wash before bed, you don't want to go to sleep smelling like food."

A terrified high-pitched squeak made me jump - it might have come from me because Kayin put his arm around me. "Don't worry Little Sister, it'll be fine."

I wasn't convinced, however the rustling of a bush did convince me that brother owl was right and we needed to head back to camp.

*   *   *

"Oh, good, you're back. I have stuff to make s'mores!" Gavin called out.

Usually sweets, especially chocolate would make me feel better, but I bet bears liked s'mores too. I tried to look through the darkness, but whatever hid in the woods I couldn't see.

"Why do we always eat s'mores when we camp with white people?" Storm asked.

"I have no idea," Rebecca answered.

"I like s'mores," Elijah said.

"What's a s'more?" Kayin asked.

"It's a graham cracker with a piece of chocolate and a marshmallow you toast over the fire," Taliesin explained.

"I like chocolate," Kayin said.

"They're good, but very messy," I added.

"Not when they're done correctly," Taliesin said in a superior tone of voice. Like he was some kind of a s'mores expert! He's as much of a city kid as I am.

"Bob and George made roasting sticks for everyone," Gavin said, handing out pointed sticks. "There are graham crackers and chocolate set up on the table here, so grab a marshmallow and have fun!" Gavin pointed to the camp table he'd set up earlier.

"Rebecca, will you bring me some?" Grandfather George asked.

"Have you checked your sugar?" Grandmother Carol asked.

"Yes, dear. I did it while Gavin set everything up. I can have one," George answered, with affection in his voice. It was sweet how much in love they still were.

It took a bit of shuffling, but soon we were all around the fire, roasting our marshmallows. Taliesin held his marshmallow several inches above the fire, and turned it slowly.

"What are you doing?" I asked bumping him with my elbow.

He snorted and wanted to scoot away, but Gavin sat on the other side of him. "I'm roasting my marshmallow. What do you think I'm doing?"

"But it won't catch on fire way up there."

"Heathen. You don't burn your marshmallow, you toast it to a perfect golden brown." Taliesin actually straightened his back so he could look down on me from a greater height, like I wasn't already short.

"You don't know what you're doing," I said and stuck my marshmallow into the fire. When I pulled it out and twisted it so the flames covered the entire treat, then I blew it out. Grinning, I pulled the crispy black coating off and popped it in my mouth. Perfect.

"I can't believe you ate that," Taliesin said, several of the others agreeing with him.

"You're a wuss," I said sucking the melted marshmallow off my fingers.

"Why? Because I don't like eating ash?"

"Now children," Paul said soothingly. "Everyone can make their marshmallow however they want."

"Yes," Gavin agreed. "And if Sapphire wants to set hers on fire and do it wrong, then she's allowed."

Taliesin laughed and raised his marshmallow. "See? Perfectly toasted. Storm, could you hand me a plate, please, I forgot to get one."

While Taliesin turned, reaching out for a plate, I used my stick and pushed his stick down, placing his marshmallow in the flames.

"For goodness sake, girl you don't shove a man's marshmallow in the fire," Gavin shouted in fake horror.

"Sapphire!" Taliesin yelped, yanking his stick back and carefully examining his marshmallow. "It's darker than it should be, and now it's uneven." He glared at me.

I stuck my tongue out and placed another marshmallow on my stick directly into the fire.

"How do you put the s'more together?" Kayin asked.

"Oh, do you have your marshmallow cooked?" I asked.

He held up his stick, which held a perfectly charred marshmallow. "Perfect." I showed him how to pull the hot marshmallow off his stick using the cracker and chocolate.

Taking a big bite, Kayin smiled around the gooey mess. Melted marshmallow and chocolate dripped on his chin. "It's good, but very messy."

"Mine isn't. A perfectly toasted marshmallow makes the chocolate soft not melted." Taliesin smirked. He took a bite of his treat and avoided getting anything on him.

I narrowed my eyes at his prissiness. Anali must have seen something in my look because she suddenly joined in the conversation. "I also like mine on fire."

"No," Gavin said, his hand against his heart. "How can we stay married with this between us?"

Anali giggled.

"Fire is definitely the way to go," Grandmother Carol agreed daintily blowing out her marshmallow.

"Now, dear, we have discussed this, and we're a toasted marshmallow family," Grandfather George added teasingly.

"Good luck, Dad," Mary said, blowing the fire off her own marshmallow.

"At least the men of this family know how to cook a marshmallow," Paul said, turning as Elijah blew out the flame on his own marshmallow with a sheepish grin.

I hoped our laughter scared away any bears, which might have been tempted by the smell of burning sugar.

After cleaning up, we sat around the fire in happy silence. I remember Grandmother Carol telling me they were going to drum, and I wondered when that would happen. Right now everyone seemed content, except for Taliesin, who kept swatting at his hair.

"What are you doing?" I asked. A piece of his white hair floated up and he swatted again.

"Faeries love my hair," Taliesin grumbled.

"Well, it is so lovely the way it glows in the moonlight," Mary said soothingly.

I could see his hair moving, one piece being separated into sections and then braided, but I couldn't see the faeries.

"You can't see them?" Kayin said.

I shook my head. I couldn't see them at all.

"Kayin, let me switch places with you," Gavin said. He sat behind me on the log. "Close your eyes."

Gavin's voice pitched low, and he spoke slowly. I wasn't sure what was happening, but I closed my eyes.

"Now breathe and let your body relax." Gavin made his own breaths slow and deep. Soon I followed along. Then a drum started softly, and a second, then a third joined in. I could feel each beat echoing in my body. The rock encasing my power thrummed and began to heat up.

"I want you to picture Taliesin in your mind as he is now. He's sitting next to you, the firelight giving his white sweater a yellow glow. The moonlight makes his hair and skin glow silver." Gavin paused giving me time to picture Taliesin firmly in my mind.

It didn't take long. Once I could see his sky-blue eyes, I nodded my head.

"Perfect. Now I want you to see what is happening to his hair. Little pieces are being lifted up, separated, and three faeries are making a braid, now that he has stopped swatting at them." Gavin's voice spoke in the same beat as the drums.

I began to feel light-headed, and part of me wanted to come out of the meditation, force my eyes open, and end this. For a moment I stiffened, and the drums sounded louder, encouraging me to relax and let go. Releasing a breath, I let go and trusted.

"In a moment I want you to open your eyes," Gavin said. "But first I want you to know there are five faeries playing with his hair. One lovely little faerie in a white dress with pale blue hair, is twisting two strands of his hair together. Three faeries are making a braid, one in a yellow dress with brown hair, another in a bright pink dress with grass green hair, and the third a boy wearing brown pants, a white shirt, and an acorn cap on his head. The fifth faerie is also a boy with an acorn cap. He's the smallest of the five and is wearing brown pants and an orange shirt."

Gavin paused letting me create the image in my mind.

"Now hold the truth in your mind. Know this image is real," Gavin said firmly, yet softly. "Ride the drum, let go and when the drum stops, open your eyes."

I let the image form clearly in my mind. I could even hear the bell-like laughter of the small faeries. I could see Taliesin's scowl at having his hair messed with, and the joy on the faeries' faces as they played with the moonlit strands.

The drum stopped and I opened my eyes. There they were: five little faeries playing with Taliesin's hair. I gasped as the surge of power released from my core. I arched and shook as a wave of heat flowed through me. The rock in my belly hummed with power and heat. It hadn't broken open but some of my power released.

The faeries flew over to me, patting my face trying to sooth me as the energy reestablished itself in my body.

"Sapphire?" Gavin asked trying to keep the worry from his voice.

"I'm okay, just a power surge," I managed to answer. "They're so pretty."

The faeries preened at the compliment, and danced around showing how pretty they looked.

My hand shook as I reached for my cup. Suddenly, Storm knelt in front of me holding the cup up. "Let me help."

Blushing, I let him hold the cup while I took a drink. In the trees I could see lights, some small like the faeries, but others were a large as a person. I could feel my nervousness building. Everyone stared at me.

"The Lakota tell a story of how White Buffalo Calf Woman brought to the people the sacred pipe and taught them the way," Grandfather Bob began.

With each word I relaxed more and let myself be taken in by his story, the newly released energy settling within me.

"Two young hunters were out searching for game when they saw a strange person walking towards them. As they got closer the hunters saw a beautiful woman wearing a white buffalo skin. One hunter let his heart be filled with lust and greed to make her his. The other hunter realized she was special and not human. The young woman opened her robes. The wise man turned his head at her naked form, but the man with lust and greed in his heart rushed forward and embraced her. The woman closed her robes around him and when she opened them again there was a pile of bones and snakes at her feet."

Grandpa Bob paused for a moment without letting go of the magic of his story. "The wise hunter ran to his village telling his people about the beautiful and powerful woman who was headed their way. They greeted her with respect and she gave the Lakota the first pipe. She taught them the way of the pipe and stayed with them for a long time. When she left, she turned into a white buffalo calf. The sacred pipe, the one White Buffalo Calf Woman gifted to the Lakota, is still used today."

When the story ended, everyone cleaned up and headed for their tents. I still felt shaky, so Gavin walked me over to mine. Faeries danced among the treetops, and I hoped they would keep the bears away.

"Good night." Gavin hugged me before heading to his own tent.

"'Night."

"Good night, Sapphire. Will you be okay by yourself?" Anali asked.

"I'm sure I'll be fine. Kayin and Taliesin will be on the other side," I said, faking a reassuring smile. Gavin bought two big tents. His and Anali's two rooms, one for them to sleep in and one to hang out in. The tent he bought for the boys and me contained three rooms. Two sleep areas, one on each end, and a hanging out room in-between.

Anali gave me a hug. "All right, sleep well. And if you need anything come on over."

"I will, don't worry."

Kayin and Taliesin were already inside taking off their shoes. "We put you in that room," Taliesin said jutting his chin to the room behind me.

"Okay thanks." Oh, great, the room pointing towards the woods! I forced my hand not to shake as I unzipped the tent flap. Crawling inside I was pleasantly surprised. Gavin bought air mattresses and they created a thick layer of cushion between the hard ground and me.

Changing into my flannel pajamas was interesting. I couldn't stand because I kept slipping on the air mattress, but eventually

I got into them. Scooting into the thick sleeping bag I began to shiver. It was cold!

"Sleep well," Kayin called from the other side of the tent.

"You, too." I didn't think I would sleep at all.

"Yes, don't let the critters bite," Taliesin teased. He's such a snot!

"Shut-up," I said turning off the flashlight. Slowly, very slowly, the sleeping bag began to warm up, and I clung to hopes of sleeping until I heard an odd rustle. Did something just bump the tent? It didn't sound like a branch. Holding my breath, I waited and jumped when I heard it again. I scooted further down into my sleeping bag.

What was out there?

I listened carefully and almost screamed when I heard something walking around outside. Soft measured footsteps, snuffling sounds, and a dark shape between the tent and the fire.

"Sister raccoon, good evening," I heard Grandfather Bob greet the mysterious dark shape.

Okay, raccoons are small. Nothing to worry about. Go to sleep and stop being such a baby. Closing my eyes, I breathed slowly and tried to ignore the deep silence broken occasionally by the wind and unknown hungry wild animals.

I dozed off and on for hours, never sleeping deeply and always being forced into consciousness by some strange noise. My eyes ached with exhaustion, but I doubted I would ever fall fully asleep. Putting my hand up into the cold air I shivered and hit the light on my phone. I almost cried. It was only three o'clock. I had to lay lie in here for at least three more hours.

All right, calm down, I told myself. Everything is fine. It's warmish in here and as long as I don't have to pee I can stay in here and be fine. And of course, I didn't have to pee until I thought about it. Sapphire, you only have to pee because you thought about it, close your eyes and go back to sleep! I lay back down and snuggled into my sleeping bag.

A few minutes later my eyes popped open. Damn it, I needed to pee now! Gasping as the cold air wrapped around me, I quickly put on my socks and coat, unzipped the flap and shoved my feet into my freezing shoes. Flashlight in hand, I unzipped the main flap and stared out into the night. The moon hung low in the sky, not giving much light. I could see the shape of the pit toilet in the distance. It wasn't that far away. I could go by myself. Turning, I looked at where the boys were sleeping. No, I couldn't wake one of them up, could I?

I flinched at the sound of the zipper being undone. "What are you doing?" Taliesin snapped.

"I have to go to the bathroom."

"So?" he asked.

I turned big pleading eyes his way. Please don't make me ask out loud, I chanted as I stared at him.

"For the love of...," he snapped, moving back into the room. I relaxed once I heard clothes rustling.

"You better be quick," Taliesin grumbled, his teeth chattering.

I nodded. Of course I would be quick. It was cold and scary out here.

As quietly as possible we walked across the campsite and down the little path to the toilet. Carefully, I opened the door and shone the flashlight in, making sure nothing scary waited to eat me.

"Sapphire," Taliesin hissed.

"I was just checking," I pouted and went inside, squeaking as I sat down. Cold seat, cold seat!

"Are you all right?"

"Cold."

Taliesin chuckled. I glared at the door.

"Your turn," I said stepping out.

He grunted and went inside. I walked out of the cover of the trees and looked up. Even though the cold made my eyes tear up, I couldn't look away.

"What are you doing?" Taliesin snapped.

"Have you ever seen so many stars?" Bright dots of light covered the sky. I could even make out some of the constellations and the Milky Way.

"No, I haven't. I can see why so many people made up stories about the stars."

Maybe I didn't have to go back inside; my camp chair had a footrest. I could bring my sleeping bag outside and stare at the sky for the rest of the night.

A lonely howl pierced the night. I jumped and grabbed Taliesin's arm.

"It's probably a coyote," he whispered. He didn't sound sure of that.

An answering howl was all it took for us to go right back to the tent.

"Thank you for going with me."

"Whatever. Go to sleep," Taliesin said, toeing off his shoes and climbing back into his side of the tent.

I lay in my cold sleeping bag listening to the conversation between several coyotes. At four-thirty I swear one of them laughed.

Chapter Twenty-Seven

"Courage is being scared to death...and saddling up anyway."
~John Wayne

As soon as the first bird chirped and the skies lightened to gray, I got out of the tent and by the fire. My body shook with the cold as I tended the fire. They banked it the night before, and it didn't take long to uncover a few red-hot coals at the bottom of the ashes. Carefully, I placed the smaller twigs over the coals and blew on them. A small flame flickered into being. With as much care as my shaking hands would allow, I placed larger twigs and branches over the small flame. Sitting back, I waited patiently for it to ignite and offer real warmth, when a gust of wind swept through camp and the little flame sputtered about to die.

"No!" My breath made a white cloud in front of me. I held out my hand as if I could force the flame to stay against the force of the wind. Power fluttered through me, strengthening the small flame. I focused and forced a little trickle of power out of my hand onto the fire, and the gift was there.

"Grow," I whispered. The flame grew steadily until I created a hot roaring fire before me. I sighed in pleasure and pulled a blanket over my back.

"Would you like some coffee?"

I jumped and turned to the voice. "Oh, hello, Elijah. No, thank you. I'm not a big coffee drinker."

"I also have tea," he said, as he set up the metal grating over the fire and placed a metal coffee pot on top.

"Tea would be great," I answered with a smile. "I hope I didn't wake you up?"

"No, the birds did that." He filled a kettle with water and placed it over the fire.

"They sound very cheerful this morning," I said looking up. The morning sun lit the very tops of the trees. Birds fluttered from one tree to another.

"It would seem so, but most of the calls are to keep other birds out of their territory," Elijah answered.

"No way. Well, there goes the one nice thing about this morning."

"Hey, what about me?" Elijah teased, flashing me a charming smile.

I eyed him carefully for a moment. "Well, you are making me tea, so I suppose you count as a good thing."

"Thank you so much for the praise." Looking up, he waved to Rebecca and Storm. "I have to go help with morning prayers. Do you need anything first? We won't be long."

"No, I'm fine. Am I in the way? Or is there something I should do?"

"No, we need to charge the medicine bags." I must have looked confused because he said, "I'll explain when I get back."

I nodded and watched as the three Guardian apprentices walked around the edge of the camp, stopping at specific spots and saying prayers. It felt rude to intrude, so I turned back to the fire, closed my eyes, and began to do the five-count meditation.

I could feel the power I released last night. It warmed and comforted as it flowed through me. I channeled it up and down my spine with each series of breaths, gaining control of my gifts. When I stopped, my powers settled in the pit of my belly, surrounding the pulsing, ashen stone. The rest of my powers pushed to be released. I hoped it wouldn't hurt too much when that happened.

Opening my eyes, I saw Rebecca and Storm getting things together for breakfast. "Can I help?"

"Not right now, but we were wondering if we could check on your blocked power?" Rebecca asked cautiously.

"I guess. What do you want to do?"

"My gift is healing," Rebecca said as she sat next to me. "I want to put my hand over where your gifts are being blocked and see what's there."

I shrugged; it sounded easy enough. "Sure, no problem."

Gently, she placed her hand on my lower belly, and closed her eyes. "You have that good and sealed up, haven't you? I can also see what you released last night. I can tell there's an emotional reason, but other than that, nothing."

"May I try?" Storm asked. "I'm empathic."

I nodded and soon a much larger hand lay on my belly. He gasped, his eyes flying open. "You were so scared. That rock which encases your powers is all fear. What happened?"

"The leader of the Sons of Belial was nearby. We needed to hide. Gavin and Anali told me to make myself small, which I did. That man, he felt so unnatural." I clasped my hands together to keep them from shaking. "I was covered in a slick, sticky, evil feeling. All I knew, I didn't want him to find me, ever."

"I can see why you wouldn't want to release your powers after that," Rebecca said, standing up and going back to making breakfast. "If you still want to help, could you grease a pan?"

"Sure." I jumped up, grateful to have something to do and for the subject change.

"You said you'd explain," I reminded Elijah when he came back over, as I coated a large cast iron Dutch oven with butter.

"Oh, yes. We are guardians for magical creatures. To make sure they know we're here, we hang medicine bags which call out to all magical creatures in the area."

"Then what?" I asked.

"We talk to them," Elijah answered with a shrug as if it were nothing. "Find out how they are doing, if they need anything, if they have enough space. Things like that."

"Oh, that's pretty cool." I looked at the tree line. "Can I see one?"

"Sure, come on," Elijah said, getting up.

I handed Rebecca the newly greased pan, and followed. A leather bag about the size of my palm hung from an oak tree with small green buds, closed at the top with a carved turquoise bird, and a thin piece of metal held it to the bag. "Is the metal from Akasha?"

"Yes, I believe it came from a bracelet. Generations ago someone melted it down and made wire out of it to make these amulets," Elijah explained.

"What's inside?"

"Pieces of magical creatures and stone."

My face wrinkled in disgust, bits of animals, gross.

Elijah laughed. "Not like that, bits of fur, feathers, and whiskers."

I blushed. "Oh, sorry."

"That's okay. I didn't explain it well the first time." Elijah flashed me another bright smile. I bet he was used to girls swooning near him. He was very handsome, but I wasn't interested in any guy. If my cheeks flushed, it was due to the cold.

Turning, I started to go back to camp, but instead I slipped and fell right onto Elijah. He caught me, hissing in pain.

"I am so sorry! Are you okay?" I asked, pushing against his chest to right myself, causing him to grimace.

"I'm okay," he answered after taking a few breaths to calm himself. "My dad and I were helping out some friends a few days ago."

"You're bleeding," I said. He wore his jacket open over a tee-shirt which was become discolored with blood in two places. I reached out to help him.

"What are you doing?" Elijah grabbed my hands.

"You're bleeding! Do you want Rebecca to heal you?"

"Sapphire, if it will make you feel better I'll put ointment on them, and clean bandages, but they can't be healed."

"Why not?" See, even yummy men aren't worth the trouble. They never make any sense. I would be mad if this was some macho thing.

"That's not how it's done," Elijah answered with a shrug.

"Can I at least help with the ointment?" I wanted to make sure the wounds weren't too bad. I felt awful for hurting him.

"You just want to get my shirt off." Elijah waggled his eyebrows at me.

Please, I lived next to Carlos for almost a year - flirting didn't affect me. I raised an eyebrow at him. He'd cave within a minute. I could do Melanie's "mom" look perfectly.

Elijah huffed. "Fine, you'll probably nag me until you're happy. Come on."

I followed him to his tent. His mom came out of the woods. She seemed very peaceful and calm.

"Good morning, you two."

"Good morning, Mary. Elijah needs a Band-aid."

Mary stopped and blinked, looking at her son in question. They stared at each other for a moment, then she began to grin. They obviously had an entire conversation looking at each other.

"I'll get a wet rag, and the first aid box. Take your shirt off, so I can wash the blood out," Mary said.

Elijah sighed, and handed me his jacket. "What happened?" I asked softly when I saw the scars. There were two sets, one much older than the fresh wounds on either side of his chest.

"I told you it's nothing. I was helping out." Elijah shrugged and looked away.

Mary cleaned off the blood, applied a thick ointment and covered the wounds with gauze pads. "There, all better. Why don't you go and help with breakfast?"

Elijah nodded and walked off.

"Was it one of the magical creatures?" I asked. I couldn't tell what made the scars. I'd never seen anything like them before. "Is it something I need to be careful of?"

"No, Sapphire, you're fine. Elijah was helping out some people." Mary patted my shoulder. "Thank you for making sure my son is safe and taken care of. I promise he's fine. Go and have something to drink while they finish making breakfast."

"Okay," I said, unconvinced. Those scars and wounds meant something.

The smell of fresh coffee and biscuits woke up everyone else. They sat around the fire with steaming mugs in their hands. Rebecca began cracking eggs while Elijah moved the kettle from the fire.

"Good morning, Sapphire," Kayin said and sat down next to me with a steaming mug of tea wrapped in his hands.

"Morning. Did you sleep well?"

"Yes, it was so quiet and peaceful." Kayin smiled happily.

"I'm glad. Good morning, Taliesin," I said.

He merely grunted and focused on the mug of coffee clutched in his hands.

"Gavin's the same way," Anali said, sitting next to me. "Don't bother them until after they have drunk a cup of coffee."

I grinned at Gavin, who looked as if he were still asleep, as he drank his first cup of coffee.

"Can I help with breakfast?" Anali asked

"No, thank you," Rebecca said as she laid out the last of the condiments. "It's all ready."

"Well, tomorrow you must let me make breakfast," Anali said with a smile. "It smells wonderful."

Those of us not needing caffeine to function got up and piled our plates with eggs and biscuits with homemade jam. I only took two of the large fluffy biscuits. Since I can easily eat my weight in homemade biscuits, it was a challenge not to take more.

"These are wonderful," I said. "What kind of jam is it?" I held up the biscuit I covered with pinkish-red jam. It tasted tart and sweet and so good.

"Oh that's rhubarb jam, one of Carol's specialties," Grandfather George answered.

"I've never tasted it before; I love it."

"I think I got some of that," Anali said looking over her biscuits. Taking a bite she smiled. "Oh, very good."

"Thank you," Grandmother Carol said with a smile. "It's something my grandmother taught me how to do. It's not very hard; the key is good rhubarb."

I ate slowly. I wanted to get seconds of biscuits, polite manners made me wait long enough until everyone got firsts.

Carol's weathered hand reached down and placed two biscuits smothered in rhubarb jam on my plate. "Don't worry, we can always make more."

"Thank you!" Grandmother Carol was my new favorite person.

Grandmother Carol smiled and did the same thing for Kayin, although his favorite jam was her bright pink prickly pear fruit jelly.

*   *   *

"Paul said you're stalking me and that I should come and see what's up," Gavin said, as he sat down next to me.

Well, that sounded a bit extreme. Granted, I kept an eye on Gavin so I could talk to him alone, but I also helped clean up. I didn't think I'd acted that obvious. "I wanted to talk to you alone."

"Okay?"

I opened my mouth when Storm and Kayin walked by with fishing poles.

"Come on, let's go for walk," Gavin suggested, pointing to a path leading away from camp.

"Thanks."

We walked in silence, until I felt sure no one was around.

"Elijah has these scars and wounds on his chest. He says they're nothing, that he was, 'Helping out some friends.' But there is more to it than that. Do you know what they're from?" I blurted out. Normally, I didn't pry into other people's business, but I worried some creature that we were going to have to deal with made the scars.

"I think so, at least I can make a guess," Gavin said. "One set on each side of the front of his chest?"

"Yes." Aha, I knew it was something important.

"It sounds like he danced a Sun Dance," Gavin said. "It's a spiritual ritual where people choose to sacrifice themselves for the good of the tribe. They suffer so the rest of the tribe doesn't have to."

"Why wouldn't he tell me that? I wouldn't have been rude or disrespectful." Had I been rude? Elijah seemed okay with my questions earlier. I twisted the hem of my sweatshirt.

"I know you wouldn't, Sapphire. The Sun Dance is a very personal choice. They see it as 'helping out,' no one is ever asked to dance, or pressured to do so," Gavin explained.

"Oh." I've never heard of anyone sacrificing themselves like that before.

"I've never attended a Sun Dance myself, but I have heard it is a powerfully spiritual event." Gavin stopped to look at a small flower growing on the side of the path. It looked like a tiny violet.

"Do you think all of the Guardians have done a Sun Dance?"

Gavin shook his head. "No, it's a Lakota ceremony. And the Guardians are made up of people from many different tribes. In fact Guardians are encouraged to marry other Guardians in order to pass their powers on, no matter what tribe they are from."

"That's interesting." I thought that over for a moment. "Are all Children of Fire encouraged to marry other Children of Fire?"

"Oh, I'm sure some are, but most of us are simply drawn to each other naturally so there isn't a lot of pressure. It's the magic in us." Gavin continued down the path.

I hummed. It was rather interesting. It never occurred to me that anyone would care whom I married, let alone care about their ancestry.

*   *   *

The cave was damp and dark. I stumbled forward towards the faint light in the distance. The steady beat of drums and the soft shaking of rattles moved me forward. I relaxed and followed the sound of the drums.

Within the rhythm of the drums I heard a woman's voice. No words, just gentle clear notes. I stood in front of the glass wall, and saw Akasha on the other side. In front of the wall laid the ash-gray rock that held my powers. It sat in a small fire from the energy that already been released.

This was all my fault, all my doing: the wall, the locking down of my gifts, and I was the only one who could fix it.

Bang. Looking up I saw Shamash knocking on the glass. He and Aya were trying to get to me. I wasn't sure what to do, or how to fix this. I pressed my hand against the glass, Shamash mirrored my action. I imagined I could feel the warmth of his hand in spite of the glass separating us.

A figure appeared next to me, a glowing human shape, and then she began to speak:

"Sapphire, my darling, fear and insecurity can be crippling. It can stop you from reaching for happiness, or trying to make your dreams become reality. Fear can make you hide when you should shine. I wish I could find a trick, or a way I could share with you, to help you overcome your fears, but sometimes you have to grit your teeth, take a step and do the right thing, even with your whole body shaking. I know it will be hard, and I wish I could hold your hand through all your hard, scary times, but know I'm with you in whatever way I can be."

Taking a step back, I reached down and picked up the rock. Heat blistered the skin on my hand. I held on and threw the rock at the glass wall with all my might. It made a sharp, perfect crack in the glass wall.

"Sapphire," Shamash called. "We are always here for you, you have to let us in!"

291

Tears ran down my face. I bent down to pick up the rock again. Steam poured out of it. My skin burned from being near it, but I pressed on. In one single moment three things happened. The drums stopped, my eyes flew open, and a new wave of power surged through me.

Curling in on myself, I gave in and let the power flow. There was nothing else I could do. It wasn't over. I hadn't broken through the glass, and the rock still sat there, although more of the power leaked out. I felt so stupid having done this to myself. All of this pain could have been avoided if only I had been braver, or smarter, or even for one moment felt excited about being the Jewel.

"Little Sister," Kayin said and placed a hand on my shoulder.

"We're all here, you're safe." Gavin wrapped an arm around me.

I wanted to throw myself into his arms. I wanted to be safe. I wanted to be accepted and loved. I stayed where I was. I couldn't move. He deserved a niece who loved him, who felt some kind of family connection, not someone looking for safety. I sat there while the tears fell down my checks.

I could hear the others moving around. Kayin and Gavin stayed with me, cocooning me from everything.

"Is this okay?" Gavin asked.

"Sapphire will be fine," Paul assured.

"Who was singing?" Kayin asked.

Oh, good, he'd heard it too.

"That was the spirit of the drum; no one sang."

I don't know how long I stayed there curled up into a ball, trying to accept what happened and hiding from it at the same time. I felt more than heard someone kneel down in front of me.

"Anali made some hot chocolate. I think it will help," Storm said.

Wiping my eyes on my sleeve I sat up, grateful when Gavin's arm didn't leave me. "Thank you."

"I try to respect people's privacy. However, your emotions are screaming out," Storm said, his eyes sad. "This isn't your fault. No one minds being here. And you never know, maybe your being here now with us is meant to be."

I took a sip of the spiced chocolate and looked away. Storm patted my head and went back to his seat near the fire.

Slowly, I began to feel better. Grandfather Bob told a Zuni legend about coyote, while everyone sipped hot chocolate and ate cookies. Hey, I want a cookie! Looking around I couldn't find a plate of cookies, but Gavin did have a pile of Oreos on his leg.

Reaching out I stole one. Gavin was too involved in Grandfather Bob's story to notice. I managed to take two more before the story ended.

That night I lay in the tent, staring at the walls and shivering inside my sleeping bag. Between the power surge and exhaustion, my whole body ached. I wished I could sleep. Maybe I could get used to the howl of the wind and the rustling of leaves.

I slowed my breath and closed my eyes. Slowly, my muscles began to relax. I smiled softly as I felt sleep overtake me.

A scream shattered the peace.

"What was that?" I clutched my pillow to me, as if a fluffy pillow would stop something terrifying enough to make that sound! I heard something moving, was it outside the tent? No something moved inside! It was here, this was it, I was going to be eaten by some hideous creature!

The tent flap began to move, and the zipper began to slowly slide up. What was it? I stared at the back of the tent wondering if I could claw my way through!

"Sapphire, Little Sister, are you okay?"

"Kayin?" Oh thank god!

"Of course, do you want to come and sleep in our tent? All of us together will be warmer." Kayin offered.

I felt like a fool, getting all worked up over nothing. I opened my mouth to say no when another scream echoed over the mountain. "Yes, here's my pillow."

I threw my pillow at him and shuffled like an inchworm across the tent unwilling to get out of sleeping bag. Kayin held the flap aside as I slid into their side of the tent.

"Hey, Sapphire, come on in," Taliesin said. I slid across the air mattress to the middle. If I slept in here, then I wanted to be in the middle. I would be warmer, and I was less likely to get eaten.

Kayin and Taliesin piled extra blankets between the tent wall and their heads to make a warm cocoon. Bliss. I was never sleeping on my side of the tent again.

"It was probably a cougar," Taliesin said.

"What?"

"The scream, it was probably a cougar."

They're big enough to eat a person right? "It sounded close."

"No, it's a long way off. I can't tell how far because things sound different here than on the plains back home," Kayin explained. "But it's at least a mile away."

"That's good to know," I said and snuggled down into my sleeping bag. "Thanks for letting me come over here."

"Of course, Little Sister," Kayin said.

My last thought as I fell asleep—never would I sleep in a tent alone again.

Chapter Twenty-Eight

"Whether you think you can or think you can't—you are right."
~Henry Ford

"Pass the prickly pear jelly, please," Kayin asked. We woke to the smell of breakfast and were currently smearing on as much jam and jelly as our pancakes would hold. There was syrup, but I could get syrup anywhere. Homemade jam, now that's something special. Can a person become addicted to homemade jam?

"That looks more like artwork than food," Gavin laughed, sitting next to me. His stack of pancakes foolishly, covered in syrup.

I looked down at my plate. Anali made large, round pancakes, and I covered mine in four different jams: blueberry, mulberry, prickly pear, and rhubarb. Not only that but each section covered exactly one-fourth of the pancake surface. "I guess."

"How did you sleep? You look better this morning," Gavin asked.

"I slept well," I answered eyes focused on my plate, and not looking up, and possibly blushing.

"Do I need to worry?" Gavin asked with a serious edge to his voice.

"No."

"Sapphire shared our side of the tent last night," Kayin told him. "It was very cold, and the cougar last night was a bit scary."

"Oh, okay." Gavin took a huge bite of food. Well, I guess that's it.

Elijah walked over to Grandfather George and Paul as soon as they came into camp. They talked, and Elijah seemed worried, but Grandfather George nodded and smiled in an annoying, all-knowing way.

"All is as it should be," Grandfather George said patting his grandson on the shoulder and coming over to the fire.

"I wonder what that was about?" My stomach fluttered a bit.

"I don't know," Gavin said. "I think Elijah has the gift of dreams, so maybe he dreamed something."

"Maybe." I would keep an eye on them.

"Let's go for a hike," Grandfather George said, after we cleaned up from breakfast.

It seemed rather sudden, and a bit random, but we all got ready. Soon we were hiking along a small and winding path. I watched where I walked so I wouldn't trip on the roots and rocks sticking up out of the dirt.

"It's good to know a piece of land. Memorize each step, how it feels under your foot, the plants and trees, any animal evidence you see," Paul explained, slowing down his steps. "Don't think about the past or the future; be here now and be one with the land."

I slowed my breathing, and placed each footstep with care and focus. I didn't understand the importance, only that it was vital to know this stretch of land. We walked about an hour before the forest path opened into a large meadow. Delicate new grass fluttered only an inch or two above the ground, mixing with a few other plants I didn't recognize.

The meadow hummed with power welcoming me. I looked to the Guardians to find out what to do. They were walking around enjoying the space.

I walked around the edge, looking at the small ferns and patches of velvety moss. I tried to stay along the edge. I felt wary of disrupting such a sacred place, but I was drawn to the meadow. Nervously, I walked to the very center. The trees formed a perfect circle around me. Bending down I placed my hand on the ground. Something lay buried under the earth. I wanted to dig for it, but it was too deep.

"Could you find this place again? This exact spot?" Paul asked, his black hair glinting red in the sunlight.

"Yes." I could feel the hum of whatever lay buried under the earth. It called to me, and I could find this place again without any trouble. "Why? What's buried here?"

"Good, remember that you know where to go," Paul said with a smile, then he got up and walked away.

"That's what I need, random riddles and half answers," I muttered as I sat down, the power in my body heating up in response to this place.

*   *   *

I could barely eat lunch, and my stomach felt squeamish. Something was going on, and I hated not knowing what. It only got worse as the afternoon wore on. I tried to distract myself. I tidied my side of the tent, made sure my dirty clothes were bagged up and organized my clean clothes. I also put on extra deodorant, to be on the safe side. Three days without a shower, not fun.

"Sapphire, come here," Grandmother Carol said after I had messed about the camp straightening things for twenty minutes. "I'm going to teach you how to knit." She handed me two long wooden needles and a ball of blue yarn.

Patiently she showed me how to cast on, how to knit, purl and cast off. I enjoyed it, and the motion felt a little hypnotic, and the feel of the soft yarn as it ran as it ran through my fingers.

"You have a good start. If you keep that up you can make a scarf," Grandmother Carol said, inspecting my first actual piece.

"Thank you, this is fun." I kept my eyes on the needles so I wouldn't mess up too badly.

"Oh, my pleasure. You needed something to do."

"I did. I don't know what's wrong; I feel so jittery!" A breeze blew over me and I shivered. Looking up, I noticed how low the sun hung in the sky. I hadn't even noticed the afternoon passing by.

"I'm sure you'll figure it out," Grandmother Carol said, patting my leg. "I'm going to start dinner."

"Okay, let me put this away, and I'll come and help," I said getting up. Once my attention wasn't focused on knitting I noticed that my stomach still felt queasy, how odd. I didn't feel sick, just queasy. I scratched my arm, and that's when realized what was happening. "They're here." No, oh please, no. The Sons of Belial found me, found us.

"Gavin, they're here. I can feel them!" I said running over to him.

"The Sons of Belial?" he asked holding onto my shoulders.

"Yes, and someone big, not as big as in San Francisco, but definitely big." I clutched at his shoulders. Where could we hide out here?

"Finally!" Elijah said. "I was wondering if you would ever figure it out."

"What?"

"I dreamed about this last night. Grandpa said you needed to figure this out on your own. That it was important somehow." Elijah shrugged.

"I don't understand. We have to run! We have to get out of here!" I said tugging on Gavin's arm.

"You can't leave," Grandfather Bob said. "They're waiting for you to send them home."

"What, what do you mean? Who's waiting?" I began to panic. Why was everyone else so calm! "I don't know how to open the doorway."

Grandfather Bob smiled, what I'm now going to call the "elder-all-knowing- smile. "You'll be fine. You're a gift to our world and to the magical beings here, it's your destiny to save them."

I opened my mouth to say something, to rage, scream, beg, but all that came out was a squeak.

"The sun is setting; the Sons of Belial will get here soon," Grandfather George pointed out. "We older people move slower, so you youngsters go ahead and get the ceremony started. You might want to run."

Gavin held my face, looking straight into my eyes. "What do you want to do? You pick and I'll support whatever you choose."

I wanted to say that I couldn't, that I felt too scared, that I wanted to get away from the evil I could feel coming, that I wasn't strong enough. Instead ,I closed my eyes and took a breath.

"You can do anything you set your mind to. Everything you need in life you already have. A brave heart. A sharp mind. A strong spirit. These qualities will see you through anything and everything. Someday people will tell stories about you and the amazing feats you accomplish. Know, for every mountain you climb, and every one you fall down, I will be so proud of you."

"I want to try. I need to try." I wanted to take back the words as soon as I said them.

Gavin crushed me to his chest. "I'm so proud of you. Okay, let's run, everyone is ready."

"Do you remember the way Sapphire?" Paul asked, slipping a backpack on and holding his drum.

"Don't you?" I whispered.

He shrugged carelessly. "I could probably find it. I've never been there before today. You said you'd be able to find it again."

Rude. Don't I have enough to deal with?

Ignoring the itchy feeling caused by the Sons of Belial, I felt for the connection I had to the meadow. It was still there, soft and fluttering, but there. "Yes, I can find it."

"Well, let's go," Paul replied with a grin.

We ran, flying over the trail. Our feet hit firm ground every time, missing tree roots and rocks. Bursting out of the trees and into the meadow, I gasped for breath. I was in good shape but I never ran, and that was obvious as others came through the trees breathing hard, but not panting like me. We were in the meadow.

"Now what?" I asked Mary and Paul.

"You go to the center. We'll get everyone else set up," Mary said. Thank goodness someone knew what to do.

I walked to the center of the meadow. I fell to my knees trying to catch my breath as the energy coming from the earth set my gifts alight within me.

The slick, oily, evil feeling slid over my body. The Sons of Belial were coming closer. They weren't at the campsite yet, but certainly headed that way.

"Elijah, you go and stand at the North point. Kayin you're in the East. Rebecca, South. Storm, stand in the West." I heard Paul directing everyone.

"Anali, stand between Elijah and Kayin, half way to Sapphire," Mary instructed. "Gavin, you go and stand between Elijah and Storm, also half way to Sapphire."

"Paul is going to drum, while I cast a circle and invite the spirits to join us. Let your gifts flow and open them to what is happening. If you need help, follow the drum, it will never lead you astray," Mary explained.

This all sounded good, but what was the point? What did they expect to happen? "What am I supposed to do?"

"Whatever feels right. I'm creating a ritual to connect all of you, to help focus your intent," Mary said. "When the time comes, you'll figure it out."

Great, yeah, I'll just magically know. Good plan. What the hell! I tried to calm my breathing, but I could feel the Sons of Belial coming closer.

Mary walked around the circle we created, sprinkling some kind of powder on the ground. Our circle stretched out big enough that I couldn't touch anyone else. I felt exposed, shivering, I hoped this magical knowledge would present itself soon.

Paul began to drum. Mary placed her hands on Kayin's back and called out in a clear voice. "Spirits of the East, we invite you into our circle. Please bless us with your knowledge and strength."

Kayin burst into flames. Fire swept around the circle, sealing us all in.

Mary walked to Rebecca, placed her hands on her back, and called out, "Spirits of the South, we invite you into our circle. Please bless us with your knowledge and strength."

Plants began to grow around Rebecca, twining up her legs, and blooming, while they also spread along the ground making a third circle.

"Spirits of the West we invite you into our circle. Please bless us with your knowledge and strength."

Water swirled around Storm, and flowed out creating a fourth circle, never ceasing its movements, but flowing along the ground.

"Spirits of the North we invite you into our circle. Please bless us with your knowledge and strength."

Elijah's hair whipped around him as he was surrounded by the wind. It moved out from him in the circle, an invisible fifth circle, which surrounded and protected us with only the waving grass to show its passage.

Mary now went to Anali. "Mother Earth, we invite you into our circle and ask that you bless us with your wisdom and love."

Anali froze and took a shuddering breath as the image of Aya appeared over her.

"You have my wisdom and my love," Aya said. Her voice came from a great distance.

Next she stood behind Gavin with her hands on his shoulders. "Father Sky, we invite you into our circle and ask that you bless us with your protection and love."

Gavin became a vessel for Shamash.

"You have my protection and my love," Shamash answered.

Mary walked over to me. "You are the Jewel, Sapphire, the spirit which will bind them all."

Mary calmly walked through the circles and sat at her husband's side, picking up her rattle.

"They're at the camp and coming this way fast," Elijah gasped.

I screamed as Grandfather George, Grandfather Bob and Grandmother Carol stepped through the trees. I clutched at my chest as if I could stop my heart from pounding. They sat down and took out their instruments. They slid right into the beat Paul established.

I saw Taliesin, his hair was long and wild, glowing in the faint light from the crescent moon. On his forehead a star shone. He crouched down and made odd noises. Animals gathered before him. None of them looked like magical creatures, but normal animals: foxes, bears, deer, rabbits, many types of birds, and more coming through the forest.

Turning his glowing blue eyes to me, Taliesin said. "They are ready."

Good for them. I wasn't ready! I still didn't know what I needed to do! I could feel the power of the circle and the elements. I could feel everyone in the circle. My gifts bubbled and raced through me. The rock bound the last of my powers, hot in my belly. I felt the oily sickness of the walk-ins and the man with them. It was so much, maybe too much. I wanted to run and hide.

"Sapphire, we are here for you," Aya said.

"You can do this; you're strong enough," Shamash said.

"What do I have to do?" I cried.

"You have to accept who you are."

My hands shook as my brow furrowed in confusion. Who I am? I'm nobody. I'm a group home kid who likes the circus and is called Sara. Right?

I jumped as I heard shouts in the distance. The Sons of Belial were so close.

"Who am I?" I whispered.

"You are my granddaughter," Shamash said. Power infused every word warming my mother's fire pendant, which sat against my chest.

His granddaughter, I am the granddaughter of the Phoenix King. The image I created of myself faded, the name Sara crumbled into dust. Who am I?

Standing tall I turned to face the center of the circle. Taking a deep breath, I let myself float on the beat of the drum.

"I am Sapphire Aya Rayner, daughter of Gabriella and Keagan Rayner, niece to Gavin and Anali Marsh and the many times great-granddaughter of the Phoenix King Shamash and the Phoenix Queen Aya. I am the Jewel. I now open this doorway to Akasha so my lost people can go home!" I said, yelling the last words into the sky.

The ash rock inside me burst open and I shouted as all of my powers were released. The swirling circles of elements came together making a brilliant white circle, the energies came into Shamash and Aya, then flowed into me.

I gritted my teeth against the intensity. The powers built and surged inside of me until I feared I would burst from them. I held my hands out in front of me, palms down. White-hot power burst from me and into the Earth.

The ground before me rumbled and exploded open as an ancient doorway appeared. The stone form was made from rocks from Akasha. They absorbed the energy flowing from my hands, and a glowing circle of purple-tipped white fire appeared. I could see the bright green grass and turquoise sky of Akasha on the other side of the doorway.

"Thank you," a voice said softly next to me. I saw a woman with the face of deer. She placed her hand briefly on my wrist. One by one the animals changed into their humanoid forms. Some still looked mostly animal, while others looked to be human wearing animal skin. I held my breath as a winged snake flew by me. Bells jingled as a group of masked beings walked past me and into the portal to Akasha.

"I know it's bright, but we're almost there, hold onto your host." A man's voice demanded.

"Pasha Yilmaz, we're trying, but it is very hard," a walk-in hissed.

Turning my head, I saw four men stepping into the meadow. The three walk-ins put their hands over their eyes, trying to protect themselves from the light. Pasha Yilmaz wasn't affected by the light of our circle and aimed his gun at Elijah.

"NO!" I screamed and flung my right hand towards the Sons of Belial, surrounding them in bright white flames.

The walk-ins screamed. The fire touched one of them, and the specter within the man was yanked out, screaming as it was forced towards the doorway.

"Find peace in our world," Aya said as it passed her.

The other two walk-ins left their hosts to crumple to the ground while they fled into the night sky.

"I am no mere specter!" Pasha Yilmaz screamed. "And I am not afraid of a fire caused by a little girl!"

"No, you are an aberration," Shamash judged. "You should not be here any longer. How does your master keep you alive?"

"You'll find out," he said taking a step forward into the flames. Screaming, he jumped back, falling to his knees. His skin wrinkled and dulled as we watched.

"You steal life which does not belong to you. Come forward and set things right. You need to continue on your journey." Shamash now projected the power and strength of the regal king he was.

"No," gasped Yilmaz. Stumbling, he hurried away.

"I can't hold this much longer," I whispered, my body shaking.

Soft hands held my face. "You are doing so well. Just a little longer. They're almost all through."

Before me stood a beautiful young Native American woman dressed in pure white buckskin.

"Help me," I begged.

She smiled and kissed my brow gifting me with some of her strength and passing along her memories.

I saw her and others like her come into our world, fascinated with the people they found here. They chose to interact with them, some teaching, some causing mischief, and other causing trouble. They were beings like us, with flaws and hurts, and both goodness and evil in their hearts.

I watched as the centuries went by, and the magical beings tried to help. Giving hope and encouragement, sitting with the People in their grief and joy, and trying to help them find their way.

All the while the animal beings walked into the doorway, each one thanking me as they passed.

"You did it," the woman in the white buckskin said. "You can let go now."

"You need to go through first," I said, forcing myself to hold the doorway open while I still blocked the path in case Yilmaz came back.

"Sapphire, my work here is not yet done. Some of us are still needed. Many of the younger ones have chosen to stay with me. They can see a new way for the People. We will call you when we're ready to go home."

With that she stepped away from me and walked out of the circle, joining a group of magical beings. As they walked deeper into the forest some of them melted into animals.

"You're done, Sapphire," Gavin said. "You can let go now."

Exhaling, I dropped my hands. I heard Gavin's shout as I fell to the ground and into the darkness.

Chapter Twenty-Nine

"We know what we are, but know not what we may be."
~William Shakespeare

No, not again. How do I get out of here? I looked around as if the dream or vision or whatever, had a door I could use to escape whatever happened next. The dream became clearer.

He sat in a steam room with a white towel wrapped around his waist. The mosaic tile of white, golden yellow, and a variety of blues so beautiful I almost forgot I was trapped near evil.

"Are you sure you're okay?" asked Lee. His bare chest was marred by thick scars.

"Yes. Sit with me, old friend."

Lee rolled his eyes as he sat. "I don't know why you like baking yourself so much."

He laughed and poured a cup of scented water on the coals. "Thank you for humoring me."

"Khan, you haven't screamed like that since they tried to burn you as a witch."

"We need to figure out what happened. I want Yilmaz brought here as soon as he is well enough to travel. Whatever he encountered stole life from him. Life that I gave him."

I gasped as I felt his anger, cold and vicious. I grabbed my fire pendant, willing Shamash and Aya to help pull me free of this dream.

"I will need another creature soon. We can't get caught in a weak moment. I fear we are at war."

Lee smiled, stroking a scar, making him looking even scarier. "I do love war."

"I know, my friend, I know. But first we must figure out what we are up against. What magical being could have done this?"

I breathed a sigh of relief as the images began to fade. He wasn't looking for Children of Fire. He still thinks we are nothing important.

"What did Yilmaz say about what happened?" Lee asked.

"All he can remember is seeing a bunch of magical creatures and a bright white and purple light," he sighed. "It reminds me of something, something from long, long before I met you."

"The Big Bang?"

He snorted and began to laugh.

My stomach rolled and my skin felt like sandpaper scraped against it. I whimpered, please, please let me go. The dream images began to fade.

I moaned. I could feel people near me, but I didn't know who they were. I couldn't see. My whole body hurt, sparks of power made my body twitch and shake. Someone cursed and the car swerved. I was in a car? Voices surrounded me, but I couldn't make any of them out. I needed to get away. I began to fight the hands that held onto me. My shaking limbs flailed about, not doing much damage.

Cool hands held my face and someone came close to me. I squirmed to get away and pushed into the body behind me. I couldn't think clearly, my chest ached. What happened? All I could remember were the Sons of Belial coming for us. I gasped for air.

"Sapphire, listen to me." The person got closer, icy blue eyes filled my vision as a forehead pressed against mine. "Calm down, it's Taliesin, you're safe. Kayin is right behind you."

"Everyone is fine." Kayin's accent slid over me, and my panic eased a bit.

"Uncle Gavin?" I choked out between gasping breaths.

"I'm here, sweetheart. So is Anali." I could hear Gavin, but I couldn't see him. A large hand awkwardly patted my leg.

"Others?" I managed to squeak out. Taliesin moved back a little bit, but I kept my eyes glued to his.

"We all got away safe and sound. You were the only one hurt." Taliesin's eyes were full of worry.

"Sapphire," Kayin whispered in my ear. "Try and breathe with us for a bit and then we will answer all of your questions, okay?"

I nodded and felt Kayin's chest rise against my back. Taliesin matched his breathing to Kayin's and soon I took slow, calm breaths. My vision cleared as my panic faded and I began to look around. We were in the SUV Gavin had rented. I could make out Gavin and Anali sitting in the front seats. Behind me all of our camping stuff was piled haphazardly in the back.

Taliesin's hands left my face. "Sit up a bit, and I'll get you some water."

I groaned. Every muscle protested the slight shift in position.

"Here, give her some ibuprofen," Anali said, handing Kayin two white pills.

Gratefully, I drank the cold water and swallowed the pain killers. Please, let them help.

"What happened?" I asked after drinking the bottle of water.

"What's the last thing you remember?" Anali asked.

I forced myself to sit up a little bit higher. "I remember opening the portal, magical creatures going home to Akasha, and blocking the Sons of Belial. I released the doorway, then woke up here."

"Good," Gavin said, and ran a hand through his hair. "Not much happened after that. We went back to camp. Packed everything and took off in case the Sons of Belial came back."

"What about the two men the walk-ins possessed?" I asked the memory of the shadow beings ripped from their bodies clear in my mind.

"George said they would drop them off at the ranger station," Anali said.

"And everyone is okay?"

"Yes, Sapphire," Taliesin said with a sigh. "In fact the others said they felt energized."

"It's true. Storm, Elijah, Rebecca and I were fine afterwards," Kayin said.

"Are we going home?" I asked trying to see into the black night so I could figure out where we are.

"No, not yet. I want to switch the rental car in case any of the Sons of Belial wrote down our license plate. Then I thought we'd spend a few days in San Diego. It's a large city and easy to hide in. We can go to Sea World," Gavin ended with a fake chipper voice.

"You are so weird," Taliesin said, staring at the back of Gavin's like he'd lost his mind.

"I would like to go to Sea World," Kayin said. I suspected he wanted to rile up Taliesin.

Anali laughed. "What about you, Sapphire?"

"Will there be a shower?"

"Of course," Gavin said.

"Then I'm fine. All I want right now is something to eat and a hot shower." I didn't mean to sound like a brat but I was hungry, smelly, and I ached.

"Well, the food thing I can fix. I'll stop at the next place that's open." Gavin leaned forward peering into the night. "There should be a truck stop or something coming up. We can at least get French fries and pie."

I liked pie. "That sounds good."

Kayin rubbed his hand down my arm. "You're shaking a lot, are you cold?"

"A little, but the shaking is from releasing my powers." I shook like this after putting on the fire pendant the first time. It was scary, but at least this time I knew what to expect.

Anali turned in her seat. "Why don't you lie back and do some five-count breathing?"

That helped before. "Okay." I lay back against Kayin and began to focus on my breath.

Taliesin shifted at my feet. I heard bags rustle. What was he up to? I tried to ignore Taliesin and count.

"I'm going to move you," Taliesin said. I winced as he picked up my feet and laid my legs over his lap. "Kayin, help me with this." A soft blanket was tucked around me.

"Thank you," I said. Maybe Taliesin wasn't so bad. I gathered my power in my belly and ran it up my spine. The twitching and shaking eased a bit, but my body still hurt.

*   *   *

You know how sometimes an injury doesn't hurt until you look at it? That happened to me as I stared at my hands. The skin on my palms was bright red and blistered, then faded pink as the burn went up my fingers. What in the world happened? I thought fire wasn't supposed to burn me? Maybe the Phoenix power did it? I channeled a lot of it, something I had never done before.

Letting the cold water run over my hands, I wished I could control the power to regenerate like I could pull up fire. Gently, I patted my hands dry and went out to the table. Gavin stopped at the first truck stop he found. The diner looked like something out of a movie. Clean, cheap, white tables, black and white checkerboard tile, and a jukebox. The waitresses wore blue dresses with white aprons and called everyone "Honey." The diner was crowded for nine on a Monday night.

When I got back to the table there were plates of fried zucchini, fried mozzarella, fried onion rings and nachos. I didn't realize I had been gone that long.

"I ordered you a garden burger and a vanilla milkshake. I hope that's okay," Gavin said.

"It's great, thanks." I looked down at my hands, checking where the burns ended and carefully picked up a mozzarella stick with the tips of my fingers.

Anali looked at me oddly. "What's wrong with your hands?"

I held up one hand, my fingers curled protectively ready to close if someone tried to touch the burnt skin.

"Sapphire, why didn't you say something? We have a first aid kit in the car," Anali said, frowning at my hand.

"I noticed it when I was in the bathroom." I reached over the table and carefully took a fried zucchini, dipping it in ranch dressing before eating it. Yum, greasy, salty, fried food and ranch dressing.

Gavin stood up. "I'll go get the kit."

"No, wait until after dinner," I said waving him back to his seat with my curled hands. "If you put ointment on my hands it will be even harder to eat."

"Here we are," the waitress said setting down milkshakes in front of everyone. I picked mine up and let the cold glass soothe my hands. "Your meals will be out in a bit. If you need anything holler."

"Thank you," we said.

"Look how polite you all are," she said her bright red lips curling into a smile. Her ponytail bounced as she walked away.

"So we're headed to San Diego?" I asked, when I could no longer stand the uncomfortable silence that fell over the table.

"Yes," Gavin answered, faking cheerful excitement again. "We'll switch cars a couple of times, check into a hotel and have fun in San Diego."

"What about credit cards?" Taliesin asked between bites of onion rings. "Won't they be able to trace you by your credit cards? We'll have to have one for the rental car and the hotel room."

"I have a second set that is attached to a private trust fund. They can't get to me or my name from those cards." Gavin dripped cheese on his sleeve as he ate some nachos.

"That seems well thought out," I said.

Gavin raked a hand through his hair. "I grew up knowing the Sons of Belial are dangerous. I always have escape plans."

"So what are we going to do while we're there?" Anali asked, turning the subject to something happier.

They began to plan. Or plot, depending on how one wanted to look at it. All the popular tourist spots were mentioned, plus the botanical gardens and a few museums. I stayed quiet, eating my food and replaying what happened in the circle. I almost killed someone. If Pasha Yilmaz had been in contact with the magical fire any longer, he would have died. I knew he stole his life from other magical beings, but still, I didn't want to kill anyone. I didn't want to hurt anyone. Would I have to kill someone someday, in order to protect my family and friends? Would I be able to? What if it were a magical creature? Could I kill to save one of my grandfather's people?

"Sapphire, are you okay?" Gavin asked.

"Hmm? Oh yeah, just tired," I said, it was half true. "Do they have pie?"

Gavin looked unconvinced but called the waitress over.

*   *   *

Shamash landed beside me on the grass, whistling a sweet song.

"Hello, Adadda, did everyone get here okay?"

Shamash stretched his neck forward and rubbed his beak against my hands until I opened them up. Large tears fell from his gold eyes. My breath caught at the beauty. A tear fell onto my palm, and the burn healed. I held out my other hand and another large shimmery tear fell from Shamash's eye.

I opened and closed my hands amazed at how good they felt. "Thank you."

"You are welcome, Sapphire." Shamash sat next to me in his human form, his flame-red hair dancing around his face as the flower-scented breeze blew by us.

"Where is Aya?"

Shamash smiled. "She is helping the people that you sent home to us. Many of them have suffered on Earth and are in need of healing. Thank you, Sapphire, thank you for sending them home to me."

"You're welcome." The screams from the walk-ins and Yilmaz filled my head.

"Sapphire, what's wrong?"

To my shame my eyes filled with tears. "I didn't mean to hurt anyone."

Shamash wrapped his arms around me making me feel safe. "Hush, my Jewel. I know you didn't want to hurt anyone. Unfortunately, there are people in the world who make choices that cannot be ignored. Choices that force you to make horrible decisions. No one blames you for protecting those you care about."

Shamash stroked my hair and rocked me while I cried.

*   *   *

I held my breath as the icy wave slammed into me.

"Woo-hoo," Kayin yelled, gripping my hand tightly.

I wasn't sure how I'd been talked into playing in the waves, but I felt pretty sure Kayin's big brown eyes were to blame.

"I wish I could swim," Kayin said. "Surfing looks like fun."

"I think it looks scary." Gavin had talked Taliesin into taking a surfing lesson with him, and they kept falling off their boards and into the waves. I couldn't even doggy paddle, no way was I going to try surfing.

"Hold on, Little Sister." Kayin pulled me close as a large wave hit and knocked both of us off our feet. We came up sputtering.

"Stand up! Stand up! Here comes another one!" I grabbed Kayin and tried to stand, both of us laughing even as we scrambled to save ourselves. The waves pushed us both towards the beach.

"This is so fun!" Kayin grinned as he coughed up sea water.

I smiled and pulled him up before the next wave hit. The boy was water crazy.

I could feel Anali wanting our attention. I saw her on the beach calling to us. Her pink and orange tunic glowed against her brown skin. "Big Brother, Anali wants us."

"You're lips are blue; both of you need to get warm," Anali said as we trudged out of the waves. "I brought towels, a change of clothes, and food."

Once out of the water the wind ripped through my wet clothes. "What about Gavin and Taliesin?" I asked through chattering teeth.

"Their lesson should end soon. Go on up to the bathrooms and get changed." Anali handed each of us a bag and towels.

In the movies walking on sand looks romantic and fun. In real life it's difficult to walk on and filled with hidden sharp things: rocks, broken shells, pieces of glass, and sticks. Kayin and I held onto each other so we wouldn't fall.

Anali bought us each sweatpants, a tee shirt, and hoodie. Kayin's sweats were brown; mine were black. Both of us wore touristy San Diego tee shirts.

Gavin and Taliesin were sitting with Anali when we got back. She must have bought them clothes, too. Gavin got navy blue sweats and hoodie, Taliesin got gray. I could imagine the look of disdain on Taliesin's face when he saw the cheesy tourist tee shirt.

"Did you two have fun?" Gavin asked. His lips were still tinted blue from the ocean water, a smear of mustard decorated his cheek from his sandwich. "Come and get something to eat."

"We had the most fun," Kayin said, sitting down and taking the sandwich Anali offered him. "How was surfing?"

Gavin went into enthusiastic detail about their lesson. Taliesin stayed quiet and huddled into his sweats. His normally pale white skin showed a definite blue cast to it. "Are you okay?"

"Y-y-y-yeessss," Taliesin stuttered through his shaking teeth. Taliesin didn't have enough body fat to insulate himself from the icy Pacific Ocean.

I felt bad. Taliesin looked painfully cold. "Would you like me to get you something hot to drink? There's a cafe over there."

For a moment I thought he would say no, but then he nodded.

"Coffee? Hot Chocolate? Tea?" I asked.

"C-Can I have a l-latte, please?" Taliesin stuttered.

"Sure." I turned to Gavin and took a deep breath. I knew he wouldn't mind, but I never asked people for money. "Gavin, can I have some money to go and get hot drinks?" I pointed to the cafe up the boardwalk.

"Of course, I'll come with you. Who wants what?" Gavin jumped up brushing sand off his butt. His damp red hair hung in clumps around his face.

"How are you doing?" Gavin asked, as we waited in the cafe for our order.

"Good. My hands are all better." I held up my hands for him to see.

Gavin sighed. "I know, I checked them this morning. I'm wondering how you're doing with having your powers back, and with what happened yesterday."

"Number 24," called the barista.

"It's a lot to take in," I said, as we walked back to the others. "I'm happy we were able to help the magical beings, but I don't like hurting people."

"I'm sorry it came to that, but I'm glad that everyone is safe," Gavin said.

"Yeah, me too, I wouldn't do things differently, but the way they screamed..." I shuddered.

"I wish I could protect you from all of this," Gavin said, his eyes bright with tears. "I wish I could keep you safe, and give you a normal life of school and friends and parties. The best I can do is help prepare you for the work we have to do. I can promise that we will have as much fun as possible wherever we go."

I could feel the truth of Gavin's words. This was the most any adult ever offered me. "That sounds pretty good."

Gavin's smile would have blinded me if I hadn't been wearing sunglasses.

*　　　*　　　*

"Hurry up, we are all waiting outside," Gavin called through the door.

"I'll be down in a minute." I snapped the barrette Rebecca made me in my hair. It was about the size of my palm. Rebecca had made it using seed beads to make a picture of the circle we created back in March. The outside circle lay swirls of clear and silver blue beads for air, next were waves of various shades of blue representing water, for earth Rebecca somehow designed vines and leaves in rich green beads, dancing flames of red, orange and yellow created the fire circle, and in the center a white circle edged with purple.

I looked around my bedroom, my mom's old room. I hadn't redecorated it, yet it began to feel like home, and now it was time to leave. School had ended and we were heading out to travel with the Cirque du Magique Feu. Taking a deep breath, I walked away from what had become my home during the past five months and headed to a new adventure.

Across the street Kayin and Gavin stuffed bags into large storage areas under the solar-powered RV Gavin managed to acquire. He kept bragging they weren't even on the market yet.

Taliesin's mom hugged him as she said goodbye. Taliesin's cheeks were pink with embarrassment but he held his mom close.

"Hey, Sara," Five said, startling me. He appeared out of nowhere. "I came to say goodbye."

"Thanks." My brow wrinkled in confusion. "You were at the going-away party Melanie held for me."

Five shrugged. "True, but I wanted to give this to you privately." He handed me a book with a worn black leather cover.

I flipped through it seeing yellowed handwritten pages. "Is this Spanish?"

Five grinned. "Yep, but you can read it."

How did he know I could read other languages? "Who are you?" I opened my mouth to call out for Gavin.

"Sorry, but I can't have you do that yet." He waved his hand. Something cool washed over me then everything went dark.

Blinking rapidly, I looked around. What happened? "Five?"

"Sara, are you okay?" he said holding me up. "I know saying good-bye to me is traumatic, but fainting seems a bit extreme."

"I didn't. Did I?" Oh, god, how embarrassing.

Five smiled, and his round baby blue eyes crinkled at the corners. "Well, I guess we could call it a swoon, or a syncopal episode."

I pushed away from him. A what episode? "You're such a brat. Thanks for coming by."

He bent down and picked up my bag tucking a book into it. "Hey, you were my favorite kid."

I rolled my eyes. "I'm sure."

"Are you ready for your new adventure?" he asked looking over his shoulder at the RV.

"I guess so. I'm all packed."

"I hope you have a wonderful time. Make sure to take care of yourself. If you need anything you can always call."

"Thanks, Five, I might do that. I have your number in my phone."

"Good." Five stepped back. "I should go. It looks like your family is ready."

My stomach fluttered. Family? I watched Gavin close the last door to the storage spaces as Anali shooed the others into the RV. This was my family? Maybe, maybe we could be.

Five tugged on my shirt. "Bye, Sara, take care and have fun."

"Bye, David, thanks for everything." He walked away. The wind blew his curls around his face and his worn jeans frayed more with each step as they dragged on the ground. He's such a goof. I hope he doesn't burn out too quickly. He'd been a good caseworker.

I hid in the shadows for a moment watching everyone and trying to wrap my mind around what my future would bring. I twisted my mom's ring on my finger. Her bracelets chimed as they fell together on my wrist.

"None of us knows how powerful, intelligent, beautiful, and compassionate we will become. Every day we grow and change as we meet new people, read new books, learn new lessons, and experience life. But more important than being able to handle every little thing that could happen is having people you can count on to help you as the future unfolds.

Surround yourself with friends and family, believe in yourself and your future will shine bright no matter what it holds."

Taking a deep breath, I walked forward to my future as a niece, a friend, a circus performer, a world traveler, and the Jewel of Akasha.

THE END

Legacy of the Feathered Serpent
Book Two in the Children of Fire Series

CHAPTER ONE

"In every conceivable manner, the family is link to our past, bridge to our future." ~Alex Haley

Llamas spit.

"Oh my god, this reeks!" my uncle Gavin said, gagging as he tried to wipe the llama spit off his face. His skin turned pink from the irritating green goo.

"Oh, gross." I tossed him a packet of wet wipes. "You were told not to scare them."

My empathy picked up the llama's happiness at his victory. The female llamas surrounded him, making odd cooing noises. Understanding what animals felt and thought didn't freak me out anymore, thank goodness. Animals have a very different view of humans than we think. It didn't surpise me to find out that when some cats when they slither around your feet while you're walking, *are* trying to kill you.

The mountains of Patagonia, Argentina loomed above us, beautiful and desolate. Craggy rocks, spindly shrubs, and grass less than an inch high covered the steep slopes. Far below, the brownish gray mountainside gave way to stripes of bright green, terraced crops.

"Is not spit," Sasha said, his Russian accent making him sound harsh and arrogant. "Is digested food."

"Thanks for sharing." I wrinkled my nose at him. Sasha looked less like a ballet dancer and more like a bear in his navy winter coat, heavy black boots, thick wool hat, and scarf.

"When is father going to be home?" Sasha paced in front of me wrapping his arms around himself.

Since Sasha's Phoenix gift of dreaming brought us here, why was he complaining? I sighed and strengthened my empathic shields against Sasha's boredom, frustration, and worry. We had a common ancestor four thousand years ago, a Phoenix King, and now our 'gifts' brought us together.

I looked over at the mother and her two young children sitting in front of their mud brick hut. They glowed against the gray rocks with their smiling dark, ruddy faces and thick wool clothes woven by the mother from bright colors.

"The sun is getting lower, and it looks like the mom started to prepare dinner, so I bet it won't be too much longer," I said.

Wind coming off the top of the snowcapped mountains of the Andes whipped around us. I snuggled deeper into the itchy wool poncho.

"Papa, he's coming. Listen," said the youngest, a girl about four or five years old.

I followed the girl's happy gaze, but couldn't see anyone.

"What did she say?" Gavin asked. A red splotch marked his face, but at least the nasty green goop was gone. His Phoenix gift of regeneration would heal that mark in a few minutes.

"She says her father is coming. But I don't see anything."

I began to get a headache as I always do whenever I translate foreign languages into English. Thank goodness my gift only works with other descendants of magical beings. Otherwise I'd have a constant migraine as we traveled.

"Can be she heard something," Sasha said.

A gust of wind blew over us from the valley, carrying with it the soft bleating of sheep.

"I think I hear them," I said.

Ten minutes later, the echo of the sheep and the sharp yips of dogs became clear. Five minutes after that, the first black-faced, woolly sheep appeared. *Sheep look so cute. And smell.* I didn't know sheep smelled. My nose wrinkled at the pungent, musky odor.

The son, who looked about five or six, ran over to the large paddock and opened the gate. The sheep trotted inside. A few tried going another way, but one of the sheep dogs herded them into the pen with little fuss.

Their father rode up over the hill on a sturdy horse with a heavy coat. He watched over his flock, sitting tall in a colorful, heavy wool poncho, a leather cowboy hat, and holding a child in his arms.

"Is everything all right?" the mom asked reaching her arms up to take the child.

"He fell rescuing a pregnant ewe. I wrapped it but haven't had time to do anything else."

Their oldest son moaned as they shifted him.

"Hello, what can I do for you?" the man called in Mapuche, an ancient language long forgotten by the Spanish-speaking people of Argentina. His wild protective energy skimmed my shield as if trying to figure me out.

"Good afternoon, sir," I said, trusting my Phoenix gift for languages would work. "My family and I would like to speak with you, if we may."

His eyes widened, and I could feel his surprise bounce off my empathic shields. "Yes, of course. Let me clean up and make sure my son is all right first."

Sasha poked me. "We must help son. He won't trust us or give us jewelry from Akasha if we don't."

I groaned and rubbed my temples. We needed the jewelry Sasha dreamed about.

Gavin sighed. "Sasha, if you knew this, why you didn't you say so? None of us is a healer."

Sasha crossed his arms. "I tell you what I remember of my dreams."

"Do you happen to remember how we heal him?" I asked. We were all learning how to manage our Phoenix gifts. I can't expect perfection, especially when I'm constantly messing up.

"Nyet."

"Sapphire, can you connect to Akasha?" Gavin asked. "Maybe we can connect to Miu somehow?"

"Then what?"

Gavin shrugged. "We hope something good happens."

I closed my eyes. "Well, I guess it's a plan. A terrible plan, but we'll see what happens."

I turned towards the fire where they placed their son. "May we try to help your son?"

His turquois eyes narrowed, his distrust pinged against my shield. "How?"

I pulled my fire pendant out, hoping he would recognize the symbol. He didn't. "We are Children of Fire, descendants of the Phoenix King. I'm hoping by connecting to him, we can heal your son."

His distrust didn't lessen. "I dreamed of this. You're here for my family's legacy, for the gifts given to my family before white man came, from the god Quetzalcoatl himself."

Not good. I hadn't meant to upset him. "Yes, I'm sorry but we are here for them. Sasha saw them in a dream given to him by Shamash."

"Our son's leg is broken and bleeding badly," the mom said.

Lichuen looked at his wife in silent communication.

"What's happening?" Sasha wasn't as patient.

"I don't know yet."

"You will heal him," the father said, a commandment not a question.

"Of course." I turned to Gavin and Sasha. "We're being given a chance. Now what?"

"We'll sit next to him and do our best to connect to the energy of Akasha," Gavin said.

Sasha dug through his pockets and pulled out three cases. "I did remember that we should take out our contacts. Seeing the fire in our eyes will help convince him."

I took a case and removed a glove, gasping as the bitter cold wind hit my skin.

"I'm not sure this is a good idea," Gavin said, as I removed my contacts.

"We need the jewelry, right?"

Gavin frowned but went along with it.

I put the case in my pocket and looked up. Lichuen's eyes widened then he nodded.

I sat next to the injured boy and almost threw up. The jagged edge of his bone tore through his lower leg. I looked up at the mountain peaks hoping the wind would blow away the coppery smell of his blood.

Once my stomach calmed, I looked down at the boy. His ruddy face looked ashy, and his eyes were bright from pain. The jewelry didn't matter.

"We're going to help you." My necklace began to warm up as the connection to Akasha opened. The boy moaned. A wave of pain and fear cut into my shield. I cupped my hands and held them up, letting the energy from Akasha fill them.

Gavin and Sasha opened their connection to Akasha and channeled more energy to me. My hands lit up with purple flames. I tipped my hands and let the flames fall like water onto the boy's wound.

He cried out as the bone snapped back into place. His dad moved closer and grasped his son's hand while his wife held onto their younger kids. The muscle and skin began to repair. My stomach churned and I looked away. *How do healers handle stuff like this?*

The energy faded as the skin finished healing over, leaving nothing but a pink scar. I slumped, trying to catch my breath. My hands, red and blistered, ached. I watched as cool blue flames danced on the red skin healing the burns.

"Thank you," his mother said as she ran her hands over her son's leg.

"I couldn't fix the blood loss," I said.

The shepherd smiled, lines carving into his weathered face, his eyes bright. "My wife knows herbs. He'll be fine. Please let us get him settled and you can join us for tea." He helped his son up, supporting him as they walked into the small home. His wife followed them.

I turned to the others and let them know what they had said.

Sasha pursed his thin lips, his thick blond eyebrows coming together as he frowned. "What do you think they will serve us?"

"We will be polite and grateful for whatever they give us," Gavin said. "They don't have a lot and what they share with us will mean less for them later."

Sasha's wind chapped cheeks turned even redder as he flushed with embarrassment. "Of course. I was curious only."

We moved to the logs which surrounded the fire. Gavin tucked his long legs close so his feet didn't land in the fire. Sasha, being five-six, didn't have as much of a problem. At five foot two I was only a little taller than our hosts, and I settled on the worn log without a problem.

The mother passed out cups of maté and plates of homemade bread and cheese made from sheep's milk. I liked the salty white cheese and chewy bread. She served the tea in gourd cups with a metal straws. The straw had a flat bottom with holes in it like a tea strainer so you didn't have to worry about drinking the tea leaves.

The little girl came over and stared into my eyes, her face so close to mine that our noses bumped.

"You have fire in your eyes."

"Let me see," said her brother.

"No." She grabbed my face, her little hand rough with callouses.

He pouted but went over to Gavin. He didn't dive in like his sister, but looked from a distance. Gavin leaned forward once I told him what they wanted. The boy gasped and moved in closer, looking into Gavin's pale green eyes.

"Children, please let our guests enjoy their tea in peace." Their father sat down and sipped his tea through the metal straw.

When finished, he picked up a small bundle wrapped in leather.

"This has been passed down in my family since the beginning of time."

He unwrapped the bundle, his thick, work-worn hands showing the greatest reverence. His family scooted closer to see. Clean raw llama wool filled the bundle. The rancher brushed the wool aside to reveal his family's treasures.

"This is a feather from Quetzalcoatl." He held out a beautiful iridescent feather. The green in the middle faded to yellow at the edges. He laid the feather against his arm with the quill at his elbow and the tip falling over his fingers.

I could feel a magical connection to Akasha radiating from the feather.

"It's beautiful, and very powerful."

"What is it?" Sasha asked, his eyes glued to the magical feather.

Oops, I need to remember to translate. "Sorry, it's a feather from Quetzalcoatl."

"These were given to my ancestor, a man from another world, who was born from people of fire."

He paused until I told the others.

"He passed these along to his son and his son to his son and now they are in my care."

He held out his weathered hands palms up. A silver arm band glinted in the pale light. The metal curved in delicate swirls with a liquid-looking red line flowing down the center of each swirl of silver. The other hand held a thick wrist cuff of hammered gold, with symbols carved into it.

The silver arm band hummed with an energy that told me Shamash had given it as a gift. The other one felt different. It vibrated with the energy from Akasha, but something more—something wild and windy.

"May I see the writing on the gold cuff, please?" I asked.

He turned it, but did not hand it to me.

"The cuff says, 'To a most treasured son, love Quetzalcoatl.'" I said first in Aztec then in English.

"I didn't know other beings brought things from Akasha to Earth," Gavin said, his fingers twitching with the desire to touch the amazing piece.

"When I received these, my father told me we needed to hold onto them until the Ones of Fire came again. The cuff from Quetzalcoatl will help you get into a secret room where he slumbers." He paused and stared at me. *What? Why is he staring at me?* Sasha nudged me. *Oh, yes.* I translated. He started speaking again as soon as I nodded.

"Many, many years ago Quetzalcoatl walked among our people. He admired the beauty of the Aztec and Toltec women and blessed many of them with children. The people built Quetzalcoatl shrines, worshiped his children, and the priests created elaborate rituals and celebrations to honor him."

"One day his red brother, Camaxtil, came and took him away. Legend says they went to battle giants and other gods who would harm the Aztec and Toltec."

His voice drew me in, and his gestures emphasized the importance of his words. I translated quickly each time he paused, so the others could follow the story.

"During Quetzalcoatl's absence, drought ravaged the land and the crops did not grow. A priest had seen Quetzalcoatl cut once, and he did not bleed. The priests decided that the gods must need blood because they didn't have any of their own. When their normal sacrifices didn't bring rain, the priests decided to hold a huge sacrifice in honor of Quetzalcoatl, hoping it would make him happy and end their suffering.

"The priests sacrificed prisoners on the summer solstice, along with the devout who felt called to offer themselves to the gods, and a virgin from each household, including the king's youngest daughter, Quetzalcoatl's great-great-granddaughter. Both Aztec and Toltec temples and pyramids ran red with blood that day. They drummed and sang to drown out the screams of terror as they took prisoners to the altar and cut their living hearts from their chests.

"During the ceremony, Quetzalcoatl did come. He flew over the people, a large magnificent feathered serpent, like a beacon of hope in the sky. Here is where the stories and the myths part ways. According to the priests, Quetzalcoatl, screamed out in joy and blessed earth with his tears. The rivers filled, the crops sprang to life, and the wells filled with sweet clean water once again. The people danced and cheered and the sacrifices continued," he said.

We leaned forward, engrossed in his tale. Even Gavin and Sasha, who had to wait for me to translate, hung on his every word.

"My ancestors knew something different. They knew Quetzalcoatl cried for his grandchild. Her lifeless turquoise eyes looked up, as if in her last moments of life she looked for Quetzalcoatl to return and save her. No one ever saw Quetzalcoatl again. People reported seeing him, and the priests still sacrificed people to honor him, but never again did he bless the people with children or wisdom."

I blinked to fight back the tears, my throat dry, and I cleared it several times in order to finish translating the story.

Lichuen leaned back and looked at the sun. He tightened his fingers around the precious family heirlooms in his hands.

"My family says that Kukulcan or Quetzalcoatl tried to find a doorway to Xilbalba, the spirit world. But something went wrong, and now Quetzalcoatl sleeps in a hidden city waiting to be sent home," she said.

"I am sad to give up my family's treasures, to not be able to pass them on to one of my own children, but this is what must happen. You need the cuff to free Quetzalcoatl." Lichuen stroked the silver arm band and beaten gold wrist cuff. His turquoise eyes were bright and watery.

Over the past few months, Uncle Gavin had taught me about our family, as he felt a strong connection to our family's history. I didn't feel that connection, but it would break my heart to have to give up the journal my mother left with me when I was five. I know from one of her entries that my mother also felt connected to our magical past.

"Family ancestry shapes who you are and who you'll become. It's more than genetics. It's quilt patterns, recipes, holiday decorations, and secrets. For some people their ancestry shows up in special gifts and abilities passed down over centuries. While I grow, learn, and try new things, the ties I feel to our ancestors ground me and help me feel connected even when I am alone."

"I'm sorry," I said. "I wish there was another way. Even if we didn't need it, there is an evil force, the Sons of Belial, who might find you and your family and try to take the jewelry."

Gavin tugged on my sleeve. "Tell him we would like to offer him a gift, for keeping these important pieces safe."

"My uncle would like to offer your family a reward for keeping the arm band and cuff safe." I twisted the hem of my poncho.

"It was an honor to have such magical items in my care," he said, his voice proud.

"We do not wish to offend you," I said. I'd managed to loosen a strand of yarn and kept wrapping and unwrapping it around my finger. "We would like to do something, a gift of friendship and family."

Husband and wife shared a look. She smiled, her teeth bright against her red-brown lips. "We could accept a gift from family, but you need to hurry. It's getting late."

Gavin practically vibrated next to me. "What did they say?"

"They said they could accept a gift from family, but to hurry."

"Tell them we'll be right back," Gavin said, jumping up with Sasha following.

Delighted squeals echoed over the mountain as the kids unpacked the baskets we brought. We gave them toys, fruit, spices, several pots, combs and brushes, beans, and grain.

"They are lovely gifts and very appreciated." She began to repack the spices. "But the sun is close to setting, and navigating the mountain is difficult in the dark."

"Yes, very difficult." Lichuen glanced at the sun sinking below the horizon and stood up. "How did you find us?"

"The family who rented us the horses drew a map to the base of your hill. They wouldn't come up, something about you both being curanderos or witches. And Sasha's dream told him where to go the rest of the way," I said.

"Ah yes, my wife is a seventh daughter, and a curandera or healer. I'm surprised you're here tonight. It is the full moon, and well known that I am a seventh son and a werewolf."

My whole body stiffened, and for a moment I couldn't breathe. *A werewolf—was he serious? Lichuen turns into a snarling vicious monster?* "What?"

"You did not know." He sighed and rubbed his rough hand over his face. "In about half an hour the moon will rise, and I will change into a werewolf. You need to be going."

"How do your family and your animals stay safe?"

And more importantly how would we stay safe?

"Sapphire, what's wrong?" Gavin asked.

"Give me a minute, he's explaining something to me," I answered, holding my hand up to keep him from talking.

"I do not become a mindless monster, wolves are not blood-thirsty animals. They do kill for food, but they also protect and nurture." He reached over and mussed his son's hair. "I could never hurt my family. However strangers on my land might not be so lucky."

I looked up at the sky. A sunset of pinks and oranges lit up the wispy clouds. "It will take us a while to get down the mountain in this dim light. We should go."

"I would invite you to stay for dinner, but I am concerned for your safety," he said.

His wife smiled and took her husband's hand in hers. "You must come back and tell us all about how you save Quetzalcoatl. Come back when there isn't a full moon, and we'll have a feast."

"Thank you, I look forward to when we can come back." I turned to Gavin, and switched languages. My head ached from switching between Mapuche and English.

"We need to leave."

"Why?" Gavin's green eyes became serious as he looked between me and the family as if he could somehow determine what was going on.

I cleared my throat. Despite everything I'd seen already, I couldn't believe what I was about to say.

"He's a werewolf, and the moon rises in less than half an hour. We have to leave his territory by then."

"Thank you for tea and for the gifts of your ancestors." The words rolled off my tongue. *Am I being taught proper manners in my dreams when I visit Akasha?*

"You are most welcome. Careful going down the mountain; the trail is narrow, and there isn't much light. You need to be quick," he said.

As we walked to the corral my stomach became nauseated with fear. I wasn't happy riding the horses during the day. I didn't know how I could cope in the dark. It felt wrong to try and force an animal that big to do what I wanted. The woman who rented them to us assured me my horse would follow the one in front of it, all I had to do was stay on.

"Come on, Sapphire, it's time to go," Gavin said, standing next to my horse. For a moment I considered seeing my first werewolf instead of getting on the horse. Gavin made the decision for me when he picked me up. I managed to keep my hands on the reins instead of clinging to the horse's mane as we started down the mountain.

A sliver of moon peeked over the horizon, and I welcomed its light while worrying about what dangers it would bring. We were not far enough from Lichuen to be safe yet. I could still hear the laughter of his children and the bleating of sheep on the icy wind.

I couldn't see the ground clearly, and the wind tugged at my clothes. "Gavin, are you sure we should be moving this quickly?"

"I have excellent night vision," Gavin bragged. "You don't need to worry. Anyway we're just going at a walk."

I didn't feel reassured. It's great that Gavin could see rocks and holes in the path, but what about me? I didn't feel like falling down the side of a cactus-filled mountain with a horse!

"Sapphire," Sasha said, "horse have excellent night vision."

I reached out a shaking hand and patted the horse's neck trying to let her know I trusted her with my safety. Maybe I should call her by name. What was it again?

"Do you remember my horse's name?" I asked. Gavin laughed.

Rude.

Sasha sighed, as if I offended him and turned in his saddle showing off his skill and comfort on the large black animal he rode. "Her name is Bonita."

"Cool, thanks." Sasha jerked his head, which normally would have made his shaggy hair flip about in a very dismissive way, but with a hat on, Sasha just looked like he had some weird tic.

The dark night encouraged silence to avoid alerting anything hiding in the inky blackness where we were. The moon rose, glowing pale yellow in the sky. Unfortunately, it wasn't high enough yet to light the rocky trail we descended.

Rocks tumbled as something large came our way.

"Gavin! Sasha! Sapphire!" Taliesin called out.

Thank goodness, maybe Taliesin could talk to the werewolf and keep us safe.

"Taliesin, what are you doing here? Is everyone okay?" Gavin said. We had left Taliesin and the others back at the ranch where we were staying since they didn't have enough horses available for all of us. I had to go, Gavin insisted on going, and since Sasha was the only one who actually knew where we were going he came along, the rest had to stay behind.

Taliesin came close enough that I could see him, and even in the cold and riding a horse, he looked GQ perfect. He's so irritating.

"Everyone's fine."

"Then why you are here?" Sasha sneered as he straightened his posture.

"Something is wrong." Taliesin looked around. "I was reading in my room."

"Our room," Sasha muttered.

Taliesin rolled his eyes. "Anyway, I knew I needed to get to you. So what kind of trouble are you in now?"

Rude! He looked right at me.

Gavin rubbed a hand over his face. "The man we visited is a werewolf, and the full moon is rising."

A howl echoed over the mountain. We all froze, maybe if we didn't move he wouldn't sense us. The sound of rocks falling down the mountain followed the next howl. The horses whinnied and began to stamp their feet, ready to get away.

"He's coming," I whispered.

"I can't reach him," Taliesin said, after a moment. "The werewolf is focused on getting the intruders out of his territory and protecting his family. We need to leave."

"We are leaving. Have you told him that?" I said.

"Of course," Taliesin flipped his white braid over his shoulder. It caught the moonlight and glowed silver. "But he doesn't care. We have to hurry."

"Can you make the horses understand what we need to do?" Gavin asked. "We need them to take over and get us down the mountain safely."

"I'll try." Taliesin bowed his head. No one moved or made a sound while we waited. After the longest minute ever, Taliesin looked up. "They understand and will help us."

We murmured our thanks and settled back into our seats. The horses took off, right down the side of the mountain. This time human cries echoed through the air.

My eyes stung as cold wind whipped around my face. I clung as well as one can to a massive beast careening down a mountain. Rocks kicked up around us, hitting our legs and the horses. They didn't want to stay around the werewolf either.

"Sapphire!" Gavin screamed. I wanted to yell that I was okay, but I couldn't breathe, couldn't move, all I could do was cling to Bonita.

She swerved to the right. I slid in the saddle and dropped the reins. I grabbed her mane, desperate to stay on. I screamed when my dangling leg hit a cactus, and the sharp spines pierced my skin through my jeans. My arms shook as I hauled myself back into the saddle. The stirrups flopped about, but I managed to shove my feet into them. I waited for my life to flash before my eyes.

"Please," I begged. "Please keep me safe."

Through the panic coming off Bonita I felt determination, strength, and a little bit of protectiveness.

Good enough for me. I put my trust in her and held on with the best of my ability. My stomach roiled again as Bonita jumped. I screamed. My legs protested as I clenched them even tighter around her back. Bonita's powerful muscles bunched and stretched under me as she ran from the monster behind us. We had to be close to the edge of its territory, right?

A fierce howl echoed around me. Nope, we weren't far enough away yet.

Bonita jerked to the right.

"Sapphire," Gavin yelled. We ran along the edge of a deep ravine. I couldn't see the bottom, only blackness. Everyone else raced down the other side of the ravine. *No. Oh, god, no.* I couldn't do this alone. Frantic, I grabbed at the reins while I tried to remember how to get the horse to go where I need to.

"I'll get her Gavin," Taliesin said. He turned his horse sharply around then headed back up the mountain.

"We're going the wrong way," I said to the horse, the reins staying just out of reach. "Please, we need to stop and go back."

Energy as soft as a moonbeam flowed over us. Bonita snorted and stopped, prancing in place, turning around. Taliesin came towards us, his forehead glowing blue-silver under his hat.

"Come on," he whispered to the horse. "Come on, girl, this way. We'll be safe, but we need to go."

Never have I felt so glad to see Taliesin. My eyes fill with tears. "Thank you."

"We're not safe yet." Taliesin turned looking up the mountain. "I don't see the werewolf, but we need to go."

"Thank you for coming back for me, and for sending the others on," I said.

Taliesin shrugged. "Their horses are listening more to me than them right now." Taliesin turned the horse's head back up the mountain to the top of the ravine.

Bonita screamed and reared up on her hind legs. My fingers tangled in her mane, holding on. I smiled as she lowered her bulk back down to the trail. *I did it! I held on! Go me!* Something slammed into me, knocking me from the horse and into the rocky ground. My chest burned as my breath was forced out of me. A snarling gray werewolf pinned me down.

ABOUT THE AUTHOR

Being told she was a horrible speller and would never learn to use a comma correctly, Alica never thought to write down the stories she constantly had running through her head. Doesn't everyone daydream about flying on a spaceship while walking to school?

Not until she was thirty did Alica dare to write down any of the people living exciting lives in her head. The relief was instantaneous. By giving them life on the page they could be released from her mind and given greater adventures.

As her books grew in size and the voices in her head learned to wait their turn, Alica found a loyal group to journey with. Women who would help her slay her commas, and use their magical gifts to traverse plot holes, transform words into their proper spelling, and release characters from any Mary Sue spells they might be under.

In-between magical adventures, Alica is mom to two personal kids, five foster kids, has one exceptional hubby, a bunny she knows is plotting her death, and some fish, aka her daughter's minions.

I hope you've enjoyed *Phoenix Child*. To find out when the next Children of Fire book will be published, learn more about my "eccentric artistic process", or to ask me questions, or send comments you can find me on-

Twitter
https://twitter.com/AMckennaJohnson

Facebook
https://www.facebook.com/AlicaMckennaJohnsonAuthor

Goodreads
http://www.goodreads.com/author/show/5755438.Alica_Mckenna_Johnson

My website/blog
www.alicamckennajohnson.com

AND to get information about my upcoming books, book signings, and talks subscribe to my newsletter. It only goes out when I have something of value to share. Cross my heart!
http://eepurl.com/bc5bzn

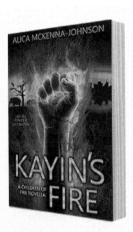

Made in the USA
San Bernardino, CA
22 June 2018